good
intentions

good intentions

A NOVEL

KASIM ALI

HENRY HOLT AND COMPANY

NEW YORK

Henry Holt and Company
Publishers since 1866
120 Broadway
New York, New York 10271

www.henryholt.com

Henry Holt® and **H**® are registered trademarks of
Macmillan Publishing Group, LLC.

Distributed in Canada by Raincoast Book Distribution Limited

Library of Congress Cataloging-in-Publication Data

Names: Ali, Kasim, author.
Title: Good intentions : a novel / Kasim Ali.
Description: First U.S. edition. | New York : Henry Holt and Company,
   2022.
Identifiers: LCCN 2021047505 (print) | LCCN 2021047506 (ebook) |
   ISBN 9781250809605 (hardcover) | ISBN 9781250809612 (ebook)
Subjects: LCGFT: Bildungsromans. | Romance fiction. | Novels.
Classification: LCC PR6101.L449 G66 2022 (print) | LCC PR6101.L449
   (ebook) | DDC 823/.92—dc23
LC record available at https://lccn.loc.gov/2021047505
LC ebook record available at https://lccn.loc.gov/2021047506

Our books may be purchased in bulk for promotional, educational, or business
use. Please contact your local bookseller or the Macmillan Corporate and
Premium Sales Department at (800) 221-7945, extension 5442, or by email at
MacmillanSpecialMarkets@macmillan.com.

First U.S. Edition 2022

Designed by Gabriel Guma

Printed in the United States of America

1   3   5   7   9   10   8   6   4   2

To Asmat Begum and Barkat Ali
Without you, there is nothing; with you, there is the world

December 2018

Nur's two weeks are nearly up, and he still hasn't said it. It's the day before he has to go back, returning to a question that he will not know how to answer.

There can only be one answer.

He is sitting at the top of the stairs, and it is nearly midnight; his parents are in the living room, waiting for the fireworks to start. He'd said he was going to get his phone. That was ten minutes ago. In a few minutes, the celebrations will begin.

Ever since he can remember, his family has sat in front of their TV together on New Year's Eve, counted down to midnight, and watched the fireworks in London. Every single year. Nur has offered to take his entire family to London before, to pay for the train tickets and the hotel, let them see in real life what they have so often watched through a screen, but each time they have refused, saying it is too much money. His mother reminds him she does not like to travel on trains, his father asking what they will get from watching it in real life that they won't get from the TV, his brother saying thanks but he'd rather stay in, his sister saying she doesn't mind, and so he doesn't offer anymore. If he's being honest, there is something about watching together, about sitting there, year after year at home, that even he likes.

But he wishes he had offered again this year. He wishes they had taken him up on it, said yes, so that he could lie when he got back after the break, say he had no time to talk, that he had taken

his family to London to see the fireworks, that he'd always wanted
to take them, that this was the first time they'd said yes and he
couldn't disrupt that by telling them his news.

Maybe that would have worked.

Maybe it wouldn't.

"Nur!" comes a shout from the living room. His mother's voice,
urgent. "It's about to begin! Come down!" Nur loves how she gets
so excited about something that could so easily become mundane
to other people, the same year in, year out. He loves that she makes
them all sit there, her husband and their three children, in a family
tradition crafted from something that only she truly enjoys.

Nur walks down the stairs, making sure to step on every creak
and warp in the floorboards, learned from all his years living here,
to make as much noise as possible. His phone is in his pocket,
heavy against his leg.

He walks into the room, three minutes left. Khalil, his younger
brother, is on the floor, sitting with his back against the wall. His
younger sister, Mariam, is on the sofa, phone on her stomach as
she lies there, watching blankly.

As always, Nani is in the other room, asleep, her light snoring
a familiar background noise for them. Every year, they invite her,
and every year she comes demanding to know why she is here,
saying this is not *her* new year, that she only celebrates the Islamic
New Year. And every year, she falls asleep long before midnight.

His mother, Hina, pats the seat on the sofa next to her, and Nur
takes it, his father, Mahmoud, on the other side of him, and all
sat there like that, they might strike an onlooker as the right kind
of family. The right kind of brown family who have stayed up to
watch the fireworks, waiting to see the celebration of the end of
one Western year and the ringing in of a new one.

The tightness in Nur's chest grows as he watches the screen. It
has been there ever since he stepped off the train onto the platform,
Uber already ordered, driven home by a stranger who looked too
much like his father, keys shaking slightly as he twisted them to
open the front door. There when he hugged his parents in the hall,
pushed Khalil affectionately, ruffled Mariam's hair, laughing at the

way she scrunched up her face in response. Each night at home, he has gone to bed with this tightness pinning him down, like his lungs can't pull in enough air.

He almost wishes that there were something wrong with him, that he might have to go to the hospital after fainting somewhere, delivered to sterile white corridors, be told there are cancerous cells swarming his body. Maybe then everything would be okay, because his secret would not be the biggest thing in their world, and maybe he would be able to make everything work.

But there is no dash to the hospital. The secret remains.

The countdown flips to the last minute, and his mother leans forward in her seat. She watches the screen as though she is trying to find something in the view of the London Eye and the city-scape, a message hidden there just for her.

Nur watches her out of the corner of his eye. They share the same nose, he and his mother; the same curve leaping downward, as if gravity had grabbed on to it with both hands. He has inherited his father's thick eyebrows but with his mother's shape. He is often told that his eyebrows are good, because there is space between them, because they look well-kept, but he tells people they are simply well-behaved. His eyes are all Nani's, a lighter brown, like gold, which marks him apart from his siblings.

The clock counts down and down until there are only single digits left, and then there is nothing and there is noise. Fireworks flash and fill their screen, are so loud that they may as well be in the room with them. His mother laughs, shouts, "Happy New Year!" and they all shout it back. Mariam takes a video on her phone, and Nur sees but doesn't mind because he knows that one day he'd like to look back at this moment and know what it was like before he changed everything. To see what his world looked like before it crumbled around him.

He waits until they get bored of the fireworks, which happens quickly. Khalil and Mariam turn to their phones, his parents watch the TV with tired eyes, waiting for it to be over.

Nur's guts twist. He glances at his siblings, fails to get their attention, so fires off a quick message to their group chat:

Need to talk to mum and dad about something
Can you guys leave
Plz
Now

Their phones buzz, and Khalil looks up at him first, eyes narrowed, questioning. Nur shakes his head a fraction, both at him and at Mariam, who is now staring at him too. But he isn't ready to explain this to them, not yet. Slowly they get up, tell their parents they'll see them in the morning, and as they leave the room Khalil locks eyes with Nur again, his curiosity burning. Regret begins to tug then, as Nur wonders if he should have told them first, tested it with them, but that moment has long passed.

"When do you go back?" his father asks. His mother reaches for the remote, muting the TV so that the fireworks continue but no sound comes from the bright lights.

"Work starts on the third, so I'll have to leave tomorrow," Nur says.

"You should have taken some more time off," his father says. "It's nice having you home, makes it feel like it used to."

"I miss having you here," his mother says, and a sharp guilt pierces Nur. Even now, after all these years living apart from his family, he still feels it. It's impossible not to.

He wishes he could stay here, not in the house itself but closer than where he is now. That he didn't have to travel for two hours to get home to see them, that he could be around his family more often.

But things are so different now, have been different for a while. He's not sure if it's him that has changed or if it's his family, or perhaps it's both, but somehow the house is still the same size it used to be when he was younger and yet there is no longer space for him here.

"I know," he says, and he leans his head on her shoulder, the way he used to when he was younger, lying against her arm, falling asleep to the sound of her breathing. "I wish I could be here all the time."

"Yeah, yeah, you're just saying that," she says, and even though she is teasing him, there is truth there. "You should sleep soon, if you want to get your train. What time is it again?"

"Midday," Nur says, left hand closed, thumb digging into his index finger.

"We'll drive you to the station—" his father begins.

The words rise up in him before he even knows what's happening. "I'm seeing someone."

All Nur can hear is the pounding of his heart. His declaration hangs in the sudden silence, and he moves away from his mother, lifting his head from her body. Rising from the sofa, he stands facing his parents, wants to see them.

His mother's face is stone, eyes on him, waiting for Nur to explain himself. His father watches him too. The air has grown thick and heavy.

"I'm seeing someone," Nur says again, stronger this time, the truth swirling through him.

"What?" his mother asks. His father is silent.

"I'm dating someone," Nur repeats. That word, so impossible to even think of saying to his parents before.

"Who is she?"

"Her name is Yasmina," Nur says. Her face floats before him, her voice whispers in his ear. "I met her at university."

"University?" his mother says, cogs in her head turning, numbers adding up. "But that was . . ."

"Theen sal," his father says.

"Four," Nur says.

"Four years," his father says, disbelief weighing down his voice. "Why did you wait so long to tell us, Nur?"

Nur shifts on his feet, but before he can answer, his mother cuts in. "Do you want to marry her?"

And there it is: hope in his mother's voice. The hope she has had for so long, because, after all, why would he be telling her this if it wasn't because he was planning to get married? She's asked him, over and over again, if there's a girl he has in mind, a suitable girl. And he's lied to her, saying no, he doesn't have time, he's always working, and anyway, where is he going to find someone, where do Muslims find people these days. Or his mother on the phone, tutting at him, rattling off a list of his cousins who have managed to find good partners. "And you, you're so smart, you're so funny, so handsome, and you're telling me you can't find anyone, but they can?" He's told her every time that she only says this because he's her son, knowing that he shouldn't continue lying but not able to tell his parents, not yet. It's not just them that ask, but Yasmina too, asking why he hasn't told them, and he tells her the same thing: not yet. She asks him why again and he says because . . . just not yet, that's why.

Now he fills in the only thing that's missing.

"Yes," he says, "but there's one other thing, Mum. Yasmina isn't Pakistani, she's Sudanese. She's Black."

November 2014

ook, all I'm saying is that if you had the option of not being white, of being brown or Black or whatever, you wouldn't want to do it. Because you know, just like every other white person on the planet—liberal, conservative, centrist—that being non-white is way worse than being one of you. It doesn't really matter how much you think you're here for us, that you voted for Sadiq or that you told your one racist uncle that all Muslims aren't terrorists or that he can't call the Sikh guy down the road a Paki because he isn't even Pakistani, he's Indian, but that's beside the point, he shouldn't be saying anything like that to anyone. Because at the end of the day, your fresh-snow-white skin means that you get to walk around without having some white woman cross the street to get away from you, clutching her bag a little tighter because she thinks you're going to rob her, without having a security guard follow you through a shop because he thinks you're going to steal something, or being searched at the airport because you look like this. Without having to be scared when passing a group of white men because you're thinking, *Wow, is this going to be the day I get my head kicked in because I look like this?* and running the rest of the way home so you don't have to find out. Constantly worrying about all these things: the way you present yourself, how you look, how you speak, how you *stand*—fuck, even the kind of music you listen to! Because, you know, you can't be too aggressive with your want for equality, you gotta say the right kinds of things, think the right

kinda way, and learn when to keep your mouth shut. So really, if
you were presented with an option to be not-white for a day or even
an hour, you would probably say no. Because you know that being
one of us is way worse than being one of you."

Nur leans against a living room wall, watching this girl, this
Pakistani girl with high cheekbones, a sharp jaw, eyelids coated in
black ink, lips a dark shade of purple, and he can't help but marvel
at her.

Her name is Saara, three *a*'s and no *h*, and this is her party. The
person she is talking at is not a person she invited to the party. He
was brought here by a friend of Saara's, an Indian girl whose name
Nur can't remember because he doesn't know her, not properly. In
fact, Saara is one of only a handful of people he knows here, but
he has come to expect this from her parties. Saara knows everyone
at their university, so Nur is never surprised that the faces are constantly changing. That is, after all, part of the appeal.

The white guy's name is Stephen; he'd introduced himself to
Saara, which was his second mistake, the first having been walking through the door. He's sitting on a sofa, face red, tips of his
ears colored pink, and he is holding tightly on to his beer bottle, as though it might save him. Nur is glad that Stephen doesn't
seem drunk, because drunk people make the wrong decisions, and
while Saara doesn't drink, she does fight. Nur has seen her before,
defending her friends from some boys at a club, all sharp edges and
no holding back, blood etched under her fingernails.

Stephen says nothing back to Saara, just looks up at her. The
truth is, there is nothing to say that would help him. If he tells her
she's right, she'll laugh at him. If he tells her that he would try to be
non-white for a day, just to know what it feels like, she will accuse
him of virtue signaling. If he tells her that this kind of hostility
only separates people more than it unites them, he'll find himself
faced with another diatribe about bad faith. There is no win here.
Even if he stays quiet, he is inferior to her, weak. But at least quiet
doesn't bring another barrage of words.

The Indian girl frowns at Saara angrily, but Saara simply shrugs.
"Rule one: Don't bring white people to my parties," she says.

The girl pulls at Stephen, who gets to his feet clumsily. He opens his mouth like he's about to say something but stops himself, clamping his lips shut, and then he's gone. The sound of the front door closing shudders over the music, but no one seems to notice. Or, if they do, no one cares.

Saara takes a sip from the glass she's holding in her right hand— Diet Coke, her choice of drink—and grins at the people around her. "Party on," she says wryly, lifting her glass high.

There are cheers and there are whoops, and the people who were gathered around to watch her pull Stephen down dissipate, the moment having passed.

All except for Nur, who stays against the wall. Saara turns to him, pulling her lips down into a frown. "Did I go too far again?" she asks.

"I think too far would have been taking him out into the garden and shooting him."

"Are you trying to argue that my activism is violent?"

"I don't think I'm trying to argue anything."

"Well, if you were going to, this would be the time for it. I invite all kinds of arguments, free speech is for everyone, et cetera, et cetera."

Nur rolls his eyes, reaches for her glass, takes a sip from it. "And now that you've chased away the white guy, what's next on the agenda?"

She pauses, finger tapping on her chin. "I don't know. Maybe I'll overthrow the patriarchy by throwing tampons at every guy that walks past the house."

"Do you even have that many tampons?"

"Every girl should have that many tampons, because they should be free. And the fact that we don't is just another example of the patriarchy keeping us vagina-having people down."

Nur laughs. "You really do have an answer for everything."

"I like to be prepared," she says, reaching for her glass back.

"Sometimes I wonder what it's like to be inside that head of yours."

She leans into him, so close he can almost count her eyelashes, thick and clumped together with mascara. "You know, you don't have to wonder. All you have to do is ask."

"Consent is important," he says.

"Oh." She sighs and closes her eyes, mock pleasure, exquisite, racing through her face. "Say that again."

"Consent is important," he whispers.

"God, isn't that what we all want to hear from cute brown boys." Saara laughs, pulling back from Nur, glass to her lips, downing the entire thing. "I will be back," she says, and walks off into the kitchen, where Nur hears her talking to other people. He stays leaning on his wall, not entirely sure what to do with himself now, because he knows she won't be back, that she will become embroiled in another conversation with people he doesn't know.

This does not happen to him enough to say it's a regular occurrence, but often enough to be noticed. He will come to a party, hosted by Saara, because her parties are the only ones he makes the effort to go to, and he will find himself enthused at being there. Then, about half an hour into it, the novelty will wear off and he'll wonder why he's there, surrounded by people he doesn't know, feeling a strange emptiness that defies definition.

He casts an eye around the room, trying to find someone he knows, but all he sees are faces vaguely familiar from other parties, ones he can't put names to, and he is too shy, too awkward, too self-conscious to go up to them. In the kitchen, he sees Saara talking away, the glass in her hand still empty, which is good, because she seems impassioned by what she's saying, waving her hands everywhere. He thinks of joining her there, but he doesn't want to be the lone puppy who trails after Saara, not able to make friends of his own.

This is the problem with coming to his ex-girlfriend's parties, he realizes. Even though the relationship was intense, lasting just under a year, and the breakup tore his heart apart, Nur somehow put himself back together and they agreed to be friends. Now they try to circle each other without thinking about all that came before. But sometimes Nur looks at her, thinks about the way she felt against him, the warmth of her. He tries to pull himself out of that, remind himself why they broke up in the first place, but it's hard to stay right here and not go there, where it felt like things were better.

Nur moves through the room, passing through people, around people, to the hallway, to the front door, and opens it. He steps out into the dark and leans against the brick wall. The cold wraps around him, thick like ice, and he closes his arms across his chest, takes in a few deep breaths, filling his lungs with it, his breath coming out gray, dissolving into the air.

He doesn't know why he does this. This is the third party of Saara's that he has been to since they broke up three months ago.

The first time she invited him, he'd stared at the message on his phone. A mistake, he thought. An attempt to get him back into her life, though he knew she wasn't the kind of person to play that game, that if she wanted him back, she would be straight about it. He'd turned up on the night, stepping into the house that felt both like a home and completely foreign to him. He'd seen her, talking animatedly off to the side. She caught his eye, walked over to him, said his name, and he could tell from the way she said it that she hadn't said his name since the last time, when they'd stretched themselves to a breaking point, snapping in two. Then she told him she was glad he had come and that he should have a good time, before walking away. He spent the night sad and alone, and when he returned home, it was as if he had swallowed all the world's grief. Rahat gave him a familiar look, eyebrow raised, arms crossed over his chest, and Nur said nothing, just went to his bed to sleep it off.

Rahat told him not to go to any others, but here he is again, going through the same motions, and if he goes home now, Rahat will be awake, that same look waiting for him.

He pulls his phone out of his pocket, starts scrolling on Twitter, when the crunch of feet on frost distracts him.

Someone is walking toward him. A Black girl wearing a yellow dress, tight against her body, and his eyes go to her bare arms, goose-bumped, then her face, her teeth chattering, jumping against one another. She stands by the open door, smiles briefly at him, and then steps inside.

Nur opens his mouth to say something, but she slips away into the party. He looks back at his phone, cheeks flushed, because he almost embarrassed himself in front of a girl he doesn't know. If she's friends with Saara, she probably knows who he is, and if she doesn't, all it would take is a quick comment, and he would be crushed with the humiliation. But there's the sharp pain of a moment missed, when he might have been able to say something, anything. She might have ignored him, but she might have said something back, sparking a bit of a conversation. Maybe he'd have got to know someone new.

He looks at the time. Just past midnight. He can't go home until at least two, when Rahat and his judgment will be asleep.

Turning, Nur pockets his phone and heads back into the house. He closes the door softly and sees Saara walking upstairs, the last of her disappearing into a bedroom.

He traces her steps, ignoring the little voice in his head that again tells him he shouldn't be following Saara around, that he should be his own person. He pushes away the memories too, of the times he has spent here, holding her hand, walking upstairs, of going into her bedroom, pushing open the door, falling together onto the bed.

There's a small collection of people in her room when he nudges the door a little, and Saara sees him immediately. "I thought you'd left," she says, a smile in her eyes.

"Only for a second."

"Everyone, you know Nur," Saara says, and the five other people look at him and all give him a gesture of something, a wave of the hand, a nod, a smile.

Out of the five, he recognizes two of them. Iman, a Black girl he'd met a few dates into seeing Saara, and Adam, someone he's known tangentially from the very beginning of university, bumping into each other here and there, neither of them quite deepening their friendship or feeling the need to.

Nur goes to sit by Adam on the floor, glad he has found someone to pass the time with.

"Hey, man," Adam says, and he lifts his hand, Nur taking it in his own and shaking it, a little awkwardly because of the way they're sitting, elbows bent crooked.

"I guess this is the part where we all come up to Saara's room and smoke," Nur says, just as Saara takes out a little box from the drawer next to her bed, pulling out a tautly rolled spliff and a lighter.

She hands both to the girl nearest her, doesn't smoke it herself, sitting on her bed cross-legged, watching and waiting.

"I bet that white guy doesn't dare come back here again," Iman says. She reaches for the spliff, puts it to her lips, inhales, holds, and then streams smoke back out.

"Or he comes back with a group of them," one of the boys offers. Nur looks at him, trying to remember his name. Something with an *H*.

"Is that what you're scared of, Hasan?" Saara asks. Hasan looks up at her. They're all sitting on the floor, with Saara regal on the bed above them, queen to their peasantry. "Retaliation?"

Hasan shrugs. "I don't know. I just hear a lot of things about white people having had enough . . ."

"Had *enough*?" Saara's voice is steel.

"I don't mean . . . I just think they can get, like, aggressive. Maybe they'll come back and break into this house and try to beat you up. Or like follow you home from university. Or something. I don't know."

"And so what?" Saara asks. The spliff continues to migrate around the circle, reaching Nur, who takes it and contemplates it for a moment before handing it to Adam. He wants to keep his mind clear tonight, feels like he needs to. "Do we stop standing up to them because we're so worried they're not going to like what we say?"

"Debate is always necessary," the girl nearest Saara says, and Nur can't remember her name either, but he has definitely seen her before, her skin light, her face long. "But I guess what Hasan is trying to say is that we don't need to provoke them . . ."

"Because they haven't spent years provoking us?"

Nur looks at the rest of them. He knows what this feels like, sitting under the intensity of Saara, pinned by her eyes as she waits for him to answer a question. Even when he knew what he wanted to say, he couldn't quite reach the words to articulate it, and maybe there was a chance that they didn't exist, that he was simply wrong and that she was right.

But Saara never wanted to hear that. She thrives on engagement. Giving in and accepting her word as truth was the worst thing to do.

Before anyone can answer her, there's a soft knock at the door, and Nur turns just as Saara steps off the bed, arms wide. "Yasmina!" she says, throwing her arms around the girl in the yellow dress from earlier. The girl smiles a little shyly, holding Saara tight. "You are very late."

"I fell asleep," Yasmina replies, and watching her, something happens to Nur's stomach, squeezes it, turns it upside down. He wants to stand too, say something, but he holds back.

Saara laughs and turns to the rest of them. "Guys, this is Yasmina," she says, and it reminds Nur of when she introduced him last year, parading him in front of everyone, hand outstretched for the world to see. "She's just moved here from . . ."

"Manchester," Yasmina says, though Nur notices that she doesn't sound like she's from there, can't quite place her accent.

Nur waves a hand at her, and her eye catches his. If she recognizes him from outside, it doesn't seem to register.

"Sit," Saara insists, and Yasmina takes the only space left on the floor, next to Nur. Her arm brushes his as she settles.

"What do you do?" Iman asks. She has the spliff again.

"What do I do?" Yasmina repeats, confusion coloring her words.

"Like, at uni."

"Oh." Yasmina chuckles, embarrassed. "Journalism."

"Nice, how do you know Saara?" Hasan asks.

Yasmina looks at Saara, a small smile on her lips. "I met Saara at a festival. Leeds, right?" she asks, even though it's clear she doesn't need the confirmation. Saara nods, and Nur looks at her, sees that distracted expression on her face, revisiting a memory, falling back into it. "I went with a few of my friends, she went with a few of hers, and we just happened to be right next to each other the entire time. I added her on Facebook, she left me hanging for a while . . ."

"I did not!" Saara says, faux outrage contorting her face. "I told you, I don't go on Facebook that much . . ."

"So she left me hanging for a while, then accepted after she deemed me worthy. We've been friends ever since."

"You moved to Bradford for her?" Iman asks.

Her smile falters. "No, I . . . I didn't like my old university, and there's a pretty good journalism course here."

"Yeah," Hasan says, and Nur remembers that he is on that course. "Our journalism course is brilliant."

"I think *brilliant* is pushing it," Iman says, offering the spliff to Yasmina, who shakes her head at it, and Iman hands it to Nur.

"You won't be saying that when I win the Pulitzer."

"For your exposé on gentrification in Birmingham's inner-city boroughs?" Iman laughs.

"Wow, you really have a thing against Birmingham, don't you?"

"I just think it's got the worst accent in the world . . ."

"The worst!"

Nur watches the two of them go back and forth, and he readjusts so that he is closer to Yasmina. "You'll get used to this," he says, low enough that no one else hears, loud enough that she can. She smiles. He turns to face her. "Nur," he says, offering her his hand.

She takes it, her skin clammy against his. "Light," she says.

"Light?"

"That's what your name means." She lets his hand go, and he pulls back, resting his hands in his lap. "Light."

"You speak Arabic?"

"A little," she says.

Her eyes are a deep brown, so dark that they might be black, but they're not. "Muslim?" he asks.

"Yeah, but I don't practice as much as I should." She shakes her head, at herself more than him. "Wow, I don't know why I said that . . ."

"Guilt, I guess. Maybe you're looking for someone to validate you."

"Oh?" She raises an eyebrow at him. "And you're going to be that person?"

"Hmm, I don't know. Do I remind you of your dad?"

"My dad?"

"Most people want validation from their dads. Others from their mums. And I really hope I don't remind you of your mum."

Yasmina laughs, and the sound burrows into his chest, knocks on his heart. "You definitely do not remind me of my mum."

"So your dad, then?"

"Not him either."

"Well, fuck. I guess I won't be able to validate you after all."

"That's a shame. I was looking forward to being able to take this weight off my chest."

"You can definitely still confess if you want to. I've been told I'm a good listener."

"Were you looking in a mirror at the time?"

Nur opens his mouth in mock shock. "Are you calling me a narcissist?"

"Hey, you said it, not me."

Nur laughs. The last time he had it this easy, the last time he found himself talking to someone this quick, it had been at a party very similar to this, with a brown girl laying into him about the patriarchy.

"So how do you know Saara?" Yasmina asks, as if she has followed his thoughts.

The question throws Nur, and he glances at Saara to find her looking at him. Something tells him she can hear everything they are saying. He turns back to Yasmina, shrugs. "Friends," he says. "From first year."

"Oh, so you go here too?"

"Yeah, I'm doing English." Nur doesn't look back at Saara, his ears burning.

"You study the same language that you speak?"

"Oh!" He narrows his eyes at her. "You sound just like my dad."

"Oh, right, do you need some validation from me?" Yasmina jokes, and a grin spreads across his face, because this is easy, because this is *so easy*. "Because, you know, most people need validation from their dads. Or so I heard, from this guy at a party who started asking me if I needed him to validate me because he thought he looked like my dad, even though he didn't know me at all."

"So he did look like your dad, then?"

"Hmm," she says slowly, as if she's casting her mind back. "Well, no, he didn't. Not at all, actually. And when I told him that, he seemed oddly disappointed."

"Maybe you should have pitied him, just let him validate you."

"I don't think I need validating from anyone."

Before he can respond, he notices movement out of the corner of his eye, Saara stepping over Iman and Hasan, over Adam and another girl talking, to sit down in front of Nur and Yasmina.

"Talking a lot here," she notes.

"Your friend is trying to validate me," Yasmina explains, with an easy smile.

Saara's eyes land on Nur, in that same face he spent so much time with, learning the contours, tracing his fingers over its lines. He could draw this face with his eyes closed, conjure it in his sleep. A face he knows better than his own.

"He does tend to do that."

"Oh, he does?" Yasmina asks, raising her eyebrows at Nur playfully.

But Nur is still looking at Saara, because he can already hear the words coming from her lips, and he is asking her not to say anything, asking without asking, and they are both trapped in this fight that isn't happening.

"I guess he succeeded with me," Saara says. "What was it, just under a year?" She looks at Yasmina, and Nur's entire body tightens. "We didn't make it, though, obviously."

"Ah."

Nur can tell from Yasmina's voice that she knows who he is now, hadn't put it together before, had assumed that Nur the ex would not be at a party thrown by Saara, that he was a different Nur, just a friend. And he recognizes too that they have talked about him, that Yasmina knows things about him he might not want her to know or that he might want her to discover for herself.

"No, we didn't," Nur says, trying his best not to appear annoyed. But he is, and he knows that Saara knows he is, and he can see a little gleam in her eye, and all he wants to do is walk out of the room, but he stays where he is. "But we're good friends now."

"The best," Saara adds. "Yasmina, have I introduced you to Iman?"

And just like that, Yasmina has been reallocated, is now sitting by Iman, who offers her a hand, asks her what her favorite thing about Bradford is. Nur's face burns, and he feels alone again, as alone as he has ever felt in this room.

The day he broke up with Saara, over the summer, he was meant to stay at her parents' house in York for a weekend. He'd been back home to Birmingham since university had ended for the year and told his parents he was going to visit a friend. It wasn't the first time he had lied to them about Saara, risking their trust in him. When he got there, he couldn't face going to her house, so he asked her if they could just walk for a while. She talked a little about her parents, about how their group of friends wanted to start a charity for homeless youths, until his quiet stopped her, his silence too loud. She asked him what was wrong, and he nearly didn't do it, almost stopped himself. But he knew he had to, that it was why he was there. So he told her things weren't great, told her he wasn't great, that he loved her but he couldn't be with her anymore, that he needed space, that he wanted to end things. It spilled out in a jumble of words, every cliché imaginable slipping through. And when he finally stopped, she was silent. Then she turned back to him and said she wasn't going to beg him to change his mind, she would never beg any man for anything, she didn't understand but she didn't want him to explain, she didn't want to hear it. She just wanted him to leave. So he did, retracing his steps, forcing himself to keep moving even though he felt like he was sinking, back to the train station, back on the train, back to his life in Birmingham, nothing changed in the eyes of his family but everything changed for him.

Nur stands, drawing Adam's eye and raised eyebrows. Then he

looks away, pulls down the hem of his hoodie, and walks out of Saara's room.

He knows he has played right into her hands, that she has won something, though he isn't sure what. His breath short, he feels nauseous, desperate to get out. He walks down the stairs, back into the kitchen, where he runs the tap, fills a glass with cold water, takes a gulp, feels the chill run down his chest.

"Nur?"

He turns at the sound of his name, glass raised to his lips.

"Bit busy?" Imran asks, that usual easy smile on his face.

Nur swallows the water hurriedly. "Little bit," he says, wiping his mouth with the back of his hand. "You're actually here. At Saara's party. Past midnight." Nur is glad for the distraction.

"Past midnight," Imran repeats. "I guess it's just been one of those terms. Cannot wait to be done with everything and not go home and do nothing."

"Not go home? You're not going home this year?"

Imran shakes his head. "My parents are going to Dubai for the holidays."

"And you don't want to go because . . ."

"Well, I got the feeling it was more of a my-parents-want-to-be-alone trip than a family thing, you know?"

Nur lets out a groan. "No, I don't know, Imran."

"Oh, come on," Imran says, and he laughs. "You know your parents fuck, right?"

"I'm well aware that my parents fuck, thank you. I just don't need to think about it. Or talk about it. Ever. Why do you want to talk about it all the time?"

"Think about it, don't think about it. It's still a thing that happens." Imran reaches over to him, puts a hand on his arm. "It's okay. I'm pretty sure they're fucking right now."

"That is so . . ." Nur shudders. "Look, my family just isn't as bougie as yours. We don't talk about this stuff. Ever."

"Ah, so you're saying my middle-class, well-educated family who can afford to take trips to Dubai and have paid for my entire education—meaning that I don't have to take loans out to pay for anything—are nothing like your working-class family who can't do any of that?" He opens his mouth, a perfect O. "Shocking."

"You are so exhausting," Nur says.

"Yeah, but you like that."

Blood rushes to Nur's cheeks, his skin flushing. "Yeah, sure," he says, and he tightens his hand on the glass. "So why are you still here past midnight?"

"Well, partly because I didn't turn up to Saara's last few parties, and when she invited me to this one, I got the sense that if I didn't come and stay for longer than an hour, I might stop getting invited." He pauses for a second. "Plus, me and Jay broke up so I needed something to take my mind off it."

Nur's world turns slow, as he digests Imran's words. "What?"

Imran looks away, pauses. "Yeah." His voice is so small, so different from the Imran that Nur knows. "Last week. He just didn't want to be with me anymore."

Nur keeps from reaching out to Imran. "How are you doing?"

Imran looks at him, exasperated grimace painted on his lips, and spreads his arms wide. "Well, I'm here past midnight, aren't I? Ain't got nowhere else to go."

Nur moves to him, halts. "It's not weird if I hug you, right?" he asks.

"Weird?" Imran asks. "We are both single again, after all."

Nur pushes him gently, hand on his chest, and then he hugs him.

"God, I'm really crying at a party," Imran says, wiping the tears away from his eyes. Nur lets him go, stands back but not too far, still close enough that he can feel Imran. "I really wish that I was drunk. But then I think I'd become too much of a cliché."

"Saara's got some weed upstairs if you want," Nur says.

"Oh, has she?" Imran looks at him, waiting for more. "And the reason you're down here and not up there is because . . . ?"

"Because . . . ," Nur says, and he thinks about Yasmina again, that feeling in his chest, that tightness. "She can be a bit much sometimes."

Imran laughs, surprised. "I never thought I'd hear you say that."

"Well, I guess I didn't see it when we were dating."

"That why you broke up with her?"

"I thought the story was that we broke up with each other."

"The only reason Saara is telling that story is because you broke up with her. It doesn't take a genius to see that." Imran puts an arm around Nur's shoulders, leads him to the back of the house, into the garden, the air crisp, their breath like steam.

"Why have you brought me out into the cold?" Nur asks, shivering. There are a few people that Nur semi-recognizes but whose names he doesn't know, sitting on the few chairs out here, next to a table of ashtrays. Their cigarettes glow in the darkness.

"Because my friend over there," Imran says, gesturing with his head, "has some non-Saara weed, and you and I are going to get high."

"Imran, you know . . ."

"I know the last time you got high, you spent your night throwing up. But look, you're with me, I'll take care of you. I promise." Imran walks him over to a guy sitting on the concrete, knees by his chest, arms hanging off them. "Hakeem."

Hakeem sees Imran and stands, reaching out for a half hug, Imran pulling Nur with him. "I did not think I'd see you here tonight," Hakeem says.

"Can't turn down Saara too many times. She might stop inviting me."

"Well, I can't deny that. Better to be on the inside than out." Hakeem puts his hand into his pocket, pulls out a spliff. "The usual, I assume?"

"As always. How much?"

"This one, on the house, for you," Hakeem says, and he glances at Nur as he speaks, winks at him.

"On the house," Imran says, and he waves the spliff in front of Nur.

"Imran . . ."

"Look, my boyfriend dumped me after eight months of being together because he said I was too much for him. Just smoke a little with me so I don't have to cry on your shoulder again."

Nur almost says no, but he recognizes the look in Imran's eyes, has been there himself. "Fine," he says.

"Perfect." Imran lets go of him. Spliff in mouth, he lights and puts his hands around it, an intimate dua, breathing in, closing his eyes for a second. "This is exactly what I needed."

The cloud of smoke dissolves into the air. Imran offers the spliff to Nur, who takes it.

The last time Nur smoked was just before the summer started, at a party for the end of first year. He'd smoked a few times before, lost his mind in it the same way everyone else did. But this time he had smoked a little and didn't feel anything for a while. And then smoked a little more . . . until his head felt so light, it was as if he was about to lose it, a balloon racing into the sky. The ground started to shift under him, suddenly alive and moving. The next thing he knew, he was on the floor, throwing up. Saara was there, helping him stand, taking him to a bathroom, staying with him while he rested his head on the toilet seat and tried not to think about who'd been there last. Then he'd told her he loved her, and she'd told him she loved him too, and he threw up a little more, dry heaves because there was nothing left in him.

Now, a term later, Nur puts the spliff to his lips, breathes in, his lungs filling, the sensation spreading through his body.

"You know," Imran says, and Nur looks back at him, "I know we're only, like, what, twenty, but sometimes I just feel so tired."

He reaches for the spliff, but Nur waves it out of reach, flame glowing in the dark. "What?"

Imran lunges and grabs the roll-up. "I mean," he says, before sucking in, "that sometimes, I feel like"—exhaling—"I'm completely exhausted by life already. And I think about people who live to be like eighty or ninety, and I think, I don't know how they get to that age. How tired they must be. How boring life must be when they get that far."

"I guess that's why people have kids, though, right?" Nur says, trying to imagine what he might be like in the future, what kind of person might inhabit his body, but he can't. That idea of him, of being older, of being an adult, feels odd, like he will never age, like he will always be this young, this old.

"So, what, they can complain about them when they're old?"

Imran laughs. "That's all my grandmother does. Complains about her bougie liberal kid who married someone else's bougie liberal kid, who raised their kid as a bougie liberal too, all going about their lives blissfully ignorant of whether they're behaving the way they're meant to, if they're living their lives the way other people want them to. Who act the way they want to, not the way they're expected to by . . ." He gestures vaguely. "By all that stuff."

Nur pauses for a second. "But those things are important too," he says. "Culture, tradition. It's what makes us who we are." A couple walk past them, heading back to the house. Nur and Imran move out of their way, farther to the back of the garden, where there are plants, dead now in the fall. Saara's plants, ones that Nur helped her with, digging in the soil with their fingers.

"Well, they're only as important as you make them, right? Our culture, tradition, religion would say that we shouldn't be smoking this. Or actually, maybe we can because we're men, so we can do whatever we want. But Saara can't, because she's a woman. And I wouldn't be standing here anyway because I would never have dated Jay, since that's against everything too, right? We have this dichotomy between what used to be important for our parents and what's important now, to us. You have to hold those two things up." He lifts both hands into the air, like arms of a scale. "And then make your choice on which one you want."

"And you want to give it up?"

"Not give it up." Long exhale. "But maybe change the terms. I don't know. Make it work for me instead of feeling like I have to change myself to work for it."

Nur casts his eyes back up to the house. The cold has settled in him, but even so, he would like to be back in the sticky heat of the party. Though that would also mean seeing Saara, and he doesn't want that.

"What are you thinking right now?" Imran asks. Nur pivots toward him, eyebrows knitting together. "Just now. What were you thinking about?"

"Nothing," Nur says.

Imran gives him a look.

"Saara," Nur says.

"You want to get back with her?" Nur shakes his head. "Has she asked to get back with you?" Another shake. "Ah, so you want to get with someone else?"

Nur hesitates at that, asks, "Why does it only have to be those options?"

"Because it's always one of those options."

"I don't know," Nur says. "What if I said I do?"

"How long has it been?"

"Three months."

"That's plenty of time."

"I don't know," Nur says, staring down at his feet, uncomfortable, because this is the first time he's had this conversation out in the open with someone else, the first time he has let himself. "Doesn't it feel a bit like betraying her?"

"Betraying her? You know *you* broke up with her, right?"

"Yeah, exactly. So she should go first. I should wait for her to start seeing someone new."

Imran lets a laugh escape. "You do realize how dumb that sounds, right? And not even like regular dumb. Just really very dumb." Nur opens his mouth to defend himself, but Imran lifts his hand to offer what's left of the spliff, plus a raised finger, silencing him. "Saara will date again when she wants to. You should do the same. If you feel like now is the right time, then now is the right time."

"And you?" Nur asks, coughing at the gritty ends he inhales. "Is it the right time?"

"For me to, what, get with someone else?" Imran asks. Nur nods. Imran sighs. "I think it's a bit too early for me to be thinking about that," he says. "I'm sure there'll be people. But I'm not ready right now, for rebounds or whatever. Jay was . . . well, a big part of my life. My first proper relationship. Nearly a whole year. Mad." He puts his hands in his pockets, shrugs his shoulders, looks away from Nur, but not quickly enough. Nur sees the glistening of tears in his eyes, a sharp wetness that fades as fast as it comes. "But it's over, right? It's done. Sorted. Gone. In the past. Now we move on and try not to think about it."

Nur flicks the end of the joint away. "Now we move on and try not to think about it," he says, reaching for Imran, arm around his shoulders. And as he does, he sees Yasmina step out into the garden, still without a jacket, and he stops, whole body tense, just for a moment.

Imran notices, follows Nur's eyes, and laughs. "So that's her?"

"I don't know what you're talking about," Nur says, waving away the suggestion, but it's too late. His body has betrayed him, and she's looking right at him now, beaming, walking over to them.

"Hey," Yasmina calls out.

"Hey." Nur is aware that he's holding Imran, that his arm is around his shoulders, and he can't seem to pull it away. A grin unfolds on Imran's face, a grin that says a lot.

"Hey," Imran says, moving so Nur's arm falls. "Imran."

"Yasmina."

"Good name," Imran says, and he nods at Nur, stepping to the side. "Well, Yasmina, enjoy Nur. I'm going in because it's very cold out here."

He jumps around her, toward the door, and Nur watches as he turns back, winking just as he steps into the house.

"So I . . ."

"Upstairs . . . ," Nur says, both of them speaking at the same time, and Nur stops, embarrassed.

"You go," she says.

"No, you go."

She bites her lip, a flash of white against her skin. "Me and Saara, we've been friends for a while, so of course I know about you. I just didn't make the connection until she . . . But I just wanted to say sorry it was awkward. I didn't mean to make you feel uncomfortable or like you had to leave—"

"You didn't," Nur says, interrupting her rush of words to make her feel better. "That was all Saara, believe me."

She's silent for a second, and he wonders what she's thinking. "But you're still friends?"

"We try to be," Nur says. "I admire her a lot. We just didn't work as . . . But that doesn't mean that we can't be friends, right?"

"Right," Yasmina says. She crosses her arms over her chest, tight. "Well, yeah, sorry. I didn't want to imply—"

"You weren't," Nur interjects. "Honestly." He glances past her head at the door to the house. "Shall we go inside?"

"Yeah, sure," she says, and she turns, both of them walking back into the party, his body so numb he can barely feel his fingertips or his nose as the warmth slams into them.

"Do you drink?" Nur asks, wanting to offer her something. The kitchen is nearly empty; a boy and a girl talk quietly in the corner.

"No." Nur looks at her, properly looks at her under the soft yellow light, how her dark skin glows. How her eyes are huge next to her small nose, her hair in long braids, scooped up in a high bun, her lips, the small rings up the edges of her ears, three in her left, four in her right. "I'm Muslim," she says.

"Oh, me too." Then he laughs. "Ah, like we discussed upstairs."

"Like we discussed upstairs."

"But you don't practice as much as you should."

"As I should?" she asks, giving him a look.

"Your words, not mine," he says, raising his hands. "I mean, I'm not the best either. Can't remember the last time I prayed." He moves slightly, a few people drifting into the room.

"I don't know if you're actually proud of that, or you're just trying to make me feel better."

"Do you need to be made to feel better about your relationship with religion?"

"Well," she says, and she tilts her head a little, narrows her eyes. "I don't know, maybe. Don't we all?"

"Hey, speak for yourself. I'm pretty content with how I go about my religious observance. I'll just get to like, what, midthirties, have a massive midlife crisis, go to Umrah, and then come back very religious, a very good Muslim man, and force my family to do the same even if they don't want to."

"You've got it all figured out," Yasmina replies with a soft laugh, her attention drifting around the room of people talking.

"So." Nur glances around too, briefly nervous. "Why this uni?"

Yasmina's eyes pull back to him. "Well, that depends."

"On what?"

"On what your stance is about introducing trauma into conversations with strangers."

"Oh, I'm all for the trauma. Start with the low-stakes stuff, like you know, my granddad doesn't particularly like me, or my cat died when I was home and I didn't know what to do with the body so I just left it there until my parents came home . . ."

"Your cat died and you just left it there until your parents came home?"

Nur can't help but snort. "No, that's just a hypothetical example."

"A strangely specific example."

"My cat is very much alive."

"So you do own a cat?"

"Four years and running."

"What's its name?"

Nur wrinkles his nose. "Look, my mum is very invested in Harry Potter . . ."

"What's it called?"

"You know, she's watched, like, all the films. She just loves the magic of it all. We even took her to the Harry Potter film studio thing for her birthday. She was so happy. All the sets and—"

"What's it called?"

He can't hide the grin on his face anymore. "Hagrid." Yasmina laughs in delight. "Look, the cat is really fluffy. And her fur is dark. She reminds my mum of Hagrid, so we named her Hagrid."

"Oh, so it's 'we' now?" she asks.

"Well, my mum likes to think we live in a democracy, and we don't like to tell her it's a dictatorship."

"Can't upset the dictator."

"Never upset the dictator."

Again, Nur is taken by how easy this is, by how little conscious effort he has to put in, how simple it feels. Like he's fallen into her, conversation flowing, found parts of himself that he didn't even know were missing.

He moves a touch closer. "So . . . your trauma?"

"I think I might wait until we've seen each other a couple of times before I begin revealing something so intimate."

He can't resist seizing on that sliver of hope. "You want to see me again?"

"All right, don't get too ahead of yourself," she says. "I'm still considering things."

They stay like that in the kitchen, talking back and forth so rapidly they barely have the space to catch their breath. As the time edges past three, Yasmina says she should probably go home, and there's regret in the air then for the night that's ending. Nur says he should be getting back too, and though he feels tired, lids heavy, he is lying. Yasmina asks him where he lives—a house just fifteen minutes away from Saara's—and she says she lives near there, so he offers to walk her home. Nur doesn't even think to say goodbye to Saara on the way out, only tips his head at Imran, who has set up camp on one of the sofas with another joint in his hand, set on blocking everything out.

Yasmina and Nur step into the night, the air colder than before. They should be in their beds, wrapped up, the world quiet. There is frost on the pavement, so their path is slow and careful. In part, it's so they don't slip, but maybe it's also so they don't have to leave each other so quickly. Yasmina's arms are crossed over her chest and against the cold as they walk up the road. Nur offers her his jacket, trying to press it on her, but she refuses, tells him she's fine. He wants to offer it to her one more time so that she'll take it home with her, giving him an excuse to see her again, but resists. They reach her house, and as she looks at him from her doorstep, shoulders still shivering, there is a moment. Then they say good night, and she opens the door, slipping in behind it. He stands there for a second, just a second, before making his own way home. Nur walks straight to his bed, lying down without taking anything off, and he thinks back to her, joy spreading through him.

January 2019

"What happened? What did they say?"

Nur is back in Nottingham sitting on the floor of their flat, shoes off by the door like always. He's looking at the art on the wall opposite him, prints Yasmina bought from a local artist she found online. She sits on the sofa, hands fluttering in her lap, waiting.

He returned yesterday evening, coming back to an empty flat. Yasmina was out with her friends, celebrating the start of a new year, and Nur was thankful she wasn't there. Not because he didn't want to see her, because he did, had missed her sorely for those two weeks. But because it meant he didn't have to explain himself.

He'd showered, scrubbing off the filth that came with traveling, but he couldn't scrub away his family's shocked faces.

"A Sudanese girl?" Khalil had asked. He punched Nur on the shoulder, light but still painful; Khalil had always been the bigger one of the two of them, the stronger one. "I never thought you'd be the rebel."

"What is she like?" Mariam asked tentatively.

Nur stood by the window in Khalil's room, pressed against the windowsill, fingers wrung, restless with nerves, trying his best not to lose it. If he wasn't careful, he was going to crack, he could feel it. "She's really great," he said, no lightness in his voice. "She's the best person I know. Good and smart, so smart, always teaching me things I didn't even know I didn't know."

"So it's been four years?" Mariam asked. Nur nodded, a lump in his throat. "And you kept it secret all this time?"

"I wanted to be sure it was for real," he said, a ready excuse prepared beforehand.

It felt odd to talk about this with his younger sister, but she was no longer that young. Nineteen years old. When she was small, her face was round and full; now she's grown into her features, the only one of them to have inherited their father's petite nose, and yet there is still a child hidden underneath.

There is a rupture between him and his siblings, the unveiling of a secret that suggests there are other secrets not being shared. "I couldn't bring her home without knowing that it was going somewhere, that we were something."

"But you know you could have told us," Mariam said.

"And are you?" Khalil asked. "Something?"

"She's the only thing I'm sure about in this world." And though the words had struck Nur as sounding disingenuous, as if lifted from some Instagram poet's profile, he meant them. "I would give up everything for her."

"Well, you might have to," Khalil muttered.

"Khalil!" Mariam elbowed him in the side.

"What?" he said. "You know how everyone gets about this stuff. Pakistani, Muslim, preferably known to the family or, even better, part of the family. That's how it goes. It's bad enough marrying an Indian or a Bangladeshi Muslim. Maybe, just maybe, they'd be okay with someone white. And you know what they always say about their kids. *So beautiful, so light.* That would be easier. But how many people in the family do we know who are married to Black people. It's just . . . harder. You guys know that."

Nur let out a hollow laugh. "Now you know why I didn't bring her around for Eid."

Mariam moved over to him, put her head on his shoulder, the same way he does with his mother, the same way Yasmina does with him. "Well, I'm happy for you, Nur. If that means anything."

If that means anything.

N ur," Yasmina says.

It's early in the morning. He'd lied to his parents about coming back. He'd taken this week off, knew he'd need the time to process. And Yasmina's PhD means she runs her own hours, so they're both here on a Wednesday morning, sun barely risen. The flat is warm and homely, and Nur wishes he'd slept in longer, pretended to be asleep. Not that he'd managed to get much rest; he'd kept himself awake going over everything again and again.

"I told them about you," he says. He chooses his words carefully, like he's sitting in front of a bomb, tweezers extended, pliers in hand, making sure that he's cutting the right wire. "Said we'd been seeing each other since university. Four years. Four whole years." It sounds surreal when he says it out loud, that he had kept their relationship like this, hidden, for so long. How did he ever convince himself this was the right thing to do?

Yasmina sighs and asks, "And?"

He turns away from her, eyes closed for a second.

"Mum said she needed some time to think about it. Dad didn't contribute much, but he's following Mum, like always . . . Mariam and Khalil are happy, though. They want to meet you." He glances at her, pushes past the lump in his throat. "But no one said anything much in the morning. Khalil made a joke, Mariam said she was excited to meet you one day, maybe, but . . ."

And he's back there again, sitting at the table. His father has gone to work, early shift at the taxi base, and Nur won't see him again before he leaves. His mother is making breakfast, roti over hot flames on the hob, the kind she made for him when he was younger, burning the white into black, spreading butter over it, and though he knows it's bad for him, he eats it anyway. He waits for someone to say something, anything. But if there are words simmering, they aren't being said aloud.

He hovers on edge all morning, until the time comes to catch his train. And when he leaves, ordering an Uber to the station, telling his mother it's fine, she doesn't have to drop him off, hugging her, saying no, it won't be that long before he returns, that he misses them all too much to stay away for long, he pauses, waiting for her to say something, but she doesn't. He sits in the car, ignoring the driver as he talks, lets the events of the past day settle in him.

"Nothing," Yasmina says. It's not a question. She falls back onto the sofa, bringing her legs up, knees pressed into her chest, curling herself up. "They didn't ask what I study, if I pray five times a day or wear a scarf, didn't want to know anything about the woman their son loves?"

"Mina." Nur climbs up next to her, puts his hand on her arm, holding it. "Look, my parents . . ." He tries to find the words that will make it better. "They'll just need some time."

"How much time?"

"Just . . . longer."

"Mine didn't," she counters, staring right ahead, hurt in her voice. There is something else too, the implication that her parents are better than his once again taking shape.

"I know," he says. "I know. I think about that all the time. You know how much I want this . . ."

"Do you?" she asks, turning her eyes to him. "So you fought for us then, when they said nothing? You said, this is really important to me, we need to talk about it, we have to."

"Well . . ."

"So no, then?"

"I didn't want to . . ."

"Are you going to call them?" she asks.

"I don't know."

"I think you should."

"I can't just force this down their throats."

"Me," she states, her voice firm. "You can't force *me* down their throats."

"Mina, I don't want to force anything down anyone's throats."

Neither of them move.

Sometimes, Nur wishes he had never met her that night, that he had made different decisions, not gone to that party or any party of Saara's. He thinks of these alternate realities, where different choices were made, where other Nurs exist who are perhaps better sons to his parents. But he can only think like this briefly, because he knows, even though things are hard for him and Yasmina now, that his life is better with her in it. There's no question at all.

"You should phone them," she says. "You don't have to talk about me. Just phone them. Make sure that they know you're not angry with them. Be their good son."

Bitterness coats those last four words.

She stands from the sofa, his hand tossed aside. He doesn't move. He hears her in their bedroom. The fast unzip of a bag, clothes landing in it, the closing of a laptop, the unplugging of a charger. He expects her to come back, but she doesn't. Instead, she heads to the door, a moment of quiet as she puts her shoes on, the turning of the handle, and then the click of the door shutting as she walks out.

December 2014

Snow has settled on the ground. Nur walks with his shoulders hunched to protect himself from the chill. He leaves footprints behind him, a trail to follow should anyone want to find him.

Fingers around his keys in his pocket, he walks up to the door of his house, takes them out, and they slip through his grasp to the ground. He swears, bending to pick them up. He stays for a second, the weight that has been there all day pressing down on him. Closing his eyes, he tries to think of something happy, of something good, but his mind is blank, a great black cloud hanging over him, blocking out the light.

The door opens, and he lifts his head to see Rahat standing over him. Rahat kneels down too, so they are eye level. "Again?" he asks. Nur nods.

Rahat extends a hand to him, and Nur takes it, walking into the house, pausing to enjoy the blood rushing back into his fingers in the heat.

"I made food," Rahat says. "Biryani."

"Biryani," Nur repeats, as if he doesn't quite understand it, needs to question it. "Sounds good."

Rahat goes into the kitchen and begins serving the food, the clatter of dishes a welcoming sound of home. Nur offers to help, and together they perform a dance, the ritual of moving in the same small space that comes from having lived together for a while. Nur takes the plates, Rahat carrying everything else, and they move back into the living room, books and papers pushed aside, plates and glasses and cutlery set down.

"Do you want to talk about it?" Rahat asks, not even waiting to taste his food.

Nur takes a mouthful of the biryani. It reminds him of home, of his mother, of sitting at Ramadan, waiting for the fast to be over so he can take a bite, of his grandmother's house on Eid Day, sitting with his cousins, passing bottles around, plastic cups raised to lips.

Rahat stays quiet, waiting for him to answer, and Nur lets the silence envelop them both.

Here is the truth.

Nur is seven, and he has broken a glass. Shattered it against the stone kitchen tiles. It slipped out of his fingers, shards scattered across the floor. He knows he should brush them all together, tell his parents that he has broken the glass. That it's fine, he wasn't hurt, but that the glass is destroyed. But he can't. There is darkness inside him, staring at the shards of glass, telling him he is useless and there is no point in trying to fix this. He wants to go and lie down, close his eyes, not open them again.

He is eleven and sitting in a new class. There are children all around him, buzzing with excitement, and a lot of them seem to know each other, while he doesn't know anyone. He forces himself to talk to someone. But what he really wants is to sit in the corner, not speak. He doesn't like to speak, doesn't think that he has anything of value to say, doesn't think anyone wants to listen.

He is fourteen, and Aqib is showing the scars on his wrist, long pale ones against his brown skin. They aren't deep, Aqib says, they'll heal. Nur traces his fingers over them, noting how smooth they are, and he asks how he did it. With the blade of my scissors, Aqib whispers.

He is eighteen, and he is sitting on the edge of his bed at university, pale scars on his thighs. Saara is tracing her fingers over them, asking him how he got them, and he can tell from her eyes that she knows already, that she has done the same to herself. But he tells her anyway. About that first time, four years ago, when he sat in the bath, water still running, and he took the razor blade he had stolen from his father's toiletry bag, the tip of it sharper than anything he had ever seen. He had pressed it to his inner thigh, let it cut through the skin, bit his lip as it stung, blood blooming into the water. He had clamped his hand over the cut, closed his eyes, let himself feel the pain because he deserved it. Saara leans closer, presses her lips to his skin.

Here is more of the truth.

Sometimes, there is an emptiness inside him so large it would take the entire world to fill. It comes and goes as it pleases, triggered by nothing specific. He feels it as much on a train going home to his family in Birmingham as he does on one coming back to university, in a lecture or in the library, lying in his bed alone or standing in the middle of a party.

Maybe some day he will become used to it, able to live alongside it, but for now, it can still take him by surprise.

You should see someone about how you're feeling," Rahat says after Nur fails to answer, the scraping of their forks against plates amplified by his silence.

"So I can get pills to fix me?"

"So you can get the help you need."

"I don't need—"

"Nur," Rahat says, and it is all there in his voice, the conversations they've had before, the attempts to make him feel better.

Nur pushes his fork through the rice and the chicken, parting them. "I don't know. I was fine. Went to my last lecture. Got the bus. Walked back. And then out of nowhere . . ."

"I heard your keys." Rahat pushes his plate away, turns to face Nur. "They dropped and then you didn't open the door."

"Thanks," Nur mutters. "For opening the door."

"Well, it could have been a con. I could have opened the door to a murderer."

Nur forces a chuckle for his friend. "When do you leave for home?" he asks.

"A couple hours. My dad's driving to get me. I told him I didn't want to carry all my books back on the train."

Nur lets the fork drop onto the plate.

"Nur," Rahat says. "You have to get help."

"I'll be fine."

"Yeah, but how long until you're fine this time? And how long will that last?"

"People get sad, Rahat."

"For a while. Maybe a day or two. A week. But you've been sad the entire time I've known you."

Nur scoffs. "Thanks."

"Do you remember?" Rahat reaches back for his plate, settling it on his lap. "The first time?"

"The first time for you."

"Okay, yes, the first time for me."

A few weeks into their friendship, secondary school, all the boys changing in the locker room for soccer, all of them excited to finally play rather than just run around the field endlessly. But Nur wasn't. He stood at the back of the room, head rushing, wanting to become part of the wall. When they all ran out, he stayed behind, and Rahat asked him what was wrong, told him he'll get the teacher when Nur couldn't reply, Nur gasping heavily, telling him no, please don't, as Rahat repeated, "It'll be fine, it'll be okay." And Nur believed him, anchored himself to Rahat's voice, went out with him, spent the hour close at his side.

It was what cemented them.

"I was right then, and I'm right now, Nur."

"I met someone," Nur says.

"You're changing the subject."

"At Saara's party. A friend of hers."

Rahat shakes his head, clearly confused. "You met Saara's friend?"

"I met Saara's friend."

"And she is a person?"

"She is a person."

"That you met."

"That I met."

"Does Saara know?"

"That I met this person? She introduced us."

"Saara introduced you to her friend. Who is now your 'person.' And she knows." Rahat gives him a what-the-fuck look.

"She is not *my* 'person.'"

"But you just said you met someone."

"I did meet someone."

Rahat jabs at Nur's arm. "Okay. Right, just tell me. What happened?"

"That party I went to a few weeks ago. I met someone and we spoke, like, the entire night. I walked her back to her house. That's it, really."

Rahat waits for more. "That's it. That's your big story?"

There is so much more to it. Nur cannot stop thinking about her, keeps replaying their conversation in his head.

"Well, I am just telling you I met someone. What else do you want?"

"Do you want to see her again?"

"I think so."

"How long has it been since Saara?"

"Nearly four months."

Rahat considers this. "Then I think you're fine. But how close are they as friends?"

Nur thinks back to the party, to the way Saara introduced Yasmina, the way they behaved around each other. "I don't know. Close enough that she came to the party. But maybe she just came because she doesn't know anyone else in Bradford. All I know is that they've been friends long enough for Saara to tell her about me."

"I don't know if that means anything, though," Rahat says. "Like, Saara would have told anyone about you guys being over."

"I guess," Nur replies, uncertainty running through him. "Saara was definitely acting like they were really close. And I don't know if I can go and, like, start something with one of her friends."

"If you dated someone I had dated, I'd definitely kill you."

"Would you do that because of the betrayal of our friendship or because you've always secretly worried I was better looking than you and this would be the manifestation of that fear?"

Rahat stretches his leg to kick Nur. "I would kill you. Does it matter why?"

"I suppose not." Nur reaches for the unfinished plate in front of him, hungry again. "So you don't think I should find out, then?"

"How much do you care about her being Saara's friend?"

"Well, it's definitely a factor, right? Like, she's Saara's friend."

"Yeah, but you and Saara are done. It's not like you guys even see each other that much, outside of her parties. Which I keep telling you that you should stop going to."

"And never fail to bring it up whenever you can," Nur says. "We're meant to be friends now. And we both know we can't be anything more, but maybe friends is good."

"Good," Rahat says, raising an eyebrow.

"Is there something wrong with 'good'?"

"I don't think you and Saara are good—" He holds up his fork when Nur opens his mouth to object. "Wait. I'm not done. I don't think you and Saara are good as friends, because you don't actually want to be friends with her at all. I think you just want to be around her even though you broke up with her."

"That's not . . ."

"Isn't it?" Rahat asks. "Why else do you go to her parties?"

"They're fun."

"There are other parties and you don't go to any of them. And you always say you never know anyone else there."

Nur looks back at his plate, frustrated, though he doesn't know if it's with himself or with Rahat. "I don't think it's a bad thing to try and be friendly with Saara."

"No," Rahat says. "But there is something wrong with living

your life thinking about her all the time. It doesn't matter what she thinks, Nur. You don't belong to her like that anymore."

"How very therapist of you," Nur says, keeping the edge from his voice.

"I'm not your therapist."

"I know." Nur pushes his polished-off plate away on the table. "Anyway. I was telling you all of this because this person added me on Facebook."

"Okay, so you buried the lede on that." Rahat extends his hand to Nur, palm open. "Show me."

"Just don't do anything," Nur says, fishing in his pocket for his phone. He pulls it out, opens Facebook, and types her name in, flushing a little when he sees it's the last thing he'd searched for.

Rahat reaches over, and Nur watches as he scrolls, looking through her posts. She hasn't posted anything since he checked last night, flipping through her photos, of which there are only a few.

"Journalism," Rahat remarks. "Moved here from Sheffield. Do you know why?" He opens her photos, swiping through them, and Nur is suddenly filled with revulsion watching him, like they have turned Yasmina into an object.

"No, I don't," Nur says, fighting the urge to grab the phone back from Rahat.

"Have you messaged her?"

"Not yet."

"How long since she added you?"

"Like, a week, I think."

"A week?" Rahat says, incredulous. "And you haven't said a single thing?"

"She hasn't said anything either," Nur says, defensive.

"She added you. Maybe she's waiting for you to make the first move. Well, second move."

Nur takes the phone back, locks it. "Okay, but I don't know what I would say."

"Just start with hello and go from there." He makes it sound so easy.

"What if she . . ."

"What if she what?"

"What if whatever we had that night, was just for that night? What if it doesn't come back?"

"You think you've lost the ability to communicate?"

"No."

"Okay. So just do it."

Nur slips the phone between his fingers, turning it over and over again.

"Look, you're the one studying English, the witty writer, the cornucopia of creativity, right? I'm sure you can come up with something relatively inoffensive."

Nur turns the screen on, looks at Yasmina's profile photo. She is smiling, right at the camera, hair braided differently, long down her back, and she is standing with a boy that looks a lot like her, maybe her brother, a friend, or maybe something more. It's dark in the photo, the moon behind her.

He brings up the chat and starts typing, backspaces, starts typing again, deletes the words. Slowly, he taps out something new, as if sacrificing each letter to some kind of god that might be able to give him what he wants.

Rahat doesn't say anything.

When Nur's done, his thumb hovers over the "Send" button. He waits, a moment, and presses it, turning his phone off immediately, not wanting to see the pathetic fruit of his labor.

•••

In some places, the snow has melted under the glare of the sun and the pounding of feet before freezing over again. These small glimpses of ice are hard to notice, sending people flailing up and down roads, arms in the air like windmills, trying to find something to hold on to. Children laugh as they run down the streets, trying their best not to fall, and when they do, there is a moment where everyone stops, waiting to see if the child is hurt. Then it lets out a giggle, and the world breathes a sigh of relief, moves again.

Nur is walking into the center of Bradford. The jacket he's

wearing is thin, more for the autumn than the winter, but he likes the way he looks in it.

It's the week before the holidays, so people are out, stuffed into their coats and gloves and hats, carrying bags and bags of shopping. Nur walks around them, through them, a little panic when his foot nearly slips beneath him, but he recovers and continues on, eager to get where he is heading.

When he reaches the restaurant, she is standing outside, in jeans and a jacket, black winged eyeliner, hat over her natural, loose hair, small curls poking out underneath it at her neck, headphones trailing from her ears. He watches her on her phone, nervous excitement pulsing through him, and steps toward her. She looks up, as if she can hear his racing heart, smiles, takes her headphones out.

"You made it," she says.

"Did you think I wasn't going to?"

He stops in front of her, not sure what to do. His first date with Saara, at the cinema, they had hugged hello, but Saara had initiated it; he hadn't known what to do then either, his body suddenly foreign.

"Shall we go in?" she asks. He nods, and they step into the restaurant. A girl, around their age, immediately comes to them, leads them to a small booth by a window.

Nur sits, sliding to the middle, taking his jacket off. "I've never been here before," he says, looking around.

"Believe it or not, not many people have." Yasmina pulls her beanie off, running her hands through her curls. "Saara told me about it."

Nur tenses at the mention of her name. "Have you been here before?"

"Once."

"With Saara," he guesses, finishing her sentence for her.

She smirks and picks up the menu. "I had fish last time. It's really good."

"Okay." He nods, surveying the assortment of Asian fusion dishes down the menu, the names he recognizes, and the ones he doesn't, until he lands on something he's had before, salmon teriyaki.

"Saara never brought you here?"

"I imagine there's a lot of places that Saara never took me," Nur says, immediately aware of how sharply that lands, and he winces. "We were only together for a year. Not even a year. Less, really."

"I know," Yasmina replies, still looking at the menu, not at him.

"Can I ask, what do you know?" The menu lowers a little, her eyes meeting his. "Like, how *much* do you know?"

"You want to know what she told me?"

"Maybe."

"Because you're a narcissist."

"Because I'm curious. Have you never wanted to know what an ex has said about you?"

Yasmina returns to the menu, eyes disappearing downward.

"You don't feel like that about an ex?" Nur continues.

A moment before she answers. "No."

"Because?"

"Because I don't date."

"You don't date? Or you never have dated?"

"I don't date," she repeats, and the menu goes back up so all he sees is her hair above it.

Nur looks down at the table, bites the inside of his cheek, wondering if he has misread the entire situation. "So what is this, then?" he asks.

The menu lowers again. "This . . . ," she says, leaving the word hanging in the air. "I'd say this was a pre-date."

"A pre-date?"

"Like a thing that we do to see if there's an actual date."

"Have you had many pre-dates?"

"I would have to say you're the first."

"I'm the first pre-date you've had?"

"Yes."

"So there's no precedent? How will you know if this is going to turn into an actual date when you don't have the data?"

A smile curls at the corner of her mouth. "Okay. I see your point. There's no criteria for this. So I guess this is pre-date zero."

"I'm pre-date patient zero?"

"You're pre-date patient zero."

"Wow," Nur says, leaning back in the booth. "I've never been patient zero for anything."

"Neither have I," Yasmina says.

"So you don't date because . . ."

"Because I'm way too insecure to ever think anyone might like me," she says. "You know, until I met a cute boy at a party and he convinced me I'm the most beautiful person he's ever seen, and we go on to have this picture-perfect life . . ."

"The cute boy being me?"

". . . because, you know, you can't abstain from dating without people asking you why. You can't just say you haven't really been interested, haven't found anyone you're into, too focused on your studying. Because that's weird, right?"

"Definitely weird. I much prefer the first story."

"You know, I didn't expect you to message me."

"I didn't expect you to add me."

"You didn't?" she asks.

"No," Nur answers. "I thought your allegiance would lie with Saara."

"Allegiance?" She stresses each syllable, the word falling heavy from her lips.

Nur considers. "Well, you're her friend . . ."

"As are you."

"Well, yeah, but I just thought maybe you might not want to talk to me because I went out with her, and . . ." His sentence trails off.

"Hmm." She traces her fingers over the menu slowly. "Well, I added you because I thought you were interesting. And when you asked me to come meet you for food, I thought, well, I want to do that, so I'm going to. Saara never came into it."

"Does she know?"

"Not unless you told her."

"So we're on a secret date."

"Pre-date," Yasmina corrects him, her eyes lighting up, the sides of them crinkling as her mouth stretches into a smile. Nur finds himself falling right into them, and he's glad that Rahat forced him to send that message, glad that he asked her out, that she said yes and they're here now. Because if he had to go home for the Christmas holidays without seeing her again, he wouldn't have been able to stop thinking about the what-ifs. Although now he won't be able to stop thinking about her no matter what.

They sit quietly, and Nur is happy to sit in silence with Yasmina. He feels perfectly comfortable but at the same time doesn't want to be complacent, feels the need to break the quiet, to entertain.

"What do people talk about on pre-dates?" Yasmina asks, interrupting his internal debate.

"I don't know. I've never been on one."

She lets loose a single chuckle. "Okay. What do people talk about on first dates?"

"I've only ever had one."

Yasmina's eyes widen a fraction. "Saara?" He nods. "Tell me about it."

"That feels a little weird."

"Oh," she says. "You don't have to."

But now he's there in his memory, waiting for Saara to arrive, watching her walk across the cinema foyer to him where he's standing, tickets in hand because he got there so early he thought he might as well get them. She leans into him, hugs him, hard, tight, and he hugs her back.

"We watched *Birdman*, at the small cinema, near uni, and Saara had a lot of opinions."

"Of course she did," Yasmina remarks, leaning toward him, her arms crossed on the table.

"So we talked and talked. And I enjoyed it. It felt like time just . . . disappeared."

"So I guess we do that, then," Yasmina says.

"Talk?" Nur asks. "We're doing that right now."

"Is it working? Do you feel yourself falling deeply in love with me?"

"No, I don't think that's pre-date stuff. That's definitely, like, second or third date stuff."

"You think you'll get a second or third date?"

"I'd say this is going fairly well."

"Fairly well. I can agree with that."

Their food arrives, and they continue to talk in between bites. Nur settles in, feeling more and more comfortable in her presence. She asks why he studies English, and he tells her it's because he hopes to be a writer one day when he grows up. She asks when that is for him, and he hesitates, says twenty-five, but he doesn't even believe that himself, can't quite see himself being anything at twenty-five, it feels so far away. He asks her why journalism, and she elaborates, explaining how she's tired of having the same out-of-touch narrative poured down her throat, that she wants more reporting from people who look like her, who look like him, instead of the predominantly white mainstream media. He listens to her speak about structural racism in journalism, why people should think about where their news comes from, that news is the way people see the rest of the world and the media has a responsibility to be as objective as possible, but where does true objectivity come from, and something fizzes in him, makes him feel so weightless, he's scared he might float away.

When they're finished, the waitress brings over a receipt, and he brings his hand down on one side just as she does the same on the other. "I've got it," he says.

"I've got it," she counters.

"This is awkward."

"Is it?"

"Well, yeah. I want to pay."

"Why?"

"Because I think it's a nice thing to do."

"I also think it's a pretty nice thing to do."

They sit there, neither hand relenting, and Nur bites back a laugh.

"So we have a stalemate."

"More of an impasse."

"An impasse, then."

"Why don't we pay for our own food? That way, you get to keep your dignity as a man and I get to keep mine as a woman."

Nur takes a second. "Okay," he concedes. "But only if I pay for your food and you pay for mine."

"What difference does it make?"

"At least it'll feel like I've paid for you."

"Wow." Yasmina waves a hand at the waitress, who comes over with a card machine, and the two of them pay, waiting silently as the machine takes their cards, spits out a receipt for each. "Wow," she says again, standing to put her jacket on, as he does the same, both a reflection of each other. "Wow," she repeats for the third time, as they step out into the night.

"You can stop now," he says. "I think I get the point."

"Are you sure? Because I don't know, I feel like you definitely didn't get the point. Might just say it one more time. Just one more . . . wow."

"Happy now?" he asks. "Got it all out?"

"As much of it as I wanted." She breathes in deeply, letting out a wavery sigh. "It's so cold."

"Is that your way of telling me that you want to go home?"

"No, that's my way of telling you that it's so cold. Aren't you freezing?"

"A little," Nur replies, and he starts walking, turning so he faces her, walking backward. "But I have something I want to show you before we both go home."

"If you take me down any alleyways . . ."

"I'm not going to take you down an alleyway." She falls in line with him, and he swivels back around, leading the way but only just. "I want to show you something."

"I don't think there's ever been a time when a Black girl has heard that and not immediately died after."

"That's true of any horror film. But I don't think we're in one of those right now."

"Definitely feels like what someone in a horror film says."

"You are . . ." He laughs, doesn't go on. "Just go with it."

"I'm going with it. Here I am, walking, going with it."

"Although it has just occurred to me, you did recently move here, don't know the city very well, and don't know me at all. So if you were going to die . . ."

"Oh, so now it's a possibility?"

"I'm saying that it might happen. I'm not saying it's *going to* happen. It's not really my style to promise things to people that I might not be able to deliver on."

"All I ask is that if you do kill me, please make sure you tell my sister what you've done. She'll probably find out anyway, but it's definitely better to be honest with her."

"You have a sister?"

A strange pause. Nur instinctively regrets asking the question, wants to retreat. "Yes," she says, after a time that is both short and long.

"What's her name?"

"Hawa," she replies, like it weighs the world.

"That's a beautiful name."

"Beautiful name for a beautiful girl," she says, as if on cue.

Nur swallows, wonders if he should go back to the jokes or if he should press her on her sister. Whether he should even continue talking. "I have a brother," he offers. "Khalil. Two years younger than me. And a sister, Mariam, four years younger."

"Two years between you all. Like your parents planned it."

"I think if you asked my parents, they'd tell you that it was all Allah's plan."

"Does that make your mother Mary?"

The line surprises Nur, eliciting a laugh. "I don't think that's the kinda question a good son should be answering about his mother."

They turn a corner, and everything goes a little quieter, the din of people disappearing. There are shops on this road, but fewer, and some of them are closed.

"Okay," Nur says, stopping. "Here it is."

She turns to face a bookshop.

Nur had just started university in Bradford, filled with people he didn't know, and he felt out of place, distant from everything and everyone. He wanted to feel like he belonged somewhere. He walked, trying to find the places he could call his own. He found many future haunts that day, but the place he ended up returning to the most was this.

An old bookshop, small and musty, run by a woman named Greta, who looked timeless, like she had just stepped out of the 1400s, or the 1600s, or maybe even the 1800s. Every time he came by, she appeared exactly the same, answering his every question, ringing up his books at the ancient till, taking his payment in cash because she didn't have a card machine.

He'd slipped into the shop that first day looking for something new but realized everything was secondhand. He asked Greta about recent books, and she told him she could order things in for him, but that she only really liked old books. Maybe if the bookshop didn't have such a rustic charm to it, if it didn't feel like he had entered a completely different world when he stepped into it, he might have found this limiting and never returned. But he loved it.

He comes back every week to browse the shelves, talk to Greta, ask after her children. She has two, one son and one daughter, both of whom live in the city with their own families. They both tell her she should close the shop, sell it, but she doesn't want to, tells them this is where she wants to be, that she will go crazy at home with nothing to do.

He feels at home when he walks into the shop, comfortable within a city that is still in many ways foreign to him.

He tells Yasmina all of this, and she looks at him as if she is seeing him differently, like he has been hiding behind a curtain that has now been pulled back. In that moment he is visible to her in a way that should make him feel anxious, but he feels nothing but relief. And when he asks her why she is staring at him like that, like she has seen him for the very first time, she tells him it is because she has.

September 2018

Nur wakes to the sound of construction work. He groans, rolling over, reaching for a pillow to shove his face into it. The construction has been going on for weeks, starting at eight a.m., even on a Saturday, like today, and he is so tired of hearing the drills go off, the ramming of metal into the ground, the breaking up of concrete.

"God, I wish they'd fuck off," he shouts into the pillow. He knows that even if he lies there, eyes closed, trying his very best, he won't be able to go back to sleep. He will not find his dreams again.

"Maybe you should wake up earlier," Yasmina says.

He lifts his head. She's on top of the duvet on her side, book in hand, glasses perched on her nose. Nur knows she has been awake since six, that she has already gone for a run, weaving through the roads she knows so well now, coming back and showering, all without waking him up.

"Not all of us are morning people, Mina." He moves the pillow slightly, folds it over so he can lean on it, and looks up at her. "What are you reading?"

"*This Must Be the Place*," she replies. "Not for work."

"Reading for pleasure?" He sucks air in through his teeth. "I didn't know you could do that."

"Neither did I." She puts the book down, glances at him. "Are you going to get up?"

"No. I'm going to stay in this bed for the entire weekend. I'm going to live here now. This mattress is my home."

Yasmina shoves him. He scowls at her, and she pushes him again, again, again, until he is half off the bed, falling, hitting the ground, wrapped in the duvet.

"You're such a dickhead," he says, standing, letting the duvet drop from him.

"Maybe, but it takes one to know one."

"What are you, five?" Nur asks, pulling at the duvet, Yasmina's body moving closer to his.

She gives him a look, the kind a parent gives their child when they're acting up. "You are so infuria—" she starts, but he jerks the duvet so she falls to her side, and Nur leaps on the bed, holding her fast to him, laughing triumphantly. "Your breath is disgusting!" she says, pushing him back, tossing a pillow at his face.

"Well, now that I've been rudely shoved out of my own bed, I guess I'll go brush my teeth." He throws the pillow back at her.

When he returns from the bathroom, Yasmina is in the living room, makeup scattered on the coffee table. "Are you going out today?" he asks, heading to the kitchen, filling the kettle with water.

"Yeah," she says, watching herself in the mirror, mascara brush in hand, eyes wide. "Gonna do some work with the others, probably go to eat after." She pauses, turns to him. "You should come with us," she says.

"No, it's okay. I'll just get in the way."

"You know that's not true."

"Except it is," Nur says, reaching for a mug, steam rising from the boiling kettle. "I never know what to say."

Once, at the very start of her PhD, Yasmina asked Nur to join her friends for dinner, suggesting he meet them, the Non-Whites as she called them: Jeremiah, Aaron, Ming, Maria. She'd left earlier to do some work with them at the library, and said he should come at around six, they'd be done by then. Nur watched the clock, waited until it was just early enough not to be weird, checking himself a few times before he left the flat. He didn't know what to expect from these people who suddenly checkered Yasmina's nightly stories.

When he got there, a Japanese restaurant, he nearly turned away at the sight of them stuffed around one long wooden table. He found a seat next to Yasmina, bags removed that had been placed to save his spot, and realized how little he fit in with these people. Yasmina introduced him to them all as a writer, and when Jeremiah asked what he'd written, a hardness settled in the pit of his stomach as he admitted nothing was out there yet, he was still finding his voice, and Jeremiah had simply nodded, like he understood. Ming interjected, asking what his real job was, and he saw the looks of feigned interest on their faces when he said he was a copywriter. He sat there, silent for most of the night, while they went back and forth about their theses, about publishing their PhDs when they were done, a few of them wanting to go into teaching afterward. Yasmina tried to bring him into the conversation a few times, lending him a crutch for him to lean on, but he still said very little.

That night, as they walked home, she had asked him what was wrong, if he was upset with her, and he told her he wasn't. That it was nice to meet her crew, but that it was okay if he wasn't friends with them too.

Yasmina turns her attention back to the mirror. "You think you don't have anything to say. But you do."

Nur pours some milk into his tea, watching the color change. "Yeah, I guess so." He stirs his tea, the spoon clinking against the mug.

"I spoke to Hawa yesterday," Yasmina says.

He takes a breath, filling his lungs. "I heard," he says, walking over to sit on the side of the sofa. "Is she all right?"

"Well, yes and no." Yasmina puts the mascara down, turns to look at him. "Mum keeps pressing her about uni."

"She still doesn't want to go?"

"Nope," Yasmina says, all her frustration embedded in that one word, her worry, her fear. "And Mum and Dad, they keep talking to her, telling her that it's fine if she doesn't want to work, but she has to do something. She's sat at home, not doing anything, not applying for any jobs, and they're driving themselves crazy about it. They've always been the kind of people who knew what they wanted to do, worked toward that. My mum always wanted to be a doctor, my dad always wanted to be a lawyer. They don't understand this lack of drive. And, with the depression, they're scared to even talk about it in case she does anything."

"She wouldn't . . ."

"No," Yasmina replies quickly, returning to the mirror, her jaw tense. "She wouldn't. She's past that now, I think. I don't know. Do you ever really get over depression?"

Nur feels something catch in his throat.

"But she's fine. She just got annoyed with them last night, because, apparently, we have another lawyer in the family who Dad wanted her to talk to, to see if she would take it seriously."

"And she doesn't want to?"

"She doesn't want to take anything seriously right now." She sighs, picking up her lipstick, following the line of her lips. "I can see it from her side. She's feels she's not ready yet and some people don't know what they want to do with their lives when the rest of us do. They're not as lucky as you or me, they take longer. Plus, she's living at home, with parents who can and do support her. It's not like they need her to work in order to survive, which I'm so grateful for. But then I get it from my parents' side too. Their daughter isn't doing anything with her life. Of course they're worried."

"It'll be fine," Nur says, and he puts a hand on her shoulder. "She'll be fine. She's only twenty. She has time."

"I know." Yasmina lets a breath out, hard and long. "I know."

"And if not, I'm sure her brilliant older sister can take her in."

"Her brilliant older sister who can barely afford to pay her own way?" Yasmina scoffs. "Sure, she can take your place in the bed."

"Hey, the sofa isn't bad at all," Nur says, giving her a slight grin.

"I just," she continues, the words heavy in her mouth, "I just never know what to do or say when she calls. Like yesterday, she was talking to me the same way anyone might talk about their parents. Like, oh, they're on my case about getting a job, what-ever. And I wanted to say, the same way I'd say to anyone, how is she going to know she doesn't like something unless she actually starts trying things? But I couldn't say that, because, because, how do you say any of that? When you know that she might . . ."

"But she won't," he responds. "Right?"

"No, I don't think so. I don't think she's there again. She doesn't feel like she's there. But how do we know? We didn't last time and look what happened. How are we supposed to spot what we're meant to be watching out for?"

"Yasmina," Nur says, and the sound of her full name makes her look right at him. "If you think there's even the slightest chance she's heading that way, you need to tell your parents."

She says nothing. He hates the way her body crumples right now, how she looks so small and sad, and he wants to reach into her, take away everything that is causing her to feel like this. "I worry about my parents. I know how hard it is for them. And I love being here with you, but sometimes I feel so . . ."

Something shifts in her face, something close to shame, embar-rassment, like she has been caught doing something she shouldn't be. "So what?" Nur asks, his pulse beating in his ears.

"Nothing." She turns her head a little, so he can't see her eyes.

"You feel guilty about being here," he says, answering for her.

The lipstick twirls in her fingers, up, down, up, down. "Well, yeah, because I could be at home with her, with them, so that they don't have to bear this on their own. But instead, I'm on the phone telling her that she needs to get a job, while I'm here in Notting-ham with you."

"They were happy when you left."

The lipstick stops moving. "They weren't happy, Nur," she snaps. "And you know that. They knew I wanted to be here, but given the choice, they'd want me at home, just like your parents would." He freezes at the mention of his parents, and he wonders if they'll go there again, if this will turn the way other arguments have. But Yasmina puts the lipstick back into the bag.

"It's just hard," she says, clearing the table, assessing herself in the mirror before putting that away too. "I want to be there for them the way I always have been, but I also know my life is here, with you." She stands, and he reaches for her hand, holds it.

"You know I don't know what it feels like with Hawa," he says, "but feeling like you've failed your family? I definitely know what that feels like."

"Nur the bad son," she says.

"Nur the bad son," he repeats, smiling weakly. "But hey, every family needs one. And you are definitely not the bad Nur of your family." He stands up, kisses her forehead. "Are you going to the library?"

"Yeah," Yasmina says, stepping past him.

"I'll come with you. Just give me a minute to get ready." She turns to him, a look in her eyes. "Don't get your hopes up. I'm not coming to hang out with you and your cool friends."

She rolls her eyes. "You know, if you just let yourself relax a little, you might find you actually like them. After all, I have impeccable taste in people."

Nur lets out a groan. "Or I can come home and watch Netflix without you sitting next to me, reciting every IMDb fact about the actors . . ."

"Hey!" she shouts from the other room. "That's cute and you know it."

"It was cute the first time you asked me if I knew that Halle Berry is the only Black woman to win an Oscar for Best Actress, but I think that wore off like two years ago." He walks into the bedroom to see her slipping a jacket on. "Now it's like, wow, please just let me enjoy the film."

"You know, that right there, that's some classic male insecurity and you should definitely see someone about it," she says, pointing a finger at his chest. He reaches for it, but she pulls back. "Now get ready if you're going to walk with me. I have to be there soon."

"Always gotta be there on time," he says, taking his T-shirt off, throwing it to the other side of the room. Yasmina looks at it, then drags her eyes over to him. "I'll pick it up when I'm back, we're in a rush."

"You are getting way too comfortable." She steps past him, and he quickly throws on another shirt, jeans, shoves his feet into some sneakers, runs a hand through his hair in the mirror, and steps out.

"Done," he announces, reaching for the keys on the kitchen counter. "Let's go."

They walk out of the flat, Yasmina first, Nur second. Summer is still lingering around them, but the leaves are changing on the trees, the days still long but the nights a little cooler.

"You know," he says, hands shoved into pockets, "with Hawa, I think you should be honest with her."

She takes a beat. "Honest?"

He gives himself a moment to choose the right words. "I think you should be honest with her about what you think. Instead of just listening, instead of just saying okay, all right, that's fine. You should tell her the truth, what you're really thinking. Otherwise it makes her feel like a child."

"I don't treat her like a child," Yasmina cuts back, familiar warning signs in her voice. "I tell her she should get a job."

"I know," he says. "But you're not saying what you really think."

"And what *do* I really think?"

"That she's giving your parents a hard time."

Yasmina stops for a moment. "I can't say that to her."

"Why not?"

"Because," Yasmina starts. "Because if I say that, she might take it . . ."

"Okay, but you said she isn't there. And you know, she's twenty now. She already knows that she's giving your parents a hard time. I bet she just doesn't know how to stop. Or maybe she doesn't think she can stop."

"And me telling her that is going to do what?"

"You being honest with her is going to help her figure it out," he says. "Treating her like an adult. Not putting on your kid gloves every time you speak to her."

Yasmina says nothing, begins walking again. He knows he is risking going too far, wants to take the words back, to say he is wrong. There is a fine line with Yasmina and Hawa, and he tries his best never to go near it.

"Maybe," she says.

"Maybe," he repeats, relieved, and slips his fingers in between hers. "And then you can blame me if anything goes wrong."

"I wouldn't do that," she says. Her hand tightens a little around his. "But I would definitely tell you that you were wrong and never trust you again."

"And that feels like a fair enough reaction," he says.

They continue walking in silence, and when the library comes into view, she lets go of his hand, moves away from him. "You know you didn't have to walk me here."

"It's a Saturday, what else am I doing with my time?"

"Well, you could come with."

"Not for a second of your life," he says.

"Infuriating," she says before kissing him. "I'll see you for dinner."

He nods and she turns, walking to the library. He watches her for a few seconds before heading back to the empty flat. There is regret in him, of not taking her up on her offer, of not spending the day with her, and there is frustration too, that she would spend the weekend without him. But he sees that table, lined with her friends, the mortification creeping into him, and he knows being alone is better than being there again.

December 2014

Nur calls his mother from Birmingham New Street station; she's surprised, and he laughs, asks her if she forgot he was coming. She says she didn't forget, just likes to hear his voice, that she's on her way and he better not have brought her anything, and he looks down at the bags he's holding and says nothing.

As he walks through the streets of his home city to their pickup point, a sadness runs through Nur, the way it does whenever he returns. Everything is changing, shops closing, new ones opening in their place, new buildings going up in the place of old ones. The city is an ever-evolving organism, different every time he walks through it, and he sometimes feels lost within it.

He wonders how he is changing too, if the younger Nur might not recognize who he has turned into.

He stands on the corner, waits for his mother.

"I told you not to bring anything," she says, as he throws his bags into the back of the car.

"Oh, these are for everyone," he says, grinning at his mother, who shakes her head at him. He sits in the passenger seat. "How are you?"

"I'm good," she answers. "Just getting on with it. Sofie gave birth last week." Something she has already told him over the phone. "A boy. She's back home now." He can almost recite this conversation word for word. "I don't know how she does it. That's three boys she has now. And I bet she tries for a girl again. One more time."

"I don't know if Hussain wants another one," Nur says.

"Did you hear what happened?" she asks. Nur shakes his head. "Well, you know Sofie's pregnant, last month of it. She's huge. Can barely walk. She hears him talking to some woman on the phone, some gori called Susan, you know how he is. She asks him who the voice is, and he screams at her, tells her that she's not giving him his space. Like *he* needs space. She's the pregnant one. Then he leaves. Doesn't come back until she phones him to remind him she's carrying his kid."

"He left her alone with their two boys?"

"With her two boys at home with her. Honestly, I don't know how she lets him get away with this stuff."

"Well," Nur starts, and he shifts a little, aware his mother isn't going to agree with what he's about to say. "You can't blame her. She got married young, didn't work, had a kid really fast. He never even wanted to marry her in the first place. They both got forced to. It was never going to work out."

"He might not have wanted to marry her, but he has a duty to her as her husband."

"I know. But that doesn't mean that he's going to do his duty."

"Well, he should," she says, and Nur bites his tongue. He resists saying more, about young men marrying young women for the sake of family, doesn't want to upset his mother.

"How are Khalil and Mariam?" he asks, even though he knows, speaks to them regularly, messages flying back and forth.

"They're good." They turn onto their street, and he sees the houses he grew up around, small to some but always just big enough for his family, pressed up against one another with no room to spare, no driveways or garages. "Khalil just sent off his applications for universities."

"Oh?" Nur asks, watching the houses pass by.

Nur has spent a few nights talking to Khalil about university, about whether or not Khalil should leave or stay at home, Khalil wondering if staying is better because it'll be easier, his friends are here, a few of them are staying home too, and he'll be with Mariam and their parents. Their conversations rarely leave the surface, but Nur knows there is another factor, of the older son who has left his family, who decided to leave even though there are good universities in Birmingham, great ones, even. He knows how his community thinks, has heard the stories of boys and girls abandoning their families for university, of the sins they're indulging in, the clubs and the alcohol and the drugs. He has heard his mother talking about other children too, wondering about the things they must be up to living apart from their families unmarried.

Is that what he has become, the cliché? Is this what his parents think of him? Do they wonder if their son has become the very thing they prayed he wouldn't?

"Two here, one away," his mother declares, pulling up to the house.

"That's good." Two universities at home, one elsewhere. At least that way, Khalil might be able to imagine leaving, see how it made him feel.

"It is good." She parks the car, reversing into her spot with the ease of it having been hers for years. "He should stay at home. Be close to his family."

"If he wants to," Nur says, swallowing the shame that has crept up his throat. He takes out his bags, looks up at the house. An average house, three bedrooms, one bathroom, normal-size kitchen. He remembers his parent's joy when they finally paid off the mortgage, his father cheering in the living room, talking about how the government couldn't kick him out now, send him back to Pakistan, because he had earned his place here, that this house was his family's and no one would ever take that away from him.

Before he can open the door, Khalil has opened it to him.

"No, thank you, we don't want to buy anything," Khalil shouts, slamming it in his face.

Nur reaches for the handle, pushes at the door. "Stop being so annoying," he says, stumbling as Khalil lets the door go. Nur rushes in, Khalil retreating to the living room.

"You're getting soft in your old age," Khalil says, and Nur pushes him, dropping his bags to the floor.

"Don't fight in my house," their mother says, closing the door behind her.

"I won't, I won't," Nur replies, falling onto the sofa. He closes his eyes for a second, breathes in the comforting smell of his childhood home.

"Are we getting food?" Khalil asks.

"Wait for your dad to get back from work," his mother says, walking into the kitchen, heading straight to the sink, washing her hands, a habit of hers, never trusting the outside world to be as clean as she'd like.

Nur notices his sister standing in the doorway to the stairs and opens his arms to her.

"I'm not running into your arms."

"Oh, come on. I'm tired, I don't want to get up."

She gives him an exasperated look and sighs, walking over to give him a hug.

Mariam sits on the sofa by him. With the four of them there, Nur almost feels like the last year or so hasn't happened, that he had never left for university.

"How's uni?" she asks.

"As thrilling as you might expect. I am excelling at writing essays about books written by dead white guys."

"I love dead white guys," Khalil adds.

"Is that why you're studying medicine at university?"

"Medicine is run by the most dead white guys you've ever seen. It's like pale zombies everywhere."

"Most dead. Does that mean, like, they're more dead than any other dead person, or is it just a lot of dead white guys?"

"I'll leave that for you to figure out, Mr. English Degree."

Their mother walks back into the room and sits on the other sofa, reaching for her phone, unlocking it to check Facebook. A new tic of hers, being glued to her phone, born from finally buying a smartphone, years after everyone else.

"I hear you've chosen your universities," Nur says, looking at his brother.

Khalil shrugs. "I thought it was about time."

"Excited?"

"I'm going to stay," he declares, preempting the question.

"Can't live without us," Mariam teases.

"Not going to follow your brother?" Nur asks.

"Probably not. I don't think I've ever known my brother to do great things."

"You're so rude. Were you this rude when I lived here? I don't think you were this rude when I lived here."

"I've always been this rude."

"I don't know, man. I think you're ruder now."

"Don't think so. But either way, get your wallet out, bhayya, you're paying for the food."

Nur laughs. "No, I am not," he says, and he grabs his bags, makes for the stairs.

His room has become Khalil's now that he no longer lives at home, though his bed is still here, trapped in the same corner, waiting for him to return in the summer. Nur sits on the edge of it, surveying and spotting the small changes around him, Khalil's touch on the walls.

It was in this room that he told his mother he was going away for university. They both sat on his bed, him holding the letter in one hand—his grades from school, three As, surprising him despite the hard work he put into them—and his phone in the other, ready to call the university, accept his place. His mother told him not to. He told her he must.

He had applied for universities outside of Birmingham in secret, filling in the application forms at school during his breaks. He tried not to feel like a traitor, telling himself he wasn't doing anything wrong, but he couldn't quiet the voice in his head that whispered that he was betraying his family. There was a reason he wasn't filling these out at home, that he hadn't even told Khalil and Mariam about his plans. He told himself that those universities weren't going to accept him, that he would stay at home. He just wanted to dream, for a moment. He repeated this, even as he confirmed an outside university as his first choice, chose another as his backup. Even as he stared at the results that confirmed he was going to go.

They'd sat there for a while, mother and son, neither knowing what to say. Nur wasn't sure if he was doing the right thing. He'd spent his entire life in this house. Eighteen years. And now he was going to leave, and he didn't know what that meant for the past. Would the future come in and erase everything that came before?

But his mother had reached over, put a hand on his, told him to phone the university, that if this is what he wanted to do, he should do it; she believed in him and knew he was going to do brilliant things. She would miss him, but she'd be happy knowing her son was out there bettering himself.

Nur lies down on his bed now, feet hanging off the end, and closes his eyes.

His city might change, but home doesn't.

A knock at the door distracts him. Mariam stands there, on the edge of his room, hovering by the door. "What's up?" he asks.

"Nothing," she says, stepping closer. "Just . . . you know, mum's really glad that Khalil is staying at home."

"For uni?" Nur sits up. "Yeah, I know. It's what she wants."

"It's what he wants too." She stops, words trapped. "Khalil thinks you might think badly of him for staying at home."

"What?"

She bites her lip. "He's scared you'll think he's not brave enough because he didn't leave. That you'll see it as him thinking you're a bad person for not wanting to stay at home."

"I don't think that at all—" Nur starts.

She cuts him off: "I know. But that's what he's scared of. I told him you'd never think that. You left because you needed to and he's staying home because he wants to. That doesn't make him the better son, and it doesn't make you the worse one." She pauses, a gap for Nur to fill, but he doesn't. "I just wanted to tell you," she adds. "He asked me not to, but I thought you should know." She takes a beat. "You're not mad, are you?"

"No," he says, but he says it too quickly, too earnestly. "I'm not mad. I just hope he's making the choice because he wants to and not because he feels like he has to."

"He is," she responds. "This is what he wants."

Nur stays quiet for a moment. "Then that's what he needs to do."

Khalil shouts for the two of them, he's hungry and he wants to eat, so they go downstairs and do what they always do whenever Nur visits home: call for takeout, rattle off the normal order, his mother paying, Nur offering to pay, his mother telling him his money is no good here, and they order something for his father too, leave it in the microwave for when he comes home. When the food arrives, they sit on the floor like they used to when the children were small, and they eat. Nur feels both at home and like a stranger, as if he is part of everything that is happening but also watching from the outside, no longer the person he used to be.

January 2015

You can't buy me that," Yasmina says, her gloved hand over Nur's, pulling him back.

He frowns at her. "You can't tell me what to do," he replies. In his fingers is a wooden elephant, immaculately carved.

"It's too much money, Nur."

Her protesting only makes him want to buy it more. He hands the tenner over to the woman in the stall, who takes it with a wink.

Nur turns to Yasmina, offers her the elephant. "It's yours now. Money has changed hands. You can do whatever you want with it."

She takes it from him, looking between the carving and him. "I cannot believe you spent ten whole pounds on this."

"Well, I guess dinner is on you next time."

"I think dinner might have to be on me for the whole week," she says, hooking her arm through his, pulling him to her, and pressing her lips against his shoulder. He knows it was worth it, that even though he doesn't really have the money to buy ten-pound elephants right now, she is worth it.

"My uncle once bought me, Khalil, and Mariam some wooden reindeer, from the Christmas market in Birmingham. My mum shouted at him, told him that it was haram, she couldn't have those things in her house." He chuckles at the memory. "Have you ever been to the Christmas market in Birmingham?" he asks, maneuvering around a group taking a selfie, six people pressed into one another, hats and scarves wrapped around them, each holding a wooden mug of something.

"Yeah," Yasmina says. "Once. It's supposed to be the biggest—"

"In Europe," Nur interjects, pride flaring in him. "It gets so busy and they open it so early, like the first week of November, and people flood the roads. You can barely move."

"We went as a family. My mum's sister wanted to go, heard it was meant to be amazing. So we drove down, had to park way out, like so far away, because we couldn't get into the actual city center. I remember walking a lot, cold, but it was worth it. It was so big, the lights strung over the roads."

"I know everyone makes fun of us for our accents—" Nur starts.

"As they should."

"—but our Christmas market is second to none."

"You should take me."

"Next year," he says.

"If we're still dating next year."

"I just bought you a very small wooden elephant for ten pounds. We're definitely staying together until next year, at the very least."

"Oh, because women can be bought?"

"I'd call it more of an investment."

"I think you should definitely stop talking because you're veering very close to straight misogyny," Yasmina jokes, nudging him.

"Well," Nur says, as they turn a corner, away from the markets behind them, the crowds getting quieter, "regardless, happy fifth date."

"Fourth date," Yasmina corrects him. "The first was a pre-date."

"Which we can now count as an actual date in hindsight, so fifth."

"Why, does something special happen on the fifth date?"

Nur gives her a knowing smile. "You'll only find out if you agree this is our fifth date."

"Well," she begins, giving a small shrug, "guess I'll have to wait until the next date to find out."

"Wow." Nur pushes her a little. "You are literally the worst person in the world." They walk slowly, the ground crackling under their feet.

"As someone who studies English, I think it's important you know the difference between *literally* and *figuratively*."

"As someone who studies journalism, I think it's important you understand the flexibility and ever-changing nature of language."

Yasmina gasps. "Okay, you got me there."

"I know journalism teaches you how to ask the most biting questions, but you should definitely not try that with me."

"Oh, because English teaches you such great debate skills?"

"If there was a debate team at this university, I would be the head of it."

"You would?"

"Name one argument I can't win."

"Literally anything to do with feminism."

"Is that you trying to call me sexist?"

"That's me telling you that I can beat you in any argument about feminism."

"Because you're a woman?"

"Yes."

"Well. I can't deny that."

"Look right here, another argument you have failed to win."

"You are literally the worst," Nur exclaims, and holds up a finger. "Do not say anything."

She raises her hands. "I won't, I won't."

They settle into a comfortable silence.

The sun is already set, the darkness circling around them, and all Nur wants to do is go home with Yasmina, get under his duvet, watch a film. He reaches for her hand, closing his fingers between hers.

"Are you going to Saara's tonight?" Yasmina asks, finally.

It's the question they've been waiting to ask each other, on the tip of their tongues, finally leaping off hers first.

A party looms, Saara's first of the year, one that he has no excuse to miss. If he doesn't go, she'll know something is wrong. And she'll start asking questions he doesn't want to answer.

"I don't know," he says, picking the easy way out. "Are you?"

"I want to." She stops walking, their fingers still intertwined. "You should come."

"I think I'd rather . . ."

"I want to tell her, Nur. About us."

His heart hammers in his chest. "What? Why? We don't need to."

"You guys have been apart for what, five months? I think that's enough time for you to move on." It sounds so simple on her lips.

"Has she?" he asks.

Yasmina lets go of his hand, leaving a cold emptiness between Nur's fingers. "I don't know."

"So then I can't, Mina. I can't be the first one to start seeing someone else. I was the one who ended things with her."

"What?" Yasmina scoffs.

He looks down at the ground, at the frost that's nearly invisible in the dark. "It just feels weird," he says.

"Are you looking for her permission?"

"Are *you* looking for her permission?"

"Of course not. But it's better to be truthful," Yasmina says.

He swallows the sigh building up inside. "I want her to know that I broke up with her because we didn't work, not because I was looking to be with someone else."

"But that is why you broke up with her," Yasmina pushes, exasperated. "Because you knew out there, somewhere, someone else was the right fit for you and Saara wasn't. Besides, we didn't even know each other when you two were together."

"You don't get it."

"Make me get it."

Nur gathers his thoughts. "Saara is brilliant. I still like her a lot, as a person. When we got together, I was . . . so incredibly lonely here, even with Rahat with me, and she settled me, made me feel less alone. But she can also be cruel and petty. For all her talk of being open-minded, sometimes she simply can't bring herself to think of the world in any way that's different to her view of it. God, we fought so much toward the end. She'd get angry whenever I wasn't around, whenever I didn't want to talk about something or go with her to a protest or want to watch another politician lying about something. She'd accuse me of not caring about these causes or even about her, and of course I did, of course—"

"I know, where is this going?" Yasmina says, an edge of frustration in her voice.

"So as much as I cared about her I couldn't do it anymore. Breaking up with her was one of the toughest choices I've made. I thought about it for weeks. She was my first relationship, and I didn't ever think I was going to break up with her. I always imagined it would end with her telling me I wasn't enough for her. So I don't know, maybe I am looking to her for permission to be with someone else. And . . ."

He stops, words caught in his throat.

"And what?" she asks.

"And it's you, right? *Her* friend. We met at *her* party. If it wasn't for her, I would never have met you."

"I can say the same," Yasmina counters. "She's my friend and I'm now secretly dating her ex-boyfriend. Did you not realize how that's going to make me feel?"

"I . . . I didn't think about that," he says.

"I want to tell her, Nur. Not because I think I need her permission, but because it'll be worse later on. I don't know how long this thing between us will last. But I can't keep it a secret. I don't want to."

Nur feels queasy, and he knows Yasmina is right, that they should tell Saara sooner than later, that he should have mentioned it to her after their first date, or the second, or the third.

"It'll be fine," Yasmina says, and she reaches for his hand again. "I'll be there."

"Okay," he says.

"Okay."

They trek back to their houses, Yasmina telling Nur she'll meet him at eight, and Nur looks at his watch; it's a couple hours away. They kiss, slowly, softly, by his door.

The first time they kissed was on their third date, earlier this month, after they each returned from the winter break, walking back from the cinema, a strange little film based on a short story

Yasmina had read. She told him all the changes they'd made in the adaptation, where they worked, where they didn't, and they came to Yasmina's house first, because he'd made a show of walking her home. It was raining slightly, a mist in the air. His eyes fell to her lips. He wanted to feel them, to kiss her. They were close, bodies pressed together saying good night, and then they were kissing, and he let himself fall into her, wanted it to last forever. Afterward, he kept replaying it, unable to process that it'd happened, the ghost of her lips still on his, and his entire body feeling like it was dissolving.

Nur watches her walk away, and then he goes into his empty house, Rahat gone home for the weekend. Nur hates the silence, hates being on his own. He wants to talk to Rahat about everything that's happened, to ask him for advice on how he should tell Saara that he's dating her friend, that he really likes her, wants to make it work. He considers calling Rahat but decides against it, afraid of making Rahat's time at home all about him.

He goes to his room, resumes the Netflix show he was watching. He's only a few minutes in when his phone rings, vibration passing through the bed. He reaches for it, hoping it's Rahat, sees Khalil's name instead, and for a moment considers not picking up, ignoring it and lying later, but then he answers. "Hey," he says, pausing the show.

"Hey, man, what's up?" Khalil asks.

"Nothing, just watching some TV." Nur stands from the bed, never able to sit when he's on the phone. "What's going on?"

"Nothing much, just at home. Mum and Mariam have gone out, Dad's at Haroon's."

"So it's just you."

"Just me," he says, small laugh. "Might start walking around naked." He pauses, and Nur hears everything in that pause. "I just wanted to say, Mariam told me she talked to you." Another pause. "About uni and everything." There's a world of unsaid things in his brother's voice.

"Yeah," Nur admits, his heart beating a little faster. "She did."

"I didn't want her to say anything to you, I told her not to . . ."

"Khalil," Nur interrupts, "I get it. You don't have to . . . You don't have to justify yourself or anything. If you want to stay at home, stay at home. It's not anyone's business, right?"

"I know," Khalil says. "I just wanted you to know that my choice wasn't about you or anything."

"Did you think about it?" Nur asks. "Leaving?"

"Yeah, for a little bit. You know Assad is leaving, to Edinburgh."

"Edinburgh? Shit, that's far."

"I know. When he told me, I thought he was joking. Eighteen years here, in Birmingham. I mean, his parents don't go anywhere but Pakistan."

"Neither do ours, Khalil."

"I know, I know," Khalil says. "But you know what his parents are like. I thought he'd stay at home with them. But Edinburgh. He didn't even apply to any schools here. Just wanted to go."

"You should visit him," Nur suggests. "Edinburgh is supposed to be beautiful."

"Oh, I told him I'll be up at some point. Scotland, though, so weird. Do you think he'll come back with a Scottish accent?"

"I think he'll come back pretending to have a Scottish accent," Nur says, and laughs.

"Don't worry, if he does that, I'll beat it out of him." Khalil pivots. "I did think about it, though. When Assad told me, I thought about going with him. School, college, why not uni too, you know? But, I don't know, I think I'd miss everyone too much." He stops. "I'm not saying you don't miss—"

"I know, Khalil," Nur says. "When I left, it felt like . . . I mean sometimes, it still feels like I've left you guys. And not just because I live here now, but because I'm not even properly part of the family anymore . . ."

"Nur," Khalil says. "That's not true."

"I know. I know it isn't true. But I feel like I'm missing out, even on minor stuff," Nur admits. "It's hard sometimes, to be so far away from all of you. I miss it. I miss you guys, like, all the time." He stops for a second, and maybe it's because he's saying it out loud, or perhaps it's because he's already lonely with Rahat gone, but he is suddenly filled with a longing for home.

"Nur, you know you're always going to be part of this family, even if you move to, like, Antarctica or something."

"Oh yeah, I don't think you guys are that easy to shake off, even if I wanted to."

"Mum would definitely come in a heartbeat and drag you home."

Nur laughs, and so does Khalil. "Anyway," Khalil says, "I just wanted to call to say that." He doesn't continue, and Nur knows he is pacing on the other end, neither of them able to stay still while on the phone, and he wishes they were having this conversation in person, sitting on their beds like they did when they were kids. "I should definitely be studying for something."

"My brother, the doctor."

"Your brother, trying very hard to *become* a doctor," Khalil says. "I'll talk to you soon, yeah?"

"Yeah," Nur says, and he keeps the phone at his cheek, Khalil hanging up, the silence of the house filling his ears.

Nur goes back to his show, letting time pass by until just before eight. He fixes his hair, sprays himself with a touch of fragrance, and when Yasmina texts him, he bounds out of the house, restless with nervous energy.

"Wow."

Yasmina is wearing the same dress she wore the first time he met her, and she looks just as amazing. The only difference is that this time he can tell her.

"Don't be weird," she warns him.

"You're wearing the same thing from the night we met."

"Is this what I was wearing? I had no idea."

"Oh, so now you're going to pretend like that night isn't etched into the back of your eyes?"

"Nur. Shut up." She reaches for his hand, and he gives it to her, fingers slotting together.

As they walk, silently, Nur's mind goes over and over what he has to say. He wishes he'd prepared something, a monologue, like he was in a film, lines written for him.

"You know, your hand is really sweaty," Yasmina says.

"Shit, sorry." Nur pulls his hand out of hers, wipes it on his jeans. But when he goes back to her with it, she pulls away.

"I'm not holding your hand if it's just going to get sweaty again."

"I can't help it. I'm nervous."

"It's not like you're telling your parents you've become an atheist or something."

"Not all of us are as cold as you."

"Oh, so I'm cold?"

Nur lets out a sigh. "No, you're not cold. I'm just very nervous. And I think it's okay to be a mess about this."

"As long as you know you're being over the top."

They reach Saara's road, and Nur stops for a second. "Fuck," he says, the word coming out like the last bit of helium in a deflated balloon.

His chest starts to tighten, as if someone has put a claw around his rib cage, talons made of metal. Nur bends, hands on knees, sees the ground but it's swaying, so he closes his eyes, tries to breathe the way he does when he's at home with Rahat, slow, steady, purposeful. But it feels like trying to breathe with a scarf wrapped over his nose and mouth, the air thinning.

"Nur?" Yasmina asks. Her voice echoes in the distance, trying to call to him.

He shakes his head at her, tries to tell her he's fine, but no words come out. She puts her hands on his shoulders, says his name again, once, twice. She lifts his head so he can look at her, and he registers her worried eyes, and air gradually comes into his lungs once again. "Nur, just breathe," she says, and he does, the world coming back to him. He straightens himself, sits down on a low wall, one hand to his chest.

He doesn't know how long he's there, Yasmina watching him, concern knitting her eyebrows together. "Nur," she says. "Are you okay?"

"I think . . ." Nur's voice comes out thin, strangled. "I get bad nerves sometimes."

"How are you feeling? Do you need to go to the hospital?" The worry in her voice triggers his guilt.

"No," he says quickly. "I'm fine. Just get overwhelmed sometimes."

"Is this because of . . ." She peers at Saara's house down the street, then back to him. "Is it really that bad? Telling her about us?"

Nur follows her gaze. "No," he says, but the word is limp in his mouth. "I just don't like confrontation." He can tell she doesn't believe him. "I want to," he continues, wishing, not for the first time and not for the last time, that he wasn't weak like this. "And we should. You're right. We have to."

He pushes himself up off the wall, his legs shaky, like he's run a marathon, like he should be headed home to lie in his bed for a while. He starts toward the house, and Yasmina joins him, her hand reaching for his, holding on. He knows he shouldn't walk in like that, knows that isn't the best way for Saara to see them, knows that people will talk as people do, but he is too comforted by the feel of her hand in this moment to let go.

They step into the house, the adrenaline running through him still, and it's like the past couple of months haven't happened and he is stepping back into that first night, except this time, Yasmina is holding his hand.

Immediately, he is surrounded by people, and it doesn't take long before he spots Imran, lying down on a sofa, legs hanging off the side of it. When their eyes meet, Imran sits up, grinning, and his gaze travels down to see where Nur's hand is, his face almost splitting in half from the laugh that comes out of it.

"I knew it!" he shouts over the music. Imran stands, walks over to them. "I fucking knew it. That night, when she came out to talk to you. I should have put a bet down."

"Yasmina, this is . . ."

"Imran," she says. "Nice to see you again."

"And you," Imran says, with another laugh, sharp in the air.

"Is Saara around?" Nur asks, looking around the room.

"Why? Are you scared that she's going to come and kill you both for betraying her?"

"I am not betraying her," Nur pushes back at the same time as Yasmina says, "He is not betraying her."

"I like the synchronicity here," Imran says, smirking.

"Is she here?"

"Upstairs," Imran says. "I think she's getting ready or something. Late for her own party. To be expected, I guess."

Nur glances up, as if Saara might be hanging from the ceiling, waiting for him. "Okay," he says, and that tight feeling comes back to him. "Okay. Okay."

Imran looks from Nur to Yasmina and then back to Nur. "Are you about to do what I think?"

"That depends. What do you think he's about to do?" Yasmina asks.

"I think he's about to go find Saara at her own party and tell her that he's secretly started dating her friend after meeting her through Saara. Close?"

"Right on," Nur says, his hand sweaty again, the clamminess collecting under his arms too, at the small of his back. "That's exactly what I'm about to do. So any words of advice would be great."

"Don't have your back to a wall when you tell her. Know where the exit to the room is at all times. Don't let her get near any sharp objects," Imran says. "And when it looks like she's about to turn on you with a knife, maybe run?"

"Maybe run. Not *definitely* run. Maybe run," Nur says.

"I don't know, seems like you have a death wish."

"Fuck you," Nur says.

Yasmina turns to Nur. "He's kidding." She casts a sharp look at Imran, who puts his hands up, tells Nur he'll be fine, before backing away into the crowd.

"Look, Nur. We're doing this."

"You want to do this together?"

She starts moving around a pair of guys behind her, one of them lifting his glass over her head so it doesn't spill. "I'm just as much a part of this as you are. So yeah." She looks up at him, and before he can say anything, she's turned the corner, heading for the stairs.

Nur climbs after Yasmina, and with every step something inside his throat grows larger and larger. He threads past people standing in the hallway, and then they are both standing at Saara's room, the door slightly open.

Yasmina pushes the door, slips inside. Nur has no option but to follow her, and suddenly, they are both standing in her room. Saara, who is talking very intensely to a girl Nur doesn't recognize, turns to them.

"You're here," Saara says. She looks ready, face made up, mascara, red lipstick, short dress, skin glowing, and Nur thinks back to the last time he saw her, that last party. How it had been weeks since then, how a year ago he could barely last a day without seeing her, trips back home hard to swallow because he would be away from her for days, phone calls snatched on the train, texts sent frantically before going to sleep. She looks at Yasmina and then at Nur. "You're both here."

That word reveals to Nur that she already knows why they're there, what they have to say, and a part of him is relieved, because at least it won't come as a shock, while another part of him is frustrated. She knows and he will still have to say it.

"Can I talk to you?" Nur asks. He moves closer to Yasmina. "Can we both talk to you?"

Saara doesn't say anything for a second, just looks at them. "Yeah, sure." She turns back to the girl, who takes the hint and leaves the room, closing the door behind her, the noise of the people below muffled.

Yasmina and Nur stay by the door, like children standing in their parents' room.

"So," Saara continues, "what is it?"

"Nur and I are dating," Yasmina says. As the words fall from her mouth, it's like the earth under Nur's feet has opened.

"Dating," Saara echoes. She looks at Nur, her face blank.

"Yes," Yasmina says. "For a few weeks. Nothing long. We wanted to tell you when it started, but we wanted to make sure that it was something real before we did."

"And is it?" Saara asks, her eyes still on Nur. "Real?"

Yasmina doesn't answer the question, and when Nur doesn't say anything, she turns to him, raising her eyebrows, giving him the go-ahead.

"Yes," he mutters. The word comes out strangled. "Yes," he says, gathering himself. "It is real."

Saara nods slowly, digesting. "I guess this is where I either tell you I'm happy for you and wish you the very best of luck, or I tell you to get the fuck out of my sight and never come back." She laughs, a hollow sound, echoing in the room. "Well, I'm not going to do either of those things."

She moves closer, and despite everything, Nur checks if there is anything sharp in the room, Imran's words in his head. But she steps around them, opening the door. Nur can't make eye contact.

Saara stops, just outside the door. "I already knew," she adds, and then she is gone, calling out names down the corridor, asking people how they are, and then her voice is swallowed up by the music.

Nur retreats out of the room, and Yasmina follows him, saying something to him, but he can't really hear her, and he says they should just leave. Yasmina frowns at him, shakes her head, arguing no, they should stay, but he feels like he's going to be sick, no longer welcome in this house anymore, even as a friend, that he has ruined it and fallen deeper into the hole he is trying to get out of. He walks down the stairs and out of the house, Yasmina trailing. Nur leaves Yasmina at her door, unable to breathe until he is back in his room, sitting on the floor, knees to his chest, head in his hands, wondering why. Why did he go along with Yasmina, why did he date Saara in the first place, why did he make any of those choices?

January 2019

Last year, Nur decided he was going to write a novel.

He'd written for as long as he could remember, short stories set in magical worlds. He submitted them to competitions, even won one, kept the check after it arrived in the post, framed it on his wall. But the novel cried out to him, a lengthy work he could call his own. And, at first, it had been easy. He would come home from work, Yasmina there most days of the week, working on her PhD, and he'd sit by her, typing away.

But now the words have stopped. As if someone had reached out and turned the flow off without warning.

He looks over the words he has already written, reading them back again, trying to figure out where everything was headed before the dam went up. He recalls just a few weeks ago, when the words came without strain, and he is bitter with jealousy at who he used to be.

"Do you want me to read it?" Yasmina offers, slipping a bag off her shoulders, standing by the doorway of the room they call a study, a room packed with books and shelves and a desk and a pair of chairs.

"I don't know," Nur says. He turns to her, pencil in mouth. "I don't know if that would help."

It's a question he's asked himself, if he should let her read what he's written, so she can bounce things off him. But part of him resents her for being able to help, that she might be the answer to his paralysis. Because this is his thing, not hers. He's the writer, she's the academic. Even though he knows how stupid that is, how hurtful it would be if he ever confessed, he can't help his frustration.

He stands from the chair, leaves the pencil on the desk, follows Yasmina through into the living room. "How are the Non-Whites?" he asks.

"They're fine," she answers. "I think everyone is stressed, though. We barely spoke. Deadline season. Ming and Aaron didn't even come, stayed at home."

"See, that's what you get for pursuing higher education. You should have been like the rest of us, found average jobs that make you fine money and settled down. Why reach for more?"

"Says the copywriter who wants to be an author, neither of which are particularly stable jobs," she says, skeptical.

"Hey, tell that to Stephen King."

"He's a white guy."

"And it's about time they got a brown one, right?" he asks, reaching for her waist, pulling her to him. "Even better when it's one as handsome as this one."

"Someone is really feeling themselves today," she says, grinning, and he kisses her, can taste the bitter coffee she had with her friends, a little sweetness under it.

"Not every day self-deprecation, you know?"

She pushes him away, escapes his arms. "Are you writing all day?" she asks. "I was thinking we could get takeout, watch a film?"

The words rise up in him. "She called today," he says, and it stops her right in her tracks, eyebrows joining.

"Your mum?"

He nods.

She'd called a couple of hours after Yasmina had left the flat. Her name on his phone forcing Nur to freeze for a moment before he picked up:

"Salaam."

"Salaam, Mum. How are you?"

"Fine. How are you?"

"I'm all right."

"And, work, kaam kehse jahraha hai?"

"It's just the first day back, so not that busy. We had a meeting to talk about plans for our clients this year, check in with them. Just the usual stuff."

"It's good to be prepared."

". . . And Khalil and Mariam?"

"Fine. They're fine."

"And Aba?"

"He's okay."

"Okay . . . Did you have time to think about what I told you?"

"Tum neh muhja kyah bethaya?"

"Are you going to make me say it again?"

"Say what again?"

"Ami."

"Yes, I have thought about it."

"Okay. So what do you think?"

"About your girlfriend who you hid from us for four years?"

"Her name is Yasmina, Ami."

"Do you want to marry her?"

". . . I think I do."

"Then we should meet her. And her parents."

"And you don't mind?"

"Don't mind what? Kyah aap neh hum seh jhoot bola?"

"Mum. I didn't lie to you."

"I don't know what else you would call it."

"Are you not happy for me?"

"I will always be happy for you, no matter what you do . . . I always want the best for you. Hamesha."

"I didn't mean to lie to you. I just didn't know how to tell you. I wanted to be sure this was important, that what me and Yasmina have is real."

"Yasmina. It's a nice name."

"Muslim name."

"Yes, a Muslim name. That's good."

"I can ask her to come and meet you. I can ask her parents too."

"You'll ask them? Aap keh aus neh ma baap seh mulakat ki heh?"

"Yes, I've met them a few times. They're really nice."

"You met her parents before you told us?"

"She told them about me as soon as—"

"So yes, then."

". . . Yes."

"Aur tum neh muhjeh nehi bethaya."

"I didn't know how to tell you. I wanted to be sure."

"You wanted to be sure."

". . . Yes."

"Okay. Well, let me know what she says."

"Okay, Mum."

"I'll speak to you later, Nur. Be safe, betah."

"I will, Mum."

"Khudafis."

"Khudafis."

Yasmina's hands flutter by her side. "What did she say?"

"She wants to meet you," Nur says.

She bites her lip, a flash of white. "Of course she does. She wants to meet the girl you've been hiding from her for years."

He doesn't rise to the bait. "Your parents too."

"My parents too?"

"Your parents too."

Yasmina's hands clench into fists, fingers digging into palms. "Okay," she says. "I can speak to them. Ask them when they're free." Her brain working, figuring out how her parents could get there, when the right time would be.

"You know." Nur closes the gap between them. "You don't have to do this." He has rehearsed this moment, honed what to say, sleepless nights coming up with a solution, an easy way out.

"Don't have to do what?"

"You don't have to meet her if you don't want to. If you want to end this now, call it quits, say we had a good time while we did, and find someone else, I understand. I get it."

Her face doesn't move. "Are you joking?"

"No," he says.

"Is that what you want me to do?"

"No."

"Then why are you suggesting it?"

"Because it's an option."

"Is that how little you think of me?"

"I don't—"

"You make me wait years to tell your family about us, even after we move in together. Tell me it's just a matter of time, year after year, and now, when you finally tell them, when you finally get the courage to do it, you tell me I have an out?" Her voice gets louder and louder, shaking in the air. "I don't have a fucking choice anymore, Nur. You made sure of that. You made me love you, so much that it can feel impossible sometimes, and *now* you tell me I have an out? You don't get to tell me all of this was for nothing." She shoves him, both hands on his chest, and he stumbles back. "I'm not leaving."

She reaches to push him again, and he takes hold of her hands. "I'm not asking you to," he says, words failing him. "I just—"

"You just what?" she asks. "Want me to leave so it's easier for you?"

Her words sit between them.

"That would not be easier for me," he says. But wouldn't it? If she walked out the door, told him she was done, even though it would be like a part of him had been ripped out, it would be easier, because maybe then he wouldn't have to change.

"Then don't suggest it," she shouts, pulling her hands back from him.

They stand there, staring at each other, and Nur is overcome with the urge to grab her, to drive to his parents' house, tell them: This is the woman I am going to marry, this is the woman I love and I am going to spend my life with, and I won't hear anything more about it.

He wants to give her his world.

If only it was so easy.

Don't make this weird."

"You've moved our sofas three times and you're telling me not to make things weird?" Rahat asks, watching him.

"Yes, because at least my weird is productive."

"How is this in any way productive?" Rahat moves to the sofa Nur is trying to maneuver and puts his hands on it, halting Nur. "You gotta stop with the sofas, man. I don't think she's going to care."

"You don't know her."

"So you're telling me she's so shallow, she'll see a bad sofa arrangement and walk out of the house?"

"I never said she was shallow."

"But she will somehow take offense at a bad sofa arrangement?"

"That's not . . . I just want things to be perfect."

"Life isn't perfect, Nur. And when it looks like it is, usually it's hiding something very bad. And can I just say, the sofas aren't bad. They're fine wherever you put them." Nur moves away from the sofas and stands back, looking at them.

"Fine." He puts his hands up in defeat. "I'll leave them like this."

"God, you're so fucking ridiculous sometimes."

"I'm just nervous."

"You've been seeing her for weeks," Rahat says, flopping down on one of the sofas, one of the legs of his joggers ridden up, the only way Rahat seems to like wearing them. "Why are you suddenly so worried about what your house looks like?"

Nur stands by the window, evaluating the room, trying to figure out what kind of impression he wants to make on her. There are books on the mantelpiece, his favorites of the last few months, ones he has talked to her about, with a couple of candles next to them, which Mariam got for him when he came to university but which he has never used. He has moved everything else out, the clothes-drying rack that usually sits in the corner shoved into his room, the vacuum that often lies somewhere mournfully picked up and taken to a closet. This is his home away from home, and he doesn't know what it says about him.

"Is it that you want to hide the abject poverty we live in?" Rahat asks, gesturing to the MacBook that sits on the table, though that belongs to Rahat himself.

"No, not that." It's odd. It feels like he is meeting her for the first time, trying to figure out what he should wear, what he should say, how he should act.

"Nur," Rahat says. "It's fine. I get it. You want to seem perfect to her. But you know she's already seen plenty of you. You're going *steady* now."

"This is also the first time she's going to see you."

"If you even think about trying to position me in this room . . ."

"I just want you to get along."

"Well, if she's anything like Saara, we won't," Rahat declares. "You know I never liked her."

"You definitely made that very obvious."

Nur remembers the two of them, sitting in the living room, their faces getting angrier, their voices louder and louder. And Nur said nothing, not knowing what side to pick: the friend or the girl-friend, his past or his future. He stayed quiet in the hope that the storm might pass him by.

"I don't know if that's meant to be a slight on my character or what, but I prefer to make it known who I like and who I don't like."

"Okay. Can I just ask that if you don't like Yasmina, you make it very obvious to me *after* the fact?"

"Do you really think I'm going to start a fight with your girl-friend for no reason?"

"I'm not saying that—"

"Then what are you saying?"

"That Yasmina is not like Saara. She's not going to attack you. I just want you to give her a chance."

Rahat looks away from Nur. "Of course I'm going to give her a chance," he says, voice low, and Nur realizes he has hurt his friend. But before he can say anything, Rahat shrugs. "But all I'm saying is, you don't have the best record when it comes to people you date," he says, with a laugh.

"I've only dated one person."

"Exactly. You're zero for one right now. You can't expect me to go into this optimistically with that kinda ratio."

"Rahat," Nur says, serious now.

"Okay, okay." Rahat stands from the sofa. "I promise to be on my best behavior. What time is she coming over?"

"In about half an hour." Nur pauses. "You're not wearing that, right?"

"There is nothing wrong with what I'm wearing," Rahat says. "And I'm not changing because your girlfriend is coming over."

"If you're fine looking like that . . ."

Rahat grits his teeth. "You're such a dick," he says, walking past Nur, out of the room.

"You're not angry, right?" Nur shouts without turning around.

"You massive fucking narcissist." A pause. "No."

Nur smiles and moves the sofas back.

But there is still a nervous ball inside his chest, and he knows why it's there. It won't go away, not until the day is over.

Why don't we ever go over to your house?" Yasmina had asked. They were sitting in her room, in an otherwise empty house, because the people Yasmina lived with were forever out. One of them was a recovering anorexic, spending all her time at the gym or at the library; the only reason she came home was to sleep, out of the house before Yasmina woke. The other was an art student, so she was always on campus, working through her numerous projects. Yasmina knew this about them when she moved in, and it was part of why she responded to the ad. She knew it meant she wouldn't have to make friends with the people she lived with.

Nur and Yasmina would hang out there often. They'd stopped calling these meetings dates anymore. The novelty had worn off, though Nur still felt a blast of nervous excitement whenever he planned to meet her. They saw each other a few times a week. He walked her to lecture halls, she walked him back. He sat in the library until her classes finished, she claimed a table in the café while waiting for his seminar to wrap up. They studied together at Starbucks, at her house, sat on the floor of her living room, books spread around them, typing feverishly on laptops to hit word counts.

They had become a couple. It had happened naturally, and though neither one of them brought it up, they referred to each other as boyfriend and girlfriend, because that's what they were to each other now.

When she asked him about his house, they were sitting on her bed, watching a Korean film. He was trying hard to keep track of the plot with the subtitles, so the question threw him a little. She repeated it.

"Why don't we ever go over to your house?" she asked.

He considered telling her the truth, that the one time Rahat met Saara, they'd got into a fight about Islam. A throwaway comment from Saara questioned by Rahat, Saara arguing that Islam was as flexible as any idea, that it should change with the times, that they couldn't keep following ideas from thousands of years ago; Rahat believing that Islam was an immovable thing, that it was made perfect, that it would stay that way, that it was up to them to follow it, not to change it. Nur had sat there, watched them fight, not knowing where he stood on the subject, seeing it from both sides, and thankfully, neither one of them had turned to him to ask what he thought. Although the argument had only lasted about ten minutes, it had felt much longer than that. Saara had left that night telling Nur she would be okay if she never met Rahat again, and Rahat had told Nur the very same thing.

He'd kept them apart because he loved them both. Though he'd hated it, convinced the charade somehow showed he was ashamed of them both.

For a second, he considered telling Yasmina all this verbatim. But instead, he hid the truth. "Oh. I never really thought about it," he said, the lie falling too easily.

"Well, maybe we should hang out at yours sometime. I want to see where you live."

Nur nodded and they returned to the film, but his attention wavered. He'd lost track of the story, and all he could think about was that fight, over and over again in his head, and he had a feeling that the same thing might happen again, and he would have to play referee once more, going to extreme lengths to keep the two of them apart.

Outfit changed, Nur idly scrolls through his phone on the sofa, waiting for Yasmina to tell him she's on her way, but she doesn't. Instead, there is a knock at the door, and when he goes to open it, Yasmina is standing right there, in a colorful dress, smiling at him.

"You didn't text me when you left," he says as she steps in.

"Was I supposed to?" she counters, amused. She stays in the hallway as he closes the door, and it reminds him of the first time he went to her house, waiting for her to lead the way.

"Maybe," he says, gesturing for her to walk through, down the small hallway at the front of the house, his and Rahat's shoes lined up by the wall, a strange picture nailed above, right next to where they hang their coats. Nur remembers when he first saw the little frame, a bird midflight, with wings too big, a moon that was too small behind it, the proportions all wrong, and he wondered what had possessed the landlord to buy it.

"So this is it," she says. They enter the living room, and he can't help but look at her face, to see if she's judging, but if she is, her expression doesn't give it away.

"This is the living room," he says. "Window, sofas, table—"

"Fireplace prepared beforehand with books," she says.

"Fireplace that shows how well-read I am, actually." He gestures with his hand for her to walk into the kitchen. "And here we have a state-of-the-art kitchen with some smoke stains just above the oven that were there before we moved in but that we'll *definitely* get charged for when we move out. Note the very clear windows through which we can see our neighbors' kitchen, which is really fun when you're cooking food and you turn to see an old man staring you down as he washes his dishes, and you can tell he doesn't want to be there, but instead of taking his anger out on the person who made him wash the dishes, he's wishing that you were dead. It also comes fully stocked with everything you'll need, including this small washing machine that can barely hold three towels at the same time without whining and breaking down, this toaster where the back part doesn't cook as fast as the front, and this electric hob that is environmentally friendly but shit at actually cooking your food—"

"Hey," Rahat interrupts. They both turn to see him hovering by the door, clothes different, sweatpants turned into jeans.

"Rahat, this is Yasmina. Yasmina, Rahat." Nur introduces them like he hasn't spent weeks talking to one about the other.

"Hey," Rahat says again, offering his hand to Yasmina. And as he does, a wave of guilt hits Nur, chastising him for the way he spoke to Rahat, not trusting his friend, thinking so little of him.

"It's nice to finally meet you," Yasmina says, voice full of warmth. "I've heard a lot about you."

"You too." Rahat looks at Nur, gesturing toward the living room, sitting down on the sofa.

"You know," Yasmina says, following Rahat in, taking a seat on the other sofa, by the window, "Nur always talks about you. But I had to push so hard to meet you. I wonder who he's more embarrassed about, me or you."

Nur moves to the doorway, leaning on the frame, arms crossed. "Both of you equally, I'd say."

"I don't think that's the right answer," Rahat responds, half laughing.

"It's definitely not," Yasmina says. Nur sits by her. "How did you guys meet?"

"It was secondary school," Rahat says. "We both went to the same secondary school, both came from other primary schools, both had no friends."

"Hey, I think I had a fair few."

"He definitely didn't. We were in English together, paired up to work on a story, and the rest is history."

"Wow. You really distilled us down to a few sentences," Nur says.

"What else do you want me to say?" Rahat asks. He moves his hands, putting them under his legs, holding them still.

"I don't know, what about all the stories we have, the years of friendship . . ."

"I think you might be a bit more of a romantic than me," Rahat says.

"Oh, but I definitely want to hear some of the stories," Yasmina adds. "Nur as a kid? I'm going to guess there's a lot of shit there I want to know."

"I don't think—"

"I can tell you about that later," Rahat says.

"No, he won't."

"Yeah, he definitely will," Yasmina counters, nudging Nur, shoulder to shoulder. "I'm just saying, Nur, I need to know where the bodies are and what lies I have to tell."

"I think it might be a bit soon for that . . . ," Nur begins.

"I feel like you're protesting too much," Yasmina says, grinning. "Rahat, please, the floor is all yours."

"Well, Rahat can tell you some of mine, but I can spill some of his."

"Mutually assured destruction, is it?" Rahat jokes.

"Always."

They slip into easy conversation, Rahat telling Yasmina about the times Nur messed up at school, Nur protesting, though he's not wrong, countering with a story of Rahat doing something incredibly stupid, Yasmina watching the two of them, her face a map of her emotions, Rahat thriving on her attention, ever the storyteller, making the anecdotes as big and grandiose as he can without stretching the truth too far. And Yasmina does the same, telling stories from her past, of childhood fights with Hawa, of her parents, of living at home, and contentment slides down Nur's throat, resting happily in his stomach. He is sitting with two of the most important people in his life, and he understands then what has been missing and what has been found.

April 2015

Nur bounds down the stairs after his lecture, narrowly missing the group of students waiting at the elevators, and walks through the foyer, scans his card at the library entrance, soft beep, glass doors sliding out of the way for him to step through.

Yasmina is bunkered down here, working on an essay. She'd sent him a text asking to meet her there, suggesting they get some food, and Nur had said yes, returning to his professor's diatribe about what stands for literature in today's world, half taking notes, half thinking about her.

He runs up the library stairs as quietly as he can, walks through the sterile aisles, shelves full of books long untouched, passing student after student, heads bent over their desks. Until he sees her, books spread out around her, writing, glasses on, and he smiles at the sight, stands there for a moment. She looks up, as if she can feel him staring, and he continues moving, sits down in front of her.

"Just give me a minute," she says quietly, before he can say anything.

"Are you not going to ask me how I am?" he whispers, taking his bag off, sliding it onto the seat next to him, leaning across the desk, resting his head on the pile of books between him and Yasmina.

She pushes his head away. "Do you need the attention straight away or can you give me a minute to take this final note down?"

"I think I'm going to need the attention right now."

"Sucks to be you, I guess," she replies, returning her attention to the page, her writing small and neat. Nur pulls back, sits there as she writes. "Okay," she says, after a minute, "I am done." She starts gathering up her papers and takes a breath.

"Okay?" he asks.

"Yeah, just end-of-year stuff," she explains, books collected. As she stands, she passes him a pile, which he takes in one hand, slightly teetering as he reaches for his bag, slinging it over his shoulder. "It always gets like this, right?"

"Right," Nur says. He has his own essays, of course, but they are more academic than Yasmina's, and he finds that easier, to apply other people's theories to works rather than having to cobble together his own opinions about things. Easier to just say dead white people were right all along than to risk being told that what he thinks is wrong.

"We can only take like an hour, if that's all right," Yasmina says. "I need to get back to work."

"Are you coming back here?"

"No, probably going to go home."

"Why don't you come over?" They proceed down the stairs. "We can work together. I've got a draft of an essay to go over today."

"Because if I come to your home, we're going to end up hanging out and doing no work."

"I'm not that bad."

She looks at him, eyes piercing. "The last time I came over to your house, we ended up watching a horror film, eating takeout, and then talked for hours instead of—"

"Which was great, I don't see the problem."

"That's exactly what the problem is."

They reach the ground floor, dump the books on a trolley, head out. "Okay, so you don't have to come over. But are you telling me all I have with you is an hour?"

"Yes, and you're wasting it," she says, exiting through the glass doors. He follows her a second later, pulling her close to him, one arm around her waist.

"Well, can I kiss you at least?" he asks. Yasmina nods, and he pulls her in. Even though they saw each other a couple of days ago, he has a hunger for her, and when she pulls away first, he stays there, tilted toward her. "I don't know how you don't want this all the time," he says.

"Because I'm not a dumb guy like you," she says, shrugging her bag up her shoulder.

"You missed a word there. *Hot.*"

"I don't think I missed any words."

"Why are you so rude to me?"

"Because I think someone needs to knock you off that pedestal you've been busy climbing your entire life."

"So you admit I've had to work to get here."

"Not as much as you'd like to think."

They cross the foyer, walk out of the university, students waiting for buses right outside, headphones in ears, phones in hands, others sitting on benches, some alone, some together. "Well, hey, if we want to get food—"

Yasmina reaches into her pocket, pulls out her phone, her sister's name floating across the screen. She gives him an apologetic look before answering it. "Hey," she says. "No, I'm not doing anything." Nur nudges her, playful, but there is something in her face telling him this is not the time. "What's up?"

Nur wishes he could hear the other side of the conversation, to hear Hawa's voice, to know more about Yasmina's life, about her family.

"I don't think . . . I don't think they meant that, Hawa. It'll be fine." Yasmina moves away from Nur, her voice dropping. "No, I know. I'm not . . . I know, but I'm saying that you might be thinking . . . I know. I know. Look, it'll be fine. No, I'm not doing anything later. Okay. Okay. Just call me. Okay. Bye. Bye."

She lets the phone fall from her ear, but keeps it in her hands, turning it over and over, and he can tell something is wrong. "Everything okay?" he asks.

"Yeah," she answers, tension in her jaw, hard. And then it disappears. "We need to go eat something!" She hooks her arm around his, and it's like nothing happened. "I was thinking, there's this Indian place, it's like a pop-up or something—"

"Indian?" he mock falters. "Whoa, I don't know if I can do that. My dad would kill me."

"Well, who said he needs to find out? And even if he did, it might be a good time to tell your dad that you're all the same anyway . . ."

"What?" Nur asks, a little laugh of shock.

"Not like that," she blurts out. "I just mean, India and Pakistan and Bangladesh all used to be the same country, right? And then you split."

"Because of a lot of shit," Nur says. "It's not like we just decided—"

"No, I know," Yasmina interrupts, and something drops in her voice, aware something has fallen in the joke. "I meant you guys all used to be part of, like, the same country. I never understood the whole falling-out—"

"I don't know, it probably has to do with the fact that millions of people were killed on both sides, forced to leave their homes because someone decided they couldn't be in their country anymore."

They fall into silence. "I'm sorry," Yasmina starts. "I didn't mean . . ."

"No, it's fine," Nur says, and it is fine, sort of, but there is a part of him that feels a little irritated. "I think this is the curse of going out with someone so smart. You know everything."

"I do *not* know everything."

"Yeah, you definitely do," he continues. "That big head of yours. Filled with so much knowledge, I have no idea how you remember it all."

"If you're nice to me, maybe I'll teach you," she says, and the conversation is back, pulled away from that brief faltering moment.

They cross at the traffic lights, heading toward the city. "So where is this Indian pop-up?" Nur asks.

"It's like right around the corner from your house, actually."

"Damn, they're getting too close. I think Rahat and I need to stand our ground, remind them where they are."

"Getting territorial?"

"I have to be. Protect my land, protect my woman . . ."

"You had better not be talking about me."

"Is that you saying you want me to have another woman?" Nur smirks.

"I don't know if you have it in you to carry two of us," she says. "I don't know if you're built for that life."

"I don't know whether to take that as a compliment or an insult."

"I think you should definitely take it as an insult. I'm insulting you."

"You know, I miss how you were when we first met, when you were trying to impress me. Now you're just rude as hell."

She lets go of his arm, pushes him away a little. "I have never tried to impress you."

"Oh, please. Telling me every fact you know about films, reeling them off like you're Google—"

"That's just because I find that stuff interesting. Who's the one who took me to a bookshop—"

"Whoa," Nur says, holding a hand up to her. "You'd better be careful with what you say next. A word against Greta is a word against me."

"I would never say anything about Greta," she says. "But you have to admit, that was a play. Taking me to this bookshop, telling me your story about finding it hard to fit in, how that place helped you feel more at home, forming this friendship with an old woman. The entire thing feels like it's ripped from a Nicholas Sparks book."

"Please," Nur says. "That would mean he'd have to write about someone brown for once, and we all know he isn't doing that anytime soon." Yasmina laughs, and he reaches for her hand. "Besides, that wasn't a play. The bookshop means a lot to me. You mean a lot to me. I wanted to show you, that's all."

"I know," she says. "And I'm glad you showed me it."

"It makes for a great story, right?" he says, and she laughs again, a little smaller.

They continue to walk, spring slowly unfurling into summer, winter disappearing under their feet. "How is she?" Nur asks.

Yasmina stiffens at the mention of her sister. "She's fine," she says. There is more to her voice, things hiding under her words. "She's just a bit . . . Hawa gets a bit anxious sometimes."

"Fights with your parents?" he asks.

"Sometimes," she replies, in a way that indicates she doesn't want to talk about it anymore.

"Mariam is the one who fights with our parents in our family," Nur offers. "Her and Dad sometimes. I think it's because she's the only girl in the family. My dad expects a lot from her."

"I thought the girls got it easy."

"Maybe for everyone else. Mariam did not get that deal," he says, half laughing. "My dad expects her to do everything: marriage, children, the really successful job. For me and Khalil, he just wants us to do well, or at least that's what he says. But with her, the moon is too low. She has to reach another galaxy."

"That's a lot to put on her."

"A lot to put on anyone, I guess." Nur thinks of his sister, young but no longer the way she used to be, becoming an adult, her own person. "They fight a lot. When Mariam talks about her future, there is no joke, not if Dad is there. I remember when she said something about how she wanted to live off the earth, get a farm somewhere, grow her own food, as a joke, and he thought she was being serious, told her he was never going to let her do that. I think she'll just rebel one day, go and live on some farm, just to spite him."

"Well, she should be able to do what she wants," Yasmina says. "And besides, it's not like you and Khalil are doing bad. A soon-to-be famous writer and a doctor? I'd be pretty happy with that."

"Yeah," Nur says, and he wants to make light of his family's expectations, but he doesn't feel like it.

"Sometimes I wish we could sit our parents down and tell them everything we're thinking." Yasmina redirects them north as the high street comes into view. "Say, this is what's going on inside my head, these are my fears, these are my anxieties, these are my hopes and dreams. Just be completely honest with them."

"Why can't you?"

She lets out a laugh, harsh in the quiet, late afternoon. "I can't tell my first-generation Sudanese immigrant parents everything in my head. Some of the things up here, I don't think they need to hear them."

"Oh, yeah? Like what?" Nur probes.

"I don't know, maybe about my boyfriend and the things we do, for example."

"I don't think I've heard about those 'things.' I might need some elaboration."

She elbows him in the side. "But maybe that's the deal we make with our parents. Keep things from them to keep them happy."

Nur thinks about his parents, about the things he has kept from them, the things he will inevitably keep from them in the future. "And what happens when they find out about all those things?"

She shrugs. "I guess you have to hope that you've built a strong enough foundation for it not to matter that much."

"Perhaps," Nur replies. He faces her head on. "But right now, my happiness is what matters, given that I only have fifty minutes left with you. And I don't know how much of that I want to spend walking."

Before she can say anything, he starts running, pulling her along with him, and when he sees her face, an irrepressible mix of annoyance and joy, bag flying behind her, he knows that this is what counts: the right now.

May 2017

D on't forget to tell Rahat to come to iftar," Nur's mother shouts from the kitchen as he heads to the front door.

"I will," Nur answers, stepping out into the heat, the sun blazing down on him. Headphones in, he walks to the bus stop at the top of his road and sends Rahat a quick text, saying he'll get there in fifteen minutes. Rahat replies almost immediately, he's on his way too, and will meet him by Starbucks.

The bus comes every ten minutes, the beauty of living so close to the city center. Nur finds a spot on the top deck so he can watch the world pass by, and he remembers taking this bus twice a day to go to school, headphones in, losing himself to music, half-asleep on the way there, half-asleep on the way back. Sometimes Rahat would tag along for the ride home, even though it never made sense given he'd have to walk ten minutes to get to his house after getting off at Nur's stop. They'd sit on the bus, talk about when they wouldn't need to catch buses anymore because they'd have their own cars, dreaming of the lives they would live when they were older, when they had jobs that paid well. The memory makes Nur cringe a little, revisiting his past self, the dreams that seemed so large then so meager now.

The city center is alive with people when Nur gets there, bustling with families and friends and lovers out shopping and eating.

Rahat is standing by the entrance of Starbucks, eyes only for his phone, and Nur nudges him gently. Rahat looks up at him, smiles. "Hey," he says, pulling his headphones out.

They hug, quickly, and start walking to the food court in the shopping center. "How's it been?"

"At home?" Rahat asks. "Good, like always. Mum continues to be very mum-like. She comes into my room every night before I go to sleep, as if I'll have disappeared or something."

"She's probably happy to have you back. Her beloved only betah. I still can't believe she let you go off without her for three whole years."

"I wouldn't be surprised if she doesn't let me leave that house ever again."

"Cute little wife one day," Nur says, waving a hand in front of him. "I can see it now. You and her, your parents, maybe some children too. All in the same house you grew up in. A beautiful, tidy story."

"Shut up," Rahat says. "How's home?"

"Fine. Mum and Dad, fine, Mariam and Khalil, fine. It's all fine." He hesitates, swallows the thing he has come here to say. "How's work?"

Rahat snorts. "Work is work is work is work. Nine months of it, and I'm done. I don't know how people do this all their lives, sit in offices every day staring at computer screens. My entire job is sending emails. That's all I do. Send an email, wait for the reply, reply to that. I'm stuck in email hell."

"Hey, you're the one who chose to do finance."

"Did I? Or did the world choose for me, through social conditioning?"

"Ah, you got me there," Nur remarks. "But you'll always make more money than me. There is very little money to be made in writing articles for the internet."

"At least you enjoy it."

"I don't know about that. I'm right there with you in email hell. But if the job helps justify my degree to my parents, that's what matters, right?"

"I'm not sure how to answer that without sending you into an existential crisis."

"Well, I guess I can hold on to the dream that one day I'll make it big as a writer. The brown Stephen King."

"And even then, your parents will only ever ask you when you're getting married." Rahat laughs. "Speaking of, how's Yasmina?"

The smile slips from Nur's face, but he quickly readjusts. "She's good," he says. "Just finishing her master's, getting ready for her PhD."

"I don't know how she went through three years of uni and decided she not only wanted to do a master's, but a PhD too."

"At least she knows what she's doing for the next three years. She'll be a 'doctor of' and I'll still be working for some dumb-ass website writing about the new Marvel trailer." Nur envies Yasmina for the surety of her future, because he doesn't have that, has never had that. Even before graduation, the future was murky to him, full of the unknown. And now, after a year of trying, he wishes he could extract something meaningful from the dark waters, something that might help him to understand what's coming next. "I don't know how she has the energy for it. I could never go back to school."

"It wasn't that bad," Rahat counters. "We had fun."

"Yeah, but I'm definitely not going back."

"You'll change your mind about that when you figure out that the only thing you can do with your degree is teach."

"Ouch." Nur winces, shoving Rahat. "Thanks, Dad, I didn't realize you were joining us today."

"I'm just being the voice you always need around you. The deeply critical, always-wanting-more voice, the voice of our parents and our ancestors, who are always looking down at us with disapproval."

"Like that voice doesn't exist inside my head already."

They enter the shopping center, more people here, all raising their voices to be heard above each other. Nur and Rahat know exactly where to go, cutting through crowds, experience paving their path.

"Every time I come here, all I can remember is that birthday of yours," Nur says. "Your sixteenth."

"Oh my God." Rahat laughs. "Do you mean when we sat in Pizza Hut for like eight hours and you stole those helium balloons?"

"The balloons!" Nur recalls grabbing them as they left, running away with the balloons bobbing behind him, Rahat shouting the entire time, telling him he was crazy. "You kept telling me not to do it because I'd get caught."

"I was sixteen! I really thought they were going to take you to jail for stealing a balloon."

"And they never did."

"You know I still have one of them. It's like on top of my wardrobe or something. Flat now, obviously."

"You kept it?" Nur asks. Though he knows Rahat has always been this kind of person, the type who keeps cinema tickets, train receipts for trips they've taken, physical objects of good times, it still surprises him.

"Yeah," Rahat admits with a shrug. "It was a moment."

"No, yeah, that's pretty cool. You should send me a photo of it."

They enter the food court, rows and rows of cuisines from all over the world, walking straight to the Pizza Hut, a staple of their friendship, their escape when they had two-hour breaks between classes. The food cheap, the booths comfortable, the staff uncaring that they stayed for so long. They pick a booth by the window, looking over Birmingham, buildings cascading.

"You should ask her to come," Rahat says, not even looking at the menu because he knows what he wants. "Yasmina. When was the last time she came here?"

Nur knows exactly when she came here last, twice in just under a year. He'd hated each visit, felt uneasy, on guard the entire time. And he knew she could sense the panic radiating from him. "It's just easier to go to hers," he says. "Like, with family around and stuff."

"Your family or hers?" Rahat asks.

Nur raises his eyebrows in a way that asks, *What do you think?*

"Are you going to tell them?"

Nur pretends to look at the printed menu he has memorized, the items rarely changing. "Tell them?"

"About Yasmina," Rahat says, deadpan. "It's been how long now?"

The same words coming out of a different mouth. "You know it's not that easy. Just because it's been two and a half years—"

"I get it," Rahat says, and he stops for a moment, Nur witnessing the hesitation in his face, that internal fight between speaking the truth and being there for his friend. "I just thought . . . Like, if you guys can get through practically living together at uni and then being away from each other for what, nine, ten months, you here in Birmingham, her there in Manchester, you must really love each other. So you should tell them."

Nur swallows his anger. "You know it's not that easy," he says again, looking back at the menu, wishing they were talking about anything else.

"Isn't it, though?" Rahat asks. "You love her, you want to spend the rest of your life with her—I'm assuming, anyway. That's it."

"You know that's not all . . ."

"So what then?"

Nur lifts his eyes to Rahat's. He doesn't want to say it, has never wanted to say it. "She's Black, Rahat."

Rahat flinches. "I know that . . ."

"So then you know what it is." His fingers curl around the laminated menu, words floating on the page. "It's not just that she's a girl who . . . who isn't related to us, who isn't from the same caste as us, who is Indian or Bangladeshi. She's Black. How many people in your family are married to Black people?" Rahat doesn't answer, and Nur recognizes the lines in his face and fears that he has said the wrong thing, feels guilty that he has made Rahat feel this way. "Sorry," Nur says. "I didn't mean to snap."

"It's all right," Rahat says, looking down at the table.

Shame lights up Nur's cheeks. He thumbs the edge of the menu, the plastic laminate on the paper curling away from itself, slowly coming apart. "I think we're going to move in together."

"You and Yasmina?" Surprise.

Nur can't look up. "Yeah."

It came up as a joke first, last week, him lamenting that he missed her so much, standing at the very end of his parents' back garden, the scent of his mother's roses in the air. Yasmina told him to stop being so dramatic, it had only been a week. But to him, the week had felt like an eternity, each day so long without her, and she told him he was being melodramatic, him replying that that's what writers are like, full of melodrama so thick they can barely feel anything else.

"We should live together," he had said. Her lack of immediate reply thrummed in his ears. "Right?"

"Nur," she started, and he knew what her arguments would be, the same ones she'd had when they graduated from university, when he'd said he couldn't bear to leave her.

"It makes sense, Yasmina. Your PhD is in Nottingham. I could come with you, live with you. I'd quit my job here. It's not like there's anything keeping me here—"

"Apart from your family."

"Well, they wouldn't be coming with us," he joked, trying to make light of it.

"But they wouldn't know."

"No," he admitted. "But they will. Just not yet."

"So you'd move in with me and lie to them?"

"It's not like I haven't lied to them before." No response. "I love you, Yasmina. I don't want to be away from you, not anymore. I've done nine months of it. I want to be with you. Living together makes so much sense."

She said she'd think about it. When she hung up, Nur wondered if he had gone too far. Before he left university for the last time, heading home to Birmingham, he'd told her they should live together, go somewhere, just the two of them. She'd laughed, saying sure, but with what money, and what about her master's, she had to go home. He'd said, "I'm being serious, think about it, it would be incredible," and the good humor had left her face. "What about your family?" she'd asked, and he'd replied that it didn't matter. She'd pushed back, told him of course they did. He'd argued he could make it work, for her, but she'd said an immovable no, that they could talk about it later, always later. Until now.

When she called him back last week, Nur was alone in his parents' house, everyone elsewhere. He picked up, voice loud, and Yasmina said yes. Yes, she would move in with him, because she missed him too, had been thinking about it herself, so maybe it could work. And he shouted, thrilled, told her it would be perfect, it would be everything.

You're moving in with her," Rahat double-checks, "and her parents in Manchester?"

Nur looks up at Rahat. "No, she's planning to do a PhD in Nottingham, so we thought it makes sense to move in together there. Like, we love each other and we both know that. It just makes sense." He speaks fast, like he needs to justify it, needs to defend himself to Rahat.

"What are you going to tell your parents?" Rahat asks, finally.

"I'll just tell them I'm moving in with a friend. Imran or someone."

"Not me?"

Nur pauses, confused. "No, because you're going to be here. That would be the easiest lie to work out."

"I guess," he says. "I just . . . It's a lot."

"For you?" Nur asks, before he can stop himself.

Rahat's eyes drift over Nur's shoulder to the waitress delivering the pizzas in the next booth. "Well, you won't be here."

"You'll visit and I'll come home all the time." Nur wonders why he has to make Rahat feel better about this. Why isn't he just supporting him?

"I know." Nur sees Rahat wants to elaborate, can feel it vibrating in the air between them. "What about your job? And money?"

"I'll get another job. It won't be that hard. Or maybe it will and I'm just kidding myself. But if it comes to it, I can get a job anywhere, like a café or something. All I need is to get the money in, and Yasmina will be helping out as well with her stipend. It's not like we're moving to London or anything. The rent won't be that bad."

"I guess," Rahat says. "I guess I should be happy for you, then."

The *should* irritates Nur, an admission of falsehood. "Are you annoyed? What's going on?" he asks.

Rahat pulls his hands back toward himself, letting them slip under the table. "I'm not annoyed," he answers. "I just . . . I don't get why you would move in with her if you're not going to tell your parents she exists. It doesn't make sense. It's such a huge risk. What happens if they come over to your place one day, just turn up unannounced. Are you going to hide her things, make her dive for cover? I don't think it's fair to any of them."

Nur's anger blazes red. "Yasmina is fine with it," he says, though he knows he shouldn't say that, knows he shouldn't speak for her. "And it's not fair that we can't see each other as much as we want to. I see her like two times a month, and it sucks. It's been a year of that. We want to be together—"

"You should tell your parents, then," Rahat says.

"If it was that easy, you know I would have."

"I wouldn't do that to mine," Rahat says. "I would tell them. If I was thinking about moving in with someone, I would tell them. Lying to them . . . I think that just makes it worse down the line."

Nur knows Rahat is wrong. It's easy for him to sit there and pretend he would make all the right choices in a situation he has never been in, but if the perspectives were reversed, Rahat would do exactly what Nur has.

"It's not . . ." Something deflates in Nur. "I love Yasmina and she's there, and every day I'm here, I see my parents and I want to tell them, desperately want to tell them, but I can't. I'm just not ready yet. What if we move in together and it doesn't work? I'd have told my parents this big thing, made them have all these difficult conversations, and it ends up being for nothing. I want to make sure that it's the right time, for all of us. Until then, I have to hide this from them. But it'll be worth it. It *is* worth it."

They slip into an awkward silence, and a waiter takes their order. After, Nur stares out the window, a dread churning inside him.

"I didn't mean to upset you," Rahat says, breaking first. "But I don't think it's fair to Yasmina. It feels like you're getting everything here and she's getting nothing." Nur opens his mouth to speak but Rahat continues. "You get to move in with her, not tell your parents anything, and she has to live there, knowing that she's still a secret, that you still see her as something to hide."

"I don't see her as something to—"

"But you do, right?" Rahat says. "Like, you say you want to

make sure it's worth it. But Nur, if you want to move in with her, it is worth it. And . . . I think you're hiding her from your family because on some level you aren't completely comfortable with the relationship and I don't know why. But I'm your friend, Nur, and I'm here for you, always. I just . . . I wouldn't be a very good friend if I didn't say something."

Nur makes a choice, opts for softness, not anger. "I know you care, Rahat. But, Yasmina and I, we've talked about it. I would never force her to do something she wasn't happy with. The last thing I want is to hurt her. But she gets it, that it's just not the right time yet. But it will be, at some point." The words taste like half-truths. "And you obviously are welcome to come visit us whenever you want. Like literally whenever. You don't even have to tell me. We'll give you a key."

Rahat lets out a laugh. "Sure," he says.

"Oh, before I forget," Nur adds, silently giving thanks to his mother for providing him with a change of topic, "Mum said to come over for iftar."

"God." Rahat sighs. "I feel like it always comes around so fast."

"Three more days."

"And then I'll be at yours all the time. You know, my mum gets so mad when I say I'm going over to your house."

"What? Why?"

"Because she thinks I like your mum's food better than hers."

"Well, she's not wrong there. My mum makes the absolute best food you've ever eaten."

"Don't tell mine that. She'd kill me first, then you, then maybe herself."

Nur snorts, and just like that, they've gone right back to where they should be. He lets Yasmina fall from his mind. They shuffle through other things, like Rahat's family drama, a cousin doing something he shouldn't have been doing, about Rahat's job, about Nur's job, a manager who can't quite figure out how to use email properly yet tells everyone how to do their jobs. They talk about everything they possibly can, and it never gets hard, their conversation never loses steam, and Nur feels safe sitting there, the friction from before evaporated but not forgotten.

May 2015

Five months pass since that first date. Nur and Yasmina spend more time together than either imagined possible. Yasmina hangs out at Nur's between lectures, preferring it to her own place, which can, at times, feel less like a home and more like a place to rest her head at night. She enjoys the homeliness of Nur and Rahat's dynamic. Sometimes Nur cooks, sometimes Rahat takes over, but Yasmina is never allowed to cook, guests never cook, and on the occasions Imran joins them, he flatout refuses to cook. She stays over often, sleeping in his bed, his arm around her, and when they wake in the morning, he makes coffee for her, drinking slowly in the hazy light, before walking her home.

•••

You didn't have to," Yasmina says when she opens the door to Nur, yellow tulips in his hand.

"I wanted to," he replies, leaning in to kiss her. Even now, all these months later, it is still a surprise that he gets to do this, the hairs on the back of his neck standing up.

Yasmina goes inside for a moment, finding the flowers a jug, and then they walk out, hands enclosed. They talk about final essays, how glad Yasmina is to have got them done, how she's trying not to get anxious about them, and Nur assures her she'll have done well, knows she will have, because he has read her essays, the two of them proofreading each other's work.

They stop to buy some snacks at the corner shop near them and head to the park near where Yasmina lives. Nur didn't know about it before, tucked away behind houses, and when Yasmina took him there for the first time, it was as if it belonged to them.

They find their tree, one they've marked as their own, a little twisted at the bottom, roots twirling over one another, and they lay the blanket down.

"There's this park near us in Birmingham," Nur says, cross-legged in front of Yasmina, a daisy in his fingers, plucking away its petals. "We used to go all the time when we were younger. Me, Khalil, Mariam, Mum, Dad. Like every weekend in the summer. There was this spot, I swear they made it for the parents, where they could sit and watch us anywhere we went, like above everything. And there was this massive spiderweb thing, like a net around a pole. Khalil and I used to climb it all the time. He'd try to beat me, but he never could."

"Used to?" Yasmina asks.

"We had to stop after Mariam split her head open." Nur recalls the short scream of his sister as she fell, legs flying in the air, the gravel crunching under her as she hit the ground, the metallic smell of blood, the glint of it on her forehead. "At least that's what Mum says happened. Really, she just bumped her head a little. But she had to get a few stitches, so Mum decided we couldn't be trusted."

"We tried taking Hawa to parks, but she'd get scared in them. Like she wanted to stay by Mum, wouldn't even come with me when I went to the swings. She didn't like the crowds. Doesn't like crowds still," Yasmina adds, looking into the distance, where a small group of friends are setting up their blankets. "She used to get so anxious when she was a kid. Anything could tip her over."

Nur imagines Yasmina as a child, holding Hawa, trying to soothe her.

"Did your parents know she was anxious?"

"I don't know," she admits, with a small shrug. "If they did, they never said anything about it to me."

A faint memory arises of how young Nur was when Mariam was born, how much smaller she was, how he was told to be careful, that babies were fragile. His parents, running to Mariam any time she cried, to see what she needed. How he knew they must have done the same thing with him and Khalil. How his parents had cared for them endlessly.

"We were really close when we were younger," Yasmina continues. "People used to think we were twins, even though I was so much older than her. Apparently, we had the same energy, whatever that means." She looks at him, gives him a small smile. "We did everything together."

"Not anymore?" he asks.

Her face shifts a little, drops. "Not so much," she replies, and that is the end of the conversation about Hawa for now.

Yasmina reaches for the bag of food, olives and sun-ripened tomatoes, sliced carrots and hummus, plain because she doesn't like the other flavors, artificial on her tongue. Nur talks about his family, about this infinite web of relatives he has, uncles and aunties and cousins, both here and in Pakistan. How he'd been tasked with making a family tree at school once and he couldn't do it, the diagram growing more twisted the further back he went, this cousin marrying this cousin, families intertwining, how everyone is related to everyone else in three or four different ways. Yasmina tells him it's the same with hers, that they have such a massive family, but most are back home, in Sudan.

She lies back and says, "My family here has always been small. Like, it's just me, Hawa, my mum, Hiba, my dad, Ibrahim, maybe a couple of cousins up north. But everyone else, so many of them, are back in Sudan, and . . . I never really feel like they're *my* family, you know? They're just people that happen to have the same grandparents as me, someone way back when connecting us. But nothing more than that."

Nur agrees: "I've always felt that way about my family in Pakistan. It's fucking awful to say, but I never think about them until they're on the phone. Like we have a fairly big family here, but there's an even bigger one over there, and I just never think of them.

And . . . my dad, he came from there, all those years ago, to come live here. He didn't know anything, didn't know the language or the people or the food, and he just created a life here for himself. Nineteen-year-old Mahmoud marries my seventeen-year-old mum, Hina, because their parents said it was best, and bang, that's it, done." He folds the stem of the daisy, a neat knot. "Sometimes, I think about it, what he did, and I know I'll never be that brave. To leave my family like that, go to a place where I don't know anything, try to make a life for myself there. The sacrifices that people made so I could live here, so I could be . . . this." He gestures at himself.

"Do you ever talk to him about it?" Yasmina asks.

"I don't know how I'd bring it up. Like, oh, Dad, thanks for coming over here, because my life is a lot better here than it would have been back home, I can never understand the sacrifices you suffered to get me here, do you want fish and chips tonight or a burger?" Nur lets the daisy go, ruined by his fingers. "Sometimes I think about that Nur, the one who was born in Pakistan, where Mahmoud didn't come here, married someone else. I have no idea who he'd be, if we'd even remotely be the same person."

"I'd like to think you would be the same person," Yasmina says.

"Yeah, maybe."

The sun moves across the sky, falling slowly. Yasmina pulls out a book and so does Nur, both of them sinking into reading, and he leans against the tree and she props herself up against him. After a while, he lets his book fall into his lap and looks out at the rest of the park. There aren't too many people here on a weekday. There are some young people, students from the look of them, congregated in groups, some of them in couples, older people walking their dogs, throwing balls, and there are parents, holding their children up as they sit on the ground, pushing them around in strollers.

"What are you thinking about?" Yasmina asks, noticing the change in him.

"The future."

She shifts, putting her book down, turns so she can face him. "What?"

He moves his eyes to her, everyone else disappearing. "I was thinking about the future," he repeats.

"Okay, Yoda, you might have to be a bit clearer than that for us mere mortals."

He lets out a laugh. "I was thinking about us. Like what we might be in the future."

"And what did you come up with?"

"Well." He moves a little, creating space. "Why don't you sit up with me and I'll show you?"

Yasmina gives him a look, but he continues to pat the space next to him, so she moves, leaning against the tree.

"Okay, so look out there. Do you see that couple, sitting together? By the tree on the right?" He'd noticed them earlier, the guy sitting up, the girl lying down, head on his lap, sunglasses on, looking up, and they aren't doing anything but just sitting there, guy propped up by his arms. "That's us, like, a year from now. Here, after we've finished our last essays, dissertations done, everything signed off and uploaded and sent, and we come here, to celebrate finishing, but it's a little bittersweet, because we don't know what the future will bring. So we sit here, where we know things, where we understand the world, and we spend hours not talking, because it's easier not to say anything."

"Nur—"

"And then," he says, ignoring her, "there's the couple over there, the ones walking slowly, in the left corner." He has been watching them for a while now, they've walked around the park twice, just started their third revolution. "That's us in a couple of years. We come back here, because we're reminiscing about the time we spent together. You're about to go to America to become a journalist over there, an amazing opportunity you can't pass up, and you've asked me to come with you, and I said I needed to think about it, and you thought that meant I was saying no, so you've been thinking about trying to live without me, trying to see if you can. But I ask you to come here, to this park, to remind you of who we were, all the hours we've spent here, and you listen to me ramble on about the past, and you think

I'm about to break things off, but then I tell you I'm in, completely, one hundred percent, nothing else exists for me, just you, just us."

He sees her turn to him, no longer looking out at the park, at everyone else, and he turns to her too, shrugs at her. "Hey, I'm a writer—"

"Shut up," she says, and she kisses him, hand pressed to his face, long, deep, and he reaches for her, hand on her waist, he never wants to stop kissing her.

"A whole life," he whispers, not wanting to open his eyes, because here, there is only her face. "We have a whole life ahead of us, and I can see every little bit. There is nothing, Mina. Nothing but you."

The world shifts underneath him.

"I love you," he says, opening his eyes, and he sees hers widen in surprise. "I love you, Yasmina."

"I love you too," she replies, no hesitation, and she laughs as she says it, kisses him again, slower this time, and he can feel a lifetime of days pressed against him.

•••

You're not allowed to help," Nur says, moving her hands away from the pan, peeling her fingers from the spoon.

"I'm just saying," Yasmina needles, "I think you need a little more salt."

"The recipe says—"

"The recipe is more suggestion than ironclad ruling, you know. You have to go by taste."

Nur looks at the pan, at the rich red sauce he has been letting simmer for the past hour. "I don't know." He takes a small spoon from the drawer next to him, puts it into the red, tastes it, and he realizes that she's right, but he put in the exact amount of salt the recipe told him to.

She puts a hand on his. "Honestly, that recipe was probably written by a white person. It's okay to add more salt."

He lets out a small laugh. "Okay, okay," he says, reaches for the salt, pours more in, white grains falling down. "It's going to taste good, though."

"I wish Rahat was here," Yasmina says. "Then I might believe you."

"That's so rude." Nur places the lid over the pan, giving her a look of hurt. "I cook all the time."

"Oh, really?" she asks. "I swear, every time I come over, Rahat has made something new for you."

"Well," Nur says, and he feels a tiny bit of guilt, "Rahat likes cooking—"

"I'm just joking," Yasmina says, touches him lightly on his arm. "You don't have to—"

"I know," Nur says. He turns a little, changes his face, so she can't see the truth on it. "Anyway, last month." Their families are coming to pick them up in a couple of weeks. Rahat has already left, his father getting him earlier in the week. When he'd asked Nur if he wanted a lift, like last year, Nur said he wanted to stay for Yasmina, and Rahat looked hurt, for just a moment, and Nur pretended not to notice.

"Last month," she repeats. "Are you guys doing anything for the summer? Your family?"

Nur shakes his head, shrugs. "We don't really do anything," he says, settling against the sink opposite her. "Like, my family don't tend to do holidays or anything like that. We go to Pakistan every so often . . . But nothing like . . ."

"No holidays?" she asks.

"Do your family?"

"Sometimes. We've been to places in the UK, for sure. My parents really like exploring. My dad always tells me, before they had us, he and my mum used to just go traveling all the time, around my mum's shifts at the hospital, my dad's long hours. He'd just take her for a road trip, go get a hotel somewhere, just so he could say he'd been there. And even when they had us, they took us with them. I feel like most of my childhood is just road trips, like all over the place. We've been to the Peak District more times than I can count, down to Devon or Cornwall, up to Scotland. My dad always says, I have a car, why not?"

"That's nice, though," Nur says, and he thinks about his family going to the beach for a day, every so often, how they have stopped doing that, how the only time they ever leave their house together now is for Eid, and even then, it's to visit their relatives' houses. "I wish my family did more things like that."

"Hey, be the change you want to see in the world, right?" she says, nudging him with her foot. "Besides, you can come with my family on our next vacation."

"Go on a trip with your family?" The idea is odd to him. To be so familiar with her family that he'd feel comfortable in a car with them, talking, laughing, playing. To have the same relationship with them that he has with his own family. Something about the image makes him feel guilty.

"Yeah, why not? Picture it: you stuffed into our family car, between me and Hawa, trying your best not to lean on us every time the car goes around a bend, being super polite if my parents ask you anything, getting freaked out when I reach for your hand or touch you . . . It would be great."

"I think I'd try to jump into whatever lake we're holidaying next to."

Yasmina laughs, hits him with her foot again. "Shut up. You'd love it."

"I don't know about that. Imagine me trying to get along with your parents."

Yasmina frowns, reaches for the salt shaker, passing it back and forth in her hands. "What are you trying to say about my parents?"

"I'm saying a lot about myself, actually," Nur responds, realizing his mistake. "I wouldn't be able to talk to them. I'd be scared shitless. The only way I could ever see you in a car with my family like that is if we're married. And like, not even just newly married, five years married."

"Surely they're not that bad . . ."

"Trust me, my family are not . . . as open as yours, shall we say." He steps back to the hob, lifting the lid. "I think this is ready to go in."

"Okay," she says. "Am I allowed to help with this part?"

"With putting cheese on top and putting it in the oven?" Nur asks, looking at her. "I think I got it."

"You know, this goes against all of my learned behavior."

"The feminist in you can thank me." Nur slides the sauce into a glass dish, throws grated cheese on top, and places it into the oven. "Okay, it'll be like fifteen minutes and then we can eat."

Yasmina heads into the living room, Nur following her. "Are you guys doing anything?" he asks. "For the summer?"

"I don't know," she says, sitting on the sofa, Nur next to her, Yasmina putting her legs over his lap. "I don't think so. Hawa is . . . I don't think she's in the mood for it."

"Not up for it?" Nur says, waiting for more.

"She's stopped caring about holidays as she's grown up," Yasmina says. Her bottom lip disappears, teeth chewing on it. "Anyway, you're going to come visit me, right?"

"Over the summer? Of course," Nur says. "Just not over Ramadan. Don't want to be too bad of a Muslim."

"You won't go see your girlfriend and make out with her while you're fasting," Yasmina says, nodding. "That's great. Your imam will definitely be proud of you."

"Hey, I have to follow some of the rules. Otherwise, I'm not getting past those pearly gates."

"I think that might be the wrong religion."

"Fuck," Nur says. "I wonder if God might be insulted by that."

Yasmina laughs, but it is a little short. She plays with her ring, turning it on her finger. "I was thinking . . . ," she starts. "And, this is definitely going to sound dumb." He waits. "But I was thinking it wouldn't be so crazy if we stayed here, over the summer." Nur doesn't move. "Well, it'd actually be very insane. But like you said, you're staying in this house next year anyway, so it wouldn't be that hard. You said your landlord couldn't find someone, right? Maybe we could get some jobs or something, like working in Tesco or Waterstones, to cover rent and have the summer together. It wouldn't be bad."

It wouldn't. Nur sees it, the two of them living here together—no Rahat, no Imran. The summer stretches out before him, endless, infinite. Their own little world. He feels a pang of envy, because he wants it but he knows he can't. His family is coming to pick him up, her parents are coming for her. What would he tell them? He imagines the sound of his mother's voice on the phone, how sad she would be, how she wouldn't understand. He knows there isn't an excuse in the world that could justify spending an entire summer in another city from them, not after being here for university the rest of the year. Part of him needs to be with his family too.

"It's dumb, I know," she says to his silence. "I'm not saying we should do it. But . . . I'm just going to miss you a lot, Nur."

His first instinct is to make a joke, but he fights it. "I'm going to miss you too," he says, and the truth feels odd coming out of his lips. It's only been six months, and yet it's like he has known her forever, can barely begin to fathom life without her, and suddenly, the idea of going home for a couple of months seems stupid. Why don't they stay here, together, cocooned away from the rest of the world, ignoring everything happening outside, focusing only on what is inside, between them? He leans forward, kisses her, because he needs to feel her before he no longer can.

When they sit down to eat, legs crossed on the sofa, Yasmina tells him how the simple pasta bake is actually good, Nur admitting that he has never made one before. They are awkward with each other, a strange atmosphere around them.

Afterward, Yasmina washes the dishes, Nur putting them away, and every time he comes near her, there is electricity in the air between them, so sensitive, anything could set it off.

They head to Nur's bedroom, and when he closes the door, his breath is fast, shallow, a ball of nerves in his chest. Yasmina stands right in front of him, pulls at his shirt. "Mina," he says, voice low. Her eyes drop to his lips, and she kisses him before pulling back. There is a script here, one she has written for him, so he follows it, takes his shirt off, arms up, nothing underneath. Nur steps to her, kisses her, hand on the back of her neck, and when he pulls back, she lifts her arms up, lets him slip her shirt slowly over her head. It joins his on the floor.

Nur's breath gets stuck in his chest. Yasmina twitches shyly, clear that she is fighting the inclination to cover herself, and Nur recognizes himself in her. He traces his fingers over her bare skin, skin he's never seen. "We can, if you want."

"You're not going to say it?" she asks, a joke, but there's a slight shake to her voice.

Her skin is so soft. A pleasurable heat runs through him, his breath fluttering, his chest tight. "We don't have to," he says, "if you don't want to. We can continue waiting—"

"I want to," she interrupts. "I've wanted to for a while." She takes his hand, presses it to her chest. "Really, come here," she says.

She leans into him, kisses him. He reaches for her, hands finding smooth skin that turns into the cotton of her bra. Yasmina takes another step back, the bed against her legs, and they fall onto it, her hands finding his jeans, unbuttoning them, the zipper, and he pushes them down. He puts his fingers on the waistband of her joggers, and he hesitates for a second. Her hands joins his, pushing them down.

"Do you have a . . . ?"

"Isn't that meant to be what you bring?" she asks, and when his eyes widen, she laughs. "I'm on the pill."

"On the pill?"

"It's not just for sex, Nur," she replies, kisses him again. He feels her urgency, and suddenly, it's like the world has fallen away and there is nothing else around them. He reaches to push his underwear down, pulls hers down too, slides his hand down past her waist, and when he feels her, she arches her back, head pushed against the bed, eyes closed. He presses his lips against her neck, feels her heartbeat pulsing against them. He has missed the way another body feels against his. She puts her hand on his shoulder, nails biting half-moons into his skin, and he lifts his head, watches her face, wants to see her while he touches her. He puts his lips to her feverish skin, tastes her sweat. She breathes heavily and he can tell she is nearly there, close, her entire body stiffening, electric, and after, when she loosens, she laughs breathlessly, opens her eyes, and kisses him again, pulling on his lips.

"Do you feel okay?" he asks, and she laughs again, pushes him away and then pulls him back, arm wrapped around his neck, kissing him. "Do you still . . . ," he starts, and she nods, moving herself back, to the pillows, head against them, and he follows her. When she takes hold of him, he lets out a small gasp, mouth near her ear, and he lets her lead the way, pushing back in tandem with him. She takes his face in her hands, so all he sees is her, and when he comes, everything pulses in waves, and he collapses on her, out of breath.

The two of them stay there, panting, until he lifts himself up, and she looks away from him. He leans over and kisses her, before she can say anything. "Good?"

"Shut up," she says, laughing, pushes him off her, the two of them lying by each other. She reaches for his hand, holds it against her chest. "Good," she says.

January 2016

She once asked why the Weeknd's hair looked like that, and when I explained that it was just his style, she said she thought it was because he didn't wash his hair. Because he was Black."

Nur sits in Imran's living room, on the floor, back to a wall, pizza boxes around them. "She did not," Imran says, sitting opposite him, legs stretched out.

"Yeah, she did. We spoke about it, a bit. I said that Black people definitely wash their hair, that maybe some of them wash it a little less regularly than we do because it damages the texture of Black hair, but we should all be washing our hair less anyway. She went quiet, so I didn't say anything else because I thought I'd upset her."

"Yeah, but she needs to be told. Everyone does."

"I know," Nur says, playing with the pizza's cardboard box, fingers fidgety, unable to rest.

"It's not like we're born with this knowledge. If she's never properly met a Black person, if she's never talked to a Black person, how is she going to know she's wrong?"

"You make it sound like she thinks being Black is like being a different species," Nur says.

Imran waves away the suggestion. "You know what I mean," he says. "It's like . . . Everyone is racist, right? We're born into a racist society. It's there from the very beginning, this unconscious set of received ideas that worm their way into your mind. They're always going to be there, latent. But it's up to us—not only to *not* be racist, but to be anti-racist. And I think that means we have to stand up when other people are being racist around us."

"Profound," Nur notes.

"I know who Audre Lorde is," Imran says, a playful look in his eyes. "I'm not just a pretty face."

"I don't know. I remember all these things they've said in the past, things that I didn't even realize were wrong when I was younger, but now, looking back, it's like, man, that's some fucked-up shit. For example, I had a friend at school who was a Black girl, Amira. She was really funny. We were twelve, younger even, maybe. I can't remember. All I know is that one day, we were walking home together, and my mum saw us, not holding hands or anything, just talking, and when I got home, she shouted at me, saying that I shouldn't be hanging out with girls like that."

"Because Black girls are what—dangerous . . . ?"

"Because Black girls are not the kind of girls that you hang around with," Nur finishes, his heart heavy as he speaks. "I remember thinking, when I was younger, that I didn't understand what the problem was; I'd thought it was because she was a girl and I was a boy, we weren't meant to be talking to each other. I knew I wasn't meant to be talking to girls anyway, but if Amira had been Indian or Bangladeshi or even white, I don't know that she would have freaked out like that."

"You know, my auntie married a Black guy." Nur raises his eyebrows at Imran. "They met working at Queen's Hospital. He was Ethiopian, had come here with his parents when he was a kid escaping the war, like a lot of people during that time. But you wouldn't guess he wasn't born here. He speaks better English than my parents do."

"Hard-working immigrants strike again."

Imran barks a laugh. "Like always. Unsurprisingly, her family were really difficult about it. This was in the nineties, and when she told everyone she wanted to marry him, they forbade it, told her if she did, she would be out of the family. But she loved him. So her parents stopped talking to her for a while. When they called asking her to come back, she thought it was to make amends, so she went. And they dropped it on her; they'd found a long list of people she could marry, good boys from good families, whatever the fuck that means."

"Like it even fucking matters," Nur says, angry.

"She married him anyway," Imran continues. "Smallest wedding ever, handful of people, mostly from work, her parents didn't go. She lives with him in Leeds now, and they've got, like, three kids, who she brings over every now and then, for Eid or Christmas, but you can tell she doesn't want to visit, that she's doing it out of like family duty or some shit."

Nur picks up a pizza slice, drooping in his hand, and wonders if that's the future lying in store for him. A voice tells him to stop being stupid, that he has only been seeing Yasmina for a year. And yet there is a part of him that can't help but think about the future, about the long-term, about marriage.

"I guess that's the thing," he wonders aloud, staring at the floor, seeing an entire life play out before his eyes. "If I brought Yasmina home, if I ever even thought about it, I just know my parents wouldn't accept her, wouldn't accept us. That the same thing would happen to me."

"But you can't keep your relationship secret forever," Imran says. "Like you're ashamed of her. You can't subject her to that."

"I know," Nur admits, lead in his heart, dragging him down. "I just think it would be easier sometimes if we didn't have all this trailing behind us, family, culture, tradition. Being the most dutiful child you can be. As if all that matters is conforming to what your parents want of you, and all they care about is what other people think of them, of you. We try so hard to be this upstanding family, just in case someone looks closely and sees the cracks."

"It's the immigrant paradox," Imran says. "We're never going to fit in in England because we're not *really* from here and we're not *really* welcome here. We'll always stick out, as much as we might try not to. So we have to be perfect, right? To show that we deserve to be here. That feeds into everything. We have to present the best versions of ourselves to this country, and we have to keep the façade up to ourselves too. We can't let it drop. Not ever."

"Not ever."

"Well." Imran readjusts his position on the floor. "At least you're not gay *and* dating someone Black. That would be hell."

"Your parents would definitely be fine with that," Nur says, rolling his eyes. "Bougie, liberal, middle-class parents, well educated with nice jobs."

"Well, just like how everyone's a little bit racist, everyone's a little bit homophobic too. You were probably homophobic as a kid."

"I was not," Nur replies, indignant.

"You definitely were," Imran says, his voice tight. "We all were. Even me. I thought being gay was one of the biggest sins. That you couldn't be both Muslim and gay, and if you were gay, you had to give up Islam. I knew early on that I liked boys more than I liked girls, that I didn't like girls in that way at all, actually. But I was terrified, convinced myself I'd grow out of it. I thought I deserved to burn in hell. I spent years like that, until I thought, this is the way Allah made me and it didn't make sense to me that he would make people like me only for us to have to fight against ourselves our entire lives. It didn't sit with the idea of him that I had. But I'm not all the way there yet. I don't know if anyone gets *all* the way there. Ever. But we're all on some kind of journey, right? You go to university and meet different kinds of people, you have eye-opening conversations and experiences you couldn't have anticipated. You learn, you grow, you evolve. We're lucky to have that. Those experiences. But have your parents ever had that opportunity to look beyond their own community?"

"So you're telling me to bring my parents to university."

"No, you dick. I'm saying to give them a chance. We put our parents into a box and keep them locked away, not letting them live or breathe beyond the four walls we put around them. But they're people too, just like us. They can learn things, if they're given the chance. Don't deny them the chance to grow and then hate them for their ignorance."

Imran's words settle inside Nur. "Ever thought about becoming a YouTube philosopher? A Socrates for our modern times?"

"I don't know if philosophy is my thing. But public speaking— I'm pretty good, right? Like, I can see it now, Imran the life coach, here to tell you how to get your shit in order."

"I wouldn't go that far."

"Didn't I just tell you how to get your shit in order?"

Nur ignores him. "I don't know why I'm thinking like this."

"Like what?"

"About the future. About having to talk to my parents about Yasmina. She could dump me right this second and it'd be over. I've only known her a year."

"Isn't that your thing, though—overthinking?" Imran says, smirking. "Do you love Yasmina?"

"Yeah," Nur says. "Yes, I do."

"Then you'll figure it out. If she means that much to you, you'll figure out how to talk to your parents about her, how to navigate it."

He responds like it is so simple, and Nur desperately wants to agree.

"I saw Jay the other day," Imran says.

"Oh?"

"He was with some white guy. Holding hands and everything. I guess he's moved on."

Anger sparks in Nur, but he pushes it to the side, wants to be helpful. "How does that make you feel?"

"What are you, my therapist now?" Imran jokes. He exhales. "I'm a little annoyed. He broke up with me because he said I was 'too much.' Too loud, too myself. But a year later, he's out there, holding hands with this white guy. I swear I hate it when people say this, but that guy looks so camp. Like, he has the hair, the face, the walk. Everything about him screams it. I don't get it. Jay said he didn't want 'too much,' but then he went for someone who is the very definition of 'too much'? And fine, fine," he says, putting his hands up. "I don't know the dude. He could be the best person out there for Jay. But I don't care about that. *I* want to be the best person for Jay."

"Imran—"

"Oh, sorry, was that too much? Should I scale my existentialism back for you?"

"I don't think it's existentialism . . ."

"Hey, hey. I don't remember *you* being our modern-day Socrates. How about letting me do that while you sit and listen?"

Nur ignores his joke. "Is there anyone else? For you?"

"For me?" Imran repeats. "I don't know. I downloaded Tinder, but it's a bit much."

"Oh, perfect for you, then," Nur says.

"Asshole," Imran replies with a smile. "I feel weird using Tinder. I'm not sure how to act on there. I don't know what kind of person to be. It feels like everyone is pretending." He presses his back against the wall. "And I know that's what happens when you meet people in real life. You fake being this heightened version of yourself, hide away the flaws and the cracks, make sure they can't see your bleeding heart and your trauma. But it's pushed to another level on apps. Everything feels manufactured. Like, dudes ask you questions and you have to respond in a certain way to get a reaction from them, which in turn makes them respond artificially."

"Got any dick pics yet?"

Imran nearly chokes. "That's where your mind goes. I'm saying all this profound shit about the state of modern dating and your mind immediately goes to dick pics?"

"I'm just asking because it felt like the direction you were going in, but you were taking a really long time. If you want to write a dissertation about dating apps and how they're taking away the romance in romancing, go right ahead. But right now, I wanna know if you got any dick pics."

Imran wipes his hands on his jeans, reaches for his phone, swipes, and then throws it to Nur. "Feel free to read the conversations if you need validation that you're in a stable relationship. But don't judge me for the things I've said."

Nur skims through the conversations, indeed grateful for having found Yasmina, for not facing this digital life. He pities Imran, but he doesn't voice it. He scrolls and he scrolls and he scrolls, until he reaches the bottom of the page, and it refreshes, revealing more and more messages that he hasn't replied to. "This is . . ."

"Hell," Imran remarks. "I know. Like I said, you should be glad you're dating in real life and not having to do this."

Nur tosses the phone back to him. "True. At least I don't have to tell my parents I found Yasmina on Tinder."

June 2015

Nur has been to Manchester before. Earlier this year, a weekend away from university at Yasmina's request. He walked around the places she'd grown up, the center loud and filled with people who looked like him and her. She pointed out places from her past, where she had found the lines of herself. He'd felt humbled that Yasmina had opened up to him in such a way, shown him a door into her past.

But even so, when his train pulls into the platform, Nur's heart jumps into his throat, lodges there, making it hard to swallow. He stands along with others in the carriage, takes his phone out, messaging her to announce his arrival.

They'd met a week ago, the day before they each went home for the summer, leaving Bradford behind, and they'd made plans to see each other after Ramadan. But that felt too long, so he booked the tickets yesterday, told his parents he was seeing Rahat, and when he told her, she said it was stupid, too much money. But he said he wanted to see her, would spare any expense.

The sun streams through the glass above onto the platform as he walks out through the gates. He scans the crowd of other people, Black, brown, white, but he cannot locate the one person he wants. Then she yells his name and her face is right in front of him, smile big. It's like someone has stuck a key into the lock of his chest, his body so light. They hug, and even though it has only been a few days, it feels like far longer.

"How was the train?" she asks, the two of them walking out of the train station, her hand in his.

"Fine," he answers. "Long. But I did some reading."

"No writing?"

"Not today," he says. "I couldn't get my head into it." He doesn't want to tell her about his odd little anxiety. "How's home?" He senses something is wrong. Her grip tightens around his fingers. "Mina, what is it?" he asks, worry filling him up.

"Let's find somewhere first." She diverts him, and he nods, knowing not to press her when it comes to home, when it comes to Hawa.

Over their first six months together he has picked up a little about Hawa, how fragile she can be, how sensitive she is, how they often fight but Yasmina always apologizes first. Once Nur joked that Yasmina should not talk to Hawa until she apologized, because that was what he did with Khalil to teach him a lesson. But Yasmina's face froze; she said she could never do that to Hawa. He recognized his misstep and their conversation cut off, a new thread emerging instead. There are other things too, like how Yasmina calls Hawa nearly every day to check in; he has been there for a few of these calls, noticing how Yasmina's brow is knitted throughout and that, whenever they finish, she seems a little worn down. He wants to ask if something is wrong, but he doesn't because he has learned that Hawa is the one subject that is off-limits.

They walk to a coffee shop. Yasmina sits as Nur orders, and he watches her in the reflection of the mirror above the counter, noticing how slight she's made herself in the booth, bag next to her.

"Here," he offers, sliding her latte across the table.

She wraps both hands around its piping hot sides. "I know you're not dumb," she starts. "I know . . . I know you've noticed about Hawa . . . I don't really talk about it to people, I don't like to . . . But you're you, and we're getting serious . . . So I want to talk to you about Hawa." She pauses, fingers tapping on the mug, trying to find the right words. "Hawa is complicated. That might be the best word, but maybe there are better words."

Nur watches Yasmina speak, her eyes unable to meet his, grief in them.

"Growing up, Hawa found things difficult, and it felt like we'd been dealt very different hands. I was the 'clever' one, always getting top grades at school, and she did . . . fine. She isn't dumb, despite what she thinks of herself, but she struggled no matter how much effort she put in. Eventually she stopped trying, gave up. She made some bad friends, got into weed, like, smoking a lot, and partying, and we didn't realize. My parents . . . they've tried their best. Both of them come from very strict, religious households, and they didn't want that for us. They're quite liberal, have always stressed we could be honest and come to them about anything. We talk to each other and don't hide things the way other families do." She taps her fingers on the cup. "But they missed this, and I did too. Hawa would return home late from school or say she was sleeping over at a friend's. She never looked that bad, but I guess she was good at hiding it. She started sleeping all the time, getting into school late. My parents would get calls, telling us that she'd missed class, and they thought it was just teenage rebellion. And then, midway through my first year of uni, she tried to kill herself."

She says it quickly, rushing the words out, and they rattle across the table, the roll of a die whose result she doesn't know. Nur tries to imagine that grief, so enormous. He sits there, lump in his throat, heavy, suffocating.

"I was in the library at uni," Yasmina says, and her voice wavers, eyes glassy, "and I get a call from my mum, and she's speaking really fast, I can't understand her, all I get is that Hawa is in the hospital. So I take the first train back to Manchester and find her lying there, tubes in her arms, looking like she's sleeping." She looks up at Nur. "She had taken a bunch of pills. Luckily, whoever she bought them from had ripped her off, because they were cut with all kinds of shit and not as strong as she thought. When she was discharged a few days later . . ." She sighs, lets the drink go, her hands shaking a little. "I was at home for a week. I didn't know what to do. I didn't know what to say to Hawa. My parents kept asking me what *they* should do. They were . . . I've never seen them like that. They were so terrified and worried we'd lost ourselves. And I thought they were going to take us back to Sudan, and I didn't know how I'd live there."

Nur reaches across the table and takes her hand, shows her he is there.

"I froze. I spent the rest of my first year at Sheffield going back to Manchester whenever I could. I let my friends go, didn't talk to anyone. I just went to lectures and then went home each weekend. Came back, went to lectures, home again on the weekend. I didn't exist there anymore. Last summer, when I moved home, I tried so hard to be the sister Hawa deserved, but I didn't know who that was. I tried to be the daughter my parents needed, but I didn't know how. I tried to be all these things, but I felt so lost." Tears on the verge of falling, she wipes her eyes with the back of her hand. "I didn't recognize who I was anymore. The smart, popular girl at university, who was strong in herself and looked out for her friends, her family. I wasn't her anymore. I was this girl so wrapped up in herself she didn't even notice her baby sister spiraling out of control."

"That's not all you are—"

"You know it was because of me, right?" she asks, stepping over his words. "That's why she did it."

"That's . . . That's not why—"

"My parents love me more than her. Or maybe they don't love me more, but I was the favorite. They showered me with attention, told me how good I was all the time, how obedient I'd been as a child, how brilliant I was. Even with all the aunties and uncles, I was the perfect one, and I loved it too. Imagine listening to that, day in, day out, and then struggling so much alone." The tears spill over, tracing lines down her face. "And I can't tell anyone. Who do I tell? Who's going to understand it? I did this to her . . ."

"You did not do this," Nur stresses, his entire body on edge. "You did not do this. Hawa did it because that's where she was. But that's not because of you—"

"It's why I left Sheffield," Yasmina says, ignoring him again, pushing her words out. "I couldn't go back. All it did was remind me of everything that had happened. My parents helped me apply to transfer. I got a spot in Bradford. Moved. Made new friends. Met you." She smiles, like seeing the sun's faint glow from behind clouds. "I met you and you made me feel like . . . like the thing that I'd lost had come back."

"I'm so sorry, Mina." Nur jumps in. He hates himself as the words come out, knowing they sound so inadequate, so clichéd, but he is sorry: sorry this happened, sorry she felt this way. Sorry, sorry, sorry.

Nur thinks of what to say, if there's anything he can add to make her feel better. He wants to help, to take every word he has and throw them at her, whatever it'll take to convince her she's not a bad person. He needs her to know that.

But he doesn't crowd her. He knows that he just needs to be here, with her. Right now, that's enough.

They stay quiet, minutes passing, people talking, cups hitting tables, coffee machines whirring and blowing and rattling, orders shouted across the kitchen, cutlery scraped against plates.

"I feel sick every time her name comes up on my phone," Yasmina admits. "I think, is this going to be another call, another text, where something has happened to her? Except that this time she's gone and I can't bring her back." She takes a shuddering breath, and her shoulders slump. Nur swings around to her side of the booth, putting an arm around her, holding her tight, so tight, against his body.

"I'm so sorry," he repeats. Tears come to his own eyes, and he tries to still himself. "I have no idea what that feels like. I have no idea . . . If Khalil or Mariam . . . I don't know. I don't know what that would do to us." But he does. It would break his entire world.

"I should have seen it coming . . ."

"But how could you?" he asks gently, peering down at her. "Maybe now, looking back, you can see things that should've told you something was wrong, but you didn't know then. You couldn't have."

Yasmina shifts away from him, toward the wall, and Nur shifts back too, a margin between them once more. He looks at the tables nearby them, weighing his words, and before he can change his mind, he's talking.

"I used to cut myself," he says. Yasmina stiffens beside him; he feels her look at him, but he can't face her, not yet. "When I was sixteen, seventeen, eighteen. On my legs." His hand unconsciously reaches for his thighs, where the lines are buried, where he has hidden them. "I don't know why I started. There was a guy at school, a friend of mine, who used to do it to his arms. He always wore these long-sleeve T-shirts and sweaters, even in summer, and I'd wonder why, and one day, he told me."

He remembers it like it was moments ago, sitting on the soccer field, Astroturf rough under them. Aqib telling him how he used to hate himself, how he still hates himself but less, him pulling his sleeve back, and Nur sees them, ridges and bumps on his arms.

"Do you still do it now?" Yasmina's voice is gentle.

"No," he says. He finally looks at her, shaking his head. "No, I haven't done it for so long. And the scars from the cuts, they're so pale now, nearly gone. No, I would never . . ."

"Okay," she says. "Okay."

They sit there together, her hand on his, his head on her shoulder, and for a moment, it feels like it is okay. They don't move or speak, letting each other's stories fold into them. When they are ready, they go find a restaurant, and sitting at a table outside, they talk and eat, everything slowly feeling good again. When they have to leave each other, Nur tells Yasmina that it'll all be fine, and he hopes she believes him.

July 2015

Nur wakes to his mother shouting up the stairs, calling Khalil to shower because his father has finished. He lies there, not moving, as Khalil gets out of bed with a soft grunt, shuffling out of the room. Nur listens to the sounds of his home, his mother in the kitchen, putting the finishing touches on the halwa she's been cooking for the last hour, the one thing she always brings on Eid Day, the smell of it wafting up to him. He likes to think how across the country there are thousands and thousands of other homes just like this, Muslims like him waking up, ready to celebrate the day ahead, happy and grateful to see another Eid arrive. He thinks about Yasmina, waking up in Manchester, wondering what she is doing right now, what she is wearing, how her family celebrate Eid, what traditions they have built up over the years.

He rises, rubs the sleep from his eyes. He fell asleep late last night, rhythm thrown into disarray by Ramadan, waking up in the middle of the night for food, too full sometimes from iftar the night before but forcing himself to eat something, drinking enough water to make his stomach feel bloated, preparation for the day ahead.

The door creaks open, and his father peeks his head in, face freshly shaved, hair wet, smiling brightly. "Eid Mubarak," he says, and Nur smiles too, can't help it.

"Eid Mubarak," he replies.

"Eid namaaz is in an hour." Nur nods, stifling a yawn. "Another year, another Ramadan done."

"I know," Nur says. "Always seems endless in those first few days, but then you get to the end and it's like you blinked and it's gone."

"Yeah." His father steps into the room and goes to the window, looking out. "I remember when we used to fast in Pakistan, so different to here. Not just how hot it was, though that made it hard, but the movement of it. The way we would stay up at night, listening to the crickets in the air, the only sound for miles, no lights because it would pull in the insects, but it was fine because the stars were always so bright. We'd sleep until midday, sun so bright, and we'd be so thirsty, we could barely move, delirious by the time it got to iftar, but somehow the women were fine, cooking for us. We'd help, only barely, getting in the way. And then we'd eat all this food, you can't even imagine. We'd be so full after, we could barely move, and then it would start all over again." He shakes his head, lets out a small laugh. "The things we did then."

"And the things you do now," Nur adds, a playful grin on his face. "Not so exciting."

"Ah, well, you learn to leave the excitement for the young after a while. You're the ones with the blood for it." He gestures with his head. "I think Khalil's getting out of the shower."

Nur pushes up from his bed, reaches for his clothes, laid out the night before, shalwar kameez for the mosque, jeans and a shirt for the rest of the day. He bounds downstairs, his mother washing up after finishing the halwa, and he kisses her on the cheek.

"Your breath stinks," she groans, and Nur laughs.

"My breath can't stink, it's Eid Day," he says, kissing her again, and she pushes him away with her elbow.

"Go have a shower. You're going to be late."

"I'm not going to be late," Nur says, rolling his eyes at Khalil, who steps out of the bathroom. "Eid Mubarak."

"And to you too, my Muslim brother," Khalil says, mock serious. "Now get your ass in the shower, so we can get this done."

By the time Nur is ready, placing a topi on his head, dressed in his shalwar kameez, the same as his brother and father, there isn't time to eat, not that Nur's stomach is used to food this early any-way. The three of them head to his father's car.

"We should get there just in time for the khutbah," Nur's father announces, settling into the driver's seat.

"Have you got any athar?" Khalil asks. His father reaches into the dashboard, pulls out a small bottle, hands it to Khalil, who opens it and puts some on the back of his wrist and the side of his neck. He offers some to Nur, who shakes his head. He finds the scent of athar overwhelming, and there'll be enough of it in the mosque, people slathering themselves with the sweet smell in celebration of today.

They drive past the smaller mosque, closer to their house, and head for the large green dome shining in the sun.

They join the queue, park, and line up again to move inside, taking their shoes off. They each have their rituals for placing them on the shelves. Khalil goes for the lowest spot, so he can reach them easily on the way out, whereas Nur settles on somewhere in the middle to avoid bending over.

Nur and Khalil take their place next to their father in the large prayer room. Around them are men they recognize, men who work in nearby shops, men who drive taxis, men who live on their road. Their faces are clean, their hair cut, new clothes, athar wafting off their skin.

They sit in a murmured quiet until the imam steps up, his voice coming out of speakers all around. Men continue to enter, fill-ing the room. This year, the khutbah is about the importance of friendship, of surrounding oneself with good people, the kind of people who want nothing but the best for others, who don't sup-port the act of sinning.

They stand to pray, and Nur is grateful to the imam for explaining how Eid prayer is different from normal prayer, because even though he is here twice a year, has been his entire life, he still forgets how many times he must raise his hands, still forgets what he has to read. Nur stands shoulder to shoulder with his father and Khalil, and when he kneels, the whole room kneeling with him, hands pressed to knees, he is swept up in a wave of gratitude, that he has this, that he belongs here. He thinks of Imran and Rahat in their own mosques, and he smiles, happy knowing they are doing this too.

"Eid Mubarak," Nur's father says when they finish praying, and they hug, Nur and his father, then Khalil and their father, then Nur and Khalil. Around them men are hugging each other, shaking hands, the quiet hum of the mosque giving way to a chorus of voices all saying the same thing, the air electric with joy.

Then there is a sudden rush to leave, to get back to their respective houses, to spend this glorious day with their families, and Nur joins the crowd, shuffling forward, reaching through a mass of arms for his shoes, clasping them to his chest and walking out with them, socks on ground because there's no space to put them on in the foyer. The three of them arrive back as Nur's mother is halfway through getting ready, looking at herself in the mirror as she applies eye shadow, one eyelid open, the other closed, being painted caramel.

"How was the mosque?" she asks.

"Same old, same old," Khalil replies, sitting on the sofa, sliding the topi off his head. "Mariam awake yet?"

"She's just getting ready." Their mother switches eyelids.

Nur decides to go bother Mariam, races up the stairs, knocks on her door, and he opens it to a grunt, sees his sister biting on a comb, French braiding her hair intricately. He's barely in the door, Khalil behind him, when their father calls for them, yelling their names up the stairs in order, and Nur gives Khalil a grin. "Eid money," he says, racing to the door.

He gets downstairs first, Khalil behind him, Mariam last. Their father stands in the middle of the living room, and beginning the same familiar charade, takes out a single pound coin and offers it to Nur, very serious face, telling Nur he won't go up, Nur negotiating, his father pulling out another pound coin with an extremely serious face. Then Nur giving his siblings a conspiratorial look, and the three of them jumping on their father, Nur and Khalil gently but firmly holding him down on the sofa, while Mariam prizes open his hands, which are full of notes. Their father laughing as he struggles, each year finding it is getting harder and harder to fight them off; when they were younger, he was able to throw them off for longer. All the while, their mother watches them from the other sofa, eyebrows raised with a hint of a smile on her face, and she plays her part too, saying "that's enough" after a few minutes, and they all stop, breathing heavily. Their father pulling himself up, breathless from laughter, and Mariam doling out the money between them, always equal, their parents never believing in tiering the money according to age as other families might.

"Now get ready," their mother announces once the three of them are successful, holding their winnings. "We'll leave in a bit."

They head back to their rooms, Nur changing from his shalwar kameez into jeans and a shirt, and Khalil does the same. Mariam appears, in a blue shalwar kameez, scarf running down pinned to her side so it doesn't move, and it is so different from the clothes she normally wears, loose sweaters and jeans, hiding her body from the world, that Nur stares for a moment.

"Don't," she threatens, preempting him.

"You look nice."

"Don't!" she repeats, but this time with a blush creeping up her cheeks.

"I'm just saying, you look really nice."

"Why do you have to do this?"

"Why can't you take a compliment?"

"Don't you know, Nur, our family is incapable of doing that," Khalil says. "I do have to say, though, looking at us, we are a pretty hot family."

"I'm glad your ego has extra space for the two of us," Mariam says. She runs her hand down the length of herself, inhales. "Does it really look good?" she asks.

"You look fantastic," Nur answers.

Back down they go, Nur glancing at the time on his phone, just before twelve, his stomach empty, a familiar sensation, but one that now can be fixed. His mother stands in the living room, one foot on the sofa as she struggles to tie her sandals, and Nur helps her, the henna on her feet mesmerizing, the patterns swirling together, a product of hours spent the night before, a friend of hers at their house, coating her skin in brown dye.

"Done," she says, and she puts a hand to his arm, rubs it in thanks. She reaches behind her for her clutch, scarf over her shoulders, draping down her arms, and lets out the breath she's been holding in all morning. "Khalil, grab the halwa. Mariam, sit in the front. I don't want your suit getting ruined. Nur, can you open the door for us?"

They move in tandem, Nur getting the front door, Mariam first, then his mother, Khalil following with the pot of halwa, their father last, closing and locking the door behind him. And when they step onto the road, Nur sees other families around them walking out into the world, everyone so clean, women draped with colors, men with the fresh look of a haircut done the night before.

Every Eid, Nur is struck by the beauty of his people. Everyone is cheerful, big smiles, and as they walk to the car, he waves at his neighbors, greeting them, Eid Mubarak. It seems the far dark edges in his mind have been pushed back for the day

But then, without any kind of push, he recognizes a melancholy creeping into his thoughts. As they drive to Nani's, a couple minutes away, his mind wanders off, and he realizes he misses Yasmina. Disappointed that he can't show her this, that he can't see her world today either.

The door to Nani's house is propped wide open, the way it always is on Eid Day, come rain, snow, or hail. Khalil barrels ahead with the pot of halwa, and from the sounds of it, there are already people here. Guests in the living room stand, greet them as they shuffle down the hallway, cousins from Dewsbury. Nur shakes their hands, with a smile that reaches his ears, strides into the kitchen, where Nani is stationed at the hob, nursing her chicken curry, the smell of it delicious in a way no other smell could be, and he wraps his arms around her from behind, lays his head on her shoulder, whispers, "Eid Mubarak," into her ear. She chuckles, tells him to stop being stupid, but he holds her a little while longer, because he has missed her so much while at university, missed coming to her house after school, eating with her, listening to her giving him the latest on family here and back in Pakistan.

"Did you make rice?" he asks, stepping back.

She scowls at him. "Of course I did, Nur, it's Eid." She hugs

Khalil and Mariam, stepping back to look at her properly. "You look so pretty, Mariam." Mariam blushes, eyes shooting to the ground. Nani puts her hand under her chin, lifts her face. "You shouldn't be shy when someone tells you that."

"Nani," Mariam begins.

"I'm being serious, darling. You're becoming quite beautiful." She lets go of Mariam and turns back to her curry. "Your mum and dad here?"

"Yeah, they're in the living room."

"Good." She scoops up some curry, putting a finger into her mouth to taste. "Tariq and Zakia should be here soon. And then we'll eat."

"Do we have to wait for them?" Khalil whines.

"Yes," she says, eyes steely.

So wait they do, sitting in the living room, the five of them and Nani, guests departing after Nur's mother serves them tea and some samoseh that Nani fried this morning, and they talk, mostly about Pakistan, Nani discussing some land problems in her cousin's town, about the legal system, the way it only cares about sucking up money. Nur's father asks if there's anything he can do to help, and she says no, her people are on it, and the phrase makes Nur think she's part of some kind of gang, which wouldn't surprise him. Nani has always acted like the godfather of their family, sitting at the head of the table since Nana died, leaving her to lead the family alone.

Nur's phone starts vibrating against his leg, and he excuses himself before daring to look at the screen to see who it is. Yasmina's name is bright on the screen, and his heart leaps for a second before being dragged down. He steps through the kitchen, outside into the garden, the sun dancing on Nani's plants, before he answers it.

"Hey," he says, and he tries to keep the stress out of his voice, the fear that someone might overhear.

"Hey," she says, and he can hear other people clatter in the background as she talks, but he focuses on the sound of her voice, on how long it has been since he saw her last. "Eid Mubarak."

"Eid Mubarak," he replies, smiling.

"How are you?"

"I'm all right. Glad to finally be able to eat." A second. "Even though I haven't eaten yet."

She laughs. "Hard to after a whole month."

"I know," he says, and his stomach turns. "But how are you? Your family?"

"We're good. I'm at my cousin's right now. She's got this barbecue set she wanted to use, so we're here, watching her husband try and fail to cook on it." He can picture the scene, Yasmina and Hawa, her parents, their family, standing together scrutinizing this man. "I just wanted to call."

"Before we meet."

"Before we meet," she responds, and she lowers her voice a little.

"I can't wait to see you," he says.

"Aren't we eager?" He hears her smile on the other end.

"When it comes to you, always."

They both pause. He imagines she is right in front of him, that all it would take is for him to raise his hand and she would be there to touch.

"I love you," she says. "I hope you have a good day—"

Footsteps reverberate behind him, and panic rises in his throat.

"You too," he replies, turning as Khalil walks to the patio door, mouth open to call for Nur. "Sure thing, I'll catch you later."

"Yeah," Yasmina says, and he hears hurt in her voice, knowing why he has ended the call in so mortifying a way. He hates that he can't keep talking to her. "Talk later."

She puts the phone down first, the sound of her disappearing, and he slowly lowers his arm. "What's up?"

"Who was that?"

"Rahat," Nur answers, picking someone Khalil knows, someone who requires no further explanation. "Just calling to say Eid Mubarak."

"Nice of him," Khalil says. "Uncle Tariq's here." He pauses. "And some other people."

Nur reenters the house, sees his uncle and his wife, Zakia, dressed in new clothes, and Tariq grins at Nur, gives him a wink. A cousin of theirs, a few years older than him, hits Nur on the back, exclaiming it's been so long since he last saw him. And so the day moves in this way, a revolving door of people, some from around the corner, some from great distances, sitting and talking to Nani, touching Nur's head, shaking his hand, hugging him, asking if he knows who they are, and he does, always remembers them, and they're surprised, even more so when he speaks Urdu with them, so used are they to children like him replying in English, and Nur basks in having surpassed their expectations, even if only in such a simple way.

At one point they eat between guests—Nur, Khalil, Mariam, Zakia, and Tariq at the dinner table, their parents and Nani in the other room—speaking over one another, Nur jumping in every so often to say something but otherwise happy to be a spectator. He's missed the way they interact with one another, knowing how long it's been since they've all been in the same place like this.

As the day wanes, Nur migrates to Nani's garden outside, finding a place for himself on the grass near the wall. Often, when it gets to this point during Eid, after all the interactions and the food, Nur veers into contemplation, considering the nature of his family. He does this now, watching the myriad of cousins, the late arrivals, the screams of the younger children. The girls take selfies, learning how to angle their phones, crowding around the phone afterward, and the boys crowd around phones too, but for different reasons, watching YouTube videos, talking about cars and soccer matches and everything else manly they've learned to discuss. The ones who are not quite adults yet stay farthest down the garden, talking about the issues plaguing their late teens and early twenties, a clique that is hard to get into, because they are bound by the secrets they keep together. The uncles stand nearest the house, some smoking, some taking photos of their children, making permanent what one day will be lost to time, discussing politics and mortgages and the things their children will not even consider for another decade or two, still free as they are.

It can overwhelm Nur sometimes, the sprawl of his family, and though he loves all of them, he's also terrified by how many people he has to please. How many people he is letting down.

It's weird to think about a space belonging to him. Nur has gone from a bedroom in his parents' house—that was never truly his, not only because he has spent so long sharing it with Khalil—to a room in the dorms, to a room in a shared house, to another room in a shared house, back to his parents', and now he stands somewhere that could be his.

He'd be renting it, of course. He doesn't have the money to buy a place of his own. That'll take a decade, maybe two.

A month ago, he and Yasmina had walked into this flat for the first time, after spending a few weeks searching for something that suited them. Something close enough for her to walk to the university for her PhD, close enough to the train station too, so they can both get home when they need to see their families. They looked and looked, and when they finally found this place within their budget, it seemed a miracle.

When they first viewed it, Yasmina said very little. As Nur asked what she thought about each room, she answered with yes or maybe, never no. He took her reticence as disapproval. The estate agent asked if they wanted to think about it, and Nur said yes, they'll go home and do that. They walked back toward the train station until he stopped her, demanding to know what was wrong.

"Do you really want to live with me?" she asked.

"Yes, I do," he said.

She nodded, arms wrapped around her chest as if shielding herself.

"Yasmina, I want to live with you," he repeated. "I want to do everything with you. There's no other answer. Ever."

They continued into the station, Nur desperately wanting to know what was happening inside her head. Their goodbye that night was painful, a short, sharp hug.

The second time they visited, Yasmina was more alive. She asked questions about bills and costs, about the tenancy agreement. She asked about the people who lived above them and the people who lived below. She asked about rubbish removal, about recycling. The questions poured out of her, and Nur watched her, impressed, because these were things *he'd* forgotten. The things that he took for granted when living with his family.

When the questions ended, the estate agent asked them, did they want the flat?

Nur held his breath, looking at Yasmina, waiting for her, and there was a second where he thought, even after all this, she might say no, but then her face broke into a smile and she said yes, yes they'll take it, and reached for his hand.

He broke the news to his mother in his family's living room. It had been just under a year of living at home after university, commuting to his job as a junior reporter, writing articles for a terribly designed website for millennials, almost ten a week, about small things happening in the entertainment sector, and he got paid enough for it. He was lucky to have the job, because opportunities like that didn't come up often in Birmingham, not full-time, not so well paid, and people at work reminded him of that, telling him as though they were terrified he'd leave. And all the while, his mother had been making remarks about him living at home, how nice it was to have him back after three years, though he mentioned that he'd always come home for the summer holidays and one weekend a month, how they'd talked on the phone all the time. She'd said, "I know, but I want my son with me *all* the time," and he'd bitten his tongue, not reminding her that she had another son.

When he told her, there was panic in his chest, a knot of thorns. He wanted to run away, tell Yasmina it was off, it was all off. Though this feeling stayed only for a moment, it was there long enough to make him disgusted with himself.

"I found another job," he said, beginning with the good thing. And it was true.

It hadn't taken him as long as he'd thought it would to find something else. There had been fear that, while he knew he could get something else, working in a café, a supermarket, he didn't want to do that, wanted to still write, because that's what he knew, and taking those jobs would have meant taking a step back. He'd scoured the internet, seeing nothing for days, and then suddenly, there was the same role, paying the same money, at a larger company that would let him work from home a few days a month. He was certain he'd flunked the interview, was worried they would take the job back, that it was all some kind of prank, but it wasn't.

"Oh?" his mother asked. "Is it better?"

"Yes," he replied, and this was a lie, it wasn't that much better. But he reframed it in his mind, argued that it was better because there was more scope for progression, that he could rise through the ranks of this new company, that there were more perks, like working from home. Better because he would live with Yasmina. "But it's not here."

"Not here?" she asked, confusion etched on her face.

He heard the concern in her voice, the fear that he'd slip away. "Not in Birmingham," he clarified. "I have to move for it."

Her eyes didn't leave his. "Where is it?" He saw it, had known her too long not to, her brain working, trying to figure out what she could and could not say, not wanting to hurt but not wanting to be hurt either.

Nur told her he'd be moving to Nottingham, not that far. He

said it made sense for his career, that he had found a place, that he would be living with a friend who was also moving there for a job.

He talked and he talked, and although he heard his voice, there was a gaping silence in the room, his mother just watching.

He ground to a halt. He asked her what she thought, and she hesitated, finally tearing her eyes away from him. "Is this really what you need to do?"

"Yes," he said. "It's a good opportunity."

From the set of her jaw, in the lines of her face, it was clear she was hurting. "Then what can I say?" she conceded. "If it's what you need, then you need it. All I ever want for you, for all my children, is the best."

Her words were kind, the words he wants to hear. But they were said with such pain that he put his arm around her, tried to shake the atmosphere in the room. "I'll be fine, Mum," he said, and he found himself aching as he spoke. "I'll be fine."

By the time he told his father, Mahmoud already knew, Nur's mother had told him, and Nur felt relieved. He didn't have to do the preamble; they could get right into it. His father asked questions about the job, the pay, the city, the living conditions. They talked about the safety of the area he'd be living in, the price of the flat. Nur showed him the place on his phone, and when his father asked if he's already gone to see it, a now familiar shame spread inside him, and he replied that yes, he'd gone with Imran, they had decided together, and his father said that was good, that he shouldn't live with someone he couldn't trust. He'd filled Khalil and Mariam in about Nottingham before he'd told his parents, sitting them down one night to say he was going to move there. They'd stayed silent when he finished talking, and he'd almost said it then, told them about Yasmina, told them the whole truth, because it might have helped them understand that he wasn't leaving them, he was going for her. But fear had held him back.

Khalil had asked if he really needed this job, and Nur had said he did, it was a good job. But something in Khalil's eyes had hinted that his lie was falling on disbelieving ears. Mariam had told him she'd just gotten used to him being home again, and Nur had felt his heart cracking. He'd said he would come back often, that they weren't going to get rid of him that easily.

Nur saved Nani for last.

He was standing in her cellar, Nani asking him to move something for her, a cabinet, from one side to the other. "Nani," he said when he was done, "I got another job."

She looked from the cabinet to him. "A new job?" she asked, her Urdu flawless to his faltering.

"Yes," he said, trying to pick the rights words. "It's better for me. But it's not here." The words tripped on his tongue, because he was out of practice, hadn't spoken it with regularity in some time.

"Not here? Then where?"

"Nottingham," he said.

She was silent for a second, just looking at him. "So you're leaving again?"

"My friend is there," he said quickly. "We'd live together, so I wouldn't be on my own." The shame of his lies spread through him again. "And Nottingham isn't as far as Bradford, I could come back all the time."

She nodded slowly, turned away from him, back to the cabinet. "It is a shame you are leaving so soon."

He said nothing but later that day, when he left her, he hugged her tight, told her it would be all right, and she said of course it would, they hadn't raised a dumb boy. When he walked out, back to his home, her disappointment was etched into his back through her fingers, her sorrow too, of losing him again, the guilt thick and heavy.

When he later told Yasmina how it had gone telling his family, he unexpectedly cried, and when Yasmina asked him why he was crying, he told her he'd always known his mother wanted the best for him but that this had been the first time she'd said it out loud to him.

What he didn't tell Yasmina was that sometimes he wondered what kind of happiness his mother wanted for him, whether it was his version or her version: go to weddings because what would people think; wear shalwar kameez because what would people think; say hello or don't say hello to someone because what would people think. The opinion of other people trumped everything, was the only thing to ever think about, hung over them like a cloud. *What will people think?*

But this had felt different. It had felt like she had accepted that her son was growing up and becoming an adult in his own right, that maybe the happiness she wanted for him was his own version of it.

So Nur stands here now, looking at the flat, at the view through the windows, and he knows this is his. Well, his and Yasmina's.

He's there before Yasmina, asked her to arrive after him. His parents had insisted on bringing everything, but he had fought them off, told them that he would hire movers; it would be easier because he wouldn't have to carry the boxes in. They relented, but said only if they could drive him there, take him to lunch before his boxes arrived.

So they all drove to Nottingham, Nur choosing a place near the flat to eat. He paid for everyone, telling his father to put his money away, saying he wanted to treat them for coming all this way for him. His father smiled weakly, and Nur registered a sense of shame for this disproportionately ostentatious show of his own wealth, of his independence. Like he was reminding them that he was no longer their baby, a man now, with a job and a life of his own, and all the secrets and lies that come with it.

"Don't forget to phone Nani," Mariam said at one point, food poised before her lips, looking at Nur.

"Is she still upset?" he asked, his response surprising him, because he hadn't automatically said thanks for reminding him or any one of the other million glib things that he'd usually have said.

"She's not upset," his mother answered, drawing his gaze to her.

"She just misses you, that's all." And there it was, a slight pout, she missed him too, even though he has barely left.

"But she's happy for you," Mariam added. "She understands that you're leaving for your career." She smiles up at him, trying to make him feel better, ease the course of the lunch, and he hates himself for lying to her. "We all do."

"Well, not all of us," Khalil said. He looked at Nur. "Why are you really leaving? Is it because you don't want to share a room with me anymore? It is, isn't it? You can just tell me."

"I don't think it's much of a secret that you're the worst person I've ever shared a room with."

"Sounds like propaganda to me, unchecked fake news."

His father cut across their sparring: "But you'll be back to visit regularly?"

The question made Nur's throat close up. "Of course I will, Dad."

"Good," his father declared, eyes right at Nur. And in that instant, he was not Nur's father but rather a man losing his son to the great wide world. "We don't want you to forget us."

"I would never forget you," Nur reassured him, wanting to stretch across the table, hug his father. But he didn't, looked down at his food. "It's not possible."

"We'll come again too," Khalil said. "Get ready for me to share a bed with you."

And as quickly as the table had groaned under the weight of a truth they didn't want to think about, it tipped back over into light.

After the meal, Nur's family suddenly needed to get out of there quickly, his father going on about beating the traffic, even though it was hours before the motorways would become congested. Khalil adding that he was tired, Mariam saying she had work to do, and so they set off, each of them hugging him: his father first, arms tight, telling him to take care of himself, Nur promising to do that if Dad took care of the rest of them; Khalil second, warning Nur not to mess around without his younger brother's wise eyes on him, Nur saying vice versa; Mariam third, not speaking as she held him, reluctant to let go, and he couldn't find the words to tell her he'd be okay, so they just stood there; and then it was his mother's turn, and she hugged him tight, arms heavy around him, silent, too. Nur wanted to tell her he wasn't leaving because he's running away from them, but rather running *to* someone, that he was building something beautiful here, and he couldn't wait to show this life to her. It all sat on the tip of his tongue. But he swallowed it, and when she pulled away from him, she laughed, wiping her tears away, telling him to be safe, to be good, and he said he would, always, and that he'd be home in no time, that she'd soon be itching for him to leave again. She readjusted his shirt lightly, told him to shut up, and as he watched them drive away, there was an emptiness inside him.

He stands in the flat—average sized, a small kitchen, living room, one bedroom, a box room they plan to make into a study—surveying the view through the windows, and he knows this is theirs.

He waits for Yasmina to burst in with her family later that afternoon. A message comes from her, soon after his boxes turn up, updating him that they have arrived in Nottingham, and he becomes giddy, wanting nothing more than to fill the flat with another person, the quiet driving him crazy.

He paces from one room to the other, arms crossed tightly, and he tries to not think about how he has left his mother not once but twice now, how he is going to continue inching away from her with every single day that he wakes up in this flat.

The sound of keys in the front door, and Yasmina is there, two bags over her shoulders, one more on the floor. He dives forward, picks up the duffel, reaches for the other on her left shoulder, freeing her arm, and Yasmina lets out a sigh of relief.

"Those stairs are not easy," she says, one arm around him, bringing him close to her. He breathes her in, her perfume familiar in his nose.

Her parents stand behind her, her mother's hair wrapped in a tight scarf, and her father smiles at him, taps him on the shoulder as they walk past him.

"Already unpacked?" Hiba asks.

"Only a little," Nur says, thinking of the boxes in the other room, his entire life jammed into those suitcases. "Is this it?" Nur asks, closing the door after Hawa, who shuffles in after her parents, holding more bags.

"This isn't even the beginning," Hiba says, and down they go again, all of them this time, carrying more bags from the car. They pile them up in the rooms, and it's crazy to think they all somehow fit into one car.

"Do you have tea bags?" Hiba asks, letting a final box drop to the floor, stretching her arms above her head.

"In the kitchen," Nur says. "There's a bag just under the cupboards toward the window. There should be sugar in there too. Milk in the fridge."

"This is why I like him," she says, nodding to Yasmina. "He knows what's important."

Hiba heads in the direction of the kitchen, Hawa following her, leaving the two of them alone with Ibrahim, who moves to the window, peering out.

Nur steps over to Yasmina, who is standing by the edge of the room, and he stands by her, sees what she is seeing; a room bigger than the living room of his parents' house, empty but for the bags lying at their feet. He pictures the room in the future, after they have unpacked, sees himself and Yasmina sitting together, watching something on TV, her working on her PhD, him working on his book. He sees them cooking in the kitchen, learning how to move around each other, routine made comfortable, breakfast after waking up, dinner before going to sleep. He flashes to them walking around this city, learning its shortcuts, the way it breathes, the way it molds to the shape of them.

This empty place, its bare walls, hollow cupboards, is going to become their home.

"Imagine this flat in a few weeks," he says. "Art on the walls, maybe a coffee table, a bookcase, we can get a rug for the floor, a dinner table by the window so you can look out when you eat."

She leans into him, shoulder pressed against his. "Yeah," she says, and sighs, and her hand slithers into Nur's. The feeling of it shocks him. Around anyone else, the feel of her body on his is not surprising. But when she makes contact with him in front of her parents, Nur is always surprised. He can't imagine being in the same room with his parents, touching Yasmina, holding her hand or kissing her—even being too close to her on a sofa. The idea of it is . . . alien. Foreign. As if touch is taboo, only for those who enjoy breaking norms. "Although I'm going to have to pick the art. No offense, but I can't trust your tastes."

"Saying 'no offense' before something offensive doesn't some-how make it unoffensive," Nur says.

"It's a pretty good flat," Hawa interrupts, reentering the room, looking around. "How many bedrooms?"

"One," Yasmina says. "But there's a sofa bed for when you come and stay with us."

"You want me to come and stay with you?" Hawa replies. The way she asks reminds Nur of Mariam when she was younger.

"Well, yeah. We both do, right?" Yasmina turns to Nur.

"Yeah, for sure, Hawa, please come stay," Nur says, a smile on his face, the kind of soft, casual smile meant to put people at ease, hid-ing the shame of not being able to offer the same to his own sister.

"All right, I'll definitely come whenever I get tired of these two jokers," Hawa says. Their mother walks back into the room with a cup of tea, both hands careful around it.

"Hey, young lady," Ibrahim warns, his arm around Hawa's shoulders, bringing her to him. "Don't be so rude."

Hawa giggles, twisting out from under her father. She heads toward the bedroom, and Ibrahim follows her, and Nur listens to them as they walk into what is going to be his and Yasmina's bed-room. Something pulls at his stomach. How is her father looking at that room? Is he thinking about the things that will happen there, about his daughter sharing that bed with Nur?

"How are your family?" Hiba asks, giving Nur a knowing look.

"Good," Nur says. "They came earlier."

"Yasmina told us," she replies, and in that, there is a question he doesn't know how to answer. "Your mum okay?"

"She got sad, like she always does."

"Well, you know, it's hard for a mum to watch her children leave," she says. She looks so much like Yasmina, the same slender face, the same dark skin, the same love in her eyes, mother and daughter like past and future. "It feels like a piece of your heart has been taken away from you."

"Mum," Yasmina says, going to stand with her, head resting on her shoulder, "you know I'm not gone-gone. I'm always coming home to visit and eat your food."

"I know, my love," she says, turning to her daughter, pressing her lips to her head, and Nur watches them, heart painful with every beat.

If only his family could have stayed, been here. If only he didn't have to hide.

•••

Nur takes one last look in the mirror, fiddling with his hair. Something about the way it stands up is wrong, but whatever he does to it isn't enough, this small imperfection frustrating him. He turns away from himself, walks out into the living room, where he sits, reaching for his phone.

Restless, he opens Twitter, Instagram, a game, whatever he can find to distract himself. He pulls at his sleeves, folds them up to his elbows, unfolds them, folds them again. He fiddles with his watch, opening and closing the strap. He glances at the door to their bedroom, *their* bedroom, and wonders what she's doing in there.

Last night, the first night, was heavy with hesitation. They unpacked their things, filled the space with themselves, dishes sliding into cupboards, clothes folding into drawers, shirts hanging in wardrobes. They moved around each other, and it was like being back at university, Nur sitting on her bed, reading something, waiting for her to get out of the shower. But this was different. Even though she had practically lived at his house, with a drawer for her clothes, her products crammed in the bathroom, her food in the fridge, it had still been his. There had been a boundary between them. But that had collapsed now. Now they existed together.

After dinner, a lamb stew her mother had made for them, Nur stood at the foot of the bed, Yasmina asked what was wrong, silk headscarf on for the night, loose shirt, bare legs poking out underneath, and he said he didn't know which side of the bed was his. She laughed out of surprise. "Whatever side you want," she replied. He pulled back the duvet, slipped in on the right, head pressed against the headboard, and she got in beside him. They lay there together, in the peace of their new life. How loud his house had been, Nur realized. Mariam on the phone, Khalil and his music, his mother watching something on the TV, his father snoring. There was constant commotion. But here it was just the two of them. A longing for his childhood home sparked in him. "This is weird," Yasmina said, turning to him. "Right?" He laughed in relief, turning to her, reminding himself why he had made this choice. "But I wouldn't want to be anywhere else," he said, and she turned the bedside lamp off as Nur curled behind her, his body fitting perfectly into the bend of hers.

The door to the bedroom opens and she stands there, face lightly made up, in a long, sleeveless red dress, with her hair natural and loose around her cheekbones. Nur gets to his feet, stutters, "You look . . ."

"Ready?" she says, approaching him. She kisses him, and when she moves away, he scoops his hand around her waist and leans down to kiss her again.

"You look incredible."

"You're not so bad yourself." He's in black jeans, white shirt, Converse. "So where are we going?"

"A surprise," he replies, takes her hand, leads her to the door.

"How long until you start work again?" she asks, the two of them walking down the stairs of their building.

"Two weeks. And then you'll never see me."

"Apart from evenings and weekends."

"Of course. I'll be expecting food every night," he says, as they step outside.

"That sounds like a great way to disappoint yourself."

"I guess I'll have to be the one who works and cooks."

"And raises the kids in the future, don't forget!" She nudges him.

"I'll happily be the househusband to your investigative journalist."

"Alongside your own fabulous writing career, right? Don't forget: Brown Stephen King. That's what we're aiming for. Nothing less." They turn the corner at the end of their road. "You're really not going to tell me where we're going?"

"That would defeat the purpose of the surprise."

"You're so infuriating sometimes," she says, pulling at his hand, but he says nothing. "Have you spoken to your parents yet?" she asks, a hard turn in the conversation.

He'd woken up to a text from his mother, telling him they missed him already, and the words sent an ache through him. He replied he missed her too, that he'd already bought train tickets for the end of the month, he'd see them soon. Another lie to add to the pile. When he told Yasmina, she told him to call her, to ease her mind.

"Not yet," he says now. "I'll do it later."

"They'll get used to it," she says. "The moving-out thing. Every child moves out eventually, right?"

"When you're Pakistani, you leave only when you're married," Nur says. "It's tradition, right? That's what kills them."

"But they let you leave," she presses. "When you told them you needed to leave, for whatever reason, they let you."

"Yeah, but . . . ," Nur starts, and he knows where this conversation will go if he lets it. He doesn't want to get into a debate, doesn't want their first real day here to turn into something sad. "I think they're still upset about it."

"Of course they are. They wanted you to be home with them. But they'll get used to it, just like mine will." He stays quiet. "I know," she says, "that my parents are different to yours, but ultimately, your parents will see that this is for the best."

"The best for me, not them," Nur says. "It's just . . . not the same, Mina. You know that."

"Yeah," she says, but she sounds a little distant, a little hollow, and there are words on his tongue, about his culture, about his parents, about the way they grew up, about their expectations of their children, but he swallows them. Not today.

They turn another corner, and the houses on one side of the street disappear, a parking lot opening up with a small building behind it.

"Okay," he announces, stopping, turning her to face him. "Close your eyes."

"Close my eyes?"

"Please."

She sighs and complies. He spins her around, then, hands on her eyes, leads her slowly, over the parking lot, until she is standing just in front of the doors of the building. "Okay," he says, pulling his hands back. "You can open them now."

He waits for a reaction.

"I looked for an independent one," he explains, wanting to fill the silence. "Because I know you wouldn't want to go to one of the big chains, and this one shows, like, all the foreign films. There's actually a German one playing tonight, subtitled and everything. It costs like seventy pounds for a ticket. But I thought it would be nice to go for a date night, me and you, some expensive cinema tickets, chocolates that I bought from Tesco snuck in, and—"

She stops him: "Nur." He realizes she's staring at him, and before he can say anything, she kisses him. He's surprised at first, but then he sinks into it, feels himself against her. He is filled with contentment, soft and easy. "I love you."

"I love you too," he says. He examines her. "You already knew, didn't you?"

She laughs, shakes her head at him. "It doesn't matter . . ."

"Oh my God, you did." He steps away from her. "All I could find on Google were the big ones. I went down a forum for this, to find a small cinema near us that plays foreign films and nothing else. It doesn't even have a website!"

"I know—"

"I thought—"

She reaches for his arm. "I know," she repeats, big smile. "I love that you did that. And we'll go here all the time, don't worry about that. But I did find it right after we said yes to our apartment."

He laughs, puts his arm around her. "I should have known. This is on me."

She puts her hand on his chest, and they both look up at the cinema, this little building. "You said something about a German film with subtitles?" Before he can reply, she starts walking, her hand wrapped around his, pulling him along with her, and when she looks back at him, grinning, he knows he has never been as happy as he is in this moment.

July 2017

The kitchen is filled with smells of pakoreh and samoseh, fried potatoes and onions and meat. It reminds Nur of home, his mother in the kitchen, sleeves rolled up, in front of the oven, frying food in oil hot enough to burn. Small marks run up and down her forearms, from drops of oil spitting out, too faint to be seen unless she points them out.

He always assumes cooking will take less time than it does, thinking he'll be done soon enough, only to glance at the clock and realize the time. He loses himself in the act, seconds and minutes becoming meaningless to him. It's less to do with the cooking itself, and more to do with Nur being a perfectionist, wanting everything to go as well as it possibly can. But his devotion is worth it, because it means the food will taste good, taste right.

He's been up since six, starting first on the samoseh, which are the most difficult things to make, since he likes to make them by hand, not just buying some from the shop, because there is nothing worse than eating inauthentic frozen samoseh from the supermarket. No, Nur makes them by hand, the way his mother taught him, which means he stands at the kitchen counter for an infinity, laying down the pastry, placing a spoonful or two of filling, wrapping them up so they look like small triangles, running his fingers along the sides to make sure they stick together, and frying them. He's done two versions, meat and vegetarian, and they are stacked on one side of the counter, opposite the pakoreh, which are both significantly easier and significantly messier to make.

Yasmina asks if she can help with anything, and he gives her a skeptical look, one that speaks of years between them. "I'm not that bad," she argues.

"There's a reason why I'm the cook in this house and not you," he says, telling her to leave him to it, and so she does, occasionally popping in to watch as he lowers his concoctions into the oil, as it spats at him the same way it does his mother. Oil doesn't respect anything but itself.

"Did you get the snacks earlier?" he calls to Yasmina, who is in the other room.

"Yes, I got the snacks."

"Yeah, but did you get *all* the snacks? Or did you just get the ones that you like?"

"I got the ones that I like and I got the ones you asked for."

It's her job to get confectionary from the shops, for when the night transitions from dinner to mindless eating. "I'll get the bowls," she says, entering the kitchen, moving around him to one of the cupboards, reaching in.

"I'll set the table in a second," Nur offers. "Do you think it's enough?"

Her eyes move from him to the food behind him. "We definitely have enough," she says.

"Okay." He turns on the running water, waits for the temperature to heat up.

"It'll be fine," Yasmina says, putting a hand on Nur's arm.

"I know. I just want things to go well."

"They will," she replies, and she reaches across, kisses him on the cheek.

She walks out of the kitchen, and he hears bowls touching the table, the clatter of sweets landing in them. Nur stays by the sink, washing the endless line of dishes he's used for cooking. He finishes, dries his hands on a towel, brings the pakoreh into the living room, places them in the center of the table, and goes back for the samoseh.

He examines the table, overspilling with food, remembering being younger, by the table in his parents' home, staring at everything he loves, samoseh and pakoreh, rasmalai and faloodah, and wanting nothing more than to eat everything. But he can't. This is for the guests, his mother would remind him and his siblings over and over. When the guests arrived, Nur would watch as they ate, not allowed to eat himself. Once, one of the guests, an old man wearing a round hat on his head, offered him food, and Nur, without thinking, took the samoseh, bit into it. His mother slid over to him and gave him a raised eyebrow, mixing guilt and fear together in his stomach.

"When do they get here?" Nur asks.

"Soon," Yasmina responds, heading toward the office.

"Where are you going?"

"I want to finish the reading I was doing earlier."

Nur lets out a groan. "But your PhD doesn't even start until September."

"I know. I just want to get ahead on some stuff."

"Okay. Well, can you at least sit with me and read?"

She smiles at him. "Is this your way of admitting you miss me?"

"This is me pointing out that you've spent the last week trapped in that study. And I'd like to have my person back, even if she is sitting in the same room as me, reading incessantly and not paying attention to me."

Yasmina raises an eyebrow. "Okay, fine. But if you distract me, I'm going back into that study and locking myself in."

"That room doesn't have a lock."

"I can move the desk."

"That, I do not deny."

"Oh"—she pauses, moving to fetch her book—"can you ask Imran if he's bringing his boyfriend? I want to meet him."

"He is, isn't he?" Nur asks.

"I don't know," Yasmina shouts from the study. "That's why I said you should ask him."

"Doing it right now." Nur reaches for his phone, typing a quick message to Imran. "How long have they been together now?"

"Six months," Yasmina says. "How do I know this and you don't?" She returns holding a thick book, Post-it notes sticking out from the sides, reminding Nur of university.

"Because I think Imran feels more comfortable talking about his boyfriend around you than he does with me."

"Maybe that's because you accused him of having too much sex?"

"I didn't . . . ," Nur splutters. "I didn't accuse him of that. I just warned him he should be careful if he was going to sleep around. Like use protection. That's all."

"Which very much sounds like your way of saying that he's having too much sex and you disapprove," Yasmina says.

She goes to sit on the sofa, choosing the corner, bringing her knees up. "And was I wrong?" Nur asks, joining her, reaching for his own book, high fantasy to her academia, on the coffee table.

"You weren't wrong, but you should have phrased it better. You know, for someone who studied English, who writes for both a living and a hobby, you tend to word these things wrong a lot of the time."

"I thought . . . ," Nur begins, but regret runs through him, black ink on white paper, corrosive. "Do you think I should apologize?"

"I thought you already did?"

"Yeah, but should I apologize again? I didn't mean it like that—"

"He knows by now. He wouldn't be coming to this party if he hadn't accepted your apology."

"Or he's just coming for you." Nur pulls out his phone. "See, he hasn't even replied to me yet!"

"Nur," she says, looking out over the top of her book, "you're beginning to sound paranoid."

"I'm just saying, have you ever known him to not respond immediately?"

"You're right. I guess he's either dead or ignoring you because you said something to him a few months ago, then immediately apologized, and even though the two of you have been friends for almost four years now, he took it personally and has decided never to talk to you again. Though of course he is still coming here, to the place you live, for a party you're throwing." She tilts her head. "Sounds plausible, right?"

"I hate it when you have that smug look on your face."

"Then you shouldn't give me so many opportunities to wear it."

She returns to her book, and Nur stares at his phone, as if he can make Imran reply by sheer force of will alone, but minutes pass and nothing comes. He returns to his book, but his mind is elsewhere, attention drained, so he puts it aside, reaches for his laptop instead.

He has an assignment from work that he should be working on, a thousand words about the future of cinema in the wake of streaming, and the email is open on his screen, staring at him, a self-inflicted reminder of how he should be spending his time. He closes his email, goes to Twitter, starts scrolling mindlessly.

He tires of that too and opens Netflix, pressing play on a true-crime documentary, the sound far louder than it should be. Yasmina glares at him, and he turns the volume down, wills himself to be consumed by it, but even that isn't enough.

He is worried he has somehow angered and insulted one of his closest friends. Though he can admit that everything Yasmina has said is true, that Imran wouldn't bother coming to their party if he were still upset, that they've been messaging back and forth at the same rate as always, he continues to feel like a line has been crossed and he will never be able to return.

Nur used to be the one Imran told things to, not Yasmina. Nur gave her updates on Imran's life, the person he was seeing, the job he had, how he was doing. They were the ones the connection existed between. And now it seems conversations run the other way, Yasmina sharing the news. Maybe that's the natural evolution of things, maybe Imran is doing what was normal, becoming friends with someone who has become a mainstay in his life, who he likes and gets on with. Or perhaps it's because Nur opened his mouth, said the wrong thing, and now Imran can't confide in him for fear of judgment.

His phone vibrates. "Imran?" Yasmina asks, looking at him, and he shakes his head.

"Rahat just got in," he replies. "He'll be here in a little bit." He stands, Yasmina reaching out for him, her hand on his arm. "I should go get ready." Her grip slips, and he walks out of the room.

He sits on the edge of the bed, and he is struck with a familiar hollowness, like someone has reached into his throat with a long spoon, the kind that comes with a sundae, and scooped all of him out. He is now a man walking without anything inside him, a paper bag with nothing to carry.

He breathes in deeply, fills his lungs with air in the vague hope that if he replaces the emptiness with something else, the feeling will fade, leave him.

Sometimes, the anxiety lasts seconds, a thought straying across the frayed edges of his mind when he is in the shower, sitting on the sofa, writing, reading. The moment he pays attention, it runs away from him, through hallways and doors, out of windows, escaping like smoke into the night air, and he wonders if it's always lurking there, only fleeing when he casts light onto it.

Other times, it lingers for hours, sometimes days, and when it decides to stay, it hurts, a dull ache in the middle of his chest. He wonders if he should tell Yasmina how he is feeling, but she is always doing something, or so he tells himself, her attention needed elsewhere, working on her PhD or out with new friends from her course. He never wants to take precedence in her life, never wants her to think she has to take care of him. So he deals with it by himself, and he's aware she notices, knows that she sees something paining him, but she never asks him about it. They dance around this emptiness, each waiting for the other one to address it, to make it go away, and it never happens. In these moments, he misses living with Rahat, who he could always go to, never worry he was interrupting, and Rahat would help, make him feel better, right the world for him once more.

Alone, Nur finds himself wondering what the point of it all is. Not specific things, like Yasmina, but bigger things, like his entire life. He questions his job, why he does it, writing article after article about things he doesn't care about, going to an office where there are people he doesn't like, coming home to a flat that he pays for but finds nothing of comfort in, at least not in those moments, and he steps into the bath, the steam of it painting the walls a ghostly sheen, and he closes his eyes, wonders what it would be like to slip under the water. But he never does. Never tries it. He casts the thought out, steps out of the bath, going to find Yasmina and hold her close. He draws his focus to what matters, and it is here, with her. Always with her.

"Is he walking here?" Yasmina interrupts. "Rahat?"

He looks up from his shoes, finds her standing by the door.

"I gave him our address. He probably got an Uber. He should be here in a few minutes," he says, keeping his voice still.

"Okay," she says. She turns, as if to leave, then walks into the room, kneeling by him, one hand on his knee. "We don't have to do this," she offers, and there it is, addressing his issues without talking about them. "They can come, but maybe not for the entire night. We can send them out, somewhere else. Say you're sick or say I'm sick. Say something."

Nur looks into her eyes, this woman he's built a life with, who is willing to tear it all down for him, and he shakes his head. "No," he replies. "I'm okay."

She stands, pressing her lips to the top of his head, pressing her hand to his face. "Okay," she says, returning to do a final once-over of the living room. He watches her, a vacuum swirling internally, dust caught in a wind.

He finishes putting himself together, walks after her. He turns on their small speaker, plugging his phone into it, and when he does, he sees a message from Imran, saying he's bringing his boyfriend to the party and is that okay, though it's too late now either way because they're basically there and he looks forward to seeing them both.

Nur smiles, closes the chat without replying, letting a playlist run, the music filling the room. Hears a knock at the door, answers, swinging it open to reveal Rahat.

"Hey, man!" he greets Nur, wrapping his arms around him, and Nur's emptiness shifts, pushed aside by love for his friend.

"God, it's been too long," Nur remarks, holding Rahat longer than he might have wanted, but he has missed his friend, missed him dearly.

"Not that long," Rahat says. They separate, and Rahat gives him a look, asking everything without words, like he did when they lived together, slipping back into his old role.

"I'm fine," Nur replies. "Just got a little . . . you know."

Rahat nods, walks into the flat, Nur behind him. "Am I the first?"

"You're always first," Nur says. He puts an arm around Rahat, eager to be around him again, surprising himself by how much he needs his company.

"Ah, you're here," Yasmina says, arms stretched out for Rahat, who glides away from Nur, going to hold her tight. "I'm so glad you could come."

"I wouldn't miss this for anything," Rahat insists.

"How are you? How's your family?" Yasmina asks, settling into the sofa, Rahat sitting next to her, Nur choosing to lean against the wall in front of them.

"Home is good, family is good." Rahat glances at Nur as he speaks. "Things are good. Though it's weird to be in Birmingham without Nur."

"You're always welcome to move in," Nur jokes. "We do have a sofa bed."

"I don't know that you guys want that," Rahat says with a smile, but there is something behind the words, hinting that he wants nothing more than to live with him again, the three of them together like at uni.

Before Nur can respond, there's another knock at the door, and suddenly the flat is flooded with people. Iman and Adam, Imran and his boyfriend, a Palestinian guy named Ramy, Aaron and Ming, another couple of friends from Yasmina's past life in Manchester. The living room bursts with people, everyone is talking, the music barely heard over the chatter of voices.

As the evening unfolds, they settle onto the floor of the living room, backs against walls and the sofa, feet splayed, full from Nur's food, snack bowls empty, and the windows are thrown open but it's still warm in the room.

"So, tell us how you met," Yasmina says.

Imran is sitting by Ramy, and Imran leans his head onto Ramy's. "Do you want to tell them?" he asks.

"Do I want to tell your friends how we met?"

"Don't you?"

Ramy laughs, blood rushing to his light cheeks. "Okay, fine. I'll do it." He clears his throat and looks right at Yasmina, but the entire room is captivated by him, a stage thrown down for him, a willing audience listening. "Well, Imran works at a start-up, coding yet another new app that's going to suck more time away from us millennials. And I work as a freelance coding specialist. Boring stuff, but if you ever need someone to look over your code, make sure there aren't any bugs in it, that's me. And one day, I get assigned to this company, have to be there for weeks, and Imran is the leader of my team. There's three of us. And, actually, Imran went after someone else first."

"I did not," Imran says.

"He definitely did. This white guy, Bryan, with a *y*, not an *i*; Imran went after him the second he saw him, and I watched them for the first few days going back and forth. Bryan is the kinda guy who gets attention wherever he goes."

"He's very pretty," Imran explains to the audience, and Ramy rolls his eyes.

"If you're into men with strong jaws and piercing blue eyes and skin paler than snow, then sure, he's pretty. But what Imran doesn't want to admit is that Bryan is also extremely dumb. I guess you wouldn't think that. Guy works for an IT company specializing in coding. He must be smart. And he is, when it comes to that. But literally anything and everything else, he's not great at. So there we are, the three of us, and Imran isn't even aware of me—"

"I was aware of you. I spoke to you. Told you to do things—"

"Imran didn't notice me beyond instructing me what to do. I'm waiting for him to realize that Bryan is just a walking bag of meat with a proclivity toward coding. And then, instead, he sleeps with him."

"You had sex with Bryan?" Yasmina asks, in a salacious way that implies she already knew.

Imran glances at Nur before he answers. "Yes," he says. "One time. We went out and got drunk, he asked me if I wanted to come back to his. I don't think that's bad . . ."

"It's only bad because Bryan has literally no personality. It's like fucking a corpse."

"It was definitely not like fucking a corpse—"

"So they come into work the next day, and Imran is wearing this huge smile on his face, like he's heard the best news of his life. And I'm not dumb. I know what's happened. So I go over to him—"

"And he asks me if I fucked Bryan the corpse."

"And I ask if he fucked Bryan the corpse. He lies straight to my face and tells me he doesn't fuck people he works with. I say sure, whatever, and go to walk away when he reaches for me, asks me if there's anything I should know about Bryan—"

"I couldn't figure him out—"

"I laugh, think he's joking, and when I realize he's not, I tell him that Bryan is fine, as far as I know, he just doesn't have a lot going on inside his head."

"At which point, I realize what I've done and—"

"He asks me out. And I say no. Because why would I date someone who had sex with Bryan. Definitely speaks to bad taste."

"But he realized he was going to miss out on something—"

"I knew there was a reason I'd been watching the two of them flirt, feeling some kinda way about it. So I doubled back, said yes."

"One date led to two led to three and now here we are, finishing off each other's sentences as a show for you all."

"Oh, like you don't love the attention," Rahat remarks.

"A romance for the ages," Yasmina says. "One to tell the kids, for sure."

"A story that's worth telling," Nur adds, and Imran looks at him. He smiles at Nur, but there is something there that Nur can't figure out before Imran turns his attention back to the others.

"What about you two?" Ramy asks Yasmina. "Imran said you guys met at university."

Nur looks at Yasmina, who gestures to the room with her hand. "Over to you, Writer Man."

He laughs, nervous. "It's definitely not as good as your story."

"Okay, maybe I should be the one to tell it—" Yasmina starts, taking over.

"We met at a party," Nur blurts out. "I was there, she was there, I made a really bad joke about looking like her dad—"

"For validation," Yasmina explains. "Because that's what every woman is looking for from a man."

"And we spent a couple of hours together, talking . . ."

"Are you forgetting my part?" Imran asks.

"And Imran was there," Nur adds, "as he always is, sucking up the air in every room he walks into—"

"The people like what they like—"

"And then I walked Yasmina home—"

"So he could find out where I lived."

"Because I didn't want to leave you," Nur says. Yasmina redirects her attention to him, with a half smile.

"Do you remember how cold it was that night?" he says. "Ice on the streets . . ."

"I remember."

"I kept offering you my jacket, hoping you'd wear it into your house," he says, "because I wanted a reason to see you again." Her face shifts, a little surprised.

"And we did," she responds. "Because I had the courage to add you on Facebook."

"Though I didn't message you for a week because I was terrified," Nur jokes, glancing at Rahat, who chuckles.

"And the rest is history, right?" Yasmina says, leaning into Nur, pressing herself into his arm.

"That's really cute," Ramy notes, shifting closer to Imran.

"I think it might be better than ours," Imran says, giving Nur a smile, but Nur doesn't return it.

The conversation drifts off, Rahat joking he isn't made for love, Yasmina still leaning on Nur. He can't follow the words anymore, his head thick. He stands. Yasmina gives him a questioning look, but he shakes his head slightly.

He goes to the kitchen, looking out the window for a moment.

It's not late enough to be entirely dark, the sun setting, streetlights yet to flicker on. He watches Nottingham, so far away from home, and it's suddenly as if he is trapped here without escape.

"Nur?" Imran says behind him. "Are you all right?"

"Fine," Nur replies, turning to him, a smile placed on his face.

"You're not fine. Anyone can see that."

"I'm sorry."

"You don't have to apologize to—"

"For what I said," Nur interrupts. Imran looks at him, confused. "Before. I didn't . . . I didn't mean that you were like a fuckboy. I was just trying to look out for you, and it came out in the wrong way. I didn't mean it."

Imran laughs, understanding the divide between them. "I know," he says, and he puts a hand on Nur's shoulder. "Please tell me this isn't what you're worried about."

"Not entirely."

"Okay. Well, let me stress that you don't have to worry about it. I was angry when you said it, but, I don't know if you remember this, you apologized right away. And I know that you meant well. You just fucked up the delivery a little."

"Just a little." Nur sighs. "Sorry, I'm not the best party host tonight."

"You don't have to be. Yasmina's pretty good at that. And if not, Ramy can command a room."

"He seems like a cool guy."

"He is. I really like him."

Nur's ears perk up. "Do you love him?" he asks.

Imran leans on the counter, shrugs his shoulders. "I think I could. But it's too early to say that now. Like socialism. I like the idea of it, but I'm not ready to dive into the details of how it'd work."

"That's a real convoluted metaphor."

Imran chuckles. "I can see myself getting there, loving him, in time."

"I'm happy for you."

Imran tips his head at Nur. "Thanks. And now we can talk

about what's really your problem." Nur looks, teeth pressing on his tongue, unsure what might come out if he lets it loose.

"It's just . . . that same old feeling," he says. "Of . . . I don't know, worry, fear, panic."

"About what?" Imran asks.

Nur stares at the counter opposite him, sees himself cooking there for hours, fumbling and redoing each step. It would be so easy to lie. "I have this constant worry that I'm going to lose her. I don't know why. It's not over anything specific. I just . . . don't know. Something will break us apart, and then what? How do I live without her? I mean, I know I can. People live without partners all the time. But what kind of life would that be."

"Do you talk to her about this?"

Nur shakes his head. "No," he says. "How could I?"

"Nur," Imran says.

"I can't tell her that," Nur says. "I can't let her know what goes on in my head. What would she think of me, if she knew this is what I'm like?"

"What you're like?" Imran asks. "You live together, Nur. She chose you."

"If I was honest with her about the way my mind works, the panic, the anxiety . . ." Nur's jaw clenches. "There's so many things I can't tell her. Like, my dad phoned the other day. Just to check in. But I spent the entire time worried Yasmina was going to walk in, back from her coffee run, and he'd hear her voice, ask who that was, and I'd have to lie in front of her. And he mentions a cousin of ours, in Pakistan, who got married to someone here, how he's younger than me, and his wife is pregnant, that they're going to have a baby. He wanted me to know because he's happy for them; it's not like he was trying to make a point or anything. But there was an opinion behind his words. There always is. Because that's what we're supposed to do, right? Go to university, find someone there, marry them, and if we don't find someone there, we can go back home to our parents and ask them to find someone for us. And I wanted to admit I'd done that, that I met Yasmina, that I love her." Her name had fluttered against his cheeks, straining to get out.

"But you didn't."

Nur lets out a sharp laugh. "But I didn't. Because I'm a coward. Because—"

"Because of what he might say?" Imran interjects.

"My parents are complicated," Nur says.

"You don't have to tell me that."

"Yasmina's parents are incredible. You know, they came to drop her off and when they were here, I wondered what I might have done if my parents hadn't left in time. If my mum had wanted to stay and help me unpack. Would I have sent Yasmina a text, told her to sit in the car with her parents? Would I have rushed my own parents, telling them to leave, making up an excuse? I don't know."

"I think it depends on who is more important to you."

"They're both important to me, Yasmina and my family."

Imran moves closer to Nur, shoulder to shoulder. "Do you remember when I called you?" he asks.

The call came late at night, midsummer last year. The phone glowed bright in the dark, and Khalil grumbled as Nur picked it up, went downstairs. Imran was on the other end and he was crying so hard that he could barely catch a breath, and Nur stood in his kitchen, feet cold on the tiles, asking Imran what was wrong, if he was okay, what had happened? Though he already knew, he knew from the very second that Imran gasped into his ear for the first time.

"I was terrified," Imran recalls. "There I was, a grown man, twenty-two, telling my parents that I liked boys, not girls. That I had never liked girls. That I was never going to like girls." His hands fidget, fingers picking at each other. "They had everything ready. All that was left was to send the text, make the call, and the marriage would go ahead. A girl was waiting for me. And you know, I can't even remember her name. I have no idea who she was. Who she is." Imran scoffs, the sound hollow. Nur's fingers find the hem of his shirt, pull at it.

"Anyway, there was my liberal father, who raised me to think independently, who looked forward, crying, yelling that I'd burned his heart out, that I'd slammed my fingers into his chest, taken it out, and stamped on it. And there was my mother, cold eyes like I'd never seen before, telling me to get out. I thought she was being dramatic, that she said it because she had to. But then she pushed me. My mum, who has never hit me before, never let my dad hit me either, shoved me. Hard. She forced me out of that house, with nothing but my phone in my pocket. And I phoned *you* first. I didn't know who else to turn to. You told me to come to Birmingham, that you'd get me a ticket, and I could hear the panic in your voice, but I could hear your love too, and, as cringey as it is, it reminded me that I wasn't alone. And I hated that I'd upset you, said it was okay, said I had a plan."

"Of course I was going to worry," Nur says, putting his hand over Imran's, squeezing it tight. "You're one of my closest friends."

"Well," Imran continues, and his voice trembles, tears hovering in his eyes, "what I'm trying to say is that family can be hard. But they can also surprise you. I walked to my grandmother's house that night. I'd assumed she didn't know, but when she opened the door, it was clear she did, that she always had. But she let me in, called my parents for me, argued when they said they didn't want me. And my grandmother, the woman who prays five times a day, who goes to the mosque every other day, who has Allah's name on her lips before she does anything, was there for me. She went and got all my things for me. She gave me shelter for weeks until I found this job. She loved me when they couldn't find the strength to. And I'd never have thought she would."

"Imran—"

"I'm not repeating this to make you feel bad. I'm just saying, sometimes family can surprise us." Imran turns his hand, holds Nur's back. "Give your parents a chance. You might discover something you don't expect."

Nur laughs. "When did you become my source of wisdom?"

"I don't know," Imran says, half joking, half not. "Maybe it's the right time in my character arc."

He nudges Nur, gestures to the party, and they head back to find Yasmina standing in front of her whiteboard, all her to-dos wiped off, replaced with doodles, and she is playing a game, everyone guessing what she's drawing.

Nur settles onto the sofa, shouts things out, the room exploding with laughter. People start to leave, and he asks them to stay as they rattle off reasons, saying their Ubers are downstairs, that they have work to handle tomorrow. He lets them disappear into the night, until the only people left are him, Yasmina, Rahat, Imran, and Ramy, the closest it's been to their old gang in ages. Nur pulls the sofa out, lets Rahat take it, gives Imran and Ramy the inflatable mattress in the study, and when it's over, he lies in bed with Yasmina, awake long after she has fallen asleep, and he stares up at the ceiling, going over Imran's words in his head, thinking maybe everything will be okay.

Everything is silent. Yasmina has gone back to Manchester to talk with her parents about meeting Nur's family. Nur asked why she wouldn't just tell them on the phone, and she snapped, saying it was a conversation they needed to have in person. He thought something else was going on, but he didn't ask, terrified of what it might be. So he watched as she packed, and when she was done, she kissed him, delicately.

They've each left to go home on weekends before, but there is something uncomfortable this time, Nur aware that he is the cause. He lies in their bed, reaching for her pillow, letting her smell invade his nose. He falls asleep, and his dreams are a tangled mess, chaotic and angry, and in the morning he can't recall the details.

Alone, Nur is struck by how he doesn't really know anyone in Nottingham, despite going on two years here. Yasmina has friends through her PhD, but he has yet to make any significant friends at work. There are people, of course, whom he enjoys spending time with in larger settings. But there's no one he feels comfortable around outside of the office, one-on-one. He finds the idea odd, to mix his personal and professional lives, though he has watched others do the same and, sometimes, wishes he could do that too.

He toys with phoning Imran but knows he'll be with Ramy, and he doesn't want to take up Imran's time. He scrolls through his contacts, passing names; Adam he hasn't spoken to recently; Iman he barely talked to even when they were at university; Rahat he can't bring himself to call. So he sits in the living room, continuing a comic-book show on Netflix, letting the plot race past him, and he thinks about leaving the flat, going for a run, something to fill the time.

What he really wants to know is how the conversation with Yasmina's parents went, if she has even had it yet. What she told them, what they said back. It's an itch underneath his skin, to know with certainty if they want to meet his family, after waiting years already.

He knows Yasmina's mother likes him, that she has told him as much. But he realizes too that, above all, she wants the best for her daughter. And he can imagine Hiba saying there is no point, that Nur waited too long, that Yasmina should leave him and move back home.

Or perhaps Yasmina's father, sitting her down, asking if she wants to be with someone who has never introduced her to his family. She might argue with him, say that he had never liked Nur, but that would be a lie. Ibrahim has treated Nur as an equal in all things, has respected his inclusion in his daughter's life.

The first time Yasmina invited him to her parents' house in Manchester, the summer after university ended, just before she started her master's, Nur feared her parents would hate him. He'd met them briefly once before, heard Yasmina on the phone with them, but they were still an unknown to him.

He'd waited on a corner just outside the center of Manchester, the same way he does for his mother in Birmingham, and her father pulled up, Yasmina in the front. He got into the back, said hello, thanked them for picking him up from the station, and when her father asked questions, he answered slowly, thinking about his response first, and he saw Yasmina grinning through the side mirror, delighting in his awkwardness. They got to the house, his chest tightening. He saw Hawa, who gave him a quick hug, and Hiba exclaimed how glad she was to see him again, inviting him inside, the smell of food coming from the kitchen, spices tingling inside his nose, shoes lined up by the door, photos of them hanging on the walls, and he felt like an intruder, seeing part of Yasmina's life he hadn't been privy to.

They sat down at the dining table, Nur taking up as little space as possible, Hiba telling the story of how they'd moved into this house years ago, when Yasmina and Hawa were babies, how they hadn't been sure of the community but it was the perfect house for them. They'd made friends with the Somalian family up the road, the only other Black family around, though more had eventually arrived, a few South Asian families too, and they'd raised money to build a mosque. After a few years the white people started to leave, the house prices going down because of it, more and more of their own moving in, and Nur thought about his own community, how it had always been people who look like him; he had never felt out of place there. He pictured Yasmina as a child, seeing nothing but difference whenever she stepped outside, and he wanted to go back in time, be there with her, make her feel less alone.

He sits, and he speculates. It might be easier, he decides, if Yasmina breaks everything off. He could go back to his parents, explain they've broken up, and his mother will say that she knew this would happen, his father adding that there are other people in the world for him, his siblings telling him it'll get better, that she is stupid for letting him go.

His phone vibrates on his lap, dragging his thoughts out of their endless cycle. He looks at the name flashing on the screen and, for a moment, considers letting it ring out. But he answers.

"Hey," he says.

"Hey," Mariam replies. She sounds hesitant. He steps back, gives her space. "How are you?"

"Good," Nur says. He starts pacing in the middle of the room. "How are things?"

"Things?" He hears her brain whirring, trying to decide how to answer. "Do you want the lie or the truth?" she asks, a game they played when they were younger, Nur asking her if she wanted the lie or the truth, Mariam always picking truth, Nur lying to her, warning she should never trust a man.

"The truth," he answers.

"Things are hard," she says. "Because you came and threw a grenade into our lives, and I don't know what to do with it." He wonders what she'd have said if he had picked the other option.

He debates asking what any of this has to do with Mariam, that it's between him and their parents, that he appreciates her being there for him but at the end of the day, it's not her acceptance he's looking for. But he doesn't want to be so blunt. "I don't know what *you're* supposed to do with it."

"I'm happy for you. That, I'm not confused about or questioning. I'm happy you found someone you love."

"But?" he asks, waiting for more.

"But . . ." She inhales, and Nur remembers when she would try to be brave, either at school or at home, and she'd stand in front of him, staring, holding a breath in until it was going to burst out of her, until finally it did and she screamed her words out. Like the pain she felt holding her breath somehow emboldened her to get the anger out. "But I can't believe you didn't tell me."

Nur knew this was coming. The way Mariam looked at him when she asked if it was true.

He lacks an answer to her question, the one she's *actually* asking. Why didn't he trust her?

"I didn't want to—"

"Until it was real," she says. "That's what you told us already." Anger flares in him, ready, easy. "But that's not why you didn't tell us. It can't have taken you four years to know if it was 'real.' You would have known before. A year, maybe two. I don't know. But you didn't. You didn't tell me until you told Mum and Dad. And that I get. The way our people talk about marriage, how important it is. The way we talk about people's wives and husbands and children. I get why you waited to tell them. But why did you feel you couldn't be honest with us? Why you couldn't tell me?"

Nur closes his eyes, tries to steady his heart rate. "I didn't know how to," he says, opting for part of the truth.

"We tell each other everything—" He scoffs. "Don't do that," she snaps.

"Do what?"

"Treat me like I'm an idiot." He hears her move, a chair squeaking, knows where she is, in her bedroom. "We always tell each other everything—"

"We *used* to," he interjects, remembering the three of them as children, nothing hidden. And he knows exactly when that changed, stepping out that door at eighteen, the moment he became one and they stayed two. "But we're adults now, there are things we don't tell each other."

"But not this," she counters, frustration coloring her voice. "Not something as big as this. You fell in love with someone. For years."

"I didn't know—"

"How to," she says, finishing his sentence for him. "You said that."

"Well, what else do you want me to say?" Restlessness rushes through him, leaves in the wind.

"I want you to explain. I want to know why you kept this from Khalil and me."

Nur walks to the other side of the room, stands by the window, looks down at the ground below him, how far away it seems. "How could I come home and tell you I met someone, had fallen in love with her, but she was Black and I thought our parents would never accept her because of that? I didn't want to think about that, about their disapproval. But I had to. All the time. Every time I looked at her. You've seen what happens in our family, the fucking stories we hear—"

"And you thought Khalil and I weren't going to accept her," she says, voice quiet.

He leans against the glass, forehead planted against the cold. "I wasn't sure, Mariam." It's the most truthful thing he has said in a while.

"We . . . Khalil and I, we don't have a problem with her. If you love her, she's a good person. I don't think you'd choose the wrong person to spend your life with. But it hurts that you didn't trust us."

"I didn't know how to, Mariam," he says, and her name comes out weird, as if he is shouting at her, berating her like a father.

"You should have known we'd be there for you."

He turns from the window, looks at the empty flat. How much simpler his life would be if he hadn't met Yasmina, hadn't fallen in love with her.

"Is Khalil there?" Nur asks.

"No, he's at uni," Mariam replies. "Studying. He's always studying."

Nur chuckles. "He's going to be the best of us. And I don't know how he got there."

"Because he works hard," Mariam jokes, and in there is a familiarity that makes Nur miss home, miss all the things he is no longer part of. "Are you going to bring her here?" she asks.

"Yeah," Nur says. "Well, if her parents want to go. I don't know if they will."

"What are they like?"

"Her parents? They're pretty cool. I think Mum and Dad will really like them, actually. I can see Mum getting along with her mum. I just . . ." He reaches for the wooden elephant on the windowsill, fingers around it. "I hope she gives them a chance."

"She will," Mariam says. "She wouldn't have asked you to bring them here if she didn't want to."

"Do you think she's okay? With everything?"

"Okay with her son lying to her for four years?" Mariam asks, a pain right to Nur's heart. "I don't know if she'll ever be okay with that. But I think she's happy you found someone. If anything, she was probably thinking it for a while. I mean, you never tell us anything about your life, so we all kinda guessed you were seeing someone."

"I'm sorry." It's the only thing Nur can think of saying, and a part of him wonders if he means it, wanting the words to be true but unable to believe it fully.

Seconds slip past them.

"I should go," she says, and he knows that whatever she says next is a lie. "Mum wants to go shopping for food and I said I'd go with her."

"Okay," Nur replies. "I'll speak to you later."

"Yeah," she says. Pauses. "Bye."

A beep, silence.

He lowers the phone from his ear, throws it at the sofa, leaves the room, stands against the kitchen counter, his breath quicker and shorter, tension in his lungs. He wishes that someone was here. Yasmina, Imran, Rahat, Mariam, Khalil. All these people and yet he is here alone, and that thought makes everything worse. He can't breathe. He slides down onto the floor, back against the cupboards, puts his head between his knees, lets the darkness soothe him.

He doesn't know how long he sits there before his phone rings, the sound entering his ears, dragging his head up, and he feels dizzy as he stands, the light in the kitchen different from when he sat down.

"Hello?" He answers without checking who's calling, the screen blurry.

"Nur." Yasmina's voice lifts him up.

"Yasmina—"

"I'm coming back in a few days," she announces.

His heart stops. "A few *days*?" The thrill of hearing her when he needed it most disappears, is replaced with terror that the thing he's been prophesying is happening, and he can see her standing outside the flat, suitcase in hand.

"Yeah, I need to be home right now. So I'm going to stay a little longer."

"*Need* to be?" he echoes, wanting to scream down the phone at her, demand she tell him the truth, admit she is leaving him.

"Yeah," she says. He hears someone else's voice in the background, too far away to understand what they are saying. But his brain fills in the blanks. Her mother, her father, her sister, urging her to get off the phone, whispering that she doesn't owe him anything.

"Is this because of me?"

"What?" she asks, confused.

"Are you staying at home because of me?" he repeats, hand tightening around the phone. He shouldn't have asked but he needs to know, because if this is why, then he has to tell his family it's over. He can already hear the relief in his mother's voice, that she doesn't have to try something she never wanted to do, change something about herself that she does not accept needs changing.

"Why would I be staying at home because of you?" Another voice in the background, the sound of a door opening and closing.

"Because . . ." They both know exactly what he means.

"Because what, Nur? Because you're the only thing happening in my life? And everything has to be about you? Every move, every single thing I say?" Her voice is tight, and he realizes he's said the wrong thing. But like a child who doesn't know better, he can't help himself.

"You know I don't think that—"

"Then why would this be about you?"

"Because I just told my parents about us."

"And?"

He laughs, baffled. "That's what we've wanted so long. That you've wanted me to do. And it's why you went to Manchester, to talk to your parents—"

"That's not the only reason I came home," she says, through what sounds like gritted teeth.

"So then why are you staying at home?"

"I'm here because my sister needs me. Hawa needs me, Nur. Like she *always* needs me," Yasmina hisses. "In the ways that I can't be here for her most of the time, because I'm with you."

His heart drops down his stomach, lands somewhere at his feet. "Hawa," he enunciates as if discovering her name for the first time. "Is she all right?"

"She'll be fine." Yasmina's voice chills.

"I'm sorry," he says, acutely aware he is apologizing for the second time this day. "I didn't . . . I didn't think. I thought—"

"You thought everything was about you," she repeats. "But it's not. Not right now. I'll be home in a few days. I've already told work—"

"Yasmina," Nur says, though he has spoken too much already, said all the wrong words.

A sigh. "It's fine," she replies. "I have to go."

He desperately wants to talk more, but he stills his tongue. He's said enough. "I love you."

She pauses. "I love you too."

She is gone. The flat is silent again. Nur wishes he could cut his tongue out, never communicate with anyone again, because it seems like all he does these days is cause hurt whenever he talks.

February 2018

Nur's mobile phone rings. He sees Yasmina's name on his screen, panic flaring through him. She never calls when he's at work. "Sorry," he whispers, the room turning to him, a presentation on the screen. "I've got to . . ." Apologetic smile, he leaves before anyone responds, door closing softly behind him. "Yasmina, what—"

"Hawa wants to visit," she announces.

"Visit?" He walks down the hallway until he sees an empty meeting room, slips inside. "Like us here, in Nottingham?"

"She just called. She's having . . . a moment. And she wants to come stay with us. I said she could. She's coming tonight."

"Tonight? Like tonight, tonight?"

"Like tonight, tonight." Worry in her voice. "Sorry, I should have asked you first. But she . . . she sounded really bad on the phone. My parents got on her case again. I think she was feeling worse than she normally does, and they pushed her over the edge. And she can't be there right now. Instead of doing something bad, she's coming to us."

"It's fine," Nur reassures her. "It's good that she's coming here, rather than going who knows where. What time does her train get in?" He makes his voice solid, dependable.

"In a couple of hours. I can go get her." She hesitates.

"But?"

"But I have a meeting with my tutor tomorrow." His heart drops. "And she'll be here . . ."

". . . while I'm working from home," he finishes. He runs through the things he has to do tomorrow. His remote workdays are his most productive, knocking out small tasks that build up through the week, no longer distracted by the hum of other people.

"I can—"

"No," he says. "You need to see your tutor. You're already stressing out about that revised abstract. She's not a kid, I can take care of her."

"Yeah, but . . ." He imagines her going room to room in their flat, worry lines on her face. "You've never seen her like this."

"It'll work out," Nur says. "And if it doesn't, we'll get through it together. You'll only be gone like a couple of hours, right?"

"Three, max."

"Hawa and I can last three hours together, at least."

Yasmina takes in a deep breath. "Okay," she says. "I need to call my parents and tell them she'll be here with us, that she's okay. They must be—"

"Go," he interrupts her. "Go call them. I'll be home at the usual time. Maybe we can order food in tonight?"

"Yeah. She really loves Chinese."

"Then Chinese it is." He pauses. "It'll be okay, Yasmina. She'll be okay."

"I know." Her voice trembles. "I'll see you later."

"Love you."

"Love you."

Nur goes back to the presentation, takes his chair, giving the room another apologetic smile, and when the meeting is done, he returns to his desk, laptop back on, replying to emails, scheduling posts to go up. And the entire time, he pretends to be paying attention, but he's thinking about Hawa. He thought she was getting better, the calls getting shorter and shorter, not every day, not every other day, a couple of times a week. When Yasmina has her on speaker, while she's doing her makeup, cooking, Hawa has sounded lighter, brighter.

It's like they've gone back to square one.

But he knows, more than anyone, that it's never as easy as it seems to get better, to become the version of yourself that you want to be.

The clock hits five. Nur waves goodbye to his colleagues, says he'll see them on Monday, and as he walks down the stairs, headphones in, a true-crime podcast in his ears, his stomach rumbles with nerves. Every step is hard.

He retraces his morning journey back to their flat, and when he turns the corner, his eyes instinctively go to their kitchen window, yellow light on, and as he crosses the street, a figure passes through it. Hawa. She is already there.

Nur forces himself onward. He fumbles his keys stepping inside the building, climbing the stairs, and he hovers outside their door, steadying himself, preparing to enter.

The sharp silence of a conversation stopped by outside interruption greets him.

Yasmina appears from the living room, hugging him tight. "Hawa's here," she says. "Are you hungry? We were thinking we might get food now."

"I could eat," he nods. And then, lower, "How is she?"

"Better," Yasmina whispers. In that word, there is a world Nur knows he will never see, though he understands, or at least thinks he does.

Nur takes his shoes off, coat hung up, swallows his nerves, following Yasmina farther into their flat.

Hawa sits curled up on the sofa, blanket over her. She gives him a weary smile as he walks in, her face drawn, cheeks thin, eyes tired. "Hawa," he exclaims, pretending everything is fine, like he doesn't realize she's turned up on short notice. "How are you?"

"I've been better," she replies, reaching over to pick up a mug on the floor by the sofa, bringing it to her lips. "The place looks nice."

"Thank you," Nur says, still standing by the door. He walks in, sits on a lounge chair in the corner of the room, facing her. "Yasmina bought some more art."

"And that's new too," Yasmina adds, gesturing to the lamp behind Hawa. "We got it for like ten quid."

"Facebook," Nur explains, proud of their steal.

Sitting there, Nur on the chair, Yasmina by Hawa's feet, it's as though they're her parents. He half expects Yasmina to pat her on the feet. And just like that, Nur imagines them in the future, Yasmina and Nur advising their own child, trying to do what's right.

"Shall we order some food?" Yasmina asks.

Nur takes his phone out, passes it over to her. She finds a Chinese place, passes the phone wordlessly over to Hawa, who looks through the menu, explains she's trying to go vegetarian, heard it improves, well, everything, then passes the phone back to Nur. He adds the same thing he always gets, chicken and noodles, can't go wrong with that, and pays. "It'll be here in half an hour," he says, standing. "I'm going to have a shower."

Yasmina nods and he walks to their room, a stranger in his own house, closing the door behind him, leaning his head against it. He doesn't know what to do. Yasmina is the one in charge here, the one who knows this battleground, and he is waiting for her orders.

He goes to the bathroom, door closed, which he and Yasmina never do, turns the shower on, and he spends as much time in there as he can without it becoming obvious he's trying to avoid them. He steps into the hallway just as the doorbell goes, delivery guy handing him a bag.

He carries the food, hair wet, back to where Hawa and Yasmina sit together, Hawa's head on Yasmina's shoulder, a film playing on the TV, Emma Watson and Tom Hanks, some evil internet corporation they're trying to take down. "Food," he offers.

"Thank you," Hawa says as he puts the bag in front of her, coffee table cleared off. "For the food. For letting me stay over."

"You don't have to—" he begins.

"No, I have to." He looks up, a familiar steel in her eyes. "Because it's rude if I don't. This is your home—"

"Hawa—"

"And I'm here now, a disruption. I know you're going to say that I'm not, that this place is mine whenever I need it, and I'm really grateful for that, I am. But you can't deny this wasn't something you were planning for this morning. So thank you. It means a lot to me, that I can come here."

Nur nods. "Then you're welcome," he says. "And in the name of transparency, your sister and I, we didn't have much planned for this Thursday night."

"Maybe some cooking. A film. Reading. Sleep," Yasmina pipes in.

"We're basically in our forties," Nur jokes, taking Hawa's food out of the bag, a big *V* scrawled on the top.

"Sounds nice," Hawa says genuinely, not joining in with their gentle self-deprecation.

Nur moves, facing the TV, the bad sci-fi film continuing to play. "Can I ask about your job?"

"You can ask whatever you want," Hawa says. "The job is fine." She'd started last year, a temporary contract working at H&M, made permanent in the new year. Hawa phoned Yasmina when she was offered the position, Yasmina telling her to take it, that it was something, and she'd have her own money, some independence from her parents, so Hawa switched to full-time, even made a few friends there.

"Do you still want to leave?" Yasmina asks.

"I don't know." Hawa shifts behind him, the shuffle of a box on the blanket. "It's an easy job. I don't have to put much mental energy into it. But I'm not sure if that's a good thing. I think I want a job like you guys do—"

"My job is not fun," Nur says.

"But you're working toward where you want to be, right? Like, you're not going to do it forever. It's a step to something else, something bigger. I'm not sure this job is giving me that."

The screen goes dark between scenes, and Nur sees their reflection, Yasmina and Hawa above, him below. "So what do you want to do?" he asks.

"I don't know . . ." She trails off, the chewing of food, the rustle of a bag. It's a warning sign, to not continue this conversation, to not go any further.

They eat quietly for the rest of their meal, watching, Yasmina resisting the urge to point out inconsistences in the film. When they finish, the two of them clean up, Hawa staying put on the sofa, tissue between her hands, wiping the grease and the dirt off.

"Do you want me to leave?" Nur says as they carry trash to the kitchen, low so Hawa doesn't hear. "Like, go into the bedroom?"

"No," Yasmina says. "She'll feel bad about making you leave."

"I can—"

Yasmina shakes her head, tight.

"Okay, fine. But what do I say?"

Yasmina opens the bin, tossing the bag of empty containers inside. "Talk about whatever you want. She doesn't need life-changing advice right now. She just wants to be away from our parents for a while. We can give her that."

"Okay," Nur says. "I can do that."

She gives him a smile, worried, and turns, the two of them reentering the living room. "Should we watch something?" she starts. "Nur and I are halfway through—"

"No," Hawa says. She shifts, sits up, pulling the blanket off her. "I want to talk about our parents."

"What?"

Nur freezes, contemplates running out of the flat, not wanting to be here for this.

"I . . ." Hawa looks at Nur. "Do you think I'm hurting them?" It's like she's asking him directly.

He sits back on the floor, slowly, but facing Hawa this time, away from the TV.

"You're not hurting them," Yasmina says. "But I think they are hurt *by* you." She glances at Nur, who gives her the smallest nod of his head. "They want the best for you, for us, and I get the sense that they feel like they've let you down. That they don't know how to make things better . . ."

"I don't know how to make things better," Hawa says. "I don't know what to do to get . . . this better." She points at herself, at her head, frustration in her fingertips. "I wish I could be, like, normal. I'm tired of waking up like this, exhausted all the time. I don't want to . . ." She closes her eyes, lets out a small laugh. "I just don't want to be like this anymore."

Nur recognizes the fear in Yasmina's eyes. Hawa runs her fingers one over another, and he sees himself when he was her age, younger, alone, no one to talk to.

He takes in a breath. "I know what you mean," he offers. Hawa looks at him. "I . . . I sometimes get panic attacks." Nur looks at the art on the wall, just by the side of Hawa. "It's like the world is pressing down on me, and nothing can fix it. I become convinced it'll last forever. Even though it always goes away, and the thing I'm panicking about turns out not to matter like I thought it would. Nothing happened to me to make me like this. It's not like I had a traumatic childhood or something. My parents are fine, my family is fine, my life is fine. But sometimes, I feel really alone. Like, *really* alone. I don't know why. It's just the way it is." Hawa stares at him, waiting for more. "I deal with it, in my own way. But you can ask Yasmina, it's difficult, and I make it a lot harder by not talking about it." He trips at Yasmina's name, still looking at the painting. "By not admitting it's real. And I don't want . . ." He takes in a breath. "I don't want Yasmina to think bad of me because of it."

"I wouldn't—" Yasmina begins.

"I know," Nur says, meeting her eyes. "But that's my fear. And it isn't your fault. It's no one's fault. It's not my fault, even. It's the way the world works, that we're meant to be ashamed of struggling. Things might be easier if we did talk about it, so we can learn to remember we aren't alone. But it's hard." He stops, finds the words. "Your parents are probably scared because they don't know how to be there for you. They want to make you feel better, happy, but they don't know how to do that. And their worry makes you worse, because you think you're this massive drain on them, this issue that's causing them so many problems. That maybe it would be better for them if you weren't here, if you left . . ." He reaches over and puts his hand on Hawa's knee. "But, Hawa, that's not true. The world would be much worse if you weren't in it. For your parents, for Yasmina, for me. We want you here."

"I need you here," Yasmina adds, putting her arm around Hawa, pulling her into herself.

Hawa closes her eyes tight. "I don't want to bring them down," she says, voice wobbly.

"You're not," Nur says. "And even if you were, it's their job to take care of you, to protect you. You just need to let them."

She sniffles. "How?"

Nur glances at Yasmina. "By talking to them," he says. "If you don't talk to them about what's going on in your head, they won't know. And if they don't know what's making you upset or angry, they're going to keep saying and doing those things, and that makes everything worse. But if you're honest with them, if you tell them how to help you, you can figure it out together. I can't promise things will improve instantly. But it'll be easier, for all of you." He half laughs. "Besides, your parents are much cooler than most parents."

"They'll get it," Yasmina says, rubbing Hawa's back. "All it takes is for you to open up. And I'll be there for you, if you want."

Hawa says nothing, wipes her eyes with her sleeve, resting on Yasmina, and Nur sits there, looking at Yasmina, trying to gauge her reaction to his words.

"I guess I can try," Hawa says, moving away from Yasmina. "I just . . ."

"I know," Nur says. "But you have us, whenever you need us. Think of me as the brother you never had."

"The brother I never wanted." Hawa laughs, the room's tension disappearing beneath them.

They move on, Yasmina picking a new film to watch, Hawa requesting something mainstream, saying that she doesn't want to use her brain, so they opt for a horror film, the lights turned off, engulfed in the winter darkness, and Nur sits next to Yasmina, at one point holding Hawa when she jumps, and he laughs, catches Yasmina smiling at him.

When the film is done, they prepare to sleep, Nur saying he'll take the sofa bed, insists on it, duvet pulled down from the wardrobe, spare pillows taken out from the storage cupboard. Yasmina walks in as he's making the bed, holding his phone charger in her hands. "I think you'll need this," she says, handing it to him, and when he takes it, she holds on to it, pulls him to her, kisses him, gentle. "Thank you," she whispers. "I didn't . . . I couldn't have done that."

"I hope it helps," he says.

She nods, lets him take the charger. "About everything else . . . ," she starts.

"I'm sorry," Nur says. "I should have talked to you about it."

"It's hard, I know," she says. "Just know that whenever you feel ready, I'm right here. And I'm never going to think you're weak for it, or broken, or whatever." She moves a step closer to him. "I'm here for you, Nur. Always."

He nods, can't say anything, because if he does, he'll cry, so he kisses her again, wraps his arms around her, hoping she knows how grateful he is for her, how he never wants to live without her. "I love you," he says.

"I love you too."

February 2019

Nur has changed his outfit three times, from a T-shirt and jeans to a button-down shirt and jeans to the one suit he owns for emergencies. He looks at himself in the mirror, suit pressed against him. He's dressed like he's going to his own funeral.

He pulls at his tie, resisting an urge to throw it across the room. He returns it to the hanger and takes off his blazer, his trousers, until he's just wearing his shirt and underwear, fixated on his reflection, pathetic.

There is a part of him that wants to call this off. He wants to ring his parents and tell them that they can't make it, that this thing they have had planned for over a month, which has had to move three times because Khalil was busy, because his father was called to work, because Yasmina's mother had something on, and it was important they all be there, wasn't going to happen this time either. Maybe in six months? Twelve months? Maybe they should meet years from now, somewhere in the future, and it can be future Nur's problem, not his problem now.

But that would make him a coward, weak for wanting to run away from it.

Trust yourself. That was what Imran said when Nur called, relaying that it was happening, the thing they'd discussed for so long, guessing every reaction his parents might have, like in chess, trying to figure out what the next move might be, and Imran had listened to Nur as he panicked, as he stressed, and when Nur was done, Imran had asked him one simple question: Did he love her? And Nur replied instantly: Yes. That's all that matters, Imran said.

Yasmina walks into the room, her eyes landing on him. "Please tell me that's not what you're wearing," she says, and cringes. She has chosen something simple, a green dress, not too tight, with a light jumper over it, her hair in braids, vanishing for an afternoon last week to get them done, cursing at her scalp all week since.

"I have no idea what to wear," he answers, retreating to sit on the edge of the bed.

"Wear something comfortable."

"I don't know what'll make me feel comfortable today."

"This is the part where I should say we don't have to do this." Yasmina runs a hand through his hair. "But the thing is, Nur, we do have to do this." She steps over to the wardrobe, roots around in it for a second, hangers rattling against one another, and she pulls out a shirt, dark blue, throwing it at him. "Wear that with your black jeans, smart shoes. And this jacket," she instructs, throwing that at him as well.

He catches them, knows that because she's picked it out, the outfit is perfect. "Okay, I'll get dressed right away."

"My parents are on their way here."

"With Hawa?" She nods. "And then we'll drive to Birmingham."

"To your house." There it is—a small wobble to her voice. He raises his eyebrows. "This is weird, right?"

"Are you panicking?"

"Aren't you?"

"Yeah, but I thought I was the one who panicked, not you."

A flash of frustration runs across her face. "I'm allowed to panic about this, Nur."

"I know, sorry," he says, and he stands up, facing her. "But it'll be fine. I met your parents and survived . . ."

"That's because my parents are cool."

"I should be insulted, but actually, your parents are pretty cool."

"They are," she says, her voice soft.

"It'll be fine," he reiterates, pulling her in close, and he shuts his eyes, praying that he is right.

"Yeah, but what if it isn't?" she asks, speaking into his chest.

They've had this conversation cyclically ever since the call came from his parents. Yasmina asks if his parents will like her, Nur not knowing how to answer because he has no idea what his parents will think, because he has never brought anyone home, because nobody has, because that's not a thing they do in his family.

"Then we'll just try again," Nur says, and he hears his words, like it's so simple. But it isn't the truth.

Yasmina doesn't say anything. She separates herself from him, walks out of the room, and he wishes he could take back what he said, alter it to be more reassuring, but the words can't be unsaid.

The knock arrives on the front door of their flat, echoing down the corridor. Nur and Yasmina both look at each other. "Well, I guess it's real now," Nur says, resigned as he walks to the door, opens it to Yasmina's parents with Hawa behind them. Their outfits are smarter than usual, a formal shirt and trousers for her father, a beautiful dress for her mother, whose face has been made up in a way Nur has never seen before. Even Hawa looks different, mascara lining her eyes, her hair in bouncy curls framing her face.

"Nur." Her father greets him with a hug, quick and tight. "Are you ready?"

"As ready as I can be," Nur says, a nervous laugh following his words.

"It'll be fine," her father says encouragingly. He steps back and so does Nur, letting Yasmina slip between them. "Wow. Is this really my daughter I see standing in front of me?"

"Don't be weird, Dad," Yasmina says, hugging him and her mother, stepping out into the hallway.

"All he's been is weird," Hawa replies, anxious smile on her face. "The entire time up here, he's been talking nonstop."

"He's just a little nervous," Hiba says, a hand stroking her husband's arm, and Nur recalls all the times he has seen his parents together, the way they stand beside each other, never really touching. He thinks of how he runs his fingers over Yasmina's in the street, the way they are still intimate and close in public. He's never seen his parents holding hands, has always taken this as normal, all the other aunties and uncles are the same, but now he wonders about their passion for each other and whether it is just part of their past. He wonders if they were ever like him and Yasmina, hungry and naïve, and if he and Yasmina will someday be like how his parents are now.

They walk to the car, Hawa rattling on about a TV show, trying to smooth the awkwardness, and Yasmina responds distractedly.

The three of them—Yasmina, Hawa, Nur—sit in the back of the car, and Nur immediately feels trapped, stuck behind Yasmina's father. Ibrahim puts Nur's zip code into Google Maps, wheels spinning on the screen before spitting up a path, lighting the way home.

Nur, eyes like saucers, stares at the winding route back from his life with Yasmina now to the house where he grew up.

The plan was made a month ago. He'd called his mother back while Yasmina was at the library. She picked up, and the very first thing she asked was whether he'd thought about her suggestion of having Yasmina and her parents to the house for tea. He resisted the urge to snap that he'd thought about Yasmina and his family meeting for years. That he'd built this moment up in his head, going over infinite variations, imagining it while he brushed his teeth, while he ate breakfast or answered emails at his desk. Since her call, it had become all he thought about, wondering what might happen when these two parts of his life collided.

In some scenarios, all went well. Their fathers liked each other easily, and their mothers quickly warmed to each other too. His mother took Yasmina's mother into the kitchen and showed her how to make Pakistani tea, how she crumbled leaves into the milk, tipped in cinnamon, added pistachio nuts for flavor. Then food was prepared for everyone too, the mothers swapping recipes, sharing secrets and tricks, and dinner was served to a happy room, everyone content.

Other variations in his mind didn't go so well. They'd sit in the same places and have the same conversations, but there was a suffocating air of frigidity. There was nowhere for any of them to hide, and things went wrong. Nur is gripped fast onto the chair he was stuck in, wondering if the greatest thing in his life would crash to an end because their families hate each other.

Yes, he answered his mother, he had thought about it and he had spoken to Yasmina too and they wanted to do it. He was careful not to mention that they'd spoken about it in the flat they were living in together, distinctly aware that his parents didn't know about that, intending that they never would. It would be a sin greater than any other he has committed, sleeping in the same bed as a woman he was not married to, and he knew to pick his battles.

His mother asked when they would like to come. They set a date. She asked him what kind of food she should make, what she should wear, and then, right at the very end of the conversation, she said, "I can't wait to meet her, Nur." And there was joy in her voice, hope, and Nur felt relief wash over him, telling her that he couldn't wait either.

"Nur!" Yasmina shouts, and he registers her voice. "Dad, ask him again."

"How are you feeling?" Ibrahim asks.

Nur nods until he realizes Ibrahim can't see him. "Yeah," he says. "I'm fine."

"You seem a little mellow."

"Big day," Nur responds, with a chuckle.

Hiba looks at him through the rearview mirror. She has the same look in her eyes that Yasmina does when about to confess something. "You know, Nur, when Yasmina told us about you, I was worried."

"Mum—" Yasmina says, but her mother holds a hand up and Yasmina goes silent.

"She told me she was seeing someone, that she had *been* seeing someone, for nearly a year and hadn't told us. My mind went everywhere. I wanted to know why she didn't feel like she could tell us about this boy, whoever he was. She said your name, Nur. But it's just a Muslim name, you know, you could have been anything, anyone. I didn't know what to expect, and I thought about telling her to end it. This person that I was thinking about had become huge in my mind. You'd changed from just a name into this boy who was leading my daughter away from me."

"And then he was fine," Yasmina says, a warning in her tone.

"And then you were fine," Hiba says, agreeing. "We met you, and you were a good boy, clearly raised well. And, more importantly, we could tell you really cared about Yasmina. But it's true, I was worried about what you'd be like. Because then what do we do as parents? Do we demand she breaks up with you? Or do we let her make her own choices, and then she falls apart, and we come in to pick up the pieces?"

Hiba trails off for a moment, the same eyes resting in an older face, and he thinks of his mother sitting on the sofa, looking up at him, asking how long he had known Yasmina and him replying since university: four years. He understands now the way she looked at him, as though he'd said he was giving up Islam or that he was emigrating, harboring this massive secret from her. Because he had. And if he had kept this from her, what else was he hiding? He'd become a stranger to her.

"I think it's fair to assume your parents are going through the same thing," Hiba continues. "We like to think our children are exactly the kind of people we want them to be, that you're going to be the same at thirty as at twenty, as you were when we raised you as children. It's hard for us to accept that you grow up into individuals with your own opinions and ideas, especially growing up here. Sometimes we say things we don't mean because we are scared you aren't the innocent child we gave birth to anymore and we can no longer protect you. It feels like a betrayal, not by you, but by time, life, God. I don't know your mum, Nur, only what Yasmina has told me. But I know what it means to be a mother and I know yours only wants the best for you. Remember that, even if she says something she doesn't mean."

Nur struggles to find the words to reply. He nods, and he turns to look out the window as the world flies past him.

They reach his parents' house too quickly. He'd hoped for more time to prepare, even though he has had four years to practice what he'll say. They pull up near the house, *his* house, and they sit, engine turned off, the air in the car still. Nur views the house through the window, the white door, the clean patio that his mother sweeps every week, the front windows, all dark now, curtains pulled, flashes of light around the edges, and he wonders what his family is doing in there.

"We should get out," Yasmina says, turning to Nur for confirmation, and he nods. He needs to get out of the car. His breathing constricted, he reaches for the handle, opens the door, lets the cold air in, steps out, hand on his chest, the pressure building inside of him, and he wishes he were stronger.

He feels a hand on his back, and Yasmina is standing next to him.

"I know," he says, finishing her thought. "Just give me a second."

The concern on her face remains, but she lets him go, moving to stand with her parents, and Nur puts one hand on the car, inhales deeply, tries to calm himself.

The world around him loosens, his heartbeat dropping slightly. His stomach still feels chaotic, like he is about to throw up what little food he has eaten, but he is fine. For now.

He looks at Yasmina at the gate, thinks back to the first time he saw her, walking up the path to Saara's house, just in her dress, shivering in the cold, teeth chattering, and he knows this is worth it. This is all worth it.

July 2016

Summer gets really busy here."

"So I see," Yasmina remarks, pushing him to the right as a woman with a baby stroller hurries past.

It's the first time Yasmina has come to him. It was her idea, not his, and he'd said yes because he wanted to show her part of his life that she'd never seen before. But now that she is here, Nur feels exposed. Yasmina can finally see where he has spent his life, and a small part of him is embarrassed to come from here rather than somewhere more exciting, like London or Edinburgh. Birmingham, after all, has very little to show off about.

But this is him. It's where he spent his days at college, going to Apple to play with the iPads on display, reading books in Waterstones, hurrying through pages so he doesn't have to buy them, sitting in a Starbucks with his own writing. There's the alley where he smoked his first spliff. The park where he fell out with a schoolmate, a stupid fight over a girl.

This entire city is dotted with parts of him, scattered everywhere.

"Are you hungry?" he asks. "We can get something to eat."

"Not really. But what about the cinema? That new *Ghostbusters* film is out."

"You came all the way to Birmingham, and you want to go watch that?"

"Do you not?"

"No, I do. But I want to go and watch it because it's going to be terrible. Why do you want to watch it?"

"Because it's going to be terrible," she replies.

"I thought ingenues like you didn't waste your time on bad films," he says, nudging her.

"The more bad films you watch, the more you appreciate the good ones. Like you'll come out of *Ghostbusters* thinking that *The Social Network* is one of the best films you've ever seen."

"Touché," Nur responds. He studies the intersection, figuring out which path to take. "There's an indie cinema about five minutes from here, if you don't mind walking. Probably has better seats?"

"I don't mind walking."

"Cool."

They weave in and out of people, and Nur relaxes, feeling less exposed as time passes, and he even begins pointing things out. Like how before that was this nice local Turkish place, and he used to go there with his friends, until suddenly, one day, he came back from university and it was closed down, wooden boards all over it, eventually turning into a Nando's, and he's not mad about it because Nando's is good and this one is halal too, but he wishes he could eat at that Turkish place again.

"The power of gentrification," Yasmina says.

"I don't know that I'd use the word *power.*"

"Curse? Is curse better?"

"Well, maybe. Scourge?"

"It feels like we're playing a word game."

"I wish they would gentrify where my parents' house is," Nur says. "I'm tired of coming to town to buy some shampoo or toothpaste. Like, I just want to go to a Boots and pick something up, have it right there for me, you know?"

"You'd want Boots rather than going to the local corner shop and supporting your fellow man?"

"I think my fellow man is doing pretty great by charging me twice the price on a tube of toothpaste."

"Hmmm," Yasmina replies. "I think you're a little spoiled. Do you even buy the toothpaste in your house?"

Nur hesitates. "No, my mum does . . ."

"Wow. How embarrassing for you."

The cinema comes into view. The last time Nur was here was with Khalil and Mariam. They'd gone together, delighting in something stupid one of their cousins had done, because their cousins were always doing something dumb and getting caught, and Nur had treated them to the visit with his new-job money, as the generous older brother. They had whispered throughout the film, some bad horror film that didn't leave a dent on them. But now he is here with Yasmina, his girlfriend, and even though his siblings aren't there, Mariam at a wedding with their mother today, Khalil at home working through his university summer reading list, it still feels as if the two worlds are crashing into each other, like they're stepping on the footprints of his brother and sister, and he senses the anxiety creeping at the back of his neck.

They cross the foyer and he reaches for his wallet, but Yasmina stops him. "It's on me," she says.

"But you took the train here—"

"And you took it to me twice in Manchester *and* paid for things. I know your family isn't rich, Nur. Stop acting like it. Upholding the patriarchy isn't worth you going broke." She pulls her wallet out, heading for the counter.

He watches them in the mirror behind the counter as she orders their tickets, the two of them reflected back at him, a tingle rushing over him, electricity pressing into each knot in his spine.

They sit together, not touching. He wonders if he should reach across with his hand, but his chest tightens at the thought of being seen, so he doesn't do anything. During the film, she puts her head on his shoulder, and his whole body becomes rigid, like he's on his first date with her, barely able to process the film they're watching.

"Well, that was not as bad as I thought it was going to be," he says as they walk out.

"I know. I think the internet might be wrong on this one."

"The internet? Wrong? That never happens."

"It is a cesspit, though. You know they've been bullying the cast."

"They?"

"Random white men on the internet, who else?"

"I think you might be being a bit racist there," Nur says, making a face at her. Yasmina nudges him with her elbow and then reaches for his hand, and he tenses again. She stops abruptly. "What is it?" she asks.

Shame trickles down him. "Nothing," he says.

"Don't lie to me," she says, annoyance in her voice. "Don't lie when I've come all this way." Nur looks away across the square, steps fully out into the balmy heat, and she follows him, one step behind. "Nur," she says, and he flinches at the sound of his name out here in the open, suddenly aware of every single person around them, a web linked to him somehow, through second- or third- or fourth-degree connections. "Nur," she repeats.

"Don't," he hisses, the word shooting out of his mouth. "Don't say my name."

"Don't say your name?" she asks, incredulous.

"I mean . . . No, I mean, of course, say my name. I just . . ." He closes his eyes, head swimming. "I feel off."

"Off? Are you sick? Was it something you ate?" The care in her voice only makes him feel worse, because here she is, come all the way to his hometown, and he can't tell her that he is terrified people will hear her calling his name. Frightened of a family member spotting them together, sending a text, the information weaving its way to his mother, who will phone him, asking why Auntie Salma from down the road is saying that her son was holding hands with a girl in the city center. What will people think about Nur, the eldest son, the one who left for university, the good son who is no longer the good son, but the son who lies to his parents, "gallivanting" with a girl, and not just any girl but a *Black* girl. They will declare that everything they feared about children going to university away from home is true. That the distance will corrupt them, that without their parents watching over them, they will become lost.

"No, not sick. It's just weird that you're here. In my city. Where I live. With my family. I thought it'd be cool, you know, showing you the places where I hung out, but—"

"But you're scared someone is going to see you." She does the one thing he was counting on her to do. She confronts the things he cannot.

"It's different at uni," he starts, immediately regretting this train of thought. He wants to wind it back. "I didn't feel like this there. I didn't feel—" He realizes he needs to stop, but he can't.

"Ashamed? Like you have to hide me?" Her frustration is gone now, replaced with anger. "Is that what you're worried about? Hiding me?"

"No, I just feel paranoid," he says, the words dropping to the ground.

"Paranoid that someone might see your Black girlfriend."

Nur has recently become acutely aware of the way some South Asians talk about race and skin tone, seen it on the lips of people in his family. The way his cousins, who have darker skin than the others, hide under long sleeves and jackets, even when it is warm outside, staying away from the sun in hopes of growing lighter. The way Bollywood films only cast extremely light-skinned women, photoshopping posters to make them look even whiter than they are. The way skin-bleaching creams fill whole shops there, a billion-dollar "fairness" industry.

Even though Nur likes the color of his skin, how it darkens in the sun, lightens in the winter, how it sits in the middle between light and dark, the golden brown of his skin the shade that white people adore, bathe themselves in the sun or in sunbeds to get, spray it on themselves, he is still aware of it.

Still aware of how white people move into the corners of lifts when he walks in, security guards trail him through shopping centers because they assume he'll steal something.

He'd always assumed that this was how it was: you were either white or not-white. That was the line that had been drawn. That no matter who you were, where you came from, what you did, if you were on Nur's side, then you were like Nur. His experiences were everyone's.

He'd never considered the nuances of racism, how insidious it is, how it operates across a spectrum, rearing different heads to different people.

He hadn't understood that it doesn't matter if you're a minority, you still live and operate within a centuries-old racial hierarchy.

But now Yasmina is in his life, now he has to consider what that means in its entirety, what it means for them. He has seen the looks he gets from other South Asian people when they walk together, hand in hand; that first glance of noting, the second of curiosity, the third of disapproval or disappointment. Like there is something wrong about them being together. Each time Nur notices these looks, all he can think about is his own parents. He knows that Yasmina is never going to be just a girlfriend to them, that there is another conversation that will take place if they see her with Nur.

And he doesn't know what he would say to them if that happened.

So, it no longer matters that Nur has "done the reading"—books pushed at him by Saara, article upon article, detailing to him the manner of microaggressions, colorism, racial privilege, how to be a better ally—because it is one thing to read these texts and another to bring their teachings into his own life.

As much as he wants to deny it to himself, to the world, he has to confront the way his family operates, the way his community behaves, the way they come together and the way they fall apart.

Because this is his failure, one he can't hide from when he is with Yasmina.

"It's not that." He hears the lie in his voice, hears how brittle his voice is.

"Oh, it isn't?" She has tears in her eyes, and before he can continue, she walks past him.

"Yasmina," he yells, but she is gone, disappeared into the crowd, a ravenous guilt bubbling up, a longing to go back and fix what he said. She deserves so much better than this, better than him. He wants to run after her. He wants to claw at his own skin.

How excited he was to see her that morning. How easily he has fucked things up.

February 2019

Nur knocks on the door. He has keys, but he assumes he shouldn't use them today. He taps knuckles against wood, steps back, waits for the door to open, Yasmina's family behind him, the five of them on his patio.

There's the sound of shuffling. Handle pushed down, door swinging open to his mother. His heart lifts at the sight of her, dressed in clothes she would normally reserve for a wedding, a dark maroon shalwar kameez, scarf hanging over one arm. Perfume comes off her, the kind that sits in a bottle on her shelves to be looked at, not worn.

"Nur," she says, and he hears how much she has missed him since last month. For a moment, it's like he is coming home from university to see his family, nothing out of the ordinary.

He gives her a quick hug, tight but fleeting. He steps back, and his mother smiles at Yasmina, and Yasmina steps into Nur's place, offers her hand.

"Yasmina," his mother greets her, saying her name carefully, as if practiced, testing how the syllables sound in her mouth. "Welcome."

"Auntie Hina. I'm so pleased to meet you." Yasmina laughs, a scared breathless noise, and his mother reaches for her, holds her close just like she did Nur, and every doubt, every fear that Nur has felt ebbs away.

Nur's parents welcome Yasmina's parents and Hawa into the

house. They enter to a table laid out in the living room, plates of food stacked high, samoseh and pakoreh and kebabs, the smell a confirmation that he is home, that this is happening. It's clear his mother has spent all day cooking because she wants to present the best version of herself and her family, but also because she needs to be busy. Her mind works in the same way Nur's does, overthinking everything if given half the chance. He glances into the kitchen, sees Khalil and Mariam standing there, the two of them joking around, Khalil mouthing something he can't quite decipher.

Nur's father stands from the sofa, wearing his Eid clothes from last year, a black sherwani, stretched around his stomach, making him almost glow pale against it. Khalil and Mariam slip into the room, hovering by the wall.

There they stand. One family on one side, one family on the other.

Their fathers shake hands, and Hiba sits, Hawa next to her, and a calm settles inside Nur. The moment has finally arrived, and he isn't sick with the anxiety of the past few days, the past few hours even. The meeting seems to be unfolding as it is supposed to.

"Nur, come sit," his mother instructs, gesturing to the seat next to her, and he sits down, thinking of the last time he sat here, two months ago, at New Year, the night he told them.

For a second, there is only silence. Nur looks at Yasmina, but she seems fixated on the table, at the food in front of her. Khalil shrugs his shoulders, glancing at Mariam. They smile politely, but no one knows what to say.

"So," Nur starts, clearing his throat, eight pairs of eyes turning to him. "Here we are."

"Yes, finally." Yasmina breathes the word out, and he wishes he was sitting by her but knows he needs to be here, next to his mother, for this.

Nur looks around the room. "So this is Yasmina, her parents, Ibrahim and Hiba, and her sister, Hawa." His hand moves, gesturing to his own family. "And these are my parents, Mahmoud and Hina, and Khalil and Mariam, my younger brother and sister." They both raise a hand, and Yasmina smiles at them. It's surreal, as though there is an audience somewhere watching them, the nine of them are on a stage.

"How was the journey?" Nur's father asks.

"Not bad," Hiba answers. "There wasn't much traffic."

"You're lucky. When we dropped Nur off in Nottingham, there was quite a bit," he says. "We got stuck in a little traffic on the return too, took us so long to get back to Birmingham."

Hiba nods, and Nur's skin prickles. He glances at Khalil, who doesn't give anything away, is still.

"So, Nur and Yasmina, you've been seeing each other for four years now?" Nur's mother asks, small talk done away with in an instant.

Yasmina looks right at his mother and nods firmly. "Yes," she answers. "We met at university, our second year."

Pride for Yasmina lights in him, because he doubts whether he'd have been able to answer if he were the one sitting where she is.

"And you both knew," Nur's mother continues, eyes gliding to Yasmina's parents, to Hiba in particular.

"Well, Yasmina told us after some time," Hiba admits vaguely, not wanting their introduction to start on a bitter note. Despite Hiba's best efforts, Nur sees his mother's lower lip tremble ever so slightly, and Nur knows she's hurt that Yasmina's family found out first, mortified that her own son didn't tell her, that he didn't tell any of them, and that she wonders why he's so embarrassed of them.

"Mum, we knew too," Mariam blurts out. "Nur told me and Khalil about it a while ago." She doesn't look at Nur as she lies to save him.

"And you didn't tell me?" his mother responds, directly to Nur, as if there is no one else but them.

"I was worried," he says as her eyes narrow slightly, her face goes still. "I didn't know how you would react. And I wanted to be sure. Be sure that Yasmina and I were serious first."

"He didn't want to upset you," Yasmina adds, the sound of her voice reminding him of the larger picture.

"It was just such a surprise," Nur's father says, "when you told us. We thought you might have someone, maybe a few months. Just testing the waters, seeing if it was serious enough to bring home. But to find out so long, it was such a shock. But," he says, reaching out, putting a hand on Nur's shoulder, "if you're happy, then we're happy."

"When Yasmina told us, we didn't know what to think either," Ibrahim ventures, his knee touching his wife's. "We didn't know anything about Nur, and we wondered why she didn't come to us sooner too, what she was hiding. She told us it was because she didn't want to get our hopes up, make us wonder if it was serious, start preparing to welcome someone new into our family, unless it was going somewhere." He glances at Nur, a small smile on his face, and Nur is awed by how Yasmina's parents can be so open and generous. "And your son is a good boy. If there's someone better out there for Yasmina, we haven't met him."

Nur's cheeks flush. "Yasmina is the very best person I know," he says, looking at her, she and Hiba holding hands, their fingers loose.

"It's hard," Hina says, "to learn your child has done something you didn't think they would." Nur's fingers find the edge of the sofa, pull at it. "When Nur told us, all I could think was, why didn't he tell me sooner? Why would he hide this from us for four years? We're not . . . I know there are parents . . . But we're not like that." The words float out toward Yasmina's parents, but Nur senses they're aimed at him. "But I know that he's sure about this relationship. I know you are, Nur," she says, now looking in his direction. "Because otherwise, you wouldn't have arranged this introduction, you wouldn't have brought the families together."

She smiles, and he glimpses something joyful behind the tears brimming in her eyes. "I'm sure," he says, and he latches onto her hand, squeezes it tight. "I'm sure."

As if a balloon has burst, the pressure drops in the room and conversation flows more easily. Nur's mother relaxes, and she starts asking Yasmina about her PhD, her research into the ethics of journalism, and she marvels at how incredible it all sounds, nudging Nur, asking why he isn't following her lead, becoming a doctor, and Nur retorts "not a real doctor," soliciting a playful scowl from Yasmina, who says that she'll be expecting everyone to call her doctor after she finishes, and Nur laughs a little, as do Mariam and Khalil. The focus pivots to them, her parents asking what they do, and as Khalil answers, underselling his performance in his degree, Nur's mother says she'll get the dishes, and Nur puts a hand on her arm, offers to do it, and as he stands, he gestures to Yasmina, telling her to follow him into the kitchen.

"The good plates," he semi-whispers to Yasmina, gesturing to the plates on the counters.

She picks one up, runs her fingers over the flowered pattern. "It's going good, right?" she asks, looking at the plate.

He puts a hand over hers, her eyes reaching his. "It's going good," he says, giving her the confirmation she needs, and he is nearly overcome with the urge to kiss her right then, but the door is still open just slightly. "Do you want to help serve?" he asks.

They move around the kitchen together, Yasmina in his space, in the home that he grew up in, and it feels so natural. When they walk back in, Mariam is saying she isn't going to get married, not yet, she'll wait for Khalil first, a scowl on her face. Yasmina reaches for Nur's hand, and between them they can feel that something is beginning here, something new, made by them.

August 2016

Nur's leg bounces up and down on the train, unable to keep still. He taps his ticket on the table, the card stiff in his hands. For what feels like the thousandth time, he checks his phone, tracks himself on the map, small blue dot glowing on the screen, inching closer and closer to Manchester.

After Yasmina had left him at the cinema, he called her, but she wouldn't pick up. He sent her a few messages that went unanswered. He phoned Imran, recounted scene by scene what he'd done, and Imran called him a fucking idiot. After he finished shouting, Imran advised Nur to give her space, said it would take a while for her to get over it.

In the week that followed, Nur had checked his phone feverishly. He stalked her on Twitter, reading her tweets repeatedly until they were carved into his brain. He felt torn apart, atom by atom. And still there was nothing.

Until the text arrived. Yasmina saying they needed to talk, not over the phone, she wanted to see him, not a question, and he replied yes, absolutely, apologizing again, asking how she was. No response. He updated her the next day, after sorting out his tickets, but there was no acknowledgment.

Now the day was here. His leg hits the underside of the table, a small burst of pain in his knee, just as the station pulls into view. "Fuck," he half whispers, hand on his knee, mind back there, in Birmingham, going over what he said.

Even though he has it memorized, he double-checks where Yasmina has told him to come, a Costa right next to the station.

She's already there, sitting with her hands around a coffee cup, hair loose, and he gives himself a second to just look at her before going in, to remind himself of who she is to him.

"I didn't think you'd come," Nur says, settling in opposite her.

"I'm not that petty."

"That's not what I—"

"Can you just stop?" she asks. "For a second. Please?"

Nur nods, bites his tongue. There is an aching distance between them, and he wants so desperately to close it.

"I love you, Nur," Yasmina starts. "Like, really love you. And I haven't felt this for someone before. I didn't think that I could. Or maybe I didn't let myself. Whatever. But I'm not going to let you do that to me."

"Do that to you?" Nur asks, even though he knows exactly what she means.

She lets the cup go, fingers playing with one another. "Nur, this is so big that I don't know where to begin. When I was a kid, we lived in the suburbs outside Manchester and everyone around us was white. I was the only Black girl in my school, no Black families anywhere near us, but I never felt different. My parents made me feel like I was just another kid who could do anything, become anything." She twists a ring, pulling it off her finger, putting it back on again.

"But when I joined secondary school, it all changed. Suddenly, I began to feel like I was on the outside. No one said anything to my face, but I could hear it in certain things teachers would say or feel it in the way the boys treated me compared to the white girls. When other non-white families started moving into our area, things shifted again. I wasn't alone anymore because there were other kids like me, but now that there were more of us, what was unsaid started to be said. They picked on the Black kids, the brown kids, the Muslim kids, the Hindu kids. We all banded together because we had to. But, you know, hearing white kids say what they'd been thinking all along . . . parroting things you knew they'd heard their parents say . . . it hurt. Even after I'd come to expect it. *Of course* they're going to say that shit to us."

Nur puts his hands under the table, fingers digging into his thighs, stays silent, as hard as it is.

"But that's just this racist fucking country," Yasmina continues, voice now hard. "I learned that studying the violence of this country's history, but also just by coming home and seeing the news each day." She slides her ring along her finger. "So, you know, I expected that racism from white people. They invented it. But it was when I started hearing that same shit from *us*, from other brown and Black kids, that was when it hurt the most. I thought we were all on the same side. That we were in this together, but I learned the truth about that too." She lets out a bleak laugh. "As a Black woman, it feels like everyone has so many preconceptions about me before I've even opened my fucking mouth. It's exhausting."

She pushes the cup away, toward Nur, her bottom lip disappearing into her mouth, eyes like glass, unfallen tears resting in them. "Nur, we both live our lives on guard, so aware of the prejudices around us, about us, but . . . I don't want to be in a relationship like that. I don't want you to look at me like I'm just my skin, because I'm not and that's not how I see you either. Yes, I'm Black, I'm a Muslim, I'm a woman, and I'm your girlfriend, but I'm so much more than any one of those things."

"I don't look at you—" Nur stops, reconfigures. "I don't think—"

She gives him a tired look. "Oh, so you were just worried that your family might see you with a girl and shout at you?"

"That's part of it, yeah," Nur says, defensive. He tries to get his words right, knowing that he can't afford a misstep. "My family is a strict, small-c conservative Muslim family. My parents don't want their kids to date. They think it's a sin to see people romantically before marriage. For a long time, I wasn't even allowed to be friends with girls, because . . . It just wasn't how my parents lived their lives, so it wasn't going to be how their kids lived either. If they knew that I was dating you, or if they knew I was friends with someone like Imran, I think it would honestly kill my mum."

"Because they—"

"Because they think being gay is a sin. That's their belief. It's not mine. And it's not the only belief on which we differ. But that's the way it's been, the way it's always been. So yeah, I said you could come and see where I live because you wanted to, and I forgot that we had this freedom in Bradford, to just be, without worrying that someone is going to see us and tell my mother that I was holding hands with a girl—"

"A Black girl."

"A Black girl," Nur continues, frustration coming through. "Because, yeah, that's part of how it looks as well. I'm not going to lie to you and say that it isn't, when it definitely—"

"And you're okay with that?"

"No, of course I'm not okay with it—"

"Well, it sounds like you've just accepted it. That your family are racist and that's not going to change—"

"Wait," Nur interrupts, slipping into panic. "I'm not saying they're racist—"

"So, you're saying what, Nur? What are you trying to say?"

"That it's complicated! If they saw me with a brown girl, of course it would be an easier conversation. Because—"

"Because they're racist." She leans back in her chair. "So, because I'm Black, I have to be your secret?"

"Not because you're Black. Because my parents . . . they don't know I'm dating before marriage, so I have to hide everything from them."

"And you're okay asking *me* to be your secret?" she asks, looking at him. "Because your family aren't okay with you dating *me*?"

Nur doesn't say anything, hands in fists between his legs.

"I really fucking love you and I know you're sorry," Yasmina says, moving closer to him, arms on the table. "But that day, when you acted like you didn't know me in the street . . . I never thought you'd ever make me feel that way. Like I was less than you." Her face goes hard, jaw straight. "I don't plan to feel like that ever again. I don't want . . ." She stumbles over her words, the lines she came equipped with falling by the wayside.

"I never wanted to make you—"

"But you did, Nur," she snaps. "It's how I felt. What we have is special. I can feel it. Every time I see you, I get this excitement, I feel the happiest I've felt in a long time. And I don't want to give that up. But . . . don't ever treat me like that again, like this is only real when it's convenient for you." He pulls a hand up, reaches for her, hand on hers, and she doesn't move it away. "I need to know that you're on my side, Nur."

Nur nods. "I am, and I'll never let this happen again," he promises. She shifts, hand turning, fingers intertwined with his. He pulls her hand to him, kisses it, and he thanks God for pulling them back when they got so close to the edge.

But as he sits there, he knows that he is lucky, lucky that this is how it's gone, lucky that Yasmina loves him so much.

Part of him knows that she wouldn't be wrong if she left him. That if it were Rahat or Imran sitting where he is, who had behaved like he did, he would have told them how disgusting their behavior was.

How they were part of the problem.

He is lucky that she loves him.

August 2017

Khalil swings the door open. "You're late."

"Don't," Nur says. "I just had another Uber driver who wanted to know everything about my life."

"Ah," Khalil replies. "Was he related to us this time?"

Nur laughs. "Oh, man, the one who turned out to be like our fifth cousin or something?"

"And he told us to tell Nani that he wanted to see her."

"So weird," Nur says, walking in to where their mum sits watching TV.

She looks up at him disapprovingly. "Did you get an Uber?" she asks. "You know I would have come to pick you up. You don't have to waste your money on that."

"You are *so* late," Mariam says as she comes into the living room. She hugs him, tight and quick. "I'm real hungry."

"How's work?" his mum asks, interrupting her children's bickering. Nur sits by her, settling in as she shifts her legs to give him room. "How's Nottingham?"

He can tell she's trying to be casual, masking her anxiety, when what she really wants to hear is that he's safe.

"It's good," he replies. "And work is going well. It's getting easier now that I know everyone."

"Good," she says, smiles at him. "The house feels so empty now. It's going to be even emptier when Mariam goes to university."

"My sister, the politician," Nur remarks, and she rolls her eyes.

"I don't know if that's on the agenda actually," Mariam says. "I'll probably just go into consulting. You make so much more money that way."

"I thought you were a socialist . . ."

"I am definitely a socialist. But I've also got to pay for things, and it's not my fault we live in a capitalist society."

Nur lets out a theatrical sigh. "Man, I was really looking forward to my sister being the anarchist we didn't know we needed."

"Way too much work," Mariam says. "Might just be a doctor, sounds easy."

Khalil barks a laugh. "Do you know how much shit I have to do before I even come close to becoming a doctor? I'm not even sure it's worth it."

"It is *definitely* worth it," their mother says. "Doctor, politician . . ." She pauses when she looks at Nur, and Mariam lets out a sharp laugh.

"The disrespect," Mariam says.

"You don't know what I do?" Nur joins the laughter, but his pride is wounded.

"Something with words and the internet," his mother replies, waving her hand.

"Is that what you tell people he does?" Khalil asks. "That he writes on the internet? Because that's not really an achievement these days."

"I don't just write on the internet," Nur replies, though that is essentially what he does.

His mother puts a hand on his arm. "Whatever it is you do, I'm proud of you. Because it's what you want to do."

"What a mum cop-out," Mariam notes, and their mother laughs, Mariam and Khalil do too, Nur relenting to join in with them, shaking off her words.

"Are you coming to the wedding?" Nur's mother asks, turning the conversation.

Nur's cousin, Sabah, is getting married to a man she met through a family friend. The story goes that she met him at an Eid party, the two of them talking over food, and he asked her if he could see her again. Sabah, never being the kind of person who dated, always kept herself to herself, said yes, because she was older, twenty-five, and marriage was a subject she had to think about now. They met a few days later, liked each other's company so much they met again, and again, and again, until six months had passed and Sabah was talking to her parents about marrying him, their families meeting, a wedding arranged.

The invitations had arrived the week after Nur had moved, gold writing on cream paper. His mother called him immediately to check if he'd come, and he said no, weddings weren't his thing, made a joke about how old women whose names he could never remember would ask when his time was, how they'd answer their own question by saying now, the time is now.

"Sabah would really like to see you there," his mother presses, squeezing his arm on the sofa.

"Mum, you know I haven't spoken to Sabah in years. We were never that close. I don't know why you're making it seem like we were."

"So she can get you to come to the wedding," Mariam says. "Classic diplomatic move."

"I'm just saying," his mother continues. "It would be nice of you to make the effort. Besides, you should be going to your cousins' weddings. It's a good thing to do. Otherwise, people forget about you."

"If all it takes is not going to weddings for people to forget you exist, then I would guess they didn't really care about you in the first place," Khalil says.

"Are you going?" Nur asks.

"I can't," Khalil says, a slight smile on his face. "It's too close to uni. I need that weekend. I need every weekend in existence."

"You?" Nur looks at Mariam, who nods.

"You know I like weddings," she says. "We're not all like you, Nur."

He bristles at her words. "I can't come back so early in December," he says, using the line he had planned, deliberately coming home now so that he could play it as an excuse. "I have a lot of work to do, new job and everything, and I should be doing that instead of going to a wedding where my presence won't even be noticed right before I come home for Christmas."

His mother's shoulders sink a little, and she lets out a sigh. "Okay then."

Shame flares in him. "It's not that big a deal, Mum, honestly. We can go out this weekend, to dinner somewhere."

"If you don't go to people's weddings or funerals, then who's going to come to yours, Nur? Who's going to come when you get married?" she asks.

"I don't want to get married," he replies, because it seems like the easiest thing to say in the moment.

"Well, you say that now, but one day you're going to want to get married. I want you to have a good wedding. I want you to get married with lots of guests—"

"Who are only there because they think they have to, otherwise who will go to theirs?" Nur interrupts.

She frowns. "No, surrounded by people who are happy for you."

"If I wanted to do that, I would have the smallest wedding in history," Nur says, and he doesn't know why he is arguing like this, but he can't stop himself.

"I don't think Mum is saying—" Mariam begins, but their mother cuts her off.

"You don't have to attend this wedding if you don't want to," she says, one of her hands wrapped around the other, fingers digging into her palm. "None of us do. But you should think about the way you want people to see you. If you don't go to Sabah's wedding, fine. But what about the next one, and the one after that, and the one after that? They're going to forget about you. They're not going to care. When you get married, whenever that is, they're not going to want to come. And I think that's sad, Nur. I think that's sad for you."

Nur suddenly loses the ability to see anything but red, anger coursing through him. "Yeah, well, isn't that the problem with our family? That we don't view one another as actual people, so we lie to each other instead just in case someone judges us or thinks we might be bad influences. You're always lying to people, telling them you can't go somewhere because you're somewhere else, or you're ill, or you're taking care of your kids, when really you just don't want to go. Like it would even matter if they knew you didn't want to go. And when someone does the same to you, you act as though it's the worst thing in the world, that they don't respect you enough to tell you the truth. But you're doing the exact same thing! All of us are, playing this stupid game, telling each other lies. What's the point of it? Why do we hide so much of ourselves to cater to what other people think? I'm fucking tired of it."

The words spill out, marbles crashing to the floor, and he can't pick them up and return them to where they came from. A quiet takes over the room, Mariam and Khalil both staring at him, but he can't look back, can only keep his eyes on his mother, who appears a mix of sad and angry.

"I don't lie to people," she says, her words coming out slowly. "But yes, Nur, sometimes you do need to think about the way your life looks from the outside. You need to consider that. It might not be the kind of life you envision for yourself, but it's the kind of life *we* live. If that's too much for you, then don't come to the wedding. But don't sit there and act like you're so high and mighty."

She leaves, her three children listening as she goes to her room, closes the door.

Nur can't believe what's he said, that he swore in front of his mother. And for some reason, that is the sticking point, that he said *fuck*, when he has never sworn in front of her before.

"What the hell just happened?" Mariam asks, and he turns back to her, to his two siblings, both of them shocked, questions on their faces.

"I don't know," he says.

"You need to go apologize," Khalil orders. "Like, right now."

Nur looks at his brother and then looks at the door his mum left through, and he feels sick. "I . . . I didn't—"

"Go say sorry," Khalil repeats, and it's as if they have switched positions, that Khalil is the older one, the one in control. "You are so lucky Dad isn't home."

Nur heads upstairs and lingers in front of his mother's door, leans his head against it, listening, but he can't hear anything. He knocks lightly and goes in.

His parents' room, unchanged for years, a double bed in the middle, facing the window, a wardrobe on one side of it, a small table on the other. He remembers a summer when his father went to Pakistan to deal with something, months without him, how his younger self used to slip into his parents' room, lie in the bed with his mum, how she would turn around and hold him, how Khalil and Mariam would come as well, the four of them in this double bed, not enough space for all of them, but a need to be together.

His mother is resting on the edge of the bed, looking down at the floor, and she doesn't look at him. He hovers by the doorway.

"Mum?"

She doesn't move. He takes a breath and goes to sit by her, leaving just enough space between them so they aren't touching. "I'm sorry," he begins. "I didn't mean . . . I don't think you're a liar. I just . . . Every time I go to a wedding, people talk about marriage and my age and it gets to me. I never know if I'm doing something wrong, and I hate feeling like my life is running off the track or something."

She turns her face to him, sniffles slightly. He hates that he is the one responsible. "You don't have to go if you don't want to, Nur. I just don't want you to forget where you come from, who we are."

"I know, Mum."

"I want the best for you and Mariam and Khalil. I know that you're all grown up now and you don't need me, but—"

Nur stops her: "I will always need you, Mum." He moves closer, puts his arm around her. "Always."

They sit like that and let the time pass, until there is a knock at the door, Khalil saying the food has arrived, and the two of them stand, his mother wiping the tears from her eyes, and he looks at her, smiles tentatively, and she bobs her head for them to go downstairs, and he knows everything is fine again. In the living room, they all sit, steam rising from their plates, and they talk, about anything and everything As he sits there, he can't help but think that it was never his mother who was the liar, but him.

February 2019

This is how it happens.

The sun has set, darkness cast around them, and Nur suggests they think about heading back, because otherwise it's going to be too late by the time Yasmina's family gets back to Manchester.

They say their goodbyes at the door, all nine of them, hands shaken, hugs administered, and Yasmina's family step out into the cold.

"Nur," his father says, "would you come here for a second? It'll just be a minute."

Nur exchanges glances with Yasmina, gives her a reassuring smile, and watches as her family make their way to the car, lights flashing in the darkness as they get in.

"What's up?" he asks, and he cringes at himself for trying to sound so casual, as if nothing strange or out of the ordinary has happened today.

Nur's father waves him back into the living room. His mother, on the sofa, Khalil and Mariam standing, his father settling down by his mother. Nur waits for them to talk. "What is it?"

"So that's her," his mother says, less a question, more a statement.

His heart leaps into his throat. "Yes, Mum, that's Yasmina." He tries to keep his voice light.

"She's very pretty."

"She is," Nur says, and he glances at Khalil, who offers him an almost imperceptible tilt of his head, and Nur understands then what's coming. "Do you not like her?"

His mother doesn't say anything, looks at her hands. "Nur, are you sure this is the girl you want to marry?" his father asks.

"So you *don't* like her?" Nur responds, his anger growing but rotten with sadness, with bitter disappointment.

"Nur, meh tumhara bap hu, so I am asking you now, are you sure this is the girl you want to marry?" his father repeats.

"Yes."

His father nods, and Nur glances back at Khalil and Mariam, a child again, standing in front of his parents, being asked whether or not he has done something he shouldn't have, his siblings made to watch as he gets punished. But that has never been him, he is the good one, the one who listens, who draws inside the lines. Panic spasms in his stomach.

"There is no reason to rush . . . ," his mother says slowly. "My friend has a daughter, Farah. She's just graduated from a law degree, she's a trainee solicitor. Very clever girl, and she likes to read, just like you. I've heard lovely things about her—"

"Mum," Nur interrupts, unable to fathom her words.

"I could call her right now, find out if she can come here and meet you. Or we can find someone else. I have other friends whose daughters are your age, and they're all good girls. If you want—"

"Mum," he says again, but she continues talking, the words leaping out of her.

"I can call them, it's no trouble. If you want. If you don't like any of them—"

He reaches over, puts a pleading hand on her arm, and the touch seems to surprise her, as if she hadn't realized he was there in person. "Mum," he repeats, and she looks up at him, eyes wide. "Please, Mum. Yasmina is the woman I want to marry. I love her."

"You—"

"I love her," he states. Only weeks ago, he was crippled by the idea of declaring his love for Yasmina in front of his parents, of defending it. Yet saying it now feels so straightforward to him.

His mother leans back, his hand slipping off her arm.

"If you're going to marry this girl," his father replies, a warning in his words, "then you better be sure you're making the right decision."

"The right decision?" Nur asks, stressing each syllable in disbelief, slowly losing his cool. "What does that mean?"

"It's a big choice, Nur," his father says. "You're going to build a life with this girl, and what do you know about her? Her family? You need to be sure—"

Nur lets out a laugh, bitter and sharp in the air. "Because we're always so sure, right?" Everything he has felt for months, all his panic, his worry, his frustrations, spill out at once. "It's not like we send boys younger than me to Pakistan to get married to girls they don't know. Not like we've watched time and time again as those marriages fail because the couple got married only to please their parents. How many of those boys turn into men who cheat on their wives, having children, because what will people say if there are no children, but then barely paying their way, filing for divorce, and leaving the woman saddled with the children—although who can trust a divorced woman's words, right? Or what about the ones who stay, hating each other their entire lives, their children growing up in a toxic home? But that's fine, because the parents made the right choice for them, right? And that's what you want for me? To go meet Farah, meet whoever else you vaguely know, even though I already love someone, someone I would be honored to spend the rest of my life with, because what—because whoever you choose would be more acceptable to the aunties and uncles back home? To Auntie Naseem down the road, to the imam at the mosque, to all the people in our family you don't even care about anyway?"

"Because you know everything, right, Nur?" his mother asks. "You know everything about everyone, how they're feeling, why they do anything, because you're so smart, right?"

"I don't . . ."

"No, you don't," she says, her voice tight. "You don't know everything. That's how *we* did it, that's how *we* found people to marry. We involved our family in it, we didn't just run off and find anyone, because we knew it was bigger than that. It wasn't just *our* choice. And that's what we want for you, but we don't want to force you into a marriage with someone you don't want to be with. You make it sound like we're—"

"You make it sound like we don't want the best for you," his father says, leaning forward, toward Nur, concern emanating from him.

"Did you ever consider that Yasmina is the best for me?" Nur is exhausted. He knew this would happen, and he is angry at Yasmina for making him think it could go well. Why couldn't she just trust him?

"Nur isn't stupid," Khalil interrupts. Nur looks at his brother and sister, had forgotten they were there. "He's known her for four years. He says he loves her. He says he wants to marry her. How many of us do that? So many of our cousins mess around with girls, like it means nothing. Mum, you were literally just telling us about Zeeshan, how he got that girl pregnant and made her get an abortion, then his parents made him move to Pakistan because they found out and were ashamed. Nur isn't like that. He has been respectful."

"I know that—"

"Then what is it?" Nur presses. "Did you not like her? Is she not good enough?"

"She's—"

"She's Muslim," Nur says, and he hates that he has to say that, that he has to use it for validation in his parents' eyes.

"I know that," his mother says.

"So what is it, then? Just say it. Is it because she's Black?" The question makes him want to break something, feel something solid snap in his hands. "Yasmina is . . . She makes me feel whole, Mum. I feel like I can do anything when I'm with her and that the world makes sense. She's brilliant, generous, kind, caring. She's a good person. Her family are good people."

Neither of his parents respond. Nur wants them to admit it's because she is Black, that they do not want her to be part of the family because of the color of her skin. He wants his parents to verbalize their fears, to say, what will people think when they find out, to say, how will she understand our way of life, how could we take her to Pakistan? But if he hears either of his parents say anything like that, he might not step back into this house.

"Yasmina is good, Mum," Mariam says, lending her voice to the conversation. "You can see that she loves Nur. There's no question about it."

"I know that!" their mother exclaims. Her eyes continue to fill, her chin quivering. "I know that," she says again, looking at him. "I just want to make sure that you're doing the best thing. For you, for everyone."

"Don't you trust me?" Nur asks. "Don't you trust that the son you raised would do the right thing?"

His mother looks to the curtains, trying to hold herself together, his father still watching him.

"I'm sorry you can't understand this, but I've made my choice," Nur says, his words hanging in the silence. "And I want you to be happy for me, for us. But if you're not going to be, then I don't know what to do."

"What do you mean?" His mother's voice wavers slightly.

He glances at the door, thinks of Yasmina and her family waiting for him in that car. "I think it means that I love Yasmina and I love you guys too. And I don't want to pick between you, but I will if you make me."

"You'd pick her over your family?"

"Do you want me to walk out that door because you think you don't like the woman I want to marry?"

His mother is quiet then. His father puts a hand on her leg. "No," she admits.

"No," Nur echoes, and he looks at Khalil and Mariam again, sees the anguish in their eyes that is mirrored in his own, and he wishes he could rewind everything, go all the way back, tell them about Yasmina from the very beginning. Because maybe if they had known this entire time, things would have been easier. Because maybe if he'd trusted them, if he'd let them in, he wouldn't be here right now.

"You're my child," his mother starts again, a resolve in her voice. "I have done everything for you. For all of you. And you, Nur— you're my first, my eldest. I thought you trusted me, respected my word. But then we find out that you've been hiding a relationship for four years. I . . ." Her hands twist around each other in her lap. "I want everything for you, Nur. I want the best match possible, someone who would make you happy—"

"Yasmina is that."

"I wanted to be the one to guide you, that is my duty," she says. "I wanted to be part of it. And you . . . you told them before us. You told those strangers before you told your own parents."

"Mum—" he says.

"You tell us about 'right choices,' but you didn't care what we thought. You made this choice without consulting us, without ever considering what we think." She stands, the two of them upright, mother and son. "If this is how little you think of your family, then you can do what you want." She walks out of the room, her steps hard on the stairs.

Nur starts to the door, but his father stops him. "I'll talk to her," he says. "But I think you should get back to the car. It's getting late." He places a reassuring palm on Nur's shoulder, gently urging him to go, but his eyes reveal his hurt and frustration. He hugs Nur quickly before heading upstairs too, following his wife.

Nur looks back at his siblings, who seem to be communicating silently between themselves. "Nur," Mariam starts, moving to him, her hand on his arm. "Nur," she says again, and he is surprised he has tears, wiping them away with the back of his hand. "We'll talk to them—"

"No one said that falling in love was going to be this hard," Nur mumbles.

"Literally every story about falling in love says it's going to be this hard," Mariam jokes.

"Let's just hope this doesn't end up like *Devdas*," Khalil says, and he laughs, and so do Nur and Mariam, finding comfort in their closeness.

"I should go," Nur says, gesturing at the door.

"It'll be all right," Mariam says. "Yasmina's a good person. She loves you, and you love her. That's it, that's all it ever needs to be."

Nur nods, throat tight. "I'll text you guys when I get back."

"You'd better." Mariam gives him a long hug, arms tight. "Tell Yasmina I think she's great."

Khalil steps in, hugs him next, his silence saying more than his words ever could, and when they break apart, Nur's eyes are glassy.

He walks out of his childhood home, avoiding looking up the stairs. He crosses the road, back to Yamina's family car, and he slips inside.

Nur clips in his seat belt, Yasmina scooting over to make room, concern in her face, and for a moment no one speaks. Yasmina's dad turns on the ignition, shifts into drive, pauses before pulling out. "All good?" he asks, looking at Nur in the rearview mirror.

"Yeah, sorry to keep you," Nur says, and he looks back at the house, sees the front door open, Mariam and Khalil watching, waving goodbye, and he raises his hand as the car pulls away, his family disappearing into the past.

September 2017

Y ou're moving in together?"

Imran rolls his eyes, waves a fry at Nur. "You're very dramatic for someone who just moved in with his girlfriend."

"I've known Yasmina for almost three years," Nur says.

"I've been with Ramy for a year now!"

"Eight months isn't a year."

"It's *nearly* a year. And besides, it's my longest relationship. And I love him. Don't tell me that it's too soon to know I love him, because you told me you loved Yasmina like four minutes after meeting her."

"I did not!"

"Oh, so you're going to lie to me now? Like you didn't see her at Saara's party and then come to me, whimpering about how you loved her?"

"Okay, first, that was three years ago, I have no idea how you remember that. Second, I definitely did not say I loved her. Third, you were high and sad at Saara's after another breakup; your memory is nothing to go by."

"That feels like discrimination."

"You mean it feels like the truth?"

"You definitely told me you wanted to see her again."

"Maybe."

"There was a look in your eyes. A look of, like, 'I've found the one.' A twinkle, if you will."

"Three years on and you're claiming to remember a twinkle?"

"I've got a great memory, Nur. Like how you kissed me in a club because you were so happy to be out from under your parents."

"I did not kiss you because I was happy to be out from under my parents."

"Right, you kissed me because I'm incredibly hot and hard to look past."

"Yeah, that's why." Nur throws a fry at him. "Anyway, don't try to change the subject: Ramy."

"I thought we were done with that. I want to move in with Ramy. You don't think I should. The end."

"You should think about it, weigh the pros and cons."

"Just tell me what you think is wrong with him."

Nur opens his mouth in protest, closes it, and then begins again. "I don't think there is anything wrong with him," he replies, choosing his words carefully, recalling what he has said in the past.

"So what is it, then?" Imran asks.

Nur leans back in his seat, crosses his arms over his chest. "How many were there before Jay, back at uni?"

Imran grits his teeth. "Two."

"And how many after?"

"Three," Imran says. "Four if you include Ramy."

"So how many is that in total?"

"Your rudimentary math can only go so far. Your point is made."

"I'm just saying, you have a tendency to go deep fast in relationships. And sometimes, it doesn't turn out well."

"Are you really doing this?" Imran sighs, defeat coating his words.

"Sorry." Nur reverses course, unsure why he thought to push. "I'm sorry. I just don't want you to rush into something too soon."

"Then trust me," Imran pleads. "I know what I'm doing. What's happened in the past happened. I'm not thinking about that now. Ramy is different. *I'm* different."

"I'm sorry," Nur repeats, because he can't think to say anything else. "I shouldn't have—"

"It's fine," Imran interrupts. "Really, it's fine."

Nur looks out the window, at the center of Nottingham outside. Even though it's only been three months of living here, everything feels familiar to him. Walk for a few minutes from where they're sitting, take a left onto a side road, and there is the office building he knows the key code to, where his desk sits, cookies in the top drawer, a photo of him and Yasmina as his laptop screen saver; he knows of a really good kebab shop in the opposite direction, where they call him by name, start on his order as soon as he walks in; he gets his haircut from that barber who asks him about his life, about Yasmina, about work; the people who live in his apartment building, whose faces he knows, who he nods at, who stop now to say hello, ask how he and Yasmina are settling in.

This part of the country, where he has never spent time before, is slowly becoming his home, and he feels himself sliding into it, the pavements and bricks and walls and windows moving out of the way to create a place for him, and he wonders, if this becomes home, what happens to his old home in Birmingham?

"How's Yasmina?" Imran draws Nur's eyes back to him.

"Stressed out. This PhD is taking it out of her. And I can't really help. The shit she's doing . . . When she told me she wanted to study the ethics of journalism, investigate it all rather than just be part of the industry, I thought it sounded incredible. And sometimes, it is. She'll come back having read something and be so excited about it. But most of the time, she's just stressed out. There's not enough hours in the day for her."

"Honestly, I continue to be glad I didn't go back to university after my degree. My dad told me to do a master's, become specialized in something, maybe even get a PhD. But . . ." Imran shrugs, makes a face. "I'm doing fine without it."

"I think you're doing pretty great." Nur picks up a fry, holds it between his finger and thumb. "How is he?"

"My dad?" Imran asks. Nur nods. "I assume he's fine. He still won't speak to me."

Two weeks ago, Imran had phoned, told Nur that his mother had invited him home, over a year after they had kicked him out. Nur had listened, kept quiet all the bad things he was thinking about Imran's mother, instead asking him what he wanted to do. Imran told him he was going, wanted to see what she had to say. The day of, Nur didn't stray from his phone, picked up immediately when Imran's name finally appeared in the middle of the night.

Imran recounted how he'd returned home, feeling like a stranger, knocking on the door even though he still had his keys. His mother had opened the door, and he'd noticed that her face was thinner, gaunt, her body smaller, like someone had compressed her. Then she'd cried, reaching for him. When she held him, Imran had felt like a child again, and he'd cried too, neither one of them able to talk.

His father had walked in on Imran and his mother sitting in the living room, talking about his new job, where he was living, his friends, his health, everything but the important things, and when his father had seen Imran, he'd looked at him, face blank, and told Imran to get out.

"Do you think he'll ever let you come back?" Nur asks.

Imran's jaw goes stiff. "My mum asked me if I wanted to move back in. I'm meant to be seeing her next month."

"I'm going to guess that's a no," Nur says.

Imran hesitates. "There's no way I could go back. My dad wouldn't let me anyway. But if he did, I don't think I'd fit inside that house, not after living by myself, not after everything." He stops, looks for the right words. "I've grown up."

"Like the house doesn't fit you anymore," Nur murmurs, the realization familiar. "You're right. We have grown up, outgrown our childhoods. And it's terrifying sometimes. I never thought I'd be living in my own place with someone long-term like this. I assumed I'd go along with my parents' wishes, living at home until they found someone to pair me off with."

"Would you have done that?" Imran asks. "If Yasmina didn't exist. Would you have let them find you someone?"

"My parents wouldn't have, like, forced me," Nur says. "They were an arranged marriage, but they would never do that to me. My parents know me well. Maybe not everything, but they're aware of how liberal I am, that I like books and writing, so I guess they'd ask around, introduce me to girls they thought would fit well. At least, I hope they'd try to match me with someone who has similar interests. And I think I'd probably go along with it."

Imran reaches for his drink, hand around it, tight. "You know, I sometimes worry I robbed my parents of that. I'm their only son, and my parents care about that kind of stuff, we all do. My mum used to tell me how big the party my grandparents had thrown for them was when she got home from the hospital, because I was the first son, the first grandchild, the one to carry on our name. They care about that kind of stuff. Even though they're so different from their parents, even though they've changed, these things are still so important to them. And my mum has definitely thought about my wedding, my dad has pictured his future grandkids. And I'm robbing them of that—"

"You didn't choose—"

"I know."

"And it's not like you can't get married, can't have kids."

"You think my parents would let me bring my husband back to their house? You think that they'd let me ever bring a child not from my marriage into that house? Not truly their bloodline? My dad would probably kill himself before he let that happen." Imran scoffs, looks down at his plate, so much bitterness leaking from his words, it breaks Nur's heart.

"You can bring your husband to our place anytime you want," Nur says, and he reaches across the table, puts his hand on Imran's. "I would never throw you out. Or kill myself. Nothing dramatic like that."

"Of course you wouldn't," Imran replies, a pained smile, and Nur hates that he can't do anything about it, because he wants to make Imran feel better. All he ever wants is for Imran to realize how great he is.

They leave, Nur taking Imran to the park where he runs, and they walk around for a while, Imran making a quip about the weather, hands firmly shoved into pockets, jackets zipped up, because even though the sun is out, there is still a chill to the air as the seasons move along, the days turning colder and shorter, before they head back to Nur's, Imran here for the weekend.

"You know," Nur starts vaguely, "I never thought I would be here." Imran looks at him. "Like, when we were at uni, I always felt that at some point it was all going to end. The freedom, the independence of it all, it was going to come to an end and I was going to return to Birmingham, to the same dictated routine, to my parents and some boring job where I sat in an office." Nur pulls at his sleeves, covers his hands with them. "Maybe I would write sometimes, like, come home and write every other evening, my future wife okay with that as a hobby. And I'd become a dad and my book would finally get published, and I'd make enough money from that to quit my job but not enough to become rich. Just enough to get by. And maybe we have another kid, my wife and me, and my parents are happy, us still living in Birmingham, and then my brother gets married and my sister gets married and we're all like happy in these small lives of ours, where nothing is too much, you know?" He glances at Imran, who is just staring ahead.

"And I was okay with that," Nur continues, looking ahead too, a couple in front of them pushing a stroller. "I was okay with that before. It seemed logical to me. But then I met Yasmina, and none of that made sense anymore. I don't want . . . *that*. I want to be with Yasmina, I want to be independent, I want to be *here* in Nottingham. And sometimes, I feel so guilty for it, because I know my parents just want to be around me, that whenever my mum calls, she worries that I won't pick up because something has happened. But I can't . . . I can't reverse time and live that life." He pauses as they reach the edge of the park, his apartment building rising in the distance. "I'm happier here. I'm, like you said, grown now," he says.

Nur's words hang over them, this great big speech. "I never had that," Imran says, stopping in front of Nur, waiting for them to continue. "An idea of who I was going to be. Because the second I realized I was gay, I knew that whatever 'normal' was, it wasn't for me. Either I was going to be who I am and disappoint my family, live away from them, or I was going to get married to someone they chose for me and we'd have an unhappy life. I used to picture it all the time when I was a teenager. A woman, whoever she was, married to me, and maybe we would have sex and I'd close my eyes, think about anything else, and she'd get pregnant and maybe my parents would be proud. But the kid would grow up in a house filled with negativity, with this bad energy around them. And I hated the idea. So I stopped thinking about the future me, about what would happen after uni." He chuckles, a little wistful. "Daydreaming is for cis straight people, I think. It's too painful for the rest of us."

"Is this the part where I apologize on behalf of all cis straight people?" Nur jokes, plowing ahead again, drawing his keys out.

"I don't think you're *that* straight," Imran says, nudging him. "But you know, I think we're there." Nur glances back at him, slightly confused. "Like, in our lives. We're there right now. When things are changing, and changing for the better. I want to move in with Ramy, not because I'm obsessed with him or I think it's going to make me happy—well, I do feel very strongly about him and I *do* think it's going to make me happy—but I'm not relying on *just* him for my happiness. And that's different from how I used to be in relationships. And, man, you and Yasmina, you're good. I'm glad that you didn't go back home and fit yourself into that life. You might have liked it, who knows. And that's fine. But you seem so solid here. Even with everything going on."

"I really like being alive right now," Nur replies, no joke, no humor. He is dizzy with joy.

"Me too," Imran says, and he puts his arm around Nur in front of the flat's entrance. "Me too."

February 2019

Yasmina's parents try talking on the drive back, remarking how nice his parents' home is, how nice Khalil and Mariam are, how nice his parents are. How nice everything is, and Nur says nothing, only nodding in response, knowing that if he opens his mouth, he will only say the wrong things. They stop talking, Hawa reaching for her phone, the light bright on the other side of the car, Ibrahim turning the radio on for some sound.

Nur doesn't look at Yasmina.

He can't.

She reaches for his hand at some point, holds it in hers, and there is a question in the way she holds him, and he senses her frustration, wants desperately to tell her everything is okay, but he can't. There is shame in the pit of his stomach, this heavy thing that makes him want to throw up. They can see it—it is in the color of his cheeks, in his silence—and he wants to apologize to them for tonight, apologize to Yasmina for having wasted four years of her life.

When the car stops outside their flat, Nur thanks them for the ride, gets out first, stepping out from the stale car air, unable to bear being in there a second longer. He takes a deep shuddering breath, and he wants to sob, heavily.

Yasmina steps out of the car a second later, her family still inside, asking them to wait a minute and she'll come back to say good night, and she approaches him, arms crossed over her chest. "Are you going to tell me what happened?" she asks.

Nur wants to laugh. "I don't know that I should."

"Don't do that to me," she snaps, the words having built up inside her this entire time, no longer holding them back for Nur's sake. "Not when my family just went out of their way. Not now, Nur. Not now."

"I know—"

"Do you?" she asks. "Do you know what it's like for me to give everything I have for our relationship? I told my family about you, Nur, without question, without hesitation. My mum, she just told you that she wanted to tear us apart at first because she didn't know you. But they gave you a chance, and you proved yourself, because you're a good person. That's why I love you. Because you're Nur, you're caring and loving and so passionate about so much. That's why they're happy for us to be together. And you—" She laughs, this strange bark, shattering the second it leaves her lips. "You've said over and over again what your family is, what their faults are. You paint them like they're this backward conservative Muslim family who are deeply racist. And maybe they are. But what I saw tonight, that's not what you told me to expect. Whatever happened, I need to know. Because you know what, Nur? Maybe if you had been honest with them two years ago, three years, four years, maybe if you had just *tried*, this whole disaster might not have happened. But instead, I've spent all this time hiding myself away, making myself small, so that your parents don't crucify you. I've become this person who doubts herself constantly. Why isn't he telling his parents about us? Does he not love me? Does he not want to take this any further? Has he been lying this entire time? Do I even know who he is?"

"Yasmina . . . ," Nur starts, but he has nothing else to add and her name sits there between them, the name that he's said thousands of times, the name that brings him joy.

"I can't," she responds, and her voice is calm, strong. "I can't do this. Four years, Nur. Four years of feeling less than. Four years of feeling like I am nothing. I can't do it anymore. You need to know what you want. Because I can't carry on like this."

"You can't?" he asks, and he is trembling, shaking. Anger, frustration, and grief too, mixing into something toxic and dangerous. "You didn't tell your parents for a year—"

"Because I wanted to be sure!"

"Exactly!" he shouts back, louder, and his voice echoes down the street, racing up and down it, smashing into windows and doors. "Because you knew your family. You knew how long they would need. And I know what *my* family needs. You're standing here, saying all this shit about me not telling them, like you know how they'd react. You don't know. You have never known them—"

"Whose fault is that, Nur?" Her voice like ice. "Whose fault is it that I don't know your family? I asked you so many times when I could meet them. I have ruined myself for you—"

"You've ruined yourself?" he scoffs, and he feels whatever is between them tearing, and he wants to stop himself, but it's been four years of secrets. "You think that you're ruined? Please. I lied to my parents, my family, for four years because of you. I lied to my mum's face! I tore apart my family for this."

"I never asked you to do that."

"Because you never ask me to do anything, right?" Nur spits the words out. "Yasmina, always there for me. Always wanting to fix me. You can't fix this, Yasmina. You can't fix my family."

"I don't want to fix shit," Yasmina says. "And even if I could, it's not like you would let me, right?"

"What's that supposed to mean?"

She lets out another sharp laugh. "What's that supposed to mean? Nur, all the times you get in your head and close off from me . . . You never let me in. I have to tiptoe around you because you won't ever admit what's wrong. I have to go to Imran, ask him how I can help, because you won't talk to me about it." Her words strike him into silence. "And I told you, I told you about Hawa."

"What does Hawa have to do—"

"Are you fucking kidding me?" she asks. "I have . . . I told you *everything* about her. You're the only person outside of my family who knows. I told you how it made me feel, being cut out. Like it was my fault. How I've tried so hard to fix things for her."

"It's not your job to fix her, to fix me, to fix anyone—"

"Oh, fuck off!"

He lets out a laugh, of anger and sorrow, mixed together to create something ugly. "You really want to know what they said when you left? They asked if I wanted to marry someone else. Girls they know who are my age, the right kind of girls." The words pummel into her but he can't stop. He is so tired of censoring himself.

Yasmina's face flickers, jaw tense, a tremble of her lips. "What did you say?"

"I told them I loved you. But you know what, maybe it's easier if I go back and tell them I want to marry whoever the fuck they have lined up for me. Because this is exhausting. I'm fucking exhausted—"

"And you think I'm not?"

"Then maybe it would be easier if I do that. Just do whatever my parents want."

"Because that's what Nur does, right? Takes the easy road?" she snarls. "Because Nur is the good boy, the one who tells his mum all these lies to 'protect' her. No, not actually protect her, but rather protect the image she has of him. The boy who sleeps in my bed, has sex with *me*, but tells them that he's living with a 'friend.' The boy who can't even face himself in the fucking mirror, who so desperately wants to be the good son that he never bothers to even question what the fuck that even means."

Suddenly, they are both spent.

He wants to tell Yasmina that everything will be fine, that there is a way, and she'll say that they will work it out together, and he will feel relieved.

But he knows he can't this time. Something has snapped. It hasn't happened suddenly, though it feels that way. There's been a rod between them since they left university, and it has been bending this entire time, backward, forward, pulled by other hands, and they have tried to keep it together for as long as they could, but now it has shattered, and the shards of it lie at their feet, and neither one of them wants to pick up the pieces.

"You know what I realised in there, in your home?" Yasmina asks, her voice quieter now. "Your parents, your family, they weren't the ones hiding me. They weren't the ones making me question everything about myself. That was you, Nur. You made me feel like that. For years. You know, it makes me wonder, is it only them who don't like that I'm Black or is it also you?" Her face is still and he can tell this isn't the first time she has wondered this, that this question has been in her for a while, maybe even from the beginning.

The question stuns Nur. His lips part for words, but he can't find anything. "I . . . ," he starts, stops. "I don't care that you're Black."

"Oh, you don't see color?"

"You know what I mean!" he says. He can't take a breath, the world is blurred at the edges of his vision. "I didn't hide you because I'm ashamed of you. I didn't hide you—"

"Then what do you call the last four years, Nur?"

He can't take his eyes away from her. "I love you, Yasmina."

"Yeah, I know," she says, and she lets out a small laugh. "I'm tired, Nur. I'm going to go back to Manchester, with my family."

"What, tonight?" he asks, confused. "Will you be back?" The thought registers that he should stop her.

"Maybe," she says, turning without saying anything else, heading back to her parents' car. The car door opens and shuts and then the car drives off. Nur watches it head down the road, turn a corner, and it is gone, those two red lights the last he sees, the image imprinted in his mind.

He lingers in the cold, hands numb. He opens his door, keys shaking in his hand, climbs the stairs, enters their flat, empty and silent.

He walks into their bedroom, falls onto the bed, and lies there for a while, her voice in his head.

Is it only them who don't like that I'm Black or is it also you?

It wasn't him. He loved Yasmina. He *loves* Yasmina. This isn't on him. This is his family, his parents, his mother.

He thinks about the day, the jokes their parents shared, the way Mariam and Hawa laughed, the questions Khalil asked. Two families coming together, bonding over their children, over their shared future.

Were his family really able to fake that?

Were his parents that good at acting?

His mother's words ring in his mind, over and over again. *Other girls, cousins, arrange. Other girls, cousins, arrange. Other girls, cousins, arrange.* They play on a loop, and every time they spin around, his anger builds and builds.

He hears himself shouting, hears Yasmina defending herself, their words equally barbed, edged with bitterness, the kind that has accumulated over years, that is not so easy to scrub away, and he starts crying. He is weak, he is a coward, unable to fight for anything he wants, always waiting for people to move him around, to make his choices for him.

Four years.

He wants to phone Imran, explain what's happened, but he doesn't know how to talk about it. He doesn't know what he wants to hear in return. Does he want pity, for Imran to say how unfair this is? He knows Imran won't do that. Does he want Imran to tell him to fight, to speak to his family properly, to push back? No, he doesn't want that either.

He reaches for his phone, turns it on, texts from Mariam and Khalil popping up, both stressing they're there for him, and though it makes him feel better, it also makes him feel worse.

Because Yasmina's words are stuck in his head.

He thinks back to the first time he spoke to her about his family, of how he described them to her, of how he painted them as if they were stuck in another era. While he still believes some of that to be true, he also knows that people can change. But he never gave his family the chance to.

She's right.

He never even tried.

June 2016

Nur is nervous. Actually, no, nervous doesn't entirely cover how Nur feels. Nervous is what he's like before he sends off an essay to his tutor; what he feels before he walks into an exam room; what he feels before he goes to the gym sometimes. That's nervous: a small bubble in his chest, his stomach turning a little, his breathing quickening.

This feels different. This is like someone taking that feeling and adding a thousand volts to it. He is charged with energy. He can't stop pacing in his room, back and forth, like a caged dog. He is sweating, beads of moisture under his arms and in the small of his back, despite his attempts not to sweat, because even though it's summer, it isn't that hot, and he's about to sweat through the only good shirt he owns before they get there.

"Can you please calm down?" Rahat calls out from the other room. "I can literally hear you stomping around in there."

"How can you tell me to calm down?"

"Really easily. Like this: Calm down."

"I can't calm down."

"You definitely can."

"I can't."

"You can."

"Fuck!" Nur steps out of his room and glares at Rahat, who is sitting against the wall, book in hand, eyebrows raised, as if he's surprised to find Nur standing there. "Can you not do this today?"

"Do what?" Rahat asks, a grin forming, but Nur doesn't return it. "It'll be fine. All you need to do is show them who you are. That's who Yasmina loves."

"So easy when you say it."

"Well, this is why I don't date. Meeting the parents? Can't be worth it."

"Oh, *this* is why you don't date."

"Don't be an asshole when I'm trying to help you. Now go away. I'm trying to read."

"You're literally sitting outside my room."

"Then go somewhere else. I would like to read my book in peace, in the space that feels the most comfortable."

"Well, you have thirty minutes to do that."

"Thirty minutes?"

"I'm not going to let you get out of this—"

"She's not my girlfriend."

"Yeah, but this is your house and I am your friend. So I'm asking you to be with me during this troubled time."

"You are the biggest pain in my ass."

"Yeah, but I'm worth it."

"Jury's out on that one, man. Now really, go away. I'll come down when you need me to."

Nur opens his mouth to continue but decides to leave it at that, heading to the living room, where he reaches for his laptop. He goes to Netflix, phone in hand, checking it every so often, but there's nothing from Yasmina. He starts tapping his feet against the table, drumming his fingers on his chest.

Rahat shouts from upstairs, telling Nur they're outside, and then there's the sound of the doorbell, Rahat walking down, poking his head in to ask if he should open the door, and before Nur can say no, Rahat is already doing it, saying hello to Yasmina, who says hello back, slightly surprised. She asks if Nur is in, and Rahat replies in the affirmative, the sounds of many feet shuffling into the house peppering the air. Nur stands from the sofa, and it's as though he is a groom at a wedding, waiting for his bride to walk in, and he tries not to laugh at the irony, until suddenly Yasmina is there, and so are her parents, and he notices that she looks more like her mother than her father, same slant of the jaw, same shaped eyes, their skin the same shade, like dark mahogany. Her father is lighter, his eyes smaller, cheeks lower. And there is Hawa, a smaller, slighter version of Yasmina. A whole family he has only heard of but never seen, and now it feels horribly real.

"Salaam," he says, instantly regretting the word choice, should have just said hello instead, and he walks forward, hand stretched out. Yasmina's father takes it in a strong grip, taller than Nur, and they shake twice, and Nur offers his hand to her mother, who smiles at him as she shakes it, and a little bit of that nervous energy dissipates.

"Sit," Yasmina instructs, directing the three of them to sit on one sofa, Yasmina settling into the other one, leaving Nur standing in the middle of the room, as if he's about to give a speech, and Yasmina looks at him, eyes slightly narrowed. "Do you want to sit down?" she asks.

"Yes," he says, and he moves next to her on the sofa.

She turns to her parents. "So, this is Nur," she starts. "And these are my parents, Ibrahim and Hiba, and my sister, Hawa."

Nur lifts a hand to wave at them, disregarding the fact that he's already shaken their hands, and immediately feels like an idiot. A smile twitches on Hawa's face, and he wonders if she's enjoying herself, watching her sister's boyfriend make such a fool of himself.

"We've heard a few things about you, Nur," Hiba says.

"Well, not a lot," her father adds. "Only enough to know you're Muslim too."

"Yes," Nur responds, and he sees Rahat standing just outside the door, looking in, clearly amused, and Nur wants to yell, *Either go away or come in*. "My parents are from Pakistan. Well, no, my dad is from Pakistan. He married my mum, who was born here, and then he moved to England and they had me and my sister and my brother. We sometimes go back to Pakistan. I think the last time I went was like three years ago. Not that I don't like going. It's nice going back, it just gets really hot." He's viscerally aware that he's talking too much and, at the same time, not really saying anything of substance, but his mouth is working overtime, and it's only when Rahat turns away from the door, hand over his mouth to stop himself from laughing aloud, that Nur stops.

"That's pretty good," Ibrahim says. "That your family goes back. We haven't been to Sudan in years. Yasmina and Hawa don't like the heat either."

"It's not that I don't like the heat," Yasmina explains. "It's fine for, like, a day or so. But four weeks of it is a bit much."

"Both our families are from there," Hiba says. "We actually lived really close to each other, when we were children, but we had no idea. And then years later, we met each other through a family friend."

"Then we found out we'd actually worked in the same place a couple of years earlier. She was a doctor in training there. I'd just started working for the hospital's foundation, as a lawyer, just making sure everything was going as well as it should."

"We never knew! We probably passed each other a few times in that hospital." Yasmina's mother says, her hand over his, squeezing a little.

"More than a few times," he says.

"A love story for the ages," Yasmina says, a big smile on her face, and Nur wants to move closer to her, put a hand on her leg, bask in her family's happiness. But he stays put, unsure if he can be that close to her, what the rules are.

"So you met Yasmina when she moved here?" Hiba continues.

Nur nods. "A friend of ours introduced us," he says, looking at Yasmina. "And we hit it off from there."

"You've been dating since?" Ibrahim asks.

Nur feels something in his throat. "Yes," he says. "I think your daughter is a brilliant person." He nearly flinches, hates using such clichés, but he can't think of anything better to say. "She's incredible."

"We like to think so too," Hiba says, and she gives off a welcome air, lets Nur think that maybe he is nervous for no reason. "How old are your brother and sister?"

"Khalil is two years younger than me, Mariam four years."

"Planned," she notes, just like Yasmina.

Nur laughs, too hard, too loud. "I think that's what Mum wants everyone to think." He worries that he has just made that joke about his parents.

"He always wanted a son," Hiba says.

"I did not—"

"But he got two girls instead—"

"Who I'm very happy with," her father says, and he's smiling as he talks, but Nur knows what has happened behind the scenes, and it's odd, picking up such intimate details about people whom he has never met before.

"Of course you are," Yasmina chimes in. "Hawa and I are perfect."

Nur glances at Hawa, who hasn't spoken yet. She is looking out the window, into the world beyond it, and Nur wonders what is going through her mind, if she wants to be there; he wonders what Mariam and Khalil would be like if they had to do this, if they had to meet Yasmina.

"Never said you weren't," her father says. He looks back to Nur. "Yasmina tells us you want to be a writer."

Nur's stomach twists. "At some point," he says, going for the easy answer, but he remembers Yasmina telling him that her parents have always been the ones with the plan, one foot always in the future. "Writing has always been important to me. It's the one thing I've always wanted to do."

"You know it's hard to make happen," Hiba says, and though there is no disapproval in her tone, Nur can't help but read into it, is back with his own parents, listening to his father tell him an English degree wasn't good enough. "You have to work pretty hard to succeed."

"Mum . . . ," Yasmina begins.

"I will," Nur says, and he is aware that, somewhere underneath her words, a different conversation is happening. "I know it's tough to make work, not everyone reaches the dizzy heights of Zadie Smith, but I'll keep trying. The only way to make sure I never get there is to never try."

Hiba smiles at him. "Exactly," she says.

"So shall we go eat something?" Ibrahim asks. "The drive was pretty long and I don't know about everyone else, but I'm hungry."

"Yeah, sure," Nur says. "Where shall we go?" He directs the question at Yasmina.

"There's a Nando's," she suggests. "Halal?"

"Perfect," her father declares, standing, and they all follow him, Nur glad to move out of the house, Yasmina reaching for his hand, squeezing it, reassuring him.

On the way to Nando's, Nur finds that he feels a little looser out of the house. He tells them about his home, where his parents live in Birmingham, and when Ibrahim asks why he came here for university, Nur explains that the course he's doing is meant to be one of the best for English.

"Were you scared of leaving home?" Hiba asks.

"Not really," Nur says. "My parents never wanted me to leave home but I knew I had to, for myself. I've learned so much here. The boring things, like how to wash my own clothes, manage my money, make my own food."

"Being away from your family you can learn more about who you are," Hiba says, voice a little distant. "When I left Sudan, my parents thought I was crazy. 'There are hospitals here.' That's what they said when I told them. Why couldn't I just be a doctor in Sudan? It would have been easier, so much easier. I'd never been here before, didn't know anyone here. But I also knew I'd have spent the rest of my life wondering what might have happened."

"I think you made the right choice," Yasmina says, leaning into her mother, arm hooked around hers.

Hiba smiles, knocks her head against Yasmina's. "Me too," she says.

"And me," Nur says, and for a second, no one says anything and he thinks he's misjudged the situation, he doesn't know them well enough to make this joke, but then Ibrahim laughs, Hiba and Yasmina joining in, Hawa stretching her lips a little.

When they get to the restaurant, Nur is openly mocked for only having medium heat on his chicken, though he argues there's no difference between medium and hot. They talk a little about Yas-mina and her master's, she reiterates that she wants to do a PhD researching journalistic ethics, to focus more on the bigger picture, and her father says it would be great to have another doctor in the family, and then, he says, reaching over to Hawa, Hawa will follow her mother and become one too, a real doctor. Hawa frowns at him, tells him she doesn't want to be a doctor, and Nur gives her a knowing smile, remembers having the same conversation with his own father before he went to college, his father telling him he needed to pick for his future, for his career, Nur telling him he didn't want to pick a career just for the sake of money. How he had realized then how different their worlds were, wondering if he was ever going to bridge that gap, and he tells them this now, joking at first, but Ibrahim tells him Nur's father was speaking from a place of worry, of care, that all parents do. But if Nur knew what he wanted to do, then his father should trust him, trust that the son he raised knows how to make the right choices, just how Ibrahim knows his daughters will, and as he speaks, it is like Nur is listening to an old family friend talk, someone he has known for years, and this all feels so easy, so simple, like Yasmina's family have already carved out a space for him.

November 2017

Nur holds the bag in one hand, knocks on the door with the other. He hears footsteps from the other side, and Ramy greets him, wearing a tight T-shirt, his arms bulging out of the sleeves, the outline of his chest visible through the jersey material, prompting Nur to compare it to his own soft body.

"Hey, man," Ramy says, holding an arm out to Nur, and they embrace each other, and Nur notices that Ramy smells good, like he's just showered.

"I'm not too early, right?" he asks, offering the bag to Ramy.

"No, Rahat is already here. And Yasmina?"

"She's coming later. She's coming from home. Like, home-home, from her parents'."

"Ah," Ramy replies, and he stands to the side, lets Nur step into their flat, two bedrooms, a balcony, much larger than the one Nur and Yasmina have. Nur remembers when Imran showed him the listing, that small spark of jealousy, of wanting what Imran has.

Ramy leads him down the hallway, into a room where Rahat sits on a sofa, rising when Nur walks in to give him a hug. "It's been a while," Nur says, suddenly realizing how long ago he last saw his friend.

"Well, people are busy, I guess," Rahat says, and he sits back down, Nur next to him, wanting to ask what that means. But he senses that the question could lead to some awkwardness, and the last thing he wants to do right now is make today about him and Rahat.

Ramy takes a spot on the opposite sofa, and then there's a shout, Nur looking to Imran by the door, massive grin on his face, and Nur gets up once more, Imran running to him, his body slamming into Nur's. They saw each other a few weeks ago, but Nur has missed his friend sorely, and they stay like that, seconds passing, only separating when Ramy says something about whether he should be worried his boyfriend is cheating on him with his best friend.

"Welcome to Casa de Imran."

"Don't ever say that again," Nur says. "Nice place, though. Big place. Maybe too big."

"Why go small when you can go ridiculously huge?" Imran jokes. "Yasmina?"

"She'll be here soon. She's coming from Manchester."

Imran nods and gestures behind him. "Want the grand tour?" he asks.

"Hell yeah." Nur looks back at Rahat, who shakes his head.

"I've already had mine," Rahat offers, his voice a little flat.

"Just you and me, then," Imran says, and he bounces away, light on his feet, leading Nur. "So this is our room," he announces, and he steps into a bedroom, filled with a bed, two wardrobes, a desk, a TV stand complete with TV, and Nur is about to remark on the lavishness of it all when Imran closes the door and turns to him, voice dropping down to a whisper.

"I have to tell you something."

"What is it?" Nur asks, afraid to hear the answer but wanting to know what has happened.

"I went home yesterday," Imran says, and Nur's chest tightens. Nur hasn't asked him about the planned visit, has been waiting for Imran to tell him what happened. "My dad was there. I didn't think he would be. But there he was." Imran talks fast. "He told me to sit down, and Mum told me it was fine, that it was okay, so I sat and we started talking. He asked how I was, and I said okay, told him I got promoted, and he seemed happy about that. I guess every parent is proud when their child gets promoted. Unless you really hate them. I thought that was all he wanted to talk about, but then his face changed, and he said that his cousin from Pakistan had gotten in contact with them, asked if I wanted to marry their daughter."

"What?" Nur says. "I thought your parents were against the whole marrying-your-cousin thing?"

"I don't know," Imran says. "I guess they're against the idea of being forced into it. Or maybe they felt like they had to offer it to me because . . . I don't know. But I listened to him talk—honestly I didn't really know what else to do—and he went on about how she was intelligent, that she'd studied at university there, that she knew English, that she wanted to come live here, and she was looking for someone to help her do that. And then he just asked me, straight up, if I wanted to marry her."

Imran pauses, and Nur's brain starts to catch up. "He asked you to marry her, to get her to the UK? That's it?"

"Well, yeah. And then stay married to her, live in the same house, though she could do what she wants and I could do what 'I want.'"

"Why would she . . ." Nur realizes what Imran is skirting around, the pieces fitting together. "She's gay too?"

Imran lets out a laugh. "According to Dad. He said her parents hadn't caught her with anyone, but they knew she was. Probably the same feeling my parents had with me. She wants to come and live here. And apparently, she's never been an easy child. Too loud, too smart, too whatever. So, to save face, they want to send her here, marry someone, so if anyone ever asks about her, they can say she's married and living here. Like disowning her without actually disowning her."

"And your parents can tell people the same thing," Nur says. "Do you want to do that?"

Imran avoids the question. "My supposedly super-liberal parents, the ones who vote for Labour, who get into arguments at Eid about free education, higher taxes, corrupt governments, offered me a beard. And not just a beard but, like, the ultimate beard. A lifetime beard. If they had done this before Ramy, I actually might have taken it. A chance for me to see them again, to be the son they wanted. Get that life back. But as my dad talked, all I could think about was Ramy, the life we have together. Even if I was allowed to stay here in our house, if she just moved in with us and did her own thing, we were nothing but roommates, it would still feel wrong. Can you imagine? Having to keep Ramy away from all of that, telling him to stay here, telling him to be the boyfriend who stays at home while I go be the child my parents want me to be?" Imran scoffs, shakes his head. "Not a chance."

Nur nearly flinches at his words, but reminds himself that this isn't about him. "You said no?"

"I said no," Imran announces, and he grins, wide. Nur almost can't believe this is the same boy from university, the boy who joked too much, who never took anything seriously. "I told them that I'd spent way too long being the person they wanted me to be, going against myself. And I love them. I love them more than words can describe. But am I going to give up myself for them? I can't. I have to be true to who I am. This is who I am."

"And?"

"My dad told me he had prayed to Allah, that he had asked for advice, from God, from friends, from family, and that he knew this was the answer he was going to get, and he would work on being okay with that. He said it was his last chance, the last thing he was going to offer me before accepting who I am."

Nur laughs, doesn't mean to, but the sound escapes him, and before Imran can say anything, he hugs him, quick this time. "I'm so fucking proud of you." Imran opens his mouth to speak, and Nur can tell what he's about to say. "No, I mean it," he adds, cutting him off. "You're one of the bravest people I know. And I want you to know that. You're incredible."

"Nur—"

"I mean it," Nur says, and he does mean it, a rush of love for his friend, so strong it makes him want to cry. "You're an amazing person. Someone should tell you that all the time."

"You're going to make me cry," Imran says, lightly punching Nur's arm. "You're the same. All those things you think you aren't, all those things the voice in the back of your mind tells you you're not, you are. Really, Nur."

"Now you're going to make me cry," Nur says, laughing, and he looks at him. "I'm really happy for you, Imran."

Imran lets out a breath, is about to say something when the sound of the front door opening runs through the flat, Yasmina's voice filling the air. "I think we should head back," Imran says, opening the door, and they walk out to see her head into the living room. Nur calls her name, and Yasmina turns, Imran sliding between them to hug her first.

"Is this it?" Nur asks. "No one else?"

"This is it," Imran confirms, and he glances at Ramy, something passing between them.

"Are you going to take me on a tour?" Yasmina asks, and Imran looks at Nur, sighing.

"I literally just took him," he replies, as if it is a great ordeal. But then a familiar smirk appears, and he reaches out his hand to her, and she takes it, heading off with him, leaving the three of them in the room.

"When did you get here?" Nur asks Rahat, just as Ramy pulls out his phone, answering a call, an apologetic look on his face as he walks out.

Rahat doesn't look at Nur as he answers. "Not long ago," he says.

Nur waits for more, but when more doesn't come, he looks around the room, at the shelves in the corner, a photograph from when they were at university, of Nur and Imran standing at a party, a few other people in the background whose hazy shapes he recognizes, and he smiles at the memory of it. There are other photos too, of Imran and Ramy, of Imran and his parents at graduation, of Imran and Yasmina, which Nur knows better than the others, because he was the one who took it.

"I have something to tell you," Rahat says, and Nur's eyes move back to him. "I . . ." He hesitates.

"Is it your parents?" Nur asks, immediately assuming the worst.

"No, no," Rahat says. "I . . . I met someone."

"What?"

"I met someone," he says again, and he lets out a small laugh. "Well, probably not the way you think. My parents, they asked if I wanted to meet some girls they knew. They first suggested it right after uni, and I said no, but then they asked me again earlier this year, and . . . it's not like I date, not like you or Imran. I can't find people the way you do. I don't . . ." Rahat pauses, fiddling with the fabric of the sofa. "I can't do that. And that's not, like, me saying what you and Imran are doing is wrong, because you know I don't think that."

"You don't have to—"

"So anyway," Rahat cuts him off. "They took me to a few houses, and I met some girls, and there were two who I thought were great. I went on dates with them, like chaperoned dates at their houses, and I really clicked with one of them. We get along so well. We've been talking for maybe three or four months now. And her parents like me, my parents like her. It might happen."

"You're . . . you're getting married?" Nur is cold with shock.

"Maybe." Rahat laughs, this small sound. "I like her. She makes me finally understand everything that I've read about. All the films, the music."

"Why didn't you tell me?" Nur hates that this is his question. That instead of feeling happy for his friend, he is confused.

"I didn't know how to."

"What does that mean?"

Rahat bites his lip. "I think . . ." He takes a breath. "I think sometimes you can be a bit self-involved." Nur holds his tongue, eyes flickering to the wall. "Like, you never asked me about dating or if I'm meeting people in Birmingham. And I'm not, but we never really talked about it. And when my parents asked me, I didn't want to tell you because . . . I knew you would say that it was dumb and backward . . . But, I don't think those things. When I met those girls, they were the same as me. They wanted to meet someone and didn't want to date around. There's nothing wrong with that . . ."

"I know," Nur says.

"But the way you talk about it, Nur, you make it sound like it's the worst thing in the world. To be set up by your parents, to live near your parents, to live *that* life. But it's not. It's actually a nice life, and I can see it for myself now, I can see myself living like that. It's not something I want to be ashamed of or feel judged for."

"Rahat," Nur says, standing, moving over to the sofa Rahat is on, sitting by him. "I'm sorry." Rahat keeps his eyes forward, hands still clutching the sofa. "I don't think that life is wrong or shameful. If that's what you want to do, then you should do it and I'm here for you, like you've been there for me." Shame pulls at him. "I'm sorry you didn't feel like you could come and talk to me about it. I should have been a better friend."

"You're not a bad friend," Rahat says. "Just . . ."

"Not a great one," Nur says, saying it for him. "Who is she? Can I meet her?"

Rahat shifts a little, releasing his grip on the cushions, the tension leaving his body. "Her name is Saliha," he says. "She actually went to our school, two years below us, but I don't remember her. She claims to remember us vaguely."

"And she's the one?"

Rahat half laughs. "Yeah," he says, just as Ramy comes back in, and he straightens, sitting up, and Nur knows this isn't the time to talk about it more, but he tells himself he will later.

Imran and Yasmina return, and the five of them order food, Imran forcing them all to eat gyros, his favorite. They sit and talk, Imran boasting about his promotion at work, which means he now has someone under him, the idea of that, Imran a manager; Yasmina saying she doesn't want to discuss her PhD before proceeding to talk about her PhD; Ramy announcing his plans to turn the second bedroom into a gym, Imran vetoing the idea before it's even out of Ramy's mouth; Rahat admitting he wants to leave his job, about being underpaid and undervalued; Nur confiding that he's started writing a book, that it's time now to leave short stories behind.

When the night turns cold and hard, the three of them leave, bidding Ramy and Imran goodbye, and hurry to the train station, eager to get back to their own homes. Nur tells Rahat he'll call him, hugging him just a fraction longer than he normally would, and his shame lessens, but a small part lingers, reminding him to be better.

February 2019

Nur wakes up alone.

Before, alone has only ever been temporary. A weekend here, an Eid there, a birthday party, a funeral. It has always come to an end. Yasmina returns, or he comes back, and it feels like a home again.

But now there is no waiting for Yasmina to return. He doesn't know if she'll ever come back.

He spent the night checking his phone to see if she'd said anything, but there was nothing, paralleling the other times they've fought. He typed his own messages, deleting and typing, deleting and typing, and he felt like he was losing his mind, splitting into different versions of himself, all of them existing at the same time, lying on that one bed, typing out different messages to her, so many voices crammed into his head.

After the alarm, he picks up his phone again to call in sick, a text sent to his boss, who tells him to get better, and he lies there, looking up at his ceiling because he can't look over to her side of the bed. Eventually, he finally gets up, stands under the shower, replaying last night in his head. Like a detective in an expensive TV show, he watches everything, trying to spot the cracks, where things began to fall apart. But he can't see anything, can't locate the answers.

He experiences a wave of rage, the kind of anger that could level a city, and it doesn't have any specificity, only that he feels so angry he might explode.

He is too angry to eat, too angry to sit, too angry to be.

What is she doing right now? What is she telling her parents? Are they telling her she has done the right thing?

Suddenly being in the flat makes him feel sick. He slams the window open, winter air coming in, but it isn't enough, his skin still unbearable, he needs to get out. He puts his shoes on, fingers fumbling over shoelaces, reaches for his phone and keys, walks out of the apartment, and he strides, unsure of where he's going. She is everywhere, the place outside their home, where he last saw her, disappearing into her parents' car, and he walks past that, turns the corner, shivering a little as he moves. He's forgotten to pull his coat on, but he can't bring himself to go back to the flat, to the space they shared together, the bed he slept in last night alone, so he forces himself onward, hands firmly shoved into his pockets.

All he sees is her face, standing by the car, anger in her eyes. Why didn't he do anything? Why didn't he say anything four years ago? Why did he always always always stay silent, keep quiet, let the thoughts stay in his head instead of letting them out? He is angry with himself, so angry it coats his throat, bitterness on his tongue, and he doesn't know where to go, doesn't know who to call, doesn't know what to do, but his feet keep moving.

He understands, on some level, that he shouldn't be alone right now, that he needs to be with someone, that he doesn't trust himself to be on his own. But he doesn't want to call anyone. Telling Imran what happened, what his mother said, the fight . . . But Imran wouldn't get it, doesn't know his family.

His gut spasms and his eyes fill. Nur wipes them with his sleeve.

He tastes that first kiss with her, feverish with joy when he walked away, unable to think about anything else for the rest of the day; when they first slept in the same bed, at his, how she fell asleep before he did, her breathing becoming deeper, heavier, and he watched her, smelled her the night after, held the pillow she'd slept on to remind his body of her; when he saw her that first summer after spending so long apart, how her presence washed over him like a warm shower after a cold day. Him in their kitchen, teaching her how to cook the things his mother made in his childhood; him watching her get ready after a shower, lining her face with makeup, asking about her outfits even though it's clear she already knows which one she wants. All these moments that make them up, crashing into one another, leading up to this one moment, always leading here.

Did he even have a chance?

He hears the horn of a car, and he looks up, then remembers where he is, who he is, and he stops, feet still, breathes, icy air in his lungs. In front of him is the cinema, *their* cinema, where he had tried to surprise her when they moved to Nottingham, but she was one step ahead of him like always. Evenings spent here, expensive tickets, films he hasn't heard of, Yasmina hushing him when they're watching because she doesn't like the interruption. He fights to keep the tears back, swallows his grief, swallows himself.

His phone rings, vibrating against his leg, and he reaches for it, hoping against hope that it's her, that she wants to speak to him, but the name that flashes up on the screen brings searing disappointment.

"It's not—" he starts, but that's all he gets to say before he's interrupted.

"Shut up," Mariam says, and she delivers it neither nicely or angrily. She sounds weary. "Just please shut up for a second. Are you okay?"

"I'm fine," Nur replies.

"Well, I'm glad to know because you didn't say anything last night. To any of us. Have you seen any of our texts?"

Nur lowers his phone, takes a look, sees messages from Mariam, Khalil, Imran. "I didn't—"

"You've scared the fuck out of us, Nur," she says. He hears the sound of a door being closed. "Mum has been up all night. When you left . . . She came downstairs, asked where you were. We told her you'd already gone, and then suddenly, Nani was here—"

"What? Why?"

"Mum asked her to come. She told her everything."

"She told Nani—"

"Wait!" Mariam exclaims. "Just wait. She told Nani everything and Nani listened, didn't say anything. When mum was done, she asked me and Khalil what we thought. We told her Yasmina was right for you, that we'd known about the two of you, you told us a couple of years ago, that you wanted to be confident in the relationship before telling Mum and Dad."

"And?" Nur pushes, eager for Mariam to arrive at her point.

"She told mum that as long as Yasmina is Muslim, that is what is important. That things are different in the UK today, not like when they first moved here. She trusts you to make the right choice." Nur's body stops. He can't breathe, can't see. "She said that's all that matters to her. Mum pressed about culture, about children, about Eid, even about the wedding, but Nani said none of that mattered, not really. That we can work on that stuff. All that matters is making sure that Yasmina is the right person for you, and she sounds like she is."

Nur holds back the wobble in his voice. "I . . ." He tries to find the words. "I always thought Nani would—"

"Be the one to say no?" Mariam asks. "I thought so too. Older people, right? But she's honestly just happy that you had found someone." She lets out a little laugh. "She asked when she could meet Yasmina and then snapped at Mum for not inviting her last night."

"Might have been a bit much to have her there too the first time."

"Maybe," Mariam says. "You should call Mum. She's really worried about you. After Nani left, she didn't sleep until the morning."

Nur kicks at the gravel, stones loose. "What she said last night—"

"She didn't mean it, Nur."

"Yeah, she did. And Dad too. When he asked me if I was sure I wanted to marry Yasmina—"

Mariam stops him. "Because you lied to them. You lied to them for four years, Nur."

"I didn't . . . I was worried that they would—"

"Don't you think it would have been easier if you told them before? Gave them time? Talked about it?"

"Sure," Nur says, "but are you telling me they wouldn't have had the same reaction they did last night?"

"I'm saying we don't know that, but you didn't give them the chance to prove themselves," Mariam says. She stops, hesitating. "You assumed the worst of them, Nur. I don't know what else they were meant to do."

"They were meant to trust me," Nur says, his words sharp.

"And that's probably what they'd say about you too. That you were meant to trust them, that you were meant to be honest with them."

Nur searches for a response, finds this conversation reverting to the same points. "It doesn't matter anyway," he says. "I don't even know if there's going to be a me and Yasmina anymore."

"What? Nur, what do you mean? What happened?" Mariam asks quietly.

"It means that I fucked everything up." The words spill out of him. "She went home with her parents last night. I don't know if she's coming back."

"Why wouldn't she come back? After all this?" Confrontation in her voice, an unspoken accusation buried in her words.

"Because . . ." He doesn't want to say it. "Because it was me, this entire time. I told her . . . I told her she couldn't meet you guys because I was worried what Mum and Dad might say, that I was keeping her safe, that I was protecting her. And I . . ." He wants to stop speaking, keep the words in, keep the truth in. "I was protecting myself. I was being selfish. I wanted to be with her but I was terrified of speaking to Mum and Dad, scared of disappointing them. I built up this . . . this thing in my head. I thought . . . I thought I could control, it would be better if I . . . And then last night, she saw us all getting along, joking with her parents, and that worry, that fear she'd been holding in her . . . She realized I was lying. It was because of me. I did this to her." Her leaving, an empty bed. His fault. It was all his fault.

"Nur, you need to fix this." Mariam's voice is hard. "You can't . . . You can't do this to us and then nothing happens. You can't build this bridge for nothing."

"I will—"

"No, Nur," she says. "No. Don't just say you will. You need to go after her. No more hiding, no more thinking that avoiding or lying is the best way forward. You are going to go fix this. Because she's worth it." Mariam lets out a sigh. "I really like her, Nur. Don't let yourself fuck this up."

Nur takes in a shaky breath. "Okay," he says.

"We're always here for you, Nur. Even if you don't think we are. I hope you realize that by now."

"I know," Nur says. "I'll tell you what happens."

They both hang on a little longer, neither of them putting the phone down, and then Mariam is gone, the noise of the world returning, the crunch of tires on gravel, people talking, a bike bell ringing.

He slips the phone back into his pocket. He wipes the tears from his eyes, starts walking, and this time he knows exactly where he's going.

He's not going to let her go, not this easily, not after all this time.

December 2017

Nur sits packed into the back of the car, Mariam next to him, his father on the other side, his mother and Nani at the front.

A couple of weeks ago, Nur called his mother, announcing he would come to Sabah's wedding after all. He'd felt bad about the way he'd spoken to her about it, told himself it wouldn't be that bad if he went. The joy in her voice was palpable, hope spilling over, because to her, this was Nur choosing to be part of their community.

He chose a sherwani for the wedding, a little ostentatious, he thought, but he knew his mother would love it. Gold on red, a gift from his uncle the last time he'd gone to Pakistan, and when he slipped it on, part of him was still surprised to find that it fit.

"I wish you could come," he said the night before he had to leave for Birmingham. Yasmina went still, and he realized his blunder, trying to spin his words, change the meaning. "I just mean—"

"I know what you mean." She flipped over, back turned to him, and he said nothing, adjusting the pillow under his head, pretending to drift off soundly.

His mother parks the car at the wedding venue and turns the engine off, each family member adjusting their clothing, making sure everything is perfect. And then Nani opens the door, and they follow her lead, stepping out. Nur turns his head to his sister and is caught off guard again by the way she looks. This morning, as he gave himself a final look in the hallway mirror, ignoring Khalil complaining that they were making too much noise, he saw her step out of her room, shalwar kameez, makeup, hair straightened, long and shiny. She looked so grown up, a woman, not a girl, and Nur felt a mourning for who she was, for who she had been, for how much of her life he was missing.

Nani reaches for Nur, holds on to his arm. "I don't know why she had to get married in the winter," she whispers, hooking her arm through his. "It's no fun. Where is the sun, the heat, the long days spent dancing into the night? That's what I want."

"There's something nice about a winter wedding," Nur replies. "Cold outside, warm inside."

"I'd rather just be warm all the time," she says, and he laughs, knows he won't get anywhere with her.

They join the line of people inside, everyone dressed beautifully, women in colors that leap from their skins, men more muted. And the sound of life hits them as they enter the hall, the chatter of hundreds of voices, children laughing and running around, music blaring from speakers.

Nani lets go of Nur's arm the second they're in the heat, spotting one of her old friends, hurrying over to reminisce about times long past, to gossip about who is marrying whom, which child is disappointing their parents, which new babies have been born. Nur is always taken by how many people Nani knows, how she manages to keep so much information about their lives in her head.

"Tell me you're not going to run up on the stage," Mariam says, joining him.

He looks at her, confused. "What?"

"To take Sabah back," she explains. "You know, the two of you, Romeo and Juliet." He groans at her. "I'm just saying, everyone thought the two of you were going to get it on, and now you're here and she's marrying another man. It must break your heart."

"Please never repeat that sentence ever again," Nur says, laughing at his sister's theatrics. But the words bring to mind being younger, him and Sabah playing with each other, always returning to each other at events like this—weddings, funerals, Eid—and he can't remember why, can't remember the first time he ever spoke to her. It's like she was always there. And then suddenly, one day, she wasn't, her family moving away, and he moved on and so did she, established their own lives without each other.

They move down the line, Nur's parents joining them, and when they reach the end, Nani suddenly reappears. Nur's father gives money to the man waiting for them, an older relative, seated by the entrance, and the man writes down his father's name, how much money he has given, and who he is here with, and when he is done, they walk into the wedding hall.

Nur looks across at the stage as he walks in, where Sabah is sitting on a white sofa, hands folded on her lap. There are pillars behind her, a red curtain hanging between them. She looks different from the image he has held of her in his mind, of the girl she used to be, toothy smile, huge eyes, fringe. Now her face is sleek, sharp, eyes still big, ringed with eyeliner, her red lehenga sparkling as the light catches the fake jewels embedded in the cloth.

She doesn't notice him, too many people crammed into this hall for her to see one single person, and he imagines she has other things on her mind than keeping an eye out for him. His family finds a table to sit at across the hall, and Nur is struck with a sudden urge to rush the stage, take the seat next to Sabah, which is empty right now, and ask her how this happened, who this man is she is getting married to, why she is marrying so young, doesn't she have a life she wants to live, but he recognizes that these questions are disingenuous, that they mean nothing, that they are the excuses he has in his own mind for not wanting to get married so quickly.

"Nur," Nani directs, offering a chair next to her, and Nur takes it, the five of them at an eight-person table, empty dishes laid out in front of them.

"I wonder how much they spent on this," his mother says, picking up the fork in front of her, sleek steel, shining in the light. "Seems like quite a bit."

"Their only daughter," Nani says.

"Their only daughter," Nur's father echoes, nudging Mariam, who sits by him, the only member of their family openly eating.

"Of course they didn't spare a single expense. What father would hold back from doing everything he can for his only daughter?"

Mariam waves a fork at him. "Whatever you're thinking, let it go. I'm not getting married anytime soon."

"Oh, you don't have to get married this year or next year. Not even the year after that. But one day, when you do get married, I'm going to spend every penny I have. Sell the cars, sell the house, sell everything. And I'll go up to the rooftops, sing to the heavens about my daughter. Oh, my daughter! Finally, marriage! Finally, happiness!"

"Dad," Mariam says, and she laughs at him. "You're so embarrassing."

"Only when you're this young," Nani says, and she looks a little wistful. "But when you grow up, you'll miss the attention. Don't turn it away so quickly."

"I wish Khalil could have come." Nur's mother sighs. "It would have been nice for him to be here with us, to see everyone."

"Oh, he'd definitely love this." Mariam gestures to the napkins, which have been folded in an overly intricate way, unnecessary for an item that will be used once and thrown away.

"I don't know why he loves weddings so much," Nur says.

"I think he just loves . . . love," Mariam says with a small shrug, but there is something underneath her voice, a yearning, and Nur thinks of her not as his sister but as a woman in her own right, recalls himself at that age, four years ago, fresh into university and dating Saara. He sees Mariam as a real person, with wants and desires and urges. As someone who might be dating already, who might be someone else's partner, someone's Yasmina.

"Go say hello to Sabah," Nur's mother suggests, lightly hitting Nur's hand with a fork. "It would be nice if she saw you were here."

"I don't know about that—"

"Stop being such a grump, Nur," Mariam says. "Go say congratulations."

He looks to the stage again, where Sabah remains by herself, a photo, unmoving. "Maybe," he says.

"Go," Nani says, and she pushes him, a nudge on his arm to get up.

Nur stands, feels a rush of adrenaline, as though he has just put a target on his back, expecting every person in the hall to turn to him. He maneuvers around the table, back to the entrance, stopping there for a moment. He grits his teeth, tells himself he's being stupid, what does he have to be scared of, all he has to do is say hello, comment on how beautiful she looks, on how happy he is for her. That's it. Nothing else.

Someone brushes past him, a cousin, older than him, whom he vaguely recognizes. Nur and Sabah sitting on a wall outside, younger, at another wedding, legs swinging, talking about something, spotting this older cousin and a girl walking toward the back of the hall, how they'd followed them, peeked around the corner, watched as the pair kissed, tentative, their bodies hesitant, laughing quietly, not loud enough to get caught, and how they didn't talk about it afterward, neither one of them able to bring it up, Nur stuck thinking about the way their older cousin had held the girl, one hand on the side of her waist, the other at the back of her neck, imagining himself there, kissing someone, the feel of it.

He approaches the stage, fighting his fear, and climbs it, Sabah turning to him, finally moving, confusion on her face giving way to surprise, her eyes going wide. "Nur."

"You're getting married!" he says, the only thing he can think to say, and she lets out a small laugh. Nur settles down by her on the sofa, not caring what the rest of the hall must be thinking, not caring that somewhere there is a man who is supposed to be sitting here with her, who is going to spend the rest of his life with her, and how people must be talking about Nur and Sabah in comparison. Remembering that they used to spend all their time together as kids: We were convinced they were going to get married, do you think he's come back to profess his love for her, how dramatic, on her wedding day. "How are you feeling? Are you terrified? Who is he?"

Sabah laughs. "Ah, it's so nice to see you, but that's a lot of questions," she says. "Let's see. He, Adeeb, is a friend of a friend. And I'm nervous, obviously, you have no idea how much time my parents put into planning this. But I'm really happy. Which is weird to admit, I think."

"I don't think that's weird," he says. "You're allowed to be happy on your wedding day."

"Maybe," she says, and she smiles, wide, that same smile recognizable from when she was little, a sign she hasn't changed. "God, how long has it been?"

"Years," Nur admits, shameful that he's never followed up with her, that he hasn't made the effort. "Years and years. I went to university."

"So did I."

"I went away, to Bradford."

"Really?" she asks.

"I know. Bit wild." Nur chuckles, self-deprecating but clearly proud. "I actually don't live with my parents anymore."

"Now that's wild," Sabah says.

"I got a job in Nottingham," Nur explains, this half-truth sliding easily into their conversation, one he has been telling for almost half a year. But Yasmina's face comes to mind, of waking up to her every day, of her reading, writing, studying, of their life together. How he chose her and is terrified, absolutely terrified, of how precious their world is.

"I'll be moving out when this is all over too," Sabah says, fingers on her bangles. "I'll be moving in with Adeeb. He's worked all his life, through college and university, and saved up for this, for a home. So instead of living with his parents, we're going to buy a house." She says it like she's still getting accustomed to the idea, can't quite believe she's saying it.

"Wow," Nur says. "You're such a grown-up now." The idea seems ridiculous to Nur, that Sabah, the girl he knew, a year older than him, is going to be married, a wife to a husband, maybe a mother one day, that she will live inside a house that she and her husband own together, that she will be a whole person.

She shakes her head. "Don't say that. It's surreal. I feel like yesterday, I was at school, watching all our cousins getting married, feeling like such a kid. I couldn't imagine doing it. And then suddenly, this guy comes out of nowhere after I graduate, and I like him. *Really* like him. And that's it, that's all it takes. I want to be with him forever, I want to have children and build a life with him. It's so strange, to not know what you want and then suddenly know exactly what you want. Right down to the last detail."

Nur knows exactly what she means. It's the same thing he felt when he sat with Yasmina in that restaurant booth, when he walked her home that first night. It was all set, they were never making choices, not really.

"Sorry," Sabah says. "I'm just a little—"

"Don't apologize," Nur says, and he almost reaches over to hug her, but he knows not to ruin her look, made aware from his mother how much time has been spent on her clothes and her jewelry and her makeup. "It's your wedding day. You're allowed to feel however you want."

"What about you? Is there anyone?"

He shakes his head. "No, not really."

"Not really or no?" Sabah asks, looking at him with a knowing smile, and he knows she sees the answer written on his face.

"No," he doubles down, grinning. "You know me. I was never really into that."

"Until you are," she says. "I had no idea that I could feel this way until I met Adeeb. And I know how lucky I am—to find someone Pakistani, Muslim, ready to get married. We even know his family from way back. But I know it's harder for other people. I guess . . . we can't pick who we fall in love with. But we can choose to be happy, right?"

Nur can't talk, afraid that if he does, he might spill his life out here, so he looks out at the hall, the world rushing back in, the spotlights on the stage, the camera aimed at them, the roar of people talking, and he processes that everyone is there to celebrate Sabah, to celebrate her and Adeeb's love, and he wonders if he will ever give that to Yasmina.

"Anyway," he says, taking a breath. "I don't want to take up all your time. Plenty of guests left to come see you."

He goes to stand, and she reaches out to him, puts a hand on his arm, stopping him. "You know," she says, "I think about you sometimes. You should come over, when Adeeb and I are settled in. It would be nice to see you again."

A tremor races through Nur, and he nods, smiles. "I will," he says, putting his hand over hers. "Congratulations on finding everything." He winks, her hand slips, and then he is gone, stepping off the stage, back to his family, who have been joined by another family, people he recognizes, and he sits back down.

More food comes out, and the day moves quickly, waiters in white shirts and black trousers placing plate upon plate down, movements practiced, people's fingers quickly getting dirty, tearing into the meat and vegetables, Nur not eating a lot, playing with his food instead. His mind keeps returning to the stage, is so surprisingly glad for Sabah that it overwhelms him, and he is grateful he came, that he is here to see this. When Adeeb comes out, tall and thin, hair slicked back, taking his place by Sabah, Nur feels pleased at the sight of them together, can't help but beam, Mariam spotting him and elbowing him, telling him, oh, so he does like weddings after all.

After dinner the music changes, solemn strings and a low voice, and everyone gets to their feet, a hush taking over the hall, watching Sabah place a veil over her head, hiding her face as she walks down the stage. He moves with his family nearer to her, a mix of mourning and happiness, watching as she hugs person after person, each interaction longer than the last, and all he can think about is Yasmina, about wanting nothing more than to be sitting on that stage with her, everyone they know coming together to celebrate their love.

"That'll be you one day," Nur's father teases Mariam again, receiving a light elbow in response, at which he laughs.

"And that'll be you too," Nur's mother whispers, holding on to his arm as Adeeb takes Sabah and they walk out of the hall, the crowd spilling into the parking lot, watching them climb into his car and drive off.

Maybe, one day, it will be him and Yasmina.

October 2018

Nur wakes to find Yasmina in the living room, laptop propped up on a cushion, reading intensely. He walks in with his cup of tea, sits on the sofa, and waits. She doesn't look up from her laptop until a few minutes have passed, raising her eyebrows at him.

"I didn't say anything."

"You didn't have to," she replies. "I can feel your eyes on me."

"It's a Saturday."

"Yeah."

"Are you really going to spend your Saturday just working?" She opens her mouth, but he interrupts her. "There's only one answer to that question, and it's no. No, you're not going to spend one of two days a week I have with you stuck inside; you're going to let me, your kind, gracious, very good-looking boyfriend, take you out."

"Nur . . . ," she starts.

"No," he says, reaches over, closes her laptop. "You're going to burn out. You have to take a break sometimes."

Her hands twitch in her lap. "Maybe, but . . ."

"No," Nur says, setting her laptop down on the coffee table. "Let's go watch a film, grab some lunch, walk around for a bit. Get out of this flat for a little while."

"There's nothing I want to watch."

Nur laughs in disbelief. "Who are you trying to trick?"

She lets out a sigh, pushes herself up. "Fine. There is a film . . ."

"There's always a film . . ."

"I don't think you're going to like it."

"Is it one of your foreign subtitled films?"

"No," she says, smirking. "It's an American film trying very hard to be one of my foreign subtitled films."

"I don't—" Nur begins, as she walks out of the room. "I don't know what that means!" he shouts to an empty room.

They get ready, Nur downing his tea and grabbing a banana before they leave, shrugging on jackets, the air outside colder now, winter coming. He reaches for her hand as they walk, the sky a hard blue, completely clear. Their cinema, so close to them, comes into view. Nur buys the tickets, pushing her hands away as she reaches for her wallet.

Nearly three hours later, they step back out, the sky still clear. "Can you get your money back for films you didn't like? Because that was fucking awful."

"Made by the guy who made *La La Land*," Yasmina says, and that smirk is still there.

"You knew it was going to be terrible."

"I'd read a few things. But you know I like to watch bad things . . ."

". . . because it makes the good things even better," he says, finishing her idiom for her. "I know that. But did you have to let me pay so much to go watch what might be the most boring film about space exploration in the history of mankind?"

"You're the one who wanted to go out today."

"So this is my punishment?" he asks, putting an arm around her shoulders, pulling her to him.

"Kinda," she says. "But I did really want to watch it. Watching you squirm in your seat for two and a half hours was just a plus."

They walk toward a café they've both been to before, a place that serves the kind of cute things people are wont to take photos of, put up on Instagram with big white smiles, gleaming teeth, a thousand likes, sponsored content; but Yasmina and Nur don't come here for that. They come here for the coffee, the service, the food, everything solid, dependable. When they sit, Yasmina reminisces about the first time they came here; Nur, listening to her recount the story, letting her voice wrap around him. Afterward, they take the route through the park, walking through it the way they have so many times before, and when they get home, Nur collapses on the sofa, pulls Yasmina down with him, the two of them just sitting there.

"You've wasted five hours of my time," Yasmina says.

"Shut up," Nur grumbles, pushing her lightly. "It wasn't a waste."

She chuckles. "No, it wasn't." She pauses. "I just . . . I know I need to give myself breaks, but it never seems justified, you know? Like I can always spend that time doing more work. So thank you for today, for making me come out."

"You can always count on me to help you not do work," Nur says, and he leans over to her, kisses her, just as his phone starts vibrating against his leg. He pulls it out of his pocket, sees the name, turns it over quickly, but he's too late, Yasmina tensing against him.

"You should answer her call," she says.

He moves back. "I'll call her later . . ."

"When I'm not here," she says, finishing his sentence.

Nur can count on his fingers the number of times he has talked to his mother on the phone in front of Yasmina. The calls are always brief, Nur making something up to end the conversation as soon as he can.

Yasmina moves, gets off the sofa, heads out of the room, and he hears her walk into their bedroom, a drawer opening and then closing, hard. He shuts his eyes for a moment and then follows her, sees her standing by their chest of drawers, a shirt in her hand, fist tight.

"Mina," he says, standing by the doorway, knowing exactly what is coming, and he doesn't know who he's angry at, only that he's frustrated the mood has changed so quickly.

"You know what I was just thinking?" she asks, eyes only for the top of the drawers, face creams and deodorants. "That I don't even have her number." She looks at him. "Your mum's number. I don't have it. And then I thought, What if something happened to Nur? I'd call an ambulance, obviously, get you to a hospital, get help. And then what? I know the passcode to your phone, so do I just call her, tell her that something has happened to her son, and, oh, by the way, the person calling is his girlfriend of the last four years that he's hidden from you; anyway, he's at this hospital, come see him?"

Nur stays in the doorway, fingers itching.

"Because you could get in touch with my family," she says, eyes back at the drawer. "You have their numbers. And even if you didn't, they wouldn't be surprised to hear from you, Nur, because they know about you. They know about us."

"I'm going to tell my family about us."

"When?" she asks, turning to him. "Do you have a timeline on that? Tomorrow? Next month? Next year? Next decade?!"

"I . . ." He doesn't know, even though he's thought about it, even though it consumes him sometimes, the burden weighing on him. Whenever he tells her about Khalil or Mariam, whenever her family calls, the weekends he spends at home, pretending he is coming from a flat he shares with Imran.

"Because, you know, it's been well over a year now, living here together." Their moving-in anniversary, June, Nur taking the day off work, Yasmina pausing her research, the day just for them. "Nearly four years since we met."

"I know."

"And they still don't know about me." Her hands still by her sides, her jaw tight. "You have to tell them. And don't say you 'will.' Don't give me that shit again, fob me off until the next time I ask and cave in yet again."

Nur can see this playing out before him. They have been here before.

"Christmas," he says, changing the script. Her brow furrows. "I'll tell them at Christmas."

"You're just saying that . . ."

"No," he says, stepping inside the room. "I'll do it. Christmas. I'm going home for two weeks, I'll do it then."

Her face flickers, her resolve wavering. "No matter what happens?"

"No matter what happens," he says. "You're right. It's time they knew, time I told them." They're the right words, and there is a part of him that believes them, but there is another part, one twisted with fear, that doesn't know what will happen when he tells them, that doesn't want to know. That wants to stay here, where it is safe, where nothing has to change.

"I just . . . ," she begins, hands wrung together. "I'm just tired of being kept out of that part of your life, Nur. I want to meet them, your mum, dad, Khalil, Mariam. I want to meet them and have our life together feel whole, finally."

"I know," he says, and he takes a step toward her, tentatively, and when she doesn't move, doesn't flinch, he takes another, reaches for her, holds her. "They're going to love you," he says, her head on his shoulder, and she lets out a small laugh, the sound echoing through him.

"They're going to love you."

February 2019

Nur looks out the café window, the Nottingham scene presented before him familiar yet different, people he doesn't know treading paths he has walked, whole dishes left untouched on the table in front of him, because though they ordered a while ago, opening the conversation with statements of how hungry they were, they do not have the appetite to eat, the food turning cold.

"So," Imran says. "Tell me what happened."

"Do I have to? Isn't the fact that I'm sitting here with you enough?"

"Not really." Imran pushes his plate away, leans forward on his elbows. "Tell me."

"Have you heard from her?"

"I don't think I should tell you that."

"So, yes."

"What happened, Nur?"

Nur looks away from Imran, casts his eye over the rest of the café. "She came back," he says. "Last week."

He'd been packing a bag in their room, throwing clothes into it, looking desperately for his wallet, because he couldn't find it, had thrown it somewhere the night before, and there was the click of the lock, the sound of the door opening. He stopped. The ground slipped from under him, and he walked out of the room to see her standing by the door, keys gripped in her hand. He took a step toward her, instinct, his body drawn to hers, wanting to be near her.

Nur didn't know if he should talk first, to explain that he was about to go to Manchester to find her, but Yasmina remained quiet, not moving, and he faltered.

"I think we should talk," she said.

He nodded, heart in his throat. He walked to the living room, her footsteps behind him, continuing all the way to the other side of the room, giving her space, more than enough space, and when he turned, she was sitting on the sofa. He remained standing, didn't know what to do with his body, didn't know if he should sit by her, unsure how to move in this space anymore.

"Can you sit, please?" she asked.

Nur sat, this time in the lounge chair, worried about getting closer. "Okay," he said. "I want to—"

"Nur, can I speak? Just me?" He nodded, lungs tight, wanted to bury his head between his knees, pause, stop. "Do you remember when I came to see you in Birmingham for the first time, that summer after uni, and we went to the cinema? I wanted to hold your hand, but you told me we couldn't because what if someone saw us and told your parents? That something bad would happen?"

"Yes," Nur answered, the memory dragging at him.

"I can't tell you how many times I've thought about that day. Every time we hold hands in public, I remember it. The way you flinched. I can picture the exact look on your face. I fucking hated you in that moment, Nur. I remember going to the train station, getting on the next train back to Manchester. I couldn't even go home. Because my whole family knew that I was out with you, and I didn't want to return upset, have to explain how you treated me to my own mum. So I sat in a coffee shop somewhere, wasting time, and I kept seeing your face. And I knew . . . I loved you. It killed me that someone who said they loved me would look at me like that—"

"Yasmina . . . ," he said. Her hands grew tight, her body tense.

"At first, when you told me your family wouldn't accept me, I thought you were exaggerating. Fuck, I even thought you were coming up with an excuse, like the wildest excuse, because you didn't want to introduce me to your parents. But you kept telling me, and I thought, man, his parents must be racist assholes. Because isn't it enough that I'm Muslim? And if that's who they are, why am I with their son? But you are so *good*. How could you come from that? So I stayed, even after you said you had to hide our relationship. I thought, it'll change. He'll change. My mum . . . she doesn't know why I'm with you. She has never said anything but I feel it whenever she asks about you, whenever she asks about your family . . . Nur, why am I with you?" The question came out like an indictment, as if she were cross-examining herself.

"Because—" Nur said, and Yasmina looked at him, stopped him.

"You've kept me hidden away," she said, eyes filling. "I told myself enough time would pass and things would get easier. That once you realized we were going to spend the rest of our lives together, we would tell your parents. But you told me to wait. Again and again. I bided my time, I got my master's, started my PhD, did what I needed to, and I assumed you would just . . . I don't know, become the person I needed you to be, in time. But you didn't."

"I told them—"

"After four years, Nur." She said it with such exhaustion that Nur felt that there was nothing left between them. He wanted to talk, knew he had the words in him if only he could let them out. "Four years waiting. Do you know what that does to a person? I spent so many nights dreaming about you coming in, telling me you've told them and that we're going to go see them, something, anything. But nothing came."

"Yasmina," Nur said, his voice cracking, splitting right down the middle, disrupted by his tears; he wanted to set this right, but she shook her head at him, not done.

"Do you remember when you asked if I wanted to marry you?"

Nur sitting on their bed, a few months into moving in together, laptop propped open, Yasmina walking into the room, towel around her hair, makeup removed, reaching for her coconut oil, rubbing some into her palms and onto her skin, flesh gleaming in the light, and Nur watches her, so overcome with this simple image of her, wants this forever, so he asks if she would ever marry him, and she stops, tells him not to say that, and he asks why, and she says, Don't say it, and he asks why again, and she says—

"You told me not to say it if I wasn't serious."

"And you still repeated it. You looked me in the eyes and said you wanted to marry me. Told me you had known you wanted to marry me since the first second you'd seen me, wanted to spend the rest of your life with me—"

"I do—" he interrupted.

"But you can't marry someone if your family doesn't know about them, right? When you told me you were going to sit them down this time, I didn't believe you. After all this time, what was different?" She sneered, shrugged. "But then you did and I thought . . . I thought I'd feel ecstatic, excited, because this is what I've wanted all this time." She let out a half chuckle. "I felt nothing, Nur. I just . . . I just went along with it. Told my mum, said he's finally told them, they want to meet us, and she replied she was happy for me. So did Hawa. So did my dad."

The words were in him, he just had to speak. To say something.

"And then we met them. We drove down. A whole day put aside. And it felt so good, to see the house you grew up in, to meet your brother and sister, to put faces to names, to see how much they looked like you, to meet your parents—"

"But then my parents—"

"No." She cut him off, slicing the air. "It wasn't your parents."

Nur knew where this was going, felt it in his chest, and the recognition of his defeat made it hard to breathe.

"It was you, Nur," Yasmina said, her voice wavering as she stood from the sofa, turned away from him.

"Me?" he echoed, eventually. He got up, a chasm between them.

She turned back to him, wringing her hands. "I thought you were conflicted. That it was a big thing, you needed to think about it, and you didn't want to lose your family. I somehow convinced myself that you were waiting *because* it was the only thing to do. I gaslit myself, Nur. For you. And this entire time, it was you. You, who didn't do the right thing. Me, my family, your family . . . We were all just waiting for you to be honest and you weren't. I've been asking myself, was it because you didn't love me enough? Was it because I wasn't good enough?"

"I couldn't . . ."

"Because you were scared? Because you didn't care enough?" Yasmina continued, oblivious to Nur's attempts to form a response.

"Because . . ." He tried to find the answer, to find the reason why, but he couldn't. There were too many reasons. There wasn't a reason.

"You don't even know," she said.

"I love you—"

"That doesn't mean anything, Nur. Not if you're unwilling to do anything about it. Not if you let me sit here for *four years*, driving myself crazy wondering if you even want me."

"I moved in with you—"

"In secret! Your parents still think you're living with a friend. How long have we been here, nearly two years, and they still think it's you and Imran?"

"They know about us now—"

"It's not enough."

"Then what will be enough, Yasmina?" Hands clenched by his sides, fingernails digging into his palms, keeping him still. "I have always wanted a life with you—"

"You're not even close to enough, Nur," she said.

"Then what is?" he asked again.

"Maybe not being in a relationship with someone who can't admit that he's the one with the problem with me being Black."

The air in the room went solid around Nur, stiff against his chest. "I don't have a problem—" he began.

"We've done this before, Nur," she said, her voice flat, and he was back there again, telling her not to call his name in Birmingham, telling her his family were the racist ones, not him, telling Rahat it wasn't time, not yet. "It's your family, right? But you're the one who hid me. You're the one who turned me into a secret. You're the one who has always been ashamed of me."

"I am not ashamed of you, Yasmina. I have never—"

"It took me a while to realize it myself," she said, ignoring him, and now he stood too, facing her. "If someone said they weren't racist, if they said they loved you and got along with your family. If they said all the right things, voted the right way, understood you whenever you talked about the experience of being Black. If they did all that but then treated you like they were ashamed to be with you, what would you think?"

"I am not a racist—"

"And yet you behave like one," Yasmina said calmly, and he knew, Nur knew from how she spoke that there was nothing he could say that would change her mind. "You say you're not racist and I believe you, I believe that you think you're not. But, Nur, it's not enough to read the right books, to say the right things, to tweet your anger about police brutality or supporting Black people if you're going to come home and make your Black girlfriend feel like she is less than you."

His breath short, Nur grasped for a response, but he also knew a small part of him agreed with her, a small part of him that stopped him from answering back.

"I think it's best if we leave this here," she said. "If we leave us here."

"Yasmina . . ." Her name left his mouth, and he was aware that this was one of the last few times he would get to say her name to her.

"Please, Nur, don't." Any sign of weakness was gone. She was still. A decision had been made, maybe last night, maybe on the train ride over, maybe just now, and there was nothing he could do to change that.

Maybe there is a story here where Nur fights harder for Yasmina in this moment, argues that he will never give up, that they are meant to be together, that whatever she has lost in feeling for him, he will earn it back, become worthy of her. That he will do the work, that he will be better. That they will fight whatever comes their way. Maybe he goes home, declares he is going to marry her, and his parents accept, push him to do whatever he needs to make himself happy, and maybe they go through the ceremony, move into a bigger house, her stomach swells, and when he presses his hand against it, he finds purpose in what is inside her, has never felt that kind of love for anyone else, and he tells her that she has given him the world, and she tells him not to be so dramatic.

Maybe that story exists somewhere. A different Nur and a different Yasmina, happy together.

But here, Nur watched Yasmina, steel in her eyes, and he knew that this had been coming, had felt it himself, was surprised she'd stayed this long, and then she packed a bag. She said she'd be staying at a friend's place, that she'd keep her things here until she could figure something out, and when she walked toward the door, bag in her hand, she looked at him, and he held himself back in that hallway, wavering, every inch of his body hot, vibrating. He wanted to stop her, pull her back. To defend himself. But he stayed still, lips glued shut. Disappointment on her face, her lips parted slightly to say something, but then she closed her mouth against it, leaving without saying goodbye, the door shut behind her. Nur stayed there, half hoping that it might open again, and when it didn't, when minutes passed and the world carried on, he knew it had all come to an end.

Nur tells this to Imran, and when he is done, Nur sags in the booth, looks down at the untouched food.

Imran twirls a knife in his hand, up, down, digests what he's heard. "You know you fucked up here, right?"

"I don't think this is the time—" Nur begins, with a small smile, but there is no humor in Imran's face.

"I'm not joking," he says. "Yasmina is incredible."

"I know that—"

"If you knew that, you would have fought harder for her."

Nur flushes with anger. "I did fight for her."

Imran's fingers tap on the table, and he hesitates. "I'm your friend. I love you," he says, looking back up at Nur, his hand no longer strumming. "But I'm not going to lie to you. I'm not going to say what you want to hear. Yasmina is one of the best people I know, and you took that for granted. You didn't want to tell your parents because you were scared of what they would say. That's fine, for a while, but four years, Nur?"

"But I did tell them," Nur argues, frustrated that he is having to explain himself. He is weary, the years of silence weighing down on him.

"Too late, Nur. You know that. Of course, you know that. You're not dumb. Listen, I am so sorry she's gone, that you've lost her. But you need to be better."

A fresh sadness thumps inside his chest. "I didn't want to hurt her."

"And that's noble. But only up to a point." Imran takes a deep breath. "You need to face that, in time."

Nur looks down, at the plate of food in front of him. He feels sick, Yasmina's words in his head, racing around and around.

Is this really the person he is?

Imran reaches over to him, puts his hand over Nur's. "This isn't the end of the world, Nur. It might feel that way for now, but I think we both know those feelings fade with time. Yasmina will always be your first real love, and you're always going to think about what might have happened. But you'll find someone else. I guarantee it. And when you do, you're going to be better to them. Because I'm not going to let you fuck the next one up."

Now Imran smiles, but Nur doesn't return it. He says they should leave, is suddenly filled with a need to escape into the street. Imran pays, and they step out, walk with no aim. This place, this city that he had made his own with her, containing all the different versions of himself, all the different versions of her, ghosts of the past. Imran puts an arm around him as they drift down familiar roads, and Nur lets himself be held. Maybe those other Nurs and Yasminas are happy together, have found their joy in one another. And though it seems impossible right now, one day, Nur will gain that sense of joy on his own. Then, he thinks, this will all have been worth it, if it means he can find the courage in himself to become the person Yasmina always believed him to be. A good man.

Acknowledgments

In no specific order:

To Shaikyla White, for being one of the brightest stars I have around me; for being one of the most important and earliest reasons this book happened. You have my eternal gratitude and my love.

To Merima Suljic, for being one of my favorite people; to your mother, who has never treated me as less than her own.

To Kairo Maynard, for being the kind of person I am honored to be around. You're going to go further than you ever dreamed; for me, I always knew you would.

To Elise Jackson, for being the fire in the cold for those two and a bit years; I am privileged to have you in my life.

To Eleanor Dryden, without you, we wouldn't be here. Carey Mulligan ain't got nothing on you.

To Juliet Pickering, thank you for everything. My life is forever changed because you are in it.

To Helen Garnons-Williams, for being the one to make my dream come true; to Kishani Widyaratna, for being the kind of editor I didn't know I needed; to Ruby Rose Lee, for being as brilliant a person as I wish I could be.

To my grandparents, Asmat Begum and Barkat Ali, who came to England with nothing and built an entire universe. Without them, there is nothing; with them, there is the world. To my own parents, for never pushing me to do the things that other parents pushed their children to do. We didn't know if it would work out; I'm so glad you let me try. To Hamzah and Maleeha, for being exactly the kind of siblings I need to be the person I am; I hope I have done you proud. To my aunty Tanzeem Begum, called Rani for queen, a queen to her father. I got here because of you. To my aunty Allia Tabassum, for being exactly the kind of crazy that inspires me. This is for you, innit.

I am nothing without you all.

About the Author

KASIM ALI works at Penguin Random House, has previously been short-listed for Hachette's Mo Siewcharran Prize and long-listed for the 4th Estate BAME Short Story Prize, and has contributed to *The Good Journal*. He comes from Birmingham, England, and lives in London.